ESCAPE
from GARTSHERRIE

A novel by AJ Morris

Published by

M℃A

M℃Alpine Media

Whilst this novel is inspired by the lives of the author's ancestors, it is a work of fiction and any similarity to actual persons, living or dead, or actual events, is purely coincidental.

First published in Great Britain by McAlpine Media, 2022

KDP ISBN: 9798803320975

Designed & Typeset by McAlpine Media, Glasgow.
www.mcalpinemedia.co.uk

CONTENTS

1   Leaving Scotland 7

2   The Blessing...........................26

3   The Voyage Continues 44

4   The Arrival................................47

5   The Next Step 54

6   The Business............................61

7   Letters 72

8   The Partnership......................79

9   Cape Town 85

10 Sad News.................................93

11 The House................................98

12 The Passing Years 103

13 Walter's Journey....................113

14 The Adventure Begins.........138

15 Life Without Walter.............148

16 The Transvaal 152

17 Letters & Repercussions 162

18 Arrival in Bournemouth......175

19 Christmas in Melbourne 178

20 Christmas in Bournemouth 185

21 The Search is Over 194

22 Melbourne and Sydney........198

23 Edinburgh 209

24 A Change of Plan 232

25 Changes in Melbourne 235

26 A New Beginning.................241

27 Time Does Not Stand Still....245

28 The End of the 1920's.........248

29 War Clouds Gather 258

30 The War Years 267

31 Peace Declared 286

32 The Circle Completed 296

33 Letters and Romance...........307

34 The Planning Meeting.........319

35 The Glorious Reunion 324

EPILOGUE 329

DEDICATION

For all the Samuel and Maria Johnstones' who
sailed from Scotland.

Thousands of Scottish emigrants travelled with
skills and a work ethic to many foreign lands.

The countries they settled in owe an enormous
debt to the Scottish diaspora.

and

Jean and Alexander (Eck) Smith, my friends
and mentors who sailed to Australia in 1949.

ACKNOWLEDGEMENTS

I offer my heartfelt thanks to:

My publishers and dear friends, Gary and Joanne of McAlpine Media. Their graphic design beautifully captures the spirit of the times I was trying to portray.

My dear friend, Jane. We share memories of schooldays in Coatbridge - Gartsherrie Primary and Clifton High. Jane is my unfailing support.

My author friend Teresa from Glenboig, skilled editor and source of excellent advice. We also laugh together.

My darling husband Paul for 'staying on my case' and making sure the book was written.

CHAPTER 1
Leaving Scotland

It was a pitch black, bitterly cold, morning in November 1917, the inside of the window in the single end tenement flat located in the east end of Glasgow was covered with an exquisite pattern of frost. The faded brown paper blind rattled against the window, waking the young couple who were lying in an old fashioned metal framed recessed bed.

They cuddled together on the lumpy feather mattress for comfort and warmth. Samuel whispered to his young wife, "Maria, darl'n are you awake, it's the morn, the morning when our dream starts."

Although it was still dark outside they rose and left the warmth of their bed. Shivering in her nightdress Maria lit the candle in its chipped enamel holder placing it on a shooglie wicker table, where it created an almost eerie glow around the room. The candle gave off sufficient light for her to trim the wick on the paraffin lamp and light it, allowing it to softly illuminate the entire room.

Before they could wash they had to break the layer of ice on the chipped Victorian ewer sitting inside its basin. They quickly washed in the cold water and dressed in their outdoor clothes which were neatly hanging on pegs behind the front door, ready for their early morning departure.

As soon as she was dressed, Maria spread the last of the margarine on four rolls bought the previous evening, and added some slices of cheese. By way of breakfast the young couple silently ate a roll each and drank a mug of black tea, the water having being boiled on a single gas ring. The remaining two rolls Maria carefully wrapped in a linen tea towel, this would be their only sustenance on the long journey ahead.

In the far corner of the room sat a wicker hamper, a leaving present from Maria's brother, Dan. He had also brought them a farewell gift from their sister Maureen, a lined notebook bound in red Morocco leather, with a card saying;

I'll miss you Sis, write your adventures in the book and remember me.
Love and God Bless
Maureen

Maria put the rolls into the hamper, together with a Barr's Irn Brew bottle filled with water to drink during the journey. The food joined all they possessed in the world. A few clothes, farewell presents they had received from Sam's family, a layette of clothes and blankets sewn and knitted by Maria for the baby they were expecting. These, together with the Morocco bound journal and a few household items gathered in the short time they had been living in Glasgow were all the worldly possessions of Samuel and Maria Johnstone.

As they quickly tidied the room Maria desperately tried not to shed the tears which were threatening to spill.

Sam put his arms around his young wife saying, "Come on my darling girl, it's time for us to leave."

With a last look around the bleak little room they took a handle each of the wicker hamper and carried it downstairs.

The great city of Glasgow was awakening, the metal shoes on the horses hooves striking the cobbled roads. The pavements were starting to fill with men in working clothes coming out of the tenement closes, either walking to work or joining the queues for trams. There were no motor cars in this poverty stricken part of Glasgow's east end, such luxuries were reserved for the rich living in the more salubrious west end of the city.

Sam and Maria joined the queue waiting for a tram heading towards the city centre, their breath was like white smoke in the chill morning air. At last the tram arrived and they managed to manoeuvre the hamper onboard, much to the annoyance of the other passengers.

Sam started to cough in the atmosphere of cigarette and pipe smoke that pervaded the tram. This cough would be his constant companion for the remainder of his life, a legacy from a mustard gas attack in France while he was serving king and country on the front line.

At last they arrived in Gordon Street. Alighting with the hamper was as awkward as boarding the tram and again there were many tuts from passengers anxious to get to work on time.

Carrying the hamper between them they entered into the noise and smoke of Glasgow's Central Station and purchased two third class tickets to Liverpool.

They found their way to the train and settled themselves into their compartment stowing their hamper on the overhead rack. Thankfully they managed to get two seats at the rear of the compartment where they at least had a back support, rather than sitting on one of the backless wooden benches.

As the train chugged out of Glasgow Central Station in a cloud of white steam, Maria gave way to the tears that had been threatening since she rose from her bed that morning. Tears stemming from the knowledge that she and Sam had now commenced on a journey which would take them to Australia, a country over nine thousand miles away from Scotland. The likelihood was that she would never again see the Lanarkshire village of Glenboig where she had grown up, nor would she again see her family. Sam was thinking similar thoughts, in his case it was Gartsherrie where his parents lived, and he had been brought up with his two sisters. Mary, who now worked at the local Post Office and his elder sister Agnes who had recently married Tom Coats, a manager at Baird's Works, moving out of the family home and into a bungalow in a more salubrious part of the town, Drumpellier.

The reason for their journey could be found in just one word, 'religion'. Sam was from a staunch Protestant family and Maria a devout Catholic. They had worked together in the Glenboig Brickworks and had fallen in love before the start of the War in 1914.

Knowing the prejudice they would face if their feelings became known they had separated on a number of occasions. However, time spent apart had simply made them all the more sure of their love for each other.

While Sam was serving in France they wrote to each other as often as they could. Maria's letters were Sam's one tiny spot of sanity in the asylum that was the Western Front. Living in the hellhole of life in the trenches crystallised his belief that if he made it home to Scotland he would do his best to persuade his beautiful Maria, the lass with the strawberry blond curls, to marry him.

While Sam's parents, Alex and Jessie had eventually accepted the inevitability of their son's love for Maria and sent them off with their blessing, Maria's father was adamant that she was dead to him.

Mrs Riley, was also devastated at her daughter marrying outside the faith, however through her son Dan she sent the young couple a short letter wishing them a good life. This was as much as she dared to do, she was so terrified of the wrath of her husband.

Dan, who was married with his own home, was the only member of the Riley family who kept in touch with his sister and he had regularly visited the young couple while they were living in Glasgow.

Maria's eloping had caused ructions in the Riley family. As well as Mrs Riley, the children who were still staying at home, regardless of their age, were too in thrall of their father to risk contact with their sister and her Protestant husband.

Maria's father, Patrick Riley was a brusk no nonsense man, he had received little formal education but due to his intelligence and hard work had reached the heights of being employed as a foreman at the Garliston Works.

Unlike many of his fellow workmates he did not spend all his earnings on drink. Every Saturday he gave his wife sufficient house-keeping money to feed the family nourishing food and ensure that every member of his household was well clothed and shod. Each of his children attended Mass every Sunday, celebrated holidays of obligation and attended St Joseph's School, until they were old enough to start work.

He ruled his little household in Glenboig with all the authority of a king over his country. Riley was a king who practiced the old religion. Of Irish descent and a devout Catholic he attended Mass, said his prayers daily, made his confession and obeyed the priest at Our Lady & St Joseph's Church in the village, in all matters temporal and spiritual.

His great sadness was that the old village church had now been replaced and he had to worship in the new building, consecrated in 1908 and which everyone seemed to warmly embrace. However, in his view the new chapel was nothing short of a monstrosity. In his opinion Glenboig should have boasted a fine Pugin building like St Patrick's, St Augustine's and St Mary's in Coatbridge even Chapelhall had St Aloysius, a fine traditional building, creating a worthy sanctuary. Yet another of his life's disappointments.

Maria eloping with a Protestant had shocked and angered him to his very core. He simply couldn't think of anything more shameful than one of his own bedding with a proddy. Except, living with him out of wedlock! Filling in a form at the registry office would never be a true marriage in Patrick Riley's eyes. His girl, and his favourite girl at that, was now nothing more than a 'bidie-in' and separated from her Catholic faith, it was a hurt not to be tholed.

For the remainder of his days Patrick lived with his bigotry and anger, it ate like a cancer into his very soul. Try as they might, his wife, children and grandchildren never succeeded in reaching him. Eventually even the holy Mass no longer gave him any real comfort.

Once they had stowed the hamper and settled into their seats Maria took her husband's hand and whispered, "Sam, are you as frightened as me at the thought of all that is before us? Sailing thousands of miles during the winter in wartime. We have precious little money, your bad chest, and a wee baby on the way? We must be right mad."

Sam tightened his grip on her hand, "Maria my girl, I know as well as you how frightening this journey is and I'm also thinking, what if I can't do my new job properly, who will provide for you and our wee baby in a strange land? This is our one opportunity to have a new life away from Coatbridge, we've just got to take our chance. I know it's earlier than we planned to leave but we have been lucky to get a passage on the SS Trojan so we must just make the most of the chance offered to us."

The carriage gradually filled with other passengers, the guard blew his whistle and with a loud hiss of steam the train chugged out of Glasgow per the timetable, at exactly 8.14am.

The train journey to Liverpool seemed never ending. Their fellow passengers were two couples with children who kept running up and down the third class carriage playing tag, or pulling on the leather strap which opened the carriage windows. The other occupants were an elderly couple who continually tutted at the behaviour of the children, whispering loudly to each other, "Honestly Jean, the weans these days have no manners whatsoever. Could you imagine us behaving like that, we would have known better."

His wife agreed, "I know George, children should be seen and not heard, if you ask me. Can you imagine weans behaving so disgracefully in the days of auld Queen Victoria?"

And, so it went on the entire journey. The parents trying their best to control the unruly children and the elderly couple constantly complaining.

At last the long journey ended and the train pulled into Liverpool Lime Street Station, it was November 1917, a date which would be forever etched in their memory. This was the first time Maria had been out of Scotland, and it was the day which would see the start of their new life.

Sam had bought their third class tickets for the sea journey from an agent in Glasgow so they were able to leave the railway station carrying their hamper and head straight for the docks. At long last they walked up the gangplank of the steamship the SS Trojan which in the early days of the war it had been used as a troop ship and was still painted a dour battleship grey.

In the gloom of a wet November afternoon the ship seemed to merge into the gloomy weather creating a monochrome world in which all sense of colour had disappeared.

Sam was ticketed to men's dormitory 2 and Maria to the female and child dormitory 4. Their hamper was stowed and they took a few possessions to their respective dormitories to see them through the journey. The dormitories were clean and well ventilated and each passenger was issued with a mattress and bedding, mess tins and cutlery.

In addition to the dormitories and a few small cabins there was a large communal dining room for third class passengers which was also used as a recreation room and a part was cordoned off as a gentleman's smoking area. There were tiled lavatories and male and female bathhouses available for all third class passengers, not luxurious but certainly clean and perfectly adequate.

Sam and Maria were reunited on the deck jostling for a place at the rail with the other passengers, each of whom had their own story as to why they were travelling from Liverpool to the Southern Hemisphere on the SS Trojan.

Many of the passengers were waving and throwing bunting to friends and family standing on the docks. As the ship pulled anchor and entered the Mersey estuary a brass band played 'Now is the hour when we must say goodbye'. The words were so emotional that very few of the people gathered on the Albert Dock or onboard the ship could hold back the tears. As they waved farewell to family and friends the words of the chorus expressed the feeling in many hearts.

> *And now is the hour when we must say goodbye,*
> *Soon you'll be sailing far across the sea,*
> *When you're away, o, then remember me,*
> *When you return, you'll find me waiting here.*

As the ship sailed down the Mersey estuary and the lights on the quay gradually disappeared from view the passengers made their way back to their accommodation.

Maria and Samuel both felt sad and dejected that although they had waved with all the other passengers they were alone and far from home and family right at the start of their big adventure.

Sam whispered to his wife, "The cost of the tickets included food. I wonder when a meal will be served, just a cheese roll with a cup of water on a long train journey leaves a man decidedly peckish."

For the first time all day Maria smiled, "Away with you Samuel Johnstone, I'm sure we will get some dinner, now let's head downstairs out of the rain."

They did in fact enjoy their first meal in the dining room, happily they had a place in the first sitting. On the menu was lamb stew with potatoes and root vegetables, thickened with barley and served with a wedge of bread and a mug of tea. Apparently Irish stew was very popular in Liverpool as there was a big Irish immigrant population in the city. It was plain fare but well cooked, most of the passengers seemed to thoroughly enjoy the food and left a 'clean plate'.

After finishing their meal Sam said, "Maria darling, I have that letter burning a hole in my pocket that my pa gave us when we met them at Sloan's bar in Glasgow to say farewell. Will we go and find a quiet spot where we can read their words from home?"

They found a seat on deck lit by a brass bulkhead lamp. Sam removed the letter from his inside pocket and opened the envelope. The letter was written in his mother's handwriting, folded inside was a Royal Bank of Scotland pound note.

Our dearest Sam and Maria

This is the hardest letter I have ever, or will ever, write.

Firstly your pa and I have enclosed a pound note for you to keep as 'emergency money' who knows what might happen and it's important that you have a wee something put past.

It was your wee sister Mary who made us realise that your emigration to a new county is not just you running away from all the silly old religious prejudices. Sam, Maria you are running towards a new and exciting life in a new country. You two young folks are worth so much more than to simply follow the restrictions of life in Gartsherrie or Glenboig.

Your father and I planned just such an adventure but it was not to be, our destiny has been to live and work in Gartsherrie. However, we have had three wonderful children and now Agnes's husband Tom and Maria have joined our family, we have five.

There is only one thing I would ask of you both. Please write regularly and tell us of your adventures in Australia, such a faraway country. We will then feel part of your new life and in return we will keep you informed of the goings on here at home.

My dears, never forget you are our children and we want all that is good for you both, and for your wee baby when he or she arrives.

Maria, women have had the right to vote in Victoria since 1908, write and tell me how it feels when you first vote in your new land.

Love and God Bless you both

Ma and Pa

* * *

After reading the letter and shedding a few tears the young
Johnstones' retired to their respective dormitories and both slept the
sleep of the exhausted. The following morning they wakened to high
seas which seemed to worsen by the hour as they travelled out into the
Atlantic and towards the Bay of Biscay.

As arranged the previous evening, they met in the dining room for
breakfast. Both Sam and Maria managed to eat a little porridge and
drink a mug of tea but there were quite a few empty seats at the tables.
By lunchtime only hardy passengers managed to eat their lentil broth
and a roll spread with margarine. By dinnertime the number of
passengers eating in the third class dining room was into single figures.

Both Sam and Maria suffered horribly from mal de mer and like
many of their fellow passengers irrespective of whether first, second
or third class they endured terrible vomiting and vertigo.

Eventually the journey through the Bay of Biscay came to an end and
although the Atlantic was still very rough Sam and Maria were still alive.

Maria was lying in her bunk in the women's dormitory worrying in
case the constant sickness she had endured had harmed the baby she
was carrying. She desperately wanted to rise from her bunk and try to
locate Sam to find out how he had tolerated the sail through the hell that
was the Bay of Biscay but her head simply would not leave the pillow.

Maria felt a tap on her shoulder, she forced open her eyes and a
middle aged woman, dressed in black, spoke to her in a soft Highland
accent. "My dear, I've brought you a plain biscuit and a cup of water,
you must try and get a little down, you have to think of your wee
babe."

Maria immediately recognised kindness in the strangers eyes and her
soft highland accent inspired confidence. Leaning on her arm she tried
to raise her head from the thin pillow. The woman who was helping
her said, "My name is Ishbel m'dear. I'm so sorry I couldn't assist you
earlier but everyone was so very sick as we went through the Bay of
Biscay. The worst is over now and in a few days we will be in calmer
waters, we're heading towards Madeira. Now you really must try to
nibble on this biscuit no matter how sick and dizzy you feel and start
drinking a little water, I've added a wee drop of ginger essence, it's
excellent to settle your stomach down. Luckily I packed a good supply
in my cabin luggage."

Nibbling the biscuit and drinking the ginger water did indeed
soothe Maria but the comfort she gained from Ishbel's presence far
outweighed the medication. Ishbel produced a damp flannel to which

she had added a few drops of lavender oil she used this to bathe Maria's face and hands. Saying in her soft lilt, "My name is Ishbel Stewart, I'm travelling with my son to Cape Town. Now, I want you to lie still, I'll leave you some barley sugar sweets to suck and I'll come back later with something else to eat and drink, and take it you must m'dear if you want to get over your seasickness."

Sam had managed to get out of his bed and dress in the men's dormitory. Before going up on deck he opened his locker and removed his trench coat, tweed bunnet and woollen Albion Rovers scarf. Wrapped up against the cold he made his way up the metal staircase.

Very few people had braved the still inclement weather and Sam was on his own holding the ship's rail, feeling the cold wind and watching the 'white horse' waves crashing against the metal hull of the SS Trojan.

As he felt the spray on his face and the cleansing smell of the sea Sam's thoughts were for his young wife. He desperately wanted to assure himself that Maria had survived the horrendous journey through the Bay of Biscay. However, this was not possible as it was strictly forbidden for men to enter the women's dormitories.

Just as he was about to head back downstairs he heard a man's voice ask, "Are you feeling better after the worst of the storms through Biscay?"

Sam turned and saw a man about his own age wearing a black coat with a black felt hat pulled down hard on his head to try and protect him from the force of the weather.

Pleased to speak to a fellow Scot, Sam replied, "Yes, thank you, I do feel a wee bit better this morning but my main worry is about my wife, she is expecting our baby and I've no idea how she is bearing up. It's so frustrating not to be able to find out what is happening down in the female dormitories."

The man agreed, "You must be very worried, tell me your name and the number of the dormitory your wife is in and I'll ask my mother to find out how she is coping. My mother comes from a fishing family in the Western Isles, the waves in the Bay of Biscay will certainly not have defeated her, she has regularly sailed across the Minch."

Sam felt the man was an answer to his silent prayer, he replied, "I'm so very grateful to you, my wife is called Maria Johnstone and she is in Dormitory 4."

Neither man knew but Ishbel Stewart had taken matters into her own hands and already appeared to Maria in the guise of a guardian angel.

Sam put out his hand saying, "We had better introduce ourselves, my name is Samuel Johnstone, Sam, and I come from Gartsherrie in Lanarkshire, iron and steel country."

The man replied, "Pleased to meet you Sam, my name is Robert Stewart and I come from Perthshire, farming and minister country. My father and grandfather were both men of the cloth. I've followed in their footsteps, a son of the kirk. I'm an ordained minister."

Sam looked amazed, as he blurted out, "What on earth is a Scottish minister doing sailing to Australia on the SS Trojan?"

Robert smiled, "Well firstly, I'm not going to Australia, I'm going to Cape Town. I've been recruited as a minister with the Dutch Reformed Church in the Union of South Africa. I'll need to learn to speak Afrikaans and then I'll be given a congregation, more than likely somewhere up country.

"Although my name is Stewart I'm no relation to the famous African missionary James Stewart. I'm just ordinary Robert Stewart, I was invalided out of the army in 1916, finished my studies in Edinburgh and saw an advertisement in a church publication for ministers to serve in the Dutch Reformed Church in the Union of South Africa. I thought, 'I've had quite enough of the old country and its politics' so I decided to apply, and here I am on the SS Trojan with my mother Ishbel. My mother is quite a character, my father passed away last year so she decided to join me on my adventure to Africa as she has always wanted to travel but never had the opportunity to leave Scotland. It must be the blood of her seafaring ancestors flowing in her veins.

"Mother is not a woman to just sit in the parlour hosting tea parties, she will no doubt get involved in all sorts of good works. I can just see the letters going back to Scotland asking my other two brothers, who are also ministers, to try and raise money from their congregations for some worthy project or another."

Sam immediately warmed to Robert, their backgrounds could not have been more different but the fact that they had both been through the war and were disillusioned with life in Britain gave their friendship a meaningful starting point.

Robert, Sam and Ishbel now ate their meals together in the dining room and Ishbel gave Sam regular reports on the state of Maria's health. "Sam, the problem is it's not just normal seasickness, expecting a wee one while riding the Atlantic waves must be truly awful. I've just got to encourage her to stay strong until we reach Madeira. Don't worry lad your lass will pull through, she is made of stern stuff."

Over the following few days Ishbel Stewart nursed Maria through a combination of sea and pregnancy sickness. Her homely remedies passed down from her mother and grandmother worked and somehow Maria survived until the SS Trojan sailed into Funchal Harbour.

Madeira was a revelation to all the passengers, after the nightmare journey from Liverpool. The warmth in the air and the fragrance from the exotic plant life gave promise of a haven of peace and beauty.

Sam and Robert were sitting on deck drinking in the scenery when Ishbel led a frail, white faced, Maria upstairs to be reunited with her husband. Sam put his arms around his wife, afraid to hold her too tightly in case she snapped, she looked so delicate.

"What an absolutely glorious day," said Ishbel. "Far too nice to be staying onboard the ship. Lets go into the town and explore, besides I've got an idea for a special treat. Robert, do you remember when Lady Jane from Deveron House used to visit the manse for afternoon tea?"

"I certainly do mother. Archie, Euan and I always looked forward to the cakes you used to bake for her monthly visits. Whatever we had in the garden, apples, rhubarb, strawberries even plums you made them into a tart and if there wasn't any fruit you used to make scones and serve them with your home made jam, and always your special shortbread. Yes, I remember Lady Jane's visits with great pleasure. Apart from when she insisted one of us should recite a poem or sing something, that part wasn't so good."

Ishbel continued, "Well before the war Lady Jane and her husband used to go to Madeira every winter and she was always telling me how truly wonderful it was and how they so enjoyed staying at Reid's hotel. According to her she used to greatly impress the staff with her knowledge of Portuguese. If you believe that you'll believe the British government will give women the vote they so richly deserve.

"Anyway, the hotel was built by a Scotsman called William Reid. Sadly he died before it was complete but his sons finished the project and according to Lady Jane it's the jewel on the island of Madeira, don't you know. Let's all go to Reid's hotel and have a scrumptious afternoon tea."

Sam and Maria looked at each other rather awkwardly. Sam broke the silence, "Mrs Stewart we would love to accompany you and Robert but I'm afraid we just don't have any spare money for luxuries."

"Nonsense," said Ishbel, "I haven't made myself clear, it's my treat. I'd really love to visit the hotel and I want company. You'd be doing me an enormous favour if you would be my guests. Now let's get away into town."

The first class passengers had already left for the port in the tender

boat so they didn't have too long to wait for a place in the small vessel
to transport them to the quayside.

After the short boat trip the sailors helped the ladies ashore and
directed everyone towards the town. Following instructions they
started to walk up the incline into Funchal town. Everything seemed so
colourful, particularly the bougainvillea covering the white walls with
their vivid pink or purple bracts. Even the local children seemed to
have taken on the hue of flowers in their pretty embroidered outfits.
The Scottish party had never seen anything quite like the island
paradise that was Madeira.

They explored the little shops, selling wine made from grapes
grown on terraces high up in the mountain slopes of Madeira and
Porto Santo. As well as shops selling supplies to the local population
there were flower sellers and tourist shops selling beautiful embroidery
and lace. Maria would love to have been able to buy a table cover but
the cost, reasonable as it was, was well outwith their tight budget.
However, just browsing in the shops and taking in the atmosphere was
enough to make Maria start to forget the horrors of the seasickness
she had endured.

They slowly followed the steep cobbled road up the hillside towards
their destination. Reid's Hotel did not disappoint, it was a magnificent
pink building with a red tiled roof set in wondrous sub tropical
gardens, with views down to the Atlantic Ocean. Both Sam and Maria
were totally overawed as they entered the hotel and were saluted by a
white gloved doorman. The receptionist then directed the party to the
Tea Terrace where afternoon tea was being served.

Maria was dressed in a jade green cotton calf length skirt which she
had made the previous summer with help from her sister Maureen. It
was topped with a white square necked blouse, bought in the Co-
operative Emporium. Ishbel was looking elegant in a long pale grey
dress, trimmed with white lace, her summer Sunday best. Before
leaving the ship Ishbel had given Maria a sun hat insisting that she
must protect her fair skin, while she wore a grey wide brimmed hat
adorned with a single pink rose.

Seated on cane chairs with comfy cushions the view over the
gardens and down the slope towards the Atlantic was magnificent. The
gardens were full of exotic shrubs and palm trees, their green fronds
highlighted against the azure blue sky. There was also quite a number
of an intriguing tree which none of the group had ever seen before.

They were seated by a waiter who brought them glasses and a jug of
iced water, together with four lavish menus. Robert couldn't resist

asking the waiter the name of the tree. The man replied, "It's called a Norfolk Pine sir, if you are travelling to the Southern Hemisphere you will see plenty of Norfolk pines."

Ishbel took charge of the ordering, "Let's have the afternoon tea for four, it will be a lovely memory and I shall so enjoy writing to Lady Jane boasting about my visit to Reid's with Robert and our new friends. Tell me, am I being very naughty?"

"Well mother," laughed Robert, "It can be your revenge for the bird."

"Oh my, I'll never forget that afternoon," said Ishbel smiling. "Go on Robert tell Sam and Maria the whole ghastly story."

Robert soon got into his stride, "Well it was like this, Lady Jane was making her regular monthly visit, the family were all gathered in the manse sitting room, mother had just brought in a trolley with all the accoutrements for a delicious afternoon tea.

"Our pa was playing the piano and I was standing with Archie and Euan, faces shining, wearing our Eton collars and singing Old Folks at Home. The Swanee river was just about to go into full flow when there was a rumbling noise, it got louder and then swoosh a crow covered in soot came tumbling down the chimney and landed on the hearth, then there was another rumble which seemed to build and build. We were all mesmerised, between the crow flapping and the noise, the next thing an avalanche of soot came down the chimney, mother and Lady Jane were covered. The piano was on the other side of the room so father and us boys just got a wee bit of fall out. However, the crow was now starting to recover and was flapping around trying to get back outside.

"Our father was not the most practical of men, he jumped up from the piano, mumbled something about an urgent errand and disappeared. By now we boys were all in fits of laughter, however Archie had the presence of mind to open the French doors and shoo the crow into the garden. What reduced us to tears of laughter was Lady Jane had a wee West Highland terrier called Lucy, we used to call it Lucifer as it was a real nippy wee devil. Lucy's beautiful white coat was also covered in soot, now she really did look like a devil dog.

"Mother here was first to recover from the shock and started to issue orders. 'Euan, scullery, bring a brush and pail. Archie close the doors and make sure that bird of satan doesn't get back into the house. We all looked towards the French doors just in time to see the Reverend Fraser Stewart, our father, and minister, scurrying down the driveway, removing himself from the disaster at breakneck speed.

"Next Lady Jane had a fit of the vapours. 'Boy, yes you boy, Robert, get my smelling salts out of my reticule. Oh dear, oh dear, I feel most unwell and look at my poor darling little Lucy all covered in soot, my poor precious.

"Ishbel my dear get one of the boys to inform Carstairs we are returning home. I expect he's in your kitchen having a cup of tea, he must bring the car round and drive me home immediately, immediately my dear, immediately!'

"Not only father but Lady Jane and Lucy deserted the scene of carnage. We boys had to help mother, who was now almost in tears, clean up the spectacular mess. Between our efforts and that of our part time help Ethel we eventually managed to get the room back to some sort of rights. The following day mother organised a visit from the local chimney sweep. After he had finished his work we had to give the room yet another thorough clean.

"The worst part for us was seeing the beautiful afternoon tea going straight into the bin as it was covered in soot, the best part was mother gave us each sixpence for all our hard work."

Ishbel joined in, "Actually the money was from your father, compensation for his act of desertion. He also bought me a large box of Terry's chocolates by way of an apology. I sincerely hope our tea at Reid's Hotel isn't covered in soot."

Everyone was now in fits of laughter as they prepared to enjoy their afternoon of luxury.

The waiters brought the afternoon tea, with not a tiny speck of soot in evidence, Firstly the table was laid with a crisp linen table cover and napkins then fine china. The tea and hot water pots were silver as was the milk jug and sugar bowl, even the posy of fresh flowers was in a silver vase.

The table looked absolutely beautiful, next a young waiter, wearing an immaculate white jacket, brought two three tier china stands. Assorted sandwiches, minus crusts, were arranged on the bottom level, scones on the middle with little bowls of butter, cream and jam. On the top plate was a selection of the most scrumptious looking dainty cakes imaginable, a real testimony to the skill of Reid's pastry chef.

The waiter poured the tea and the party started to enjoy the lavish treats. For a time the only conversation was, 'mmm delicious, have you tried the smoked salmon sandwiches, the cucumber ones are really tasty, excellent tea, look there is even a dish of lemon slices, mmm perfection' etc. etc.

Eventually the conversation restarted, Ishbel asked Sam and Maria how long they had been married and why they were going to Australia. Robert interrupted her, "Honestly mother you are much too inquisitive, you really mustn't be so nosy."

Sam interrupted, "Robert I think your mother has every right to ask the question, after all she probably saved Maria's life. Come Maria let's tell our new friends how a young couple from industrial Lanarkshire find themselves heading to Australia to start a new life."

Together they told their story of how they had worked together at the brickworks in Glenboig but because Maria was a Catholic and Sam a Protestant they had tried to deny their love. However, the war had changed everything. After being invalided out of the army due to injuries from a gas attack Sam returned home and proposed to Maria. On telling her parents the news her father was furious and had cut Maria off from all contact with her family.

Sam explained how initially his family were not greatly pleased with them either but eventually all was well and his parents came to Glasgow to see them before they left for Australia.

"We had a lovely farewell meal with them in Sloans Bar in the Argyll Arcade. It was wonderful, the most delicious steak pie. They brought presents from my sisters and the Law family who are really close friends. My ma and pa also gave us money to help with the fares to Australia. They are not at all wealthy so it was real evidence that they had accepted our decision to run off and marry.

"We had simply cut out the church service, we eloped to Glasgow and wed in the registry office. Then we rented a tiny single end flat and worked to save enough money to emigrate. For months we earned as much as we could, and spent as little, every penny was a prisoner.

"A real stroke of luck was the Manager of the Glenboig Brickworks recommended me for a job at a brickworks in a place called Northcote, situated in the outskirts of Melbourne. So that is why we are heading to Melbourne in Victoria. Well that's the edited version of our story.

"We just couldn't live with the religious prejudice. Do you know when a Catholic marries a Protestant in our town it's called a 'mixed marriage.' If they have any children the boys take the fathers religion and the girls take the mothers. It's absolutely mad, hopefully Australia will be a much more understanding place for us to bring up our family."

Ishbel was shocked at the level of prejudice experienced by Sam and Maria but she just said, "We must enjoy our sojourn here in Madeira. It's a fair sail to our next port of call at Cape Verde, actually it's a group of about ten islands. Mind you they also speak Portuguese, so perhaps it was another Atlantic paradise for Lady Jane to enjoy, and practice her language skills."

Robert laughed, "I very much doubt it mother. In the past Cape

Verde had a bit of a sad history resulting from the transporting of slaves. I think we will probably stop there just to replenish the stores, I very much doubt there will be a Reid's hotel on Cape Verde. As far as our final short stop for provisions is concerned its Jamestown, on St Helena. St Helena was where Napoleon spent his second exile, after the wee Frenchman escaped from Elba, and it was where he died in 1821. I can't imagine we will find any luxury hotels there either. If we are allowed off the ship perhaps we can find a nice cafe for a cup of tea or coffee."

The food at Reid's was absolutely delicious and a huge treat for Maria and Sam after many months of skimping and saving to fund their journey.

Maria had been pondering on a comment Ishbel had made earlier, "Ishbel, I couldn't help notice you mentioned earlier about women getting the vote. Sam's mother is a suffragette and I was wondering if you were one too."

"Oh my dear what a laugh!" answered Ishbel. "Can you just imagine me chairing the Women's Guild meeting then coming home and saying to my husband, 'Well Fraser, I'll just away upstairs now and pin on my purple and green rosette then I'll go off and smash some windows. Do you think you can get your own dinner tonight dear?' No, that was never going to happen.

"I'm afraid I've had to support the suffrage cause from a distance without actually getting involved, at times it's been really difficult for me. I would love to have attended protest marches, but a minister's wife in rural Perthshire must keep her private opinions to herself. That's one of the reasons I am accompanying Robert to Africa, now I am a widow I can do exactly what I want, well within reason.

"Women don't have the vote yet in the Union of South Africa, perhaps I'll break a few windows in Cape Town. Maria, the State of Victoria granted women the vote away back in 1908 so you will be able to vote when you get to Australia. Use it, and use it wisely my dear."

"Sam, I told you my mother was a formidable woman didn't I?" said Robert. "Come on now, spill the beans what's all this about your mother being a suffragette?"

Sam answered, "My ma is a very bright woman, she's also a trained milliner, but for various reasons her and my father ended up living in the Rows of Gartsherrie. The Rows are wee houses built by the Baird family, the owners of a huge iron and steel works. Just about everyone who works at Bairds lives in tied housing in the Rows.

"Around the turn of the century the Baird family opened a school for the workers' children in the Gartsherrie Institute, the two teachers Jennie and Margaret Mathieson were both suffragettes. I very much doubt that the Bairds' knew of their political leanings when they employed them. They were wonderful teachers and many bairns from Gartsherrie owe them a great deal, including me and my two sisters.

"Well it was Jennie who introduced my mother to the movement and over the years they've become great friends. Jennie lives in a fancy house in Blairhill and the Johnstones' in a tiny wee house in the Long Row but their fight for the vote has brought not only them but other ladies from very different backgrounds together.

"My mother has seen a lot of poverty and the ills that come from it. She would dearly like to see women treated as equals in society.

"Our father, Alex, is a wonderful man. He has supported my mother every step of the way. He too is clever but he was brought up on a farm in Ulster and there is a lot of prejudice in Scotland against the Irish immigrants, so he has had to work as a labourer. The Irish are always overlooked when it comes to any promotions.

"After many years of struggle my mother hopes that the enormous contribution made by women during the war will be the trigger for the granting of the vote. Ma sees the vote simply as the first step to gaining rights for women, that's what is really important to her.

"Everything I've said sounds as though she is a very serious woman. Honestly my ma is anything but serious, she is great fun! We might have been poor as children but we were incredibly happy. Can you believe our house had just two rooms and a scullery, with an outside toilet and coal cellar. We slept in the kitchen, the Law family were our lodgers and they slept in the other room. We were brought up as one big family until they moved to their own wee house in the Herriot Row."

The conversations continued and the glorious afternoon passed, the shadows lengthened and sadly it was eventually time for the party to leave the opulence of Reid's hotel and walk back down into the town and board the ship.

The following morning was Sunday, and the SS Trojan was still anchored in Funchal harbour.

Notices had been put up around the ship informing all the passengers that a church service would be held in the first class dining room at 11.00am to which all passengers would be very welcome.

Maria and Ishbel were really looking forward to seeing how the first class passengers travelled, as well as attending the service, and they were not disappointed. The room was magnificent with wood panelled walls, thick Axminster carpet and gleaming crystal chandeliers. The tables had been moved and the dining chairs arranged in a horseshoe fashion. The table facing the congregation was covered in a white linen cloth and was dressed as an alter with a beautiful flower arrangement and a silver cross. The bread and communion wine for the celebration of the Eucharist were covered in snow white napkins.

An Anglican vicar, Rev. Williams-Danvers, who was travelling first class led the service. The music was provided by a member of the orchestra who played the piano. The congregation sang Christmas carols, it being close to the celebration of the birth of the Christ child.

The four friends sat together and entered into the spirit of the Anglican service which was very different to Protestant worship. Maria, with her Catholic background enjoyed the form of the service and the fact that the Mass was in English rather than Latin she found totally fascinating.

After singing the final carol, *In The Bleak Midwinter,* a strange choice in the sunshine of Madeira. Tea, coffee and delicious little biscuits was served to all those attending the service. The ladies enjoyed drinking their tea out of fine china cups, decorated with the ship's name. Ishbel whispered to Maria, "All a bit different to the tea served in mugs in 3rd Class, is it not?"

On their final day in Funchal, the four friends explored the old town and visited some of the local churches. Before rejoining the ship the friends enjoyed a glass of Madeira wine and a slice of cake in a little street cafe. They toasted the forthcoming Christmas and new year and wished for an end to the war. They also toasted the writing of a new and exciting chapter in each of their lives.

That evening the SS Trojan sailed out of Funchal Harbour and the glorious Madeira idyl was over. Maria found the next leg of the journey much easier, her seasickness abated, she still had problems with sickness due to her pregnancy but nothing like the horrors of the Bay of Biscay. The days passed and the friends spent many happy hours together playing card games or dominoes and chatting.

The ship docked briefly in St Vincent one of the Cape Verde Islands at the town of Mindelo to take on supplies before the final leg to the Union of South Africa and the beautiful Cape. Although it was a brief stop the foursome did manage to go ashore and explore the town.

With its cobbled streets, Portuguese language, flowers in abundance and small Catholic churches Mindelo had a flavour of Funchal but Robert had been reading about its grim history during the years of the slave trade and found the island strangely depressing after the joy of Funchal. However, they all enjoyed walking on dry land and drinking coffee in a small local cafe.

The final provisioning stop was at St Helena and the four friends were lucky enough to be able to disembark from the ship and spend a few hours in Jamestown.

Robert would like to have stayed longer on St Helena to track down where Napoleon had stayed but the SS Trojan was only berthed for the one day.

The ship now entered the final phase of its journey down the west coast of Africa to Cape Town where the goodbyes would be said and Sam and Maria would continue with the second half of their voyage to their new life in Australia.

Christmas day 1917 was celebrated at sea, fortunately conditions were not nearly as rough as in the North Atlantic. Everyone enjoyed a delicious Christmas lunch after the church service, which was once again held in the first class dining room. Lunch consisted of turkey, with all the trimmings, followed by plum pudding and custard. Neither Sam nor Maria had ever enjoyed such a Christmas feast. Christmas in Scotland was just another working day. However the tradition in both Glenboig and Gartsherrie was a special dinner of steak pie with mashed potatoes in the evening after work. Neither of their families had ever seen a plum pudding, their Christmas dinner would be finished off with a pancake or scone, if they were lucky, and a mug of tea.

The afternoon onboard was spent playing board games, laughing and chatting. The atmosphere on the ship was jolly and it helped to alleviate the homesickness which many people were feeling, including Sam and Maria. Teatime, and again the chefs on the ship put on a delicious spread; turkey sandwiches and mince pies with a real treat, bowls of dried figs, dates and apricots. Sam and Maria had no idea such things existed, never mind having tasted them.

To round off the day there was a jolly sing song then the pianist was joined by a fiddler and the duo played dance music to the delight of the passengers. Captain Thorn ensured that all his passengers had thoroughly enjoyed their Christmas Day, whether first or third class. Perhaps this was because he too had known days when there was very little food on the table and he had a long memory.

CHAPTER 2
The Blessing

It was the final night at sea before the ship docked in Cape Town. Ishbel was in her tiny cabin which she had been sharing with a young lady from Berkshire who was going to work as a governess in Cape Town. Maria was in dormitory 4 and Sam and Robert were talking on deck as the ship steamed down the West Coast of Southern Africa towards their final farewell.

"How are you feeling about starting your training as a Dutch minister and your new adventure?" asked Sam.

His friend replied, "Excited, scared, apprehensive, I honestly don't know. My mother on the other hand is totally calm and enthusiastic about our arrival in Cape Town.

"You know Sam I have so appreciated the friendship of you and Maria during the voyage. You are indeed a very lucky man to have married such a lovely woman. I really hope one day I meet my own Maria, it must be wonderful to have a soul mate to walk with you on life's journey."

Sam spoke diffidently, "Robert, can I ask you something? It's, well it's a bit awkward really. I told you Maria and I married in a registry office and the reasons why we had to get wed as we did. Well, both Maria and I are believers and somehow it doesn't seem right and proper not to have been married by a minister in the kirk. I was wondering, when we arrive in Cape Town, as a man of the cloth would you give us your blessing?"

Robert smiled, "Of course, I would be delighted to bless your union in the eyes of the lord. During my time in Cape Town I will be affiliated to The Groote Kerk. It's the oldest kirk in the Union of South Africa, it's even had Scottish minsters in the past, Dr William Robertson and the famous Dr Andrew Murray.

"Look Sam, we have a few days to get organised before the good ship Trojan sails on from the Cape to India. As soon as I get ashore and introduce myself to the present minister, a Dr Hausman, I'll ask him if I can use the church for a wee blessing service. Samuel Johnstone, my friend, it would be an honour to bless your union to Maria as my first act of worship in Cape Town.

"Like you and Maria my life is about to change enormously. As we enter 1918, I will be embarking on a real life changing adventure. There is a seminary in Stellenbosch where I will have to spend some time but I will mainly be stationed in Cape Town learning the language, and assisting at the church. After my probationary year I'll be sent to a church I know not where. I really will be in the hands of the Lord.

"Meantime the church have organised a wee cottage for us to live in. It's located in an area called Oranjezicht. Mother will no doubt make it into a home during our time on the Cape. You know Sam I'm not entirely sure what my mother intends to do in Cape Town. You do know she is not accompanying me to Africa because she can't thole losing her youngest son and wants to run his life. It's more because she wants an adventure of her own.

"My parents complimented each other, he was a wonderful minister to his congregation but as you heard at Reid's not the most practical of men. Mother on the other hand is amazing at all things practical, my father's stipend was not large but she magically stretched it to cover all our requirements, and there was always a meal at our table for anyone in need.

"My parents were devoted to each other, after he passed away her life changed completely, she had to leave the manse and not only had she lost her beloved husband, she had lost her job as a minister's wife and her three boys were now adults and living their own lives. Mother could have stayed with either of my brothers, but she chose to be independent and rented a little cottage.

"After I was invalided home from France, and like you, not the man who left Scotland, she looked after me until I was well enough to go back to Edinburgh and finish my degree. When I told her I had secured a post with the Dutch Reformed Kirk in Africa she was thrilled and before I could say 'Jack Robinson' she was packing our trunks. Truth to tell my brothers are not wondrously pleased that their mother is gallivanting off to Cape Town, they are not that approving of me either. They would much rather I had found a nice respectable parish in Scotland. But here we are Ishbel and Robert Stewart and Maria and Sam Johnstone all travelling to distant parts of the British Empire with no idea what the future will hold.

"Sam, I'll bid you goodnight. Tomorrow the adventure begins and my first task will be to arrange to bless your union. Good night my friend."

The following morning was Hogmanay a special day in the calendar of all Scots, wherever in the world they find themselves. After a final breakfast together, Robert gave Sam a piece of paper with the address of the cottage where they would be staying. Saying, "Come about seven o'clock tonight, I'm sure we will manage to organise some supper and you can stay for the bells, the four of us will see in 1918 together with a wee dram and a toast to a speedy end to the terrible war in Europe."

Maria and Sam watched as Robert and Ishbel disembarked, leaving their friends and the ship that had been their home during the past weeks, the SS Trojan.

Sam and Maria sat on deck and marvelled at the sight of Table Mountain rising up behind the city, flanked by Devil's Peak, the Lion's Head and Signal Hill. They couldn't imagine that any other city in the world could possibly look as breathtakingly beautiful as Cape Town.

After leaving behind the bleak winter of the northern hemisphere, they gloried in the blue southern summer sky. The sun was shining and warm, the Atlantic waves were stilled and the city appeared lush and full of trees. It was like arriving in paradise.

Sam took Maria's hand, saying, "M'darling girl, I spoke to Robert last night and asked him if he would bless our marriage. I know we wanted to get wed by the registrar to avoid all the religious prejudice in Coatbridge but in my heart of hearts I believe in the Lord and I would like to have a blessing on our union."

Maria squeezed his hand, "Yes Sam, you know I believe in the Lord, I just wish everyone could go to the church they choose without all the small minded backbiting. Robert is a good man and I would count it a privilege for him to give us the blessing of the church, besides if it hadn't been for his mother I doubt if you would have a bride after the storms on Biscay. I remember when we were all bairns at school we used to sing a song, I can't remember it all but it was something like:

> " *Loud roared the dreadful thunder*
> *The rain a deluge showers*
> *The clouds were rent asunder*
> *By lightning's vivid powers*
> *The night was dark and drear*
> *Our poor devoted bark*
> *There she lay, 'till next day*
> *In the Bay of Biscay oh.' "*

From then on the words just get worse and worse, while I was seasick I kept hearing it over and over in my head. Sam I honestly thought it was my end, I'll never forget Ishbel and how she got me through the hell of Biscay. You know Sam I rather wish we were going to settle here on the Cape rather than travel all the way to Australia, I'm sure we would be happy surrounded by all this beauty and the nearness of friends."

Sam agreed with her sentiments but he had a job and there was a home waiting for them in Northcote, near the Australian city of Melbourne, so he simply said, "Come on darling, all the people who are disembarking here have left, as visitors we can now join the queue to go ashore and explore Cape Town."

After leaving the ship and completing the customs formalities Robert and Ishbel had taken a horse drawn cab to the cottage in Alexandra Avenue, Oranjezicht which had been allocated to them by the church. Their first impression of the thatched white cottage, with its green shutters and walls draped in vivid pink bougainvillea was very favourable. As arranged they found the door key in a plant pot beside the front door and entered what was to be their home for the next twelve months. As soon as they opened the door into the hallway they were aware of the unique smell of a home with a thatched roof, it was like entering into a country barn full of straw.

The ladies of the congregation had left them a wonderful welcome gift. Throughout the cottage were vases filled with flowers, mostly proteas and the local fynbos but on the dining table was displayed a large vase filled with vivid blue agapanthus.

The pantry was stocked with food, and inside the cool box, with its muslin lined door, Ishbel found a melk tert, which she thought was a custard tart. There was also a plate of another sweetmeat, the likes of which Ishbel had never seen, little did she know that over the following months she would become a dab hand at making the delicious sweet of twisted doughnuts dipped in sugar syrup then finished with coconut called koeksisters. On top of the coal range in the kitchen sat a black cast iron pot, it looked like a witch's cauldron. They would later learn it was called a potjie, it contained a delicious stew, made from lamb, called a bredie.

After they had explored the cottage Robert told his mother about agreeing to Sam's request that he bless his friend's marriage to Maria before they sailed off to Australia. "Hopefully I'll manage to make the arrangements today and we can update them tonight. Mother, do you think the pot of stew will be enough for a Hogmanay dinner for four?"

Ishbel laughed, "Robert just think of me as the quartermaster, when it comes to catering all will be well."

While she was making a cup of tea and slicing the melk tert Ishbel agreed with her son that a blessing would be a lovely act. However, in her head she was already planning a delicious celebration feast for after the service and what they would all have to eat for the Hogmanay supper.

After enjoying his tea and cake Robert set off to find his new church and hopefully his new superior Dr Hausman.

Ishbel had scarcely washed the tea cups when their luggage arrived loaded on a horse drawn wagon. The driver and his mate carried the heavy trunks and cases into the cottage and asked Ishbel if they could be of further assistance. For the first time Ishbel heard herself addressed as 'Madam'. Her first instinct was to laugh and say, 'I'm not a madam, I'm Mrs Stewart', but the men were so respectful that she didn't want to hurt their feelings. Instead she offered them a cup of tea and a slice of melk tert. The men thanked her but said they had to leave as they had many more deliveries to make.

Isabel set to unpacking the trunks, by the time Robert returned the clothes were all in the wardrobes and chest of drawers, books neatly arranged on the shelves and family photographs displayed on the piano.

Able to have first choice Ishbel had chosen the bedroom facing out onto the back garden with a magnificent view of Table Mountain as a backdrop. On the bedside table she had placed a photograph of her husband Fraser and her bible. She stroked his well loved face saying aloud, "My darling man, what would you say to me for upping sticks and coming to Africa? I've asked myself so often 'would Fraser approve'? I'm not yet fifty, our boys are men, and men we can be proud of, three sons of the kirk. Fraser my dearest, now I want to do something for me, I'm not entirely sure what yet but I know with all my heart that I do not want to spend my remaining years in that draughty cottage in Scotland, spinning out my pension from the church and watching our savings disappear."

Ishbel's musings were interrupted by a chap on the door. Answering the knock Ishbel saw a middle aged coloured woman standing on the step. Seemingly without pausing for breath Ishbel heard her say.

"Morning Madam, I'm Sophie, I've been hired by the church to be your housekeeper and cook. I live in District Six, it's not far away so I'm not a live in you understand. My hours are eight in the morning until four in the afternoon but if you occasionally want me to do an evening I can stay late. I'll also see to the chickens. Your gardener and odd job man, Thomas April will start back next week, he just comes in three days a week, he is also a fine cobbler and he mends shoes and boots the rest of the time. Thought I'd give you time this morning to settle in before I arrived, I came in yesterday and baked you a melk tert and prepared a bredie for your supper tonight. Can I come in now Madam?"

Astonished, Ishbel invited Sophie into the cottage, where she headed straight for the kitchen. There she removed a flowered pinafore overall from her bag which she put on over her simple calico dress. "Right Madam, that's me all ready. Now, what would you like me to do?"

Ishbel instantly liked Sophie and realised she would be a real asset to the Stewart household. "Well Sophie, I've just finished tidying everything away after emptying the trunks and our cases. As they say in Scotland, 'I'm fair wabbit!' How about we have a nice cup of tea to revive us and one of the little cakes you left?"

Sophie filled the kettle and started setting a silver tea tray, "Oh no Sophie, don't go to all that bother," said Ishbel. "We will just sit in the kitchen and have a cup at the table."

Sophie was horrified, "Madam WE can't sit at the table drinking tea. The Dutch and English ladies have tea in the sitting room and I have my tea in the kitchen or out in the garden. That's the way it's done here Madam."

Ishbel couldn't help but speak with a smile in her voice as she said, "Sophie, firstly I'm neither Dutch nor English, I'm Scottish and I'm not some grand madam. I'm a widow living on a small pension. My husband was a minister and I am perfectly used to cooking and doing housework. When I lived at the manse we used to have a girl, Ethel, who came in a few days a week to help me and WE always had tea together in the kitchen. Now you make the tea and I'll get the cake."

Sophie did not know whether to be horrified or intrigued. Sitting in the kitchen having tea and cake with your Madam? 'Hmmm, Scottish people were obviously very strange people indeed.'

Robert arrived back home around lunchtime to find his mother and a lady wearing a bright floral pinny washing up in the kitchen. Ishbel introduced her new friend to Robert. "Sophie, this is my youngest son, Robert Stewart. Robert meet Sophie, she will be coming in every day to help us and she has promised to teach me Afrikaans, so it won't just be you who will understand the language of our new country".

"Pleased to meet you Sophie," said Robert. "I hope you will be very happy with us, now can I tear my mother away from the washing up I've got some news for her?"

Ishbel and Robert went through to the sitting room where they both tried to update each other on their news at the same time. Robert exclaimed, "Mother will you haud your wheesht? You can tell me all about your morning later. I have important news to tell you. I met my new superior, he took me on a tour around the kirk, it's an incredibly beautiful building and then we went to the manse where I had some coffee. He was very welcoming. Now the bad news, apparently as neither Sam nor Maria are members of the church, I can't give a formal blessing in the church building. However, he has no objection to me informally blessing them. He has suggested here in the cottage, what do you think? And, he has also said he would like to attend."

Ishbel didn't need to think twice, "Oh Robert, what a beautiful idea! Why don't you do the service in the garden? It's so lovely and colourful and with the mountain as a backdrop what better place.

"I've been discussing the blessing with Sophie, she knows a man who will come and take some photographs, wouldn't that be wonderful? And she's also suggested we go to a hotel called the Mount Nelson for tea afterwards. I was telling her about our adventure at Reid's Hotel in Madeira and she says that the Mount Nelson is THE place to go in Cape Town for a special celebration. It's very near here, it's the big building at the bottom of the hill."

Robert laughed, "Really mother, I leave you for a couple of hours and you have acquired an oracle called Sophie. However I think going out for a celebration tea would be an excellent idea as we don't really have time to arrange something special here at the cottage. I thought the 2nd of January at about two o'clock would be good and I have agreed that time with Dr Hausman. We can tell Sam and Maria tonight.

"I think I'll walk down to the hotel now and book a table for afternoon tea on the 2nd. I hope it lives up to its reputation and it's not a let down after Reid's," said Robert.

"Good idea," agreed his mother. "Sophie is going out to get some messages and I'm going to make a tray of shortbread. No respectable Scottish household can welcome in the New Year without shortbread and a sultana cake. Mind you, I didn't take a chance on that, I made a rich fruit cake months ago and brought it, well wrapped in brown paper, in my trunk."

Robert left the cottage laughing and thinking to himself, what a mother, baking a fruit cake, carefully packing it and bringing it all the way from Scotland to Africa in order to be organised for the New Year. Nothing, but nothing, will ever daunt that woman.

Eventually Sam and Maria managed to leave the ship and set foot on African soil. It was not at all what either of them imagined it would be like. Their thoughts of Africa mainly centred around the stories of the missionaries and abolitionist like Dr David Livingstone. Conjuring up pictures of Victoria Falls, Lake Malawi, and the Nile, thick jungle and native people wearing hardly any clothes, or desert - that was their idea of Africa.

Instead they found that Cape Town was a busy prosperous looking city, the people were dressed as they would be in any city in Great Britain in summertime, and while it was very pleasantly warm the climate was certainly not tropical.

A map of the city had been pinned to the notice board in the ship's dining room. Sam had drawn a copy of the map showing the city centre so that they would be able to find their way to the Stewart's cottage in Oranjezicht.

After leaving the ship they started to walk up Adderley Street, looking in the shop windows and admiring the beautiful buildings. Sam stopped at a jewellery shop, the window was full of exquisite rings, not only diamonds but rubies, sapphires and other semi precious stones. Sam questioned Maria, "Go on tell me, which is your favourite ring?"

Maria laughed, "Samuel Johnstone, it makes not a whit of difference what my favourite is, we definitely can't afford to buy a ring."

"I know that but just tell me anyway, I promise you Maria one day we will go into a shop just like this and I'll buy you a ring that reflects my love for you. Now, tell me which ring speaks to you, which one says Sam and Maria Johnstone?"

Maria looked carefully at the vast array before pointing to a blue sapphire ring with a diamond set at either side. "I love that ring Sam. The diamonds represent you and me and the sapphire the blue sea journey to reach our new life in Australia."

Sam held his wife's hand and made a promise, "Maria Johnstone, I vow one day I will buy you a ring just like the one in the window to represent our love and remind us of our journey together to the other side of the world."

Adderley Street in the heart of the city was vibrant and noisy but Sam and Maria felt entirely alone, just them and a vow. Holding hands they slowly walked up the hill towards the Company Gardens.

Before exploring the Gardens they found a small cafe with outdoor tables and ordered two teas and cheese sandwiches, the cheapest items on the menu. The food was served by a pretty young coloured girl. As she put the tea tray down she said, "I hope you don't mind me saying but you have a very strange accent, it's certainly not English, it's not by any chance German is it?"

"No it's Scottish," they laughed in unison, Sam reassured her, "Please don't worry we are not here spying for Germany."

After enjoying their lunch they spent the remainder of the day just taking in the sights of Cape Town, including walking up Signal Hill. Maria found the walk relatively easy but Sam with his damaged lungs struggled along gamely. Fortunately they got talking to some soldiers at the summit and they kindly gave them a lift back down into the city, dropping them off in Wale Street.

Sam consulted his makeshift map, they walked through the Company Gardens and headed towards Oranjezicht and their friend's cottage. When they arrived, tired out after all the walking Ishbel immediately made them welcome, taking them through the cottage and out the back door. They sat out on the stoop where she had set out a table with a large pitcher of home made lemonade and glasses. Robert joined them and while he poured the cool drinks Ishbel told them all about her day and meeting her new friend the redoubtable Sophie.

"She really is incredible," enthused Ishbel. "Sophie has even organised a photographer to come to the cottage and take a few photographs before Robert performs the blessing. The church are paying her to come in every week day from eight o'clock until four and there is an odd job man coming in three days a week. I never expected all this help but having Sophie come in every day will allow me to get a job or do some charity work. I'm really excited, no idea yet what I'll do but I've no intention of sitting around when adventures abound.

"Oh dear, I'm so very sorry I've just realised I've let the cat out the bag on the arrangements for your blessing. Robert, tell Sam what you have organised and Maria come with me and I'll show you around the cottage and then we can rejoin the men in the garden."

Maria was thrilled with the cottage, from the beautiful polished furniture made of Cape stinkwood, which looked majestic against the simple whitewashed walls to being able to look up and see the inside of the thatched roof. The floors in the hall and kitchen were terracotta tiles and the other rooms were all wooden scattered with a few occasional rugs.

As she walked Maria around the cottage Ishbel told her the arrangements for the blessing. "I hope you are not too disappointed not to be able to have the blessing in the actual kirk building, but to be honest if it was me I think I would prefer the cottage garden in the shadow of God's magnificent mountain."

The ladies joined the menfolk in the garden. Robert exclaimed,

"Isn't it truly wonderful, sitting outside on Hogmanay, who would have believed it possible, certainly not when you are born and bred in Scotland."

The four friends sat chatting with Table Mountain as their backdrop. There was so much to discuss, the arrangements for the blessing on the second of January, their journey from Liverpool to Cape Town and their plans for the future. They blethered until well after eight o'clock and as the sun started to set they retired to the dining room where Ishbel served the lamb bredie with some of Sophie's home made bread to soak up the gravy, the stew was followed by a platter of dried and fresh fruits.

As the clock struck midnight church bells rang out, sirens sounded and Cape Town welcomed in 1918. Before following Scottish tradition and singing Auld Lang Syne Robert offered a prayer. From the depth of his soul he prayed for all the men and women on the Western front, be they friend or enemy, he prayed that the war would soon be over and peace and plenty reign.

They toasted the incoming year, the ladies with sherry and the men whisky, they sang Auld Lang Syne, ate shortbread and fruit cake and remembered loved ones. Traditions from home celebrated, it was soon time for Sam and Maria to make their way back to the ship.

As they walked down Long Street they gained comfort from holding hands. Maria was thinking and feeling so many emotions, she remembered celebrations in years past, attending midnight Mass and sharing fun times with her brothers and sisters, particularly Maureen.

New year in Coatbridge often heralded snow after the crisp frosts of December. In Cape Town even after one o'clock in the morning Maria could feel the warmth in the air, she still could not fully comprehend how she came to be walking down Long Street in Cape Town with the man she loved by her side, and that they would soon be heading towards Australia and a completely new life.

Little did she realise Sam was having exactly the same homesick thoughts, the same emotions of their new reality were coursing through him too.

The following day was spent with Robert and Ishbel, Robert took them to see his church which was truly breathtaking in its beauty. The threesome sat in a pew and prayed together before walking back to the cottage to have lunch with Ishbel.

Once again they sat under the stoop this time to enjoy their lunch of tea and sandwiches and the remains of the melk tert and fruit cake.

Apparently Sophie had turned up for work, even though it was New

Years Day. Ishbel explained, "Honestly Sophie is an education. She told me that the workers new year holiday here on the Cape is on the second of January. Tt's called Tweede Nuwe Jaar, the second new year, and apparently it's all very jolly. Mind you I don't think it has a great history, I think it's something to do with the slave trade. When I asked her Sophie just said in her own unique way, 'Madam, it's better days now, I'll be back to work on Wednesday morning but I'll pop in tomorrow to introduce Mr Adams the photographer.' I didn't feel I could pry too much with us just being off the boat.

"Sophie has made something called bobotie for our supper tonight, it's a local speciality, and it smells lovely, all spicy. Best of all I just have to heat it up in the oven and make a salad. I'll need to find something productive to do soon or I'm going to become very lazy indeed with all the help from Sophie.

"I'm ever so glad we booked tea for tomorrow afternoon at the Mount Nelson, it will be such a treat to relive our tea at Reid's Hotel in Madeira, the kitchen will be firmly closed at Chez Stewart. Now Sam, please don't concern yourself about the cost, Robert and I are your hosts while you are in Cape Town."

Sadly Sam explained his feelings, "Maria and I truly appreciate all your kindness but Ishbel we can never repay you and Robert. We will shortly be sailing on to Australia and it will take a time for us to get ourselves established."

Before Robert, Sam or Maria could say anything else Ishbel interjected, in her best motherly voice, "Sam, Maria, now look here you two, this is how it works. At the moment it is our great pleasure to be able to do a kindness for you, that kindness does not have to be repaid to us. However some day you will be in a position to help somebody else, when you do so you will have repaid us a hundredfold. Now no more of this talk let's just finish our lunch and I'll let you in on the plan the wonderful Sophie suggested for this afternoon. Apparently we can take a tram ride along the coast to a place called Camp's Bay. According to Sophie the scenery is breathtaking and there are a number of cafes including one that is famous for delicious ice cream. Does anybody fancy a wafer or perhaps a pokey hat?"

They finished lunch and walked down to Victoria Road where they caught a tram to Camp's Bay. Sophie was right, the scenery was breathtaking and with the help of Robert's map they were able to work out exactly where they were in relation to the mountains.

The friends spent another memorable afternoon together, drinking in the beauty around them. The blue Atlantic with its choppy waves contrasting with the golden pristine beach edged with palm trees. Forming a backdrop to the village was the Twelve Apostles mountain range which seemed to enfold the houses between their peaks and the ocean. The painted bungalows with their colourful gardens made Camp's Bay seem like the most wonderful place to live in the whole world. Truly a seaside idyll but conveniently close to the city of Cape Town.

Sam and Robert left the ladies sitting on a bench looking out to sea while they went off to try and find the legendary ice cream seller and purchase cones or wafers.

Ishbel took the opportunity to give Maria some advice, "My dear a lot is being asked of you, while expecting your first baby you have to continue sailing thousands of miles until you reach Australia and then set up home in a country where you don't have any family or connections.

"Maria, I want to speak to you about beyond the initial time of getting established in your new country. You are a clever girl, Australia gave women the vote years ago which makes me think it is well ahead of Great Britain regarding women's rights. You are intelligent, don't just be Sam's wife, be his equal. I would love to think that you can make your mark in an exciting young country.

"I don't regret a moment of my life with Fraser, I loved him very much but there was never a ME, and I truly think I could have contributed so much more if I had not concentrated one hundred percent of my efforts towards my husband and family.

"I came from a fishing family in the Western Isles, my father was away on the boats a lot of the time with his brothers. My mother looked after the money as well as the family, she bought up little parcels of land, several cottages and a shop. We became a wealthy family on the island entirely due to her efforts. I am not saying money is the most important thing in life Maria, it's not, but you have to feel fulfilled. If you are confident in your life choices it will rub off on the rest of your family.

"Here comes the menfolk. Now Maria what are you going to wear tomorrow?"

"Same as at Reid's, my jade skirt. I don't have a lot of clothes and it's not exactly the weather for my good bottle green wool costume with the velvet collar, the one that I used to wear to church every Sunday at home."

"Perhaps I can help, shhh, we can talk after supper," whispered Ishbel.

They all enjoyed their ice cream, the conversation, the laughter and the companionship - sitting on a bench in Camp's Bay and looking out over the Atlantic waves was just bliss.

Eventually it was time to return to the city. The journey back along Victoria Avenue was if anything more spectacular, with views of the Lion's Head and Signal Hill as well as Table Mountain.

After arriving back at the cottage Robert and Sam sat in the garden enjoying a glass of Ishbel's home made lemonade.

Ishbel beckoned Maria, "Maria, perhaps you can give me a wee hand in the kitchen." When they arrived in the kitchen Ishbel said, "I've got something to show you, come into my bedroom and see what I unearthed from my trunk and tell me if you would like to wear them for the blessing tomorrow."

Lying on the bed was a silk calf length tea dress in a lovely shade of soft turquoise blue, trimmed with ecru lace. There was also a band of a matching moire ribbon and a spray of cream silk roses.

"I thought you could dress your sunhat with the ribbon and flowers and you would be most welcome to the afternoon dress. What do you think Maria?"

"I think it's the most beautiful outfit imaginable. And, you don't mind if I borrow it for the service, och Ishbel you are too too kind!"

"I'd like you to keep the dress not borrow it," said Ishbel. "When you wear it in Australia it will always remind you of your time in Cape Town. Now come away let's put the bobotie in the oven to warm while we make the salad and slice up some bread."

After supper Sam and Maria walked hand in hand down Long Street to the docks, Maria carrying a brown carrier bag, the contents of which she refused to reveal to Sam.

As the following morning dawned Maria lay on her berth thinking about the service later that day. Her actual wedding day had been grey and joyless without family or friends, the witnesses being two strangers whom Sam had treated to the price of a pint after the formalities. Their wedding breakfast was fish and chips eaten out of newspaper and a mug of tea in their rented room.

Now thanks to Robert and Ishbel they were going to have a beautiful wedding. Maria's heart was full.

Before getting ready Maria decided she would write a short letter to both her mother and her mother in law telling them that today they were going to have their marriage blessed. Sadly her letter to her mother would have to be sent via her brother Dan.

Dearest Ma
I just wanted you and the family to know that our registry office

wedding is going to be blessed today by a minister we met on the ship, his name is Robert Stewart and he was travelling out to Cape Town with his mother Ishbel. Ma, I don't know how I would have got through the past weeks without Ishbel, truly she was an angel sent to protect me. I hope you are praying for us to St Joseph and don't forget I'm Maria called for Mary the holy mother.

Sam is wonderful and I don't regret for a minute eloping with him but I do miss you all, especially our Maureen. Sam and I really appreciated Dan's support when we were in Glasgow but it's all the wee things I miss. I even miss my pa, I know he is not an evil man really but he is a bully and he uses the church to control the family. I know you are never going to change him and it's not worth trying.

But today Ma, we are going to have our union blessed in the garden of a perfect cottage, under Table Mountain. Afterwards we are going to a hotel for afternoon tea. Ishbel has even given me a lovely afternoon dress, it's a beautiful turquoise colour, just lovely.

Ma, I really just wanted you to know we are safe and happy, the first part of our journey complete.

Remember when you attend Mass keep Sam and Maria in your silent prayers.

All my love
Maria

* * *

She then penned another letter, this time to Sam's family in Gartsherrie.

Dear Ma and Pa
We have arrived safely in Cape Town and I just wanted you both to know that our marriage is going to be blessed today by a minister we met coming out on the ship, Robert Stewart. He is a Church of Scotland minister but has taken a post working for the Dutch Reformed church.

Robert travelled out to Africa with his mother Ishbel. Ishbel was my saviour on the voyage she nursed me through terrible sea sickness and has been so very kind.

The service will be held in the garden of their cottage and

Ishbel has given me a lovely turquoise afternoon dress to wear. The lady who works for them is arranging a photographer so we will be able to send you a photograph.

Sam is well and the climate here suits him. Please forgive us for leaving. We both miss home very much and our families, with me it's Maureen and Sam misses his father terribly.

You would love Ishbel Ma, she wanted to be a Suffragette but couldn't because her husband was a minister, now she is a widow she can do what she likes, I think she will join the movement in the Union of South Africa. I won't need to join, I'll have the vote in Victoria.

Love to all the family, including the Laws - Sam often tells me tales about all the Law family when they stayed with you in the Long Row.

All our love
Sam and Maria

* * *

Sam was up on deck, sitting on the bench which he had come to think of as 'our bench' waiting for his wife. After writing the letters Maria had spent several hours washing and arranging her hair then dressing carefully in her new outfit. As she walked towards Sam he was once again stunned by her beauty but he had not expected her to be wearing such an exquisite ensemble.

"My darling lass you are so beautiful! I'm the proudest man alive." Sam kissed his wife and hand in hand they walked towards the gangplank.

A lady passenger from first class approached them, she said to Maria, "My dear I heard your news from the Captain at dinner last night, no secrets on a ship. I understand you are going to have your marriage blessed today, please accept this little bouquet of fresh flowers, a bride must have flowers you know."

They both thanked the woman, who was a complete stranger, but a stranger with a heart of gold.

Sam insisted that they take a horse drawn cab to the cottage as it was such a special day. When they arrived Ishbel welcomed them, she looked beautiful in an afternoon dress in a shade of blue that exactly matched her blue eyes. "Come away in my dears, we've got plenty of time for a cup of tea before the reverend arrives." They went through

to the garden and sat out on the stoop which now seemed so familiar
to them.

Sophie brought out a tea tray, and said to Maria, "You look beautiful
Mrs Johnstone your husband is a very lucky man. My friend Mr Adams
will be here shortly with his camera, he has promised me he'll develop
the photographs later this afternoon so that you will be able to take
them back to the ship tonight."

Robert arrived dressed in his dog collar and clerical robes. They had
just started drinking their tea when the bell pull rang. Sophie showed
the photographer Mr Adams into the garden. As he was setting up his
equipment Ishbel took Maria's hand, "Come into the cottage with me
for a moment my dear I want to give you something." They went into
the sitting room and Ishbel handed Maria a small box.

Maria protested, "Ishbel you have given me so much already I can't
possibly accept anything else."

"My dear it's just a wee something and it's not terribly valuable, just
silver gilt jewellery but I thought it would set off your dress nicely and
something blue is traditional." Maria opened the box and it contained a
beautiful pendant, a central blue stone surrounded by seed pearls and
small blue stones, it might not have been a real sapphire but it was
extremely pretty. Ishbel fastened it around Maria's neck saying, "My
dear if I had been blessed with a daughter I would have wanted a girl
just like you."

The door bell rang again, this time it was Reverend Dr Hausman.
Ishbel welcomed him into the cottage and then through to the garden
where she introduced him to Sam and Maria.

Mr Adams had now set up his photographic equipment and took a
series of photographs of the assembled company. When he had finished
the formal pictures Ishbel asked if she could have a photograph taken
with Sophie and Maria. He took a lovely portrait of Ishbel sitting with
Sophie and Maria standing behind her, the background being a vibrant
bougainvillea. If Dr Hausman thought this informality a little strange he
said nothing but he quietly thought Mrs Stewart is certainly one to
watch, an independent woman if ever I saw one.

Mr Adams left and Robert carried out a beautiful service of
blessing with the mountain as a backdrop and Dr Hausman and Ishbel
sitting on chairs as witnesses.

Afterwards Sophie brought a tray of sherry out to the stoop for a
celebration toast. Dr Hausman made a kindly speech wishing the
young couple safe travels and good fortune in their new land. Sam was
not used to speaking in public but he felt he had to reply in order to

show his appreciation for all the kindness shown to him and Maria by Robert and Ishbel and also wish them well in their new life in the Union of South Africa.

Formalities over Robert suggested they all walk down to the Mount Nelson for tea. Dr Hausman thanked them for the invitation but sadly had to decline as he had another engagement.

The four friends walked down the hill towards the hotel with memories of Reid's in Funchal firmly in their minds. The Mount Nelson certainly did not disappoint. They were welcomed by a uniformed concierge who showed them to the tea lounge which was situated through the main lobby lined with elaborate mahogany reception counters at either side, all the staff were immaculately uniformed and the clientele elegantly dressed. On entering the tea lounge they were shown to their table by a tail coated maitre d. He introduced them to their waitress, "This is Noreen, she will look after you this afternoon." Noreen indeed looked after them, she spoiled them splendidly.

Noreen laid the table with the crockery and cutlery and served the beverages, however unlike Reid's in Madeira where they were presented with cake stands here they helped themselves to food from a huge mahogany table positively groaning with all things delicious both savoury and sweet. In the centre of the table raised well above the food was a beautiful floral arrangement the colours of which complimented the chintz curtains and soft furnishings in the lounge.

Throughout the afternoon Noreen brought fresh pots of tea and hot water and encouraged them to try the different treats on offer. "Sir, have you tried the little savoury puffs and squares of bacon quiche? They are both delicious! Mam, the chocolate cake is divine!"

Maria thought, 'If I live to be a hundred I'll never experience anything quite as wonderful as this ever again'.

In an act that completed the day Noreen handed Sam a large brown envelope. "This was left at reception for you Mr Johnstone." Excitedly Sam opened the envelope and saw the beautiful photographs taken by Mr Adams. There was also a note saying that he would get Sophie to deliver a set to Rev. Stewart the following day. The beautiful photographs were passed around to be admired, Maria could hardly speak for the lump in her throat.

At five o'clock they left the Mount Nelson lounge feeling replete and happy and then had a walk through the hotel gardens. Reluctantly the afternoon had to end, both Ishbel and Maria openly wept as they said their goodbyes. Robert and Sam did the Scottish thing, firm handshakes and extended best wishes. But in their hearts they too both felt very emotional.

After saying their final farewells Ishbel and Robert walked up the hill to their cottage and Sam and Maria down through the Company Gardens towards the Strand and the SS Trojan.

At the top of the gangplank a young officer met them saying, "Captain's compliments sir. Captain Thorn has arranged for you to enjoy a first class cabin tonight. Follow me and I'll shown you to your suite."

Amazed, Sam and Maria followed the officer to a beautiful double en suite cabin fitted out with every luxury imaginable, including lots of little soaps and bottles of bubble bath, cologne and creams. And, joy of joy, thick Turkish towels. There were even towelling dressing gowns and slippers hanging in the bathroom. Sam and Maria enjoyed a perfect end to a perfect day.

—

CHAPTER 3
The Voyage Continues

As the ship sailed out of Cape Town on the morning of Wednesday 3rd January 1918 towards her next port of call, Bombay, Sam and Maria stood on deck, first waving goodbye to their dear friends and then as Robert and Ishbel disappeared from view they watched Table Mountain, wearing its white table cover of cloud, until it too grew small and eventually vanished from sight.

They held hands, neither of them saying what was in their hearts, but with tears in their eyes. Leaving beautiful and vibrant Cape Town, a place where they had both renewed their faith and their marriage commitment was harder than they could possibly have imagined. However, the passage was paid and employment awaited Sam in Northcote, there was no option but to leave Africa and head for their destiny in Australia.

After Bombay the last stopping place would be the port of Columba in Ceylon before eventually reaching their final destination up the Yarra River to the Victoria Dock and the City of Melbourne.

The ship only stopped at Bombay for two days. The atmosphere was very different to that of Cape Town. The docks had an industrial feel and the people they could see from the ship looked thin and poorly nourished. The smell which seemed to pervade the atmosphere declared poverty.

Thankfully they had arrived in the Bombay winter so they were not subjected to monsoon or humidity, however it still seemed very hot to people used to a Scottish winter. Although, the morning smogs were certainly reminiscent of Glasgow.

The passengers were advised to remain onboard the ship due to the high possibility of contracting disease, as Bombay had regular cholera epidemics and apparently twenty years previously bubonic plague had been rife in the city. Notices were put up around the ship instructing that on no account had any passengers or crew member to buy anything, particularly food, from the people who congregated around the port.

Sam and Maria were mighty glad when their ship set sail away from the terrible poverty and disease of Bombay.

What they did not know was that there was quite another Bombay, a colonial Bombay where European expats lived in considerable luxury with armies of servants to cater for their every whim.

Impossible as it seemed, these people were living through the beginning of the final years of Empire. A time when great swathes of the world map were coloured pink and English was the predominant world language. Times were about to change.

The sea on the journey from Bombay to Colombo was relatively calm, However Sam and Maria were now having to get used to the heat of the tropics which was very different to living in a cold climate.

Sailing into the Port of Colombo was like landing in an oasis of civilisation and beauty after the overcrowding and stench of Bombay. Now part of the British Empire, the island of Ceylon still retained signs of previous European cultures, namely the Portuguese and Dutch. The multi-cultural inhabitants of the island were in the main well educated and there was an air of prosperity quite unlike Bombay.

There was no advice to stay on board the ship at Columba and Sam and Maria enjoyed a day exploring the town. Everything was new and interesting but they both missed the companionship of their friends Robert and Ishbel.

Although neither of them verbalised their thoughts they both wished it had been possible for them to settle in Cape Town. Lying alone on her bed in the dormitory Maria often looked at the photographs taken at the lovely little cottage in Oranjezicht with its beautiful garden, where under the backdrop of Table Mountain they had renewed their marriage vows. Every day she thought of Ishbel who felt like her second mother.

The final leg of the voyage from Columba to Melbourne seemed to take forever, the food, although filling and well cooked, had a sameness. Porridge for breakfast, soup and bread or a sandwich at lunchtime and a hearty dinner which was usually boiled mutton, stewed sausages, or scouse, the vegetables were always, potato, carrot, turnip or cabbage. Friday was fish day, but sadly not a chip in sight.

Sam often thought of his mother's delicious baking and Maria longed for scrambled eggs, the way her mother made them, cooked slowly and served with toasted soda bread.

The other passengers were mostly pleasant, Sam and Maria would pass the time of day with them but they did not make any other close friends. They spent their days walking along the deck talking and planning or reading from the limited library available for third class passengers. Not so much a library, more an old bookcase.

Maria decided to read 'Swiss Family Robinson' and then had nightmares about boa constrictors. Sam had never been a great reader before the voyage but during his time at sea he developed a love for literature that lasted the remainder of his life. His favourite authors were Charles Dickens, Thomas Hardy and Leo Tolstoy. He also read some Sir Walter Scott, although he found the style of the language a bit challenging.

At last the end of the voyage was in sight. One morning far in the distance they sighted the coast of Australia. At long last Melbourne felt almost within touching distance.

—

CHAPTER 4
The Arrival

After landing and going through the emigration control procedures, Maria and Samuel Johnstone arrived in their new country of Australia in the month of February 1918. Now reunited with their wicker hamper they found themselves on the quay alone and friendless and not entirely sure what to do next.

A tall, heavily built man approached them, wearing khaki shorts and short sleeved shirt. He spoke with a strong Australian accent, "You the couple from Scotland, Johnstone by name? If you are and the name on your travel hamper gives the clue you are, I've been sent to take you out to Northcote. Someone will meet you there and give you the keys for your weatherboard. My name's Bob by the way. Now folks I'll give you a hand with your things, m'lad Vinny is looking after the pony and trap." Sam and Maria were relieved beyond measure to meet Bob and promptly introduced themselves.

The ride to Northcote seemed to take a very long time in the summer heat and Maria was glad of the sun hat Ishbel had given her. The two men chatted as they rode but Maria was silent, just taking in the concept that she was literally on the other side of the world from Scotland. Summer here, winter at home, day here, night at home. Indeed while they were riding on the pony and trap her parents and siblings were no doubt fast asleep back in the village of Glenboig.

At last they arrived at the Northcote Brickworks. Bob went inside the imposing office building and returned with a rotund smartly dressed gentleman who introduced himself to Sam as Mr Perkins, the General Manager. He handed Sam a set of keys saying, "Bob will take you to your new weatherboard house, I've arranged for some basic furniture until you get settled in and your own things arrive from Scotland." Little did he know their 'own things' were all in the small hamper in the back of the trap.

When they saw the delightful little house Sam and Maria could not believe their good fortune. Bob opened the door then handed Sam the key saying, "Welcome to Australia Sammy my man. I'll leave you now to settle in, I live down in Andrew Street with the missus and our two littlies. If you need anything we are at number 42."

Left alone Sam and Maria started to explore their new home. It seemed enormous for just the two of them, there was a living room with a separate kitchen, and joy of joys a gas cooker. Two bedrooms and an inside bathroom, there was also a separate toilet and storeroom out in the garden which backed onto the bush. The only furniture was a double bed and wardrobe in the bedroom, the kitchen had a wooden table with two bench seats and in the living room there was a settee in front of the fireplace.

The furnishings might have been sparse but the bungalow was airy and spacious and the height of luxury after the single end flat in the east end of Glasgow where they had lived at the start of their married life.

The following day Sam reported for work while Maria started to make their house into a home. One of the first tasks Maria did was take the small statue of Robert Burns given to them by Sam's sister Mary as a farewell gift and display it in pride of place on the mantelpiece.

Every day she accomplished another project, she sewed gingham curtains for the windows and a curtain to hide the pipes under the sink in the kitchen. Maria used her skills to make chintz curtains for the living room, pink damask for the bedroom, the spare bedroom would have to wait. Every spare minute she worked on a rag rug for the bedroom, using oddments of material she bought very cheaply in a local second hand shop.

Every weekend Sam and Maria scoured the second hand shops and auctions where they bought a few pieces of furniture, the only new purchase was linoleum. That was their biggest expense so far and they had to break into their emergency savings to fund the purchase but it was well worth the expenditure and by getting the whole house done in a parquet pattern at the same time a good saving was made. They were also thrilled to see the label 'Made in Kirkcaldy' on their purchase, a wee link to Scotland and home.

The baby's birth was slightly earlier than expected. One morning Sam left for work and on his return found himself the father of a perfect baby boy. Their neighbour Jeanie had sent her daughter to get the midwife and between them they had helped bring baby Johnstone into the world.

Northcote

Dear Paw and Maw

The Johnstone name will carry on through to the next generation. Maria has given birth to a grand wee boy. Well not so wee, he weighed in at over eight pounds. Mother and baby are both well and we have decided to call him Alexander, after you Paw.

We just hope he turns out as decent a man as you are, and I hope to be as good a father to young Alexander as you were to me and the two girls.

The job is going well and although we both get a bit homesick at times we think the move was definitely for the best.

We are living in a little rented bungalow, one of the new weatherboard ones, it is painted white, can you imagine a white hoose in Gartsherrie? However we are saving every penny for a deposit to eventually buy our own place.

As far as religion is concerned we have decided that we will teach our wee lad, Alexander, right from wrong, a belief in God and simple Christian prayers and stories but he will not be brought up as either a Billy or a Tim.

We have both seen enough of religious bigotry to last a lifetime and we have no intention of bringing up our lad to judge people by what church they attend.

Hope all went well for our Agnes and that her and Tom have had a healthy bairn, the mail is dreadful, but we hope to hear news from Scotland soon.

We trust you are both well, and your youngest bairn, my wee sister Mary, is behaving herself.

With all our love

Sam, Maria and wee Alexander

* * *

One morning Alexander was still sleeping in his cot while Maria prepared breakfast and the sandwiches for Sam's packed lunch. Looking out of the window she saw the postman put something into the metal mailbox at the bottom of their garden path.

She immediately called, "Sam I've just seen the postman put something in the box, can you please go down and see what he has delivered?"

Sam returned to the house holding a letter written in his mother's hand, the envelope was crumpled and covered with many postage marks. Before even opening the envelope he just sat down on the kitchen chair, stroked the envelope and allowed the tears to fall.

Coatbridge

My dear Sam and Maria

Goodness knows when you will receive this letter. But I had to put pen to paper and let you know that your Pa and I are now the proud grandparents of a beautiful wee lass. Our Agnes and Tom are delighted, they wanted to call the wee one Jessie after me but we have now decided to call her Emily, after the suffragette Emily Davidson, you know, the one who was killed by the king's horse in 1913 at the Derby. However, your big sister insisted that she has Jessie as her middle name. So you are now Uncle Sam and Aunt Maria to Emily Jessie Coats.

As you will probably know the Representation of the People Act was passed at the beginning of this month, it only gives the vote to women over 30, a very poor showing indeed after all women have done, and are still doing, for the war effort.

The fight is not over by a long way. Hopefully Maria, you will be able to cast your vote in your new home, exciting. We will continue to strive for the equal franchise, a vote is just the start, equality is more than a cross on a ballot paper, sadly it's going to be a long haul I fear.

Other news, the Law family are all well, Rab is as crusty as ever. I think Agnes misses her eldest Charlotte, who is now settled at a farm in Condorrat with her own brood. Mary Law is still working in the brickworks in Glenboig. James, Jessie and Robert are doing well at school, although Robert is still a terrible wee mischief. Their youngest, Alexander is a right bonny wee lad, I sincerely hope he is the last bairn Agnes will ever have.

I pray every night that this terrible war is over soon, such sorrow. I met a girl in the store the other day called Sarah, she told me that her fiancé had been killed in France and she would now devote herself to her work and looking after her parents as she would never marry and have bairns, isn't that tragic. There are a lot of young men returning from the front, Coatbridge is full of men with terrible injuries, lives ruined.

Your sister Mary has been demoted from her position at the Post Office, so have several other girls, their jobs have gone to returning soldiers. I suppose we should be grateful she still has a job, albeit at a reduced wage. But, there is also good news about Mary, she is going to Pitman's College in Glasgow to train as a secretary. My friend Liz is paying her fees and after she qualifies Mary will work for Liz to enable her to devote more time to 'the cause'. Meantime, Mary is studying like mad to get up to speed before starting her course. We are so pleased for her, it was a blow losing her job but she now has a wonderful opportunity to get a good education. As they say, the Lord works in mysterious ways his wonders to perform. Or as your pa says, 'as one door closes another opens'.

Well my dears I will close now, your father and I are well and think of our Sam and Maria every day. We know you are at the start of an exciting adventure and we are happy for you, however we miss you and wish you could be with us as you prepare to welcome your new wee baby into the world.

With all our love
God bless
Ma and Pa

* * *

After writing the letter Jessie had carefully folded it and, placed it in an envelope, addressing it to Mr & Mrs Samuel Johnstone at the brickworks in Northcote where Sam had told her he would be working.

The letter left Coatbridge in February 1918 but Sam and Maria did not read it until the end of June, wintertime in Melbourne and the birth month of their son, Alexander Johnstone.

After reading the letter several times Maria said, "I wonder if your parents have received the letters we posted in Madeira, Cape Town, and Colombo as well as the ones we have sent since we arrived? Goodness knows when they will receive the one I posted last week telling them about the birth of wee Alexander. It just emphasises how many miles are between us and our kith and kin.

"Sam, I can close my eyes and picture my family's house in Glenboig. The wee garden at the front with flowers and the carefully planted rows of vegetables at the back. In my minds eye I can walk along the gravel path to the front door. I open the door and see the brown linoleum that looks like wood on the hall floor and the framed picture of Our Lady on the wall, and yet I know I'll never see it with my eyes again in this life. Alexander will never see his grandparents or his aunts and uncles or his new wee cousin Emily. Sam, if you had been a Catholic or I had been born a Protestant I doubt if we would have ever left Coatbridge. The children would have grown up together, played games, probably got up to all sorts of mischief and we would have been surrounded by family.

"Sam sometimes I get really frightened. Here we are in Australia, thousands of miles from home completely on our own with a new wee baby. Do you know I often wish we had stayed in Cape Town with Ishbel and Robert?"

"I know it's not easy my love," said Sam. "But it is as it is, we are here and we have to make the best of it. Now I've got to make tracks to my work or I'm going to be late. We can talk again tonight. I can't wait to get home to be with you and our grand wee baby boy."

After Sam left to start his day Maria fed her young baby then started her work for the day, cleaning the bungalow and preparing the evening meal. After drinking a cup of tea with a slice of toast and cheese at lunchtime she once again fed Alexander and changed his nappy. The afternoon rolled out before her and the return of Sam at around six o'clock.

Since the birth of Alexander Maria had felt what could only be called an anti-climax. Since the day when Sam had met her outside Glenboig Brickworks after he returned injured from France, life had moved at a breakneck speed. First eloping from Coatbridge followed by their registry office wedding, then their time staying in Glasgow where she had worked as a bus conductress and they had both concentrated all their energy on working, saving money and excitedly planning their move to Australia. Then the journey by ship to Australia, apart from the Bay of Biscay, that had been a great adventure and a real eye opener into a very different world. The highlight being their stay at Cape Town and the blessing of their union by Robert.

After their arrival in Australia there was the joy of being given the keys to the white weatherboard bungalow in Northcote, with its corrugated iron roof and wee garden. Making their house into a home was another adventure, finding second hand shops to buy some basic furniture. And, using a little of Sam's wages each week to purchase material and bits and bobs to enhance their wee bungalow.

Alexander's birth had not been easy but worth all the pain to have such a beautiful wee lad and to see the pride in Sam's face every time he looked at their son.

Maria had made the little bungalow homely, she kept it clean and tidy but as her home life became organised Maria found herself thinking more and more 'what now' and she oft remembered her conversation with Ishbel in Camp's Bay as they looked out on the white waves of the Atlantic Ocean.

Sam was kept busy all week at the brickworks, working hard learning a new job while earning a decent wage. Maria's life was now centred around baby Alexander and routine household tasks. It wasn't enough. Maria needed a challenge.

During the voyage Maria had developed a great fondness for Ishbel. Several letters had arrived from Cape Town and Maria was not surprised to learn that Ishbel was working in the administrative office at Cape Town's Somerset Hospital and involved with several charities.

Sam's mother Jessie was also an influence, the more Maria heard about her from Sam the more she wished there had been time for her to get to know the remarkable woman that was Jessie Johnstone wife, mother, friend, milliner and suffragette.

The first part of the adventure was now over, part two was in God's hands.

—

CHAPTER 5
The Next Step

One day when Alexander was settled in his crib and the chores for the day complete, Maria decided to treat herself to a cup of tea and a quiet read of the local newspaper, the Northcote Leader.

As she read through the paper an advert in the 'Employment' section caught her eye.

Wanted Urgently
Home workers to assemble umbrellas and parasols.
Piecework, Good rate of pay.
Apply to Box No 2659

Maria read the advert several times thinking how hard can it be to make an umbrella if you are given all the parts and you just have to put them together. Before it was time for Alexander to waken up and demand attention Maria got out her pen and notepad and wrote a letter applying for work. She quickly stamped the envelope put on her jacket and ran down to the bottom of the street to post it in the letterbox before she could change her mind.

A few days later while she was peeling potatoes for the dinner there was a knock on the door. Maria looked out of the window and saw a pony and trap standing at the kerb with a young lad holding the pony's reins. When Maria answered the door she was faced with an elderly lady dressed in a long black bombazine dress topped with an old fashioned black bonnet.

The woman addressed Maria in a precise English rather than an Australian accent. "My dear, are you the Mistress Johnstone who wrote to me with regards to carrying out some piecework?"

Maria asked the woman to come inside and offered her a cup of tea. "Thank you my dear that would be most welcome it's a long drive from Flinders Lane, and I'd be much obliged if you would also give a taste to young Walter who is holding the pony outside.

"Now while you make the tea I'll tell you what I do. I'm an agent who organises finishes on a piecework basis carried out by home workers, depending on the job you can earn 2p a unit or 2/6 a unit, it all depends on time and skill. At the moment I need workers to assemble umbrellas but I also have gloves which require pearl buttons and shoes which require buckles or diamanté fancies. Well Mistress Johnstone do you think you would like to join my ladies? I require high standards but you will find me very fair, very fair indeed."

Maria prepared the tea, as she listened to the lady explaining her business, "Tea Mrs... sorry I didn't catch your name."

"It's Harris, my name is Mistress Harris. That looks a lovely cup of tea Mistress Johnstone and if I'm not mistaken a delicious home made scone."

Maria served Mrs Harris then took a cup, together with a buttered scone, out to young Walter.

Mrs Harris seemed to Maria to come from another era but she was certainly businesslike. Maria listened quietly as she said, "Well that was indeed a refreshing cup of tea Mistress Johnstone. Now would you like me to leave some work for you to complete then we could see if we are mutually compatible. I have an excellent reputation in the trade for providing quality products, I pay a bit more than most others but in return I expect perfect work with a pernickety attention to detail."

Maria didn't hesitate, "Mrs Harris I would certainly like to try my hand at working for you. What would you like me to start with?"

"Oh I think something straightforward to start with, don't you? Can you please go out to the trap and ask Walter to bring in the large box with the slippers and the one with the appropriate finishing materials?"

Maria did as she was bid and went out to speak to the young driver. "Walter, can you bring the boxes of slippers and finishing into the house for Mrs Harris please?"

As Walter got the boxes down from the trap he whispered to Maria, "Thanks for the tea and scone Mistress. Now Mrs H will offer you 3d or 4d a unit, stand out for 6d, it's a good deal for you both, but don't say I told you. Promise?"

Maria helped Walter carry the boxes into the house, thinking 'well that was my first lesson into the world of business and from a young lad of fourteen or fifteen'.

The larger box contained an assortment of felt slippers in varying sizes, the smaller ones held insoles, tissue paper, pom-poms and little calico bags with size numbers on them.

Mrs Harris explained exactly what she required to be done. "Mistress Johnstone, firstly you must attach a pom pom to the front of each slipper in the place I'll mark, put in the correct insole, then match them into sized pairs and wrap them carefully in tissue paper before putting the slippers into the correctly sized bag. Now we must discuss payment. I see you have made very neatly stitched curtains so I'll give you 4d for each completed unit. Any rejects will not be paid for and I will also deduct 4d for each rejected unit from your total payment. Is that satisfactory to you?"

If she hadn't received the whispered advice from Walter Maria would have accepted 4p and been delighted to find a way to supplement the family income. However she mustered all her courage and said, "Mrs Harris I was thinking perhaps 6d might better reflect the amount of work I would need to do and bearing in mind I will carry out everything to meet your precise requirements."

"Mmmm," said Mrs Harris. "6d per unit for a new worker seems like a great deal of money to me. However, I like you and you make a very light scone, so I'll agree to 6d per unit on the understanding that this is a trial and if my standards are not met there will be no more work. Now let's shake hands on the deal and Walter and I will be off. I have some more jobs to deliver and collect in Northcote. I will return Wednesday next to collect the completed work."

Maria waved them off her heart fluttering in excitement at the thought of contributing to the family income while still being able to stay at home to look after baby Alexander.

Maria prepared the evening meal of mince and potatoes, followed by apple pie and custard. As soon as Sam came into the bungalow she threw her arms around him saying, "My darling Sam I've had the most wonderful, wonderful day!"

"Well if that's how you are going to greet me I hope you have more wonderful days," laughed Sam. "And, the dinner smells right good too! You dish up the food while I get washed and you can tell me all about what happened to make your day wonderful over supper."

Maria could hardly eat for telling Sam all about Mrs Harris and Walter and her pride at negotiating 6d a unit. "Sam, the extra money will make such a difference it will help us save to buy rugs and perhaps a couple of easy chairs. I thought we could buy some tools for the garden so that we can plant vegetables and perhaps some fruit, what do you think?"

"I think I've married the cleverest, as well as the most beautiful girl in the whole of Scotland and now in the whole of Australia. I'm so proud of you Maria Johnstone.

I also had a good day. As you know next year the company are opening a new steam works, well Mr Hodges called me into his office today and asked me if I'd like to be part of the new team to set up the project. Well he didn't have to ask me twice, I've jumped at the chance, promotion and a bit more money. Maria this is what we dreamed of, a chance to better ourselves and live without the old Billy and Tim prejudice found in Coatbridge."

During the following week Maria never seemed to stop working, fortunately Alexander was a contented bairn and as long as he was well fed and had a clean nappy he was not given to crying.

Each day after Sam left for work Maria quickly carried out the household tasks so that the afternoons were free to work on her finishing project. Initially she was quite slow but as she worked she got faster but she never allowed speed to hamper quality.

The following week Mrs Harris arrived promptly at the appointed time. Maria had the kettle on and a fresh batch of scones prepared. Seeing the trap pull up outside Maria opened the door and welcomed Mrs Harris into her home.

"Is that scones I can smell?" asked Mrs Harris.

"It certainly is," replied Maria, "And if you would like to sit down I'll prepare a cuppa for you and Walter." As she prepared the tea Mrs Harris started to inspect the work. Maria could hear little noises, mhm, mhm, uhh, uhh, but she was quietly confident about the standard of her work.

Maria took a cup of tea and this time two fruit scones spread liberally with butter and home made jam out to Walter. As she handed them to him she whispered, "Thanks Walter, I did manage to negotiate 6d a unit."

After she had served the tea to Mrs Harris and the older woman had yet again complimented Maria on the lightness of her baking, Mrs Harris said, "Mistress Johnstone, I have checked random samples from each of the boxes and I must say you have been as good as your word every unit is just as it should be. Now by my calculation you have completed 200 units, so I owe you the grand total of four pounds.

"Now Mrs Johnstone tell me would you like to become one of my regular ladies? If so I can deliver you a batch of work every week. As you will appreciate I cannot guarantee the rate or amount of work available, it all depends on my clients but as I said last time, I have high standards but I'm always fair.

"Now this week I have two projects for you, firstly, binding together pieces of leather which have been cut to size into purses and affix a stud closure using a special little gadget which I'll loan you. I also have a small quantity of evening gloves which require to be trimmed, bit of a fiddly job but well within your capabilities".

Maria did not hesitate, "Yes Mrs Harris, I would be delighted to become one of your ladies. I'll just go out and collect the cup and plate from Walter, why don't you enjoy another scone."

"Good, that's settled. Yes I will have another scone and perhaps a little more tea and then we can talk business."

As she collected the crockery, Maria smiled at Walter and asked, "Well, any tips for the rate this week? It's binding the purses and trimming the evening gloves."

Walter laughed, "Mrs Johnstone paying me in scones well spread with jam works very well. I'd say 9d for the gloves, and 6d for the purses, that's fair all round."

Maria returned to the house where Mrs Harris was brushing the last crumbs from her mouth. "Can you go back outside to Walter and tell him that we require the purses and the evening gloves please and then we can look at the rate."

Mrs Harris offered a flat rate for both jobs of 6p per unit. However, taking Walter's advice Maria asked for 9p for the gloves. There was only about 20 pairs but an extra 3d a pair amounted to another five shillings in her pocket.

Maria's life was now set on a new and busy path. Mrs Harris became a permanent feature, every week she called with a new project and every week Maria returned her completed work and received her payment, the date and amount meticulously entered into the back of the lined notebook which had been her sister Maureen's leaving present.

Mrs Harris enjoyed her weekly visit to Maria. The Johnstone house was always her first call after the long drive out to Northcote, knowing it was where she would receive a cup of tea accompanied by home baking. While riding in the trap Mrs Harris often contemplated exactly what treat would be in store for her, treacle or fruit scone, sponge cake, perhaps a slice of fruit loaf, whatever it was it would be delicious and Maria was always generous with a second portion.

As well as the refreshments, the other joy about visiting Smith Street was the quality of Maria's work, everything immaculate, never a rejection.

Over the months Mrs Harris gradually started to give Maria more intricate work and she was not disappointed with the results. A kind of formal relationship developed between the two women, friendship would have been an exaggeration but they were more than mere business acquaintances. Each week as they conducted their business transaction they also had a blether about local goings on, what work would shortly be coming up, the war, how young Alexander was doing, but Mrs Harris never gave anything away about her personal life.

Maria also developed a 'big sister' relationship with Walter. Every week she gave him a special baked treat and always had a warm and encouraging word with him. He no longer needed to give her advice on pricing, Maria was a quick learner.

The Johnstone account at the National Bank of Australasia grew steadily. Initially Maria felt nervous going into the imposing building each week with her passbook. However, as the balance column steadily grew pound on pound she looked forward to her weekly visit and got to recognise the tellers.

As the Johnstone family in Australia slowly prospered they received letters from home telling of lives that now seemed so very different from their life in Northcote.

Gartsherrie

My dear Sam and Maria and our wee grandson Alexander

Your father is proud fit to burst that you've named your wee one after him.

About a week or so ago we received your letter from Cape Town telling us about your blessing. Ishbel and Robert sound really lovely people, and we are so glad that they have given you both so much support. Then a few days later we received your letter from Madeira. What an adventure you are both having. Hopefully when the war ends the posts will be more reliable.

No great adventures here, certainly no fancy teas. Our idea of a fancy tea is a cup of Liptons finest and one of Agnes Law's pancakes. So many shortages, butter, tea, everything. Cooking wholesome meals was always a challenge but now with shortages it's so difficult to get a decent meal on the table. You might remember Jimmy Christie, well him and his elder brother Andy go out and trap rabbits up at the lochs. They sell them for threepence each, it's wonderful when I manage to get one, not only a lovely stew but I cure the pelts and I can use them in my millinery work.

We have heard of quite a few cases of this new flu that is going around. Joan Hosie was visiting her sister in Carluke and she heard that a whole lot of kids in an orphanage over that way died from peritonitis after getting the flu. Not much about it in the newspapers, it's just what you hear on the rumour mill.

You know our Mary was real hurt about being demoted, losing her position in the Post Office to a returning soldier was a blow. Not everyone has been as lucky as her, getting a place in college paid for by my friend Liz is exceptional. However, she is not the only one to have lost her job and the Representation of the People act giving the vote to women over 30 is a poor return for all the work carried out by women during the war. Besides I have heard a lot of the men are telling their wives not to vote or are instructing them who to vote for. It won't surprise you to know Agnes Law told me that your Uncle Rab had told her when she gets a vote she must use it to vote for the Unionist party, I think he is carried away by the name Bonar Law, perhaps Rab thinks he is one of his far out relatives.

Returning soldiers, not all of them are lucky enough to get a job, it would break your heart to see some of the boys who went away singing now returning home minus limbs. Sam, I know you had a terrible time in France but you are now in a good job with a lovely wife and bairn, my prayers have been answered.

Agnes and Tom are so happy with wee Emily, she is as pretty as a picture and such a good natured wee thing, so like our Agnes.

I have been getting quite a lot of millinery work since the war started, more money about with the men getting extra shifts in the Gartsherrie Works. However, Agnes's husband Tom says he thinks that after the war there will be a depression so I'm trying to save while things are reasonably good financially.

We miss you all but know in our heart of hearts you made the right decision.

All our love
Maw and Paw

CHAPTER 6
The Business

Summer 1918 in Northcote was extremely hot, even during the journey out to Australia on the SS Trojan Sam and Maria had never felt so uncomfortable.

Keeping cool in a Melbourne summer seemed impossibly hard and they were very grateful for the salad vegetables Maria had planted in the garden. Family meals were now so very different from a Scottish diet of porridge, soups, mince and root vegetables. They dined on egg salad, cheese salad, cold meat salad, salad with salad. Maria felt a working man needed heartier fare but when it came to meal times all they wanted was light food, perhaps with a bread roll. However, Maria had not entirely given up on her Scottish heritage and chips or fritters (sliced potato dipped in batter and deep fried) regularly accompanied the salad.

The nights too were uncomfortable and even sleeping, without as much as a sheet, was still difficult. Then there was the creepy crawlies. Maria had a morbid dread of spiders, snakes or lizards sneaking through an open window and, despite Sam's pleading, she refused to sleep with the window ajar. Wee Alexander slept with just a nappy and he was the only member of the family who slept soundly.

The war at long last ended on the 11th of November 1918 and everyone was looking forward to celebrating the first new year of peace. The only worry on the horizon was newspaper reports about a flu epidemic that people were calling the Spanish flu.

It was almost Christmas, Maria was lying awake in bed running over her plans for the festive celebration. Over the previous weeks she had been gathering in a stock of baking ingredients and she had placed an order with the local fish and poultry shop for a chicken as a special treat. Maria had no idea how to cook a whole chicken but a visit to the local library had provided recipes on how to roast the bird and also ideas on what to do with any leftovers.

In between working for Mrs Harris, Maria had managed to knit a sweater for Sam and a jacket and hat for Alexander as the winters in Victoria could be cold.

Suddenly her thoughts were interrupted by a loud knocking on the door, she immediately turned and shook her husband awake. "Sam, Sam, someone is battering on the front door, get up before the noise wakens Alexander." As they headed towards the front door the urgent knocking continued.

Sam called out, "Who's there, who on earth is knocking us up at this time of night?"

A voice Maria immediately recognised answered, "Mrs Johnstone, Mrs Johnstone it's me, Walter. Can you please help me?"

Maria turned the key and let him in. The poor boy seemed distraught as she guided him into the living room and sat him down on the new fireside chair. "Whatever is the matter Walter?" asked Maria.

"Oh Mrs Johnstone, I didn't know who else to come to. You have always been so kind and she thought such a lot of you and I just don't know what to do."

Sam knelt down in front of the boy, saying, "Right son, calm yourself down and tell us what is the matter slowly and clearly and we will do our very best to help you."

Walter took a deep breath and started to speak.

"I live with Mrs Harris, everybody thinks I'm her driver and odd job boy but I'm really her grandson. Her daughter had me out of wedlock, the family were very respectable back in England. Mrs Harris must have been mortified, she could not have stood the disgrace so her and my mother emigrated to Sydney. My mother died in Sydney when I was born so Mrs Harris then moved to Melbourne and told people I was her maid's son who had died with no family, and she was acting as my guardian through the goodness of her heart. Our cook Mrs Wilson and various maids brought me up and there was nothing to make me believe anything otherwise. Our relationship was always very formal, I never called her anything else but Mistress Harris.

"When I was fourteen I left school and she told me that I could be her driver and she would train me to help her with the business. I've been doing that for the past year or so. A few months ago she sent me up to her bedroom to collect a box. I saw a photograph on her dressing table of a young woman, it was signed 'To Mama Love Vicky'. I never knew she had a daughter, I know I shouldn't have but when I gave her the box I mentioned the beautiful lady in the photograph.

Well she was furious, told me not to interfere in things that were none of my business.

"But she is dead, Mrs Johnstone she is dead and I don't know what to do."

Maria interrupted him, "Walter, keep calm, just tell us how you know Mrs Harris is, was, your grandmother."

"Well, I couldn't get the lady in the photograph out of my mind for some reason. One day when Mrs Harris was out meeting some of her clients I went back into her room and looked at the photograph. I was curious, I know it was wrong but I opened her dressing table drawer I found a miniature picture of the lady in the photograph edged in black with a lock of hair encased in glass on the back, the hair was the same sandy blond as mine. I still never guessed but now I had started I couldn't help myself, Mrs H was always so mysterious. I found an envelope with a whole lot of certificates, her husband's birth and death certificates, their marriage certificate and a death certificate for their daughter, Victoria Mary. It showed cause of death as complications following childbirth. Behind it was another certificate, my birth certificate, Walter John Harris, illegitimate son of Victoria Mary Harris, with my date of birth. I've always been known as Walter McDonald and Mrs Harris told me my mother was her maid called Kirsty.

"I hardly slept for days, every night I just lay in bed trying to make sense of it all. Eventually tonight I went into her parlour and asked if I could ask her a question. She sat me down and said. 'Ask away Walter.' As I told her what I had done I watched the colour drain from her face.

"Mrs Johnstone, you know how confident Mrs Harris was, always in charge. Well, she spoke in a quiet voice, almost trembling, she said, 'Walter, what you say is true, I am your grandmother but I simply couldn't thole the shame of my daughter having an illegitimate child, and one that took my darling Vicky away from me. I moved here to Melbourne and started a new life. I always intended to look after you and I've just started teaching you the business. One day it will be yours but you will inherit as Walter McDonald, the name of your father. He was an engineer, he proposed to Vicky, then went off to Africa. Allegedly to make money so they could marry. She received a few letters then Vicky never heard a word from him again, my Vicky was heartbroken. It was a very bad time, I had not long been widowed then I had a terrible shock when Vicky confessed to being in the family way. We had to get away from England and everyone we knew so we moved to Australia. Now you know everything boy'.

"She then said, 'Walter I feel somewhat faint, go and get me a glass of water, I need to take one of my pills, you have shocked me to the very core with all your meddling.'

"I went down to the kitchen and got a glass of water. When I went back up to the parlour she was sitting in the chair struggling for breath and then she just fell forward. Mrs Johnstone I've killed her! Mrs Harris is dead and it's all my fault, whatever should I do? Should I go and confess to the constable?"

Sam immediately took control of the situation, "Walter, you did not kill Mrs Harris, she obviously had a bad heart and I've no doubt she could have passed away at any time. Now you must get back to Flinders and make contact with Mrs Harris's doctor and do you know if she has a solicitor?" Walter nodded.

"Look I'll come with you for a bit of support. Now I'm away to get dressed, the quicker we contact the professional men the better. Maria you had better try and get a bit of sleep, tomorrow you can take the train up to Flinders railway station with wee Alexander and help Walter get matters sorted out. I'll get an early morning train back to Northcote for work. Walter, write down the address and directions to the Harris place from Flinders station and leave them with Maria."

Within five minutes Sam and Walter were in the trap and heading back into the city. Maria went back to bed and desperately tried to get some sleep, not only was she worried about Walter she was concerned about their loss of income without the finishing work from Mrs Harris.

On the way back to the Flinders Lanes Walter told Sam that no servants lived in the house, just him and Mrs Harris. "On the ground floor there is a little shop from where she transacts her business, behind the shop is the kitchen and my room. On the first floor is the parlour and dining room, lavatory and bathroom. On the top floor is Mrs H 's bedroom and another room where she stores completed orders and other bits and bobs. There is also another lavatory just outside the kitchen in the yard. I look after the pony Paddy, he is stabled in the yard and there is also a small garden area."

The roads were quiet and they made good time reaching the home of Mrs Harris. Walter stabled Paddy and gave him some feed and water while Sam went up to the parlour. He found Mrs Harris just as Walter had described to them, fallen forward in her chair.

Sam's thoughts seemed to fly to his parents in Gartsherrie and his mother's voice came to him over all the thousands of miles. 'Sam always tell the truth and shame the devil or you will be found out'. By the time Walter came up to the parlour Sam had made up his mind as to exactly what they must do.

"Walter lad, firstly we are going to the doctor and you are going to tell him what happened. Say you were talking with Mrs Harris when she felt unwell, she wanted to take a tablet and you went downstairs to get her some water. When you found her dead you didn't know what to do so you came out to Northcote to get help from Maria and me. In other words the truth, you just don't need to tell him about Vicky. After all you are only a lad of fifteen it's hardly surprising you didn't know what you should do. Now let's get away to the doctor."

Doctor Saul was not best pleased at being woken up well after midnight but he roused himself and opened the door for Walter and Sam. Sam explained the events of the night and the doctor put on his jacket, lifted his medical bag and joined Sam and Walter in the trap.

After examining Mrs Harris he confirmed that she did in fact die from a heart attack. He explained that she had been suffering from angina and high blood pressure for years, saying, "I always knew that the lady was not going to make old bones but the blessing is, it was very quick at the end.

"Mr Johnstone, Mrs Harris used a Mr Green as her solicitor. I think it would be helpful if an adult accompanies the boy to see him first thing tomorrow. Meantime I'll issue the death certificate, nothing more I can do. You must now contact the undertakers, they will deal with the body. Mrs Harris was quite a character, a woman who made a success of business in a man's world. But she was her own person and wouldn't follow my medical advice on diet and lifestyle, it's a miracle she has lived as long as she has done.

"Mrs Harris was a non practicing Jew, can I suggest you use Bergman the undertaker and tomorrow morning you can ascertain from Mr Green her funeral wishes."

Dr Saul took his leave saying, "No need to drive me home it's only a ten minute walk and the exercise will do me good."

As soon as the doctor had left Sam lifted the telephone and asked the operator to connect him to Bergman the undertaker. Sam explained the situation and Mr Bergman promised to collect Mrs Harris's remains within the hour.

Sam took Walter down to the kitchen and made a pot of good strong tea. He could see the lad was still in shock over the nights events. As they sat drinking the welcome brew, Sam spoke to Walter. "Now lad you heard Dr Saul. Mrs Harris died of a heart attack, if it hadn't happened tonight it would have been tomorrow or next week or next month. You did not kill her so get that right out your mind. I suggest after Mr Bergman has left we try and get a bit of rest. I'll leave for an early train home, I have to get to work tomorrow, well today. Maria will come and take you to see the lawyer before you do anything else. However, I suggest you get all the paperwork you were telling me about looked out before Maria arrives in the morning."

As promised the undertaker arrived and was discrete and efficient. Sam confirmed that his wife would call into their offices the following day with Walter to finalise the arrangements.

Walter went to his bed and Sam took some throws and cushions from around the parlour and made himself a makeshift bed on the sofa.

By the time Walter wakened up Sam had left for work and Mrs Wilson the cook, together with Alice, the young parlour maid had arrived. As he walked into the kitchen still wearing his clothes from yesterday Mrs Wilson immediately berated him, "Walter! What on earth are you doing in that state? You look like death warmed up lad! Where is Mrs Harris? Alice took up her morning cuppa and she is nowhere to be found, her bed hasn't been slept in."

Walter couldn't find the words to explain the situation, his throat seemed to constrain and he couldn't say anything. Just then the shop bell rang, heralding the arrival of Maria carrying wee Alexander.

Just as Sam had done the previous evening Maria now took charge. She explained to Mrs Wilson and Alice the edited version of the events of the past hours and instructed Walter to go and get washed and changed as they had a great deal to do.

Mrs Wilson made a pot of tea and some sandwiches. By the time Walter had returned the two woman had offered to look after Alexander while Maria accompanied Walter to arrange the formalities.

Sam had briefed Maria on the events in Flinders before he left for work so she was able to get the outline of a plan formulated as she travelled into town by train. Feeling very nervous about dealing with professional people Maria had dressed in the afternoon gown Ishbel had given to her in Cape Town, somehow wearing a nice outfit made her feel more confident.

As soon as Walter was dressed and had managed to drink a cup of tea they set off, first to see Mr Green who had kindly agreed to see them without a prior appointment.

Before they could say anything the solicitor said, "I received a telephone call from Dr Saul early this morning, he told me that Mrs Harris has passed away and to expect a visit from you Master Walter.

"Now Walter, Mrs Johnstone, this is a very awkward situation. Knowing of her medical condition some months ago I asked Mrs Harris to clarify her wishes on a number of counts and give me detailed instructions. Unfortunately she did not heed my advice.

"Walter you are the sole benefactor of Mrs Harris's estate but you will not receive your inheritance until you are twenty one years of age. As her executor I would strongly recommend that I liquidate all her assets, which I will invest on your behalf, meantime I can arrange for you to attend an excellent place of education which provides boarding facilities.

"Now with regard to funeral arrangements, Mrs Harris was a non practicing Jew, but a Jew nonetheless. I respectfully suggest you advise Mr Bergman that you wish her interred in the Jewish section of the Melbourne General Cemetery."

As he was speaking Maria was thinking, 'this is not a good plan for Walter, no business to take over when he reaches manhood, besides a young man of twenty one inheriting a lot of money it could all vanish like snow off a dyke'. There was also the question of how she was going to earn money for the Johnstone family without regular work from Mrs Harris. Gathering all her courage, and with the confidence of knowing she looked the part, Maria offered an alternative plan.

"Mr Green I would like to offer a suggestion that will allow Walter to carry on working and learning the business as Mrs Harris intended. As the executor would you consider allowing my husband and myself to become Walter's legal guardians. I would work with him in the business for a salary and provide you with monthly accounts. When he is twenty one he can then make up his mind what he wants to do with his life but it seems to me that selling a prosperous business, a business that he was being groomed to inherit, makes no sense."

Walter piped up, "Sir, I don't want to go to a boarding school, I want to work and I would really like Mr and Mrs Johnstone to be my guardians, they are good decent people. Besides if you sell the house and business Mrs Wilson and Alice will lose their jobs."

Mr Green had listened carefully to Maria and thought there might be some merit in her plan but he simply said, "Go to see Mr Bergman and make the necessary arrangements, I'll arrange for you to have some money to cover the funeral costs and for your needs over the following days. Make an appointment with me for sometime next week by then we will all have had more time to think out the practicalities of your suggestion Mrs Johnstone."

Knowing Mrs Harris was Jewish, Mr Bergman had already arranged for the service to be conducted the following day and had ensured that word of the funeral had been circulated within the clothing district. Maria and Walter had very little to do by way of arrangements with the undertaker.

The hours until the funeral flew past. In what seemed like the blink of an eye Mrs Wilson, Maria and Walter were all dressed in somber clothes and leaving for the funeral service, before they had even come to terms with the death of Mrs Harris. Alice had agreed to look after wee Alexander in order to let Maria and Mrs Wilson attend the burial service.

They travelled to the cemetery in a car arranged by Mr Bergman. On arriving at The Melbourne General Cemetery they were met by a rabbi who led them into the Jewish chapel. The earthly body of Lavinia Harris was contained in a plain pine coffin which was sat on top of a trolly.

Walter was amazed to see so many people from the Melbourne clothing industry in attendance. It was only then that a realisation of just how much his grandmother had been respected dawned on the boy.

After the committal they returned to the house where Alice had prepared sandwiches and tea. Mr Green joined them and Maria thought this might be an opportunity to ensure that the solicitor was aware of Walter's true relationship to Mrs Harris As Mrs Wilson cleared away the tea things Maria said, "Walter I think you have some paperwork that you should discuss with Mr Green. Why don't you go upstairs and get the certificates?"

While he was away Maria confided in the solicitor, "Mr Green, I feel a bit out of my depth here. My husband and I have recently emigrated from Scotland and I simply carried out work for Mrs Harris. Over the past months I became friendly with her and Walter, but other than that I have no connection, except that I'm fond of Walter and if there's anything my husband Sam and I can do to help him we will."

Mr Green replied, "My dear Mrs Johnstone, we are all emigrants here. I'm from Poland, Mr Bergman is from Austria, Dr Saul's family brought him as a baby from France. We are all first, second or third generation Australians, if you go back too far it's convict blood. It shows great tenacity and strength of character to emigrate, if you and your husband work hard in your new country of Australia Mrs Johnstone you will certainly reap your reward."

Walter returned clutching a large brown envelope which he handed over to Mr Green. The solicitor carefully read through the contents.

"Young man this puts an entirely new light on your relationship to Mrs Harris, it was my understanding that you were her ward, the son of her maid. Actually I'm quite annoyed at Lavinia for not ensuring that your future was better secured, particularly as she knew full well the state of her health.

"I'll have a serious think over the next few days. Mrs Johnstone would it be possible for you and your husband to come and see me with Walter late on Sunday afternoon, shabbos will be finishing and your husband will be on his day off?"

Maria immediately agreed to his suggestion, Walter sat quietly and said nothing.

After Mr Green had taken his leave and it was only Maria and Walter sitting in the parlour Walter started to speak but his words turned to sobs. Maria put a comforting arm around him and gave him her handkerchief but she let him cry, knowing sometimes tears just have to be shed.

Eventually she said, "Walter I have to go now and Walter, you heard what Mr Green and the doctor said. Mrs Harris was living on borrowed time. You were not to blame and you had every right to ask her the questions you did. Mrs Harris should have told you that you were her grandson many years ago.

"Now I really must collect Alexander from Alice and get myself away to Flinders station, I'll have to get back to Northcote to make Sam's tea. We will come to Flinders on Sunday about two o'clock. Can you ask Alice if she would come in and look after Alexander for a couple of hours while we all go to see Mr Green?"

Sunday dawned and the Johnstone family boarded the train to Flinders railway station. Walter was at the station to meet them dressed in his Sunday best, with shoes polished to a perfect shine. Maria was again dressed in what she always thought of as her blessing dress.

Maria had been thinking a great deal about what to do about Walter's situation and she had spent hours discussing with Sam the best way to approach Mr Green with her plan.

When they met up with Walter, Sam suggested that they all go into the station tearoom and discuss the forthcoming meeting with Mr Green over a cup of tea.

Maria congratulated Walter on looking so smart, "Well done Walter, you look like a businessman already. Now I'm going to tell you my thoughts and you must consider them carefully before we speak to the solicitor.

"If Sam and I become your guardians we suggest that you stay on in the Flinders property during the week and you can come out to Northcote at the weekends. We have a spare bedroom which you can use, we will buy a single bed and make it comfortable for you. I will come up to town every week day and between us hopefully we can

Escape from Gartsherrie

manage to run the business and turn in a decent profit. We will both take a fair salary for our work and carry on employing Mrs Wilson and Alice, however they will have to be willing to take on different duties, Alice will have to help with looking after Alexander and Mrs Wilson will have to take on housekeeping duties as well as the cooking.

"That is the gist of my idea, we will just have to figure out the details as to how we will actually run the business as we go along. Now if you have anything else you want to discuss with Mr Green Walter don't hesitate to do so, remember we are talking about your future.

"I know it seems like a lifetime away at the moment but in just over five years time you will be twenty one, able to claim your inheritance and make your own way in life. Mr Green is your solicitor and trustee, if he agrees to our idea over the next few months we will have to work out a plan where I can also feel secure. Remember I will be giving over five years of my life to your business. Do you fully understand what I'm saying Walter? I have to look after my own family as well as you and your business."

"Yes Mrs Johnston, I do understand, we have to work together if we are going to make the business work, I am sure we can make a plan that is fair for us both."

They left the tearoom and headed back to the house where they left Alexander with Alice. As they walked towards Mr Green's office Maria's tummy was full of butterflies, she realised that this was an incredible opportunity, not just to help Walter but a chance to get a toehold into the world of business in Australia.

Thankfully all went well at the meeting and Walter and Maria could now commence their journey on this exciting new turn on their life's pathway.

Monday morning started a new routine for the Johnstone family. Sam prepared his own breakfast and Maria fed and dressed Alexander in preparation for the train journey into Flinders station.

Alexander fell asleep to the rhythm of the train and Maria gathered her thoughts and planned how she would approach her first day managing Harris Finishings.

Sunday's meeting had gone better than she could ever have hoped, Mr Green had arranged for a Mr Goldberg, Mrs Harris's accountant, to join them. He promised to send one of his clerks to teach them how to take care of the bookkeeping and arranged to give Mr Green a copy of the monthly figures. Mr Green had agreed to her idea that Walter would live in the Flinders house during the week and spend weekends at Northcote. He also agreed that Maria would receive a generous salary of twenty pounds a month and that Walter would receive three pounds a week which would be reviewed on his birthday each year.

Both Sam and Maria felt that the two professional men genuinely wanted them to succeed and that they would do all in their power to provide help and encouragement.

Maria's thoughts were interrupted as the train pulled into the station and the commuters poured off ready to go to their places of work. And in that moment Maria realised that she too was going to paid employment, her first day managing Harris Finishings. Maria Johnstone from the wee village of Glenboig in Scotland was now a woman of commerce and her not yet a year in her new country of Australia.

CHAPTER 7
Letters

Gartsherrie

My dear Sam and Maria

Your last letters have been quite amazing, first your promotion Sam, your pa and I are so proud. The Laws also send their congratulations, mind you. Rab Law said, 'I jist hope the lad disnae get above himself, so I dae'. Just what I would have expected from him. Your Uncle Rab really is a caution, although I wouldn't want to be married to him that's for sure!

And Maria, your exploits, what a lot for us to take in. We are so glad the business is going well and you and Walter are working hard together. What an opportunity for you to enter into a man's world. Fat chance of that happening here, we are as far away as ever from getting the vote Maria, never mind any other rights for women. After all we did during the war, the sacrifices we made, and we are still second class citizens. Maria Johnstone cherish your vote in Australia and use it wisely. Although you seem to have an awful lot of elections, can they no make up their minds in Australia? Sorry, enough of me blethering on about politics.

On a worrying note, work is really starting to dry up in the town, and all over the country for that matter. Lots of returned soldiers, many of them crippled have no chance of employment. A land fit for heroes, I think not.

We have had quite a time of it recently, my suffragette friend Liz, the one who is going to be sponsoring your wee sister Mary at Pitman's College, well she has had that terrible Spanish flu, between the three of us, our Mary, her housekeeper Mrs Armstrong (yes, I ken people who have a housekeeper) and me, we pulled her through. Agnes Law was wonderful looking after your pa's meals and washing, you know how the Gartsherrie folks rally in times of need. Liz is over the worst but a lot of people have been infected in Lanarkshire. It's random, but younger folk seem to be more likely to get it for some reason, although not bairns particularly. Take care it seems to be smitting people all over the world.

We thought our troubles were over when the war finished. Can you believe when I was down the Main Street recently there was a group of folks with banners 'The End is Nigh'. I thought 'Jessie, don't take this on, keep your spirits up' it would be so easy just now to give in between the aftermath of war and this terrible disease. I told Agnes Law about them, she just shook her head and said, 'Jessie, we are all going to hell in a hand cart'.

On a positive note our Mary's starts her course in March, all being well she will graduate from Pitman's College in March next year, now that will be another achievement for the Johnstone clan. And, another opportunity for Rab to use that guid auld Scottish phrase, 'aye no bad but mind you, I know her faither'.

Must go now, I have a hat to finish for Mrs Cumming, her son is getting married next week to a wee lass from the Herriot Row, the family live near the Laws. There was a right stooshie, she is from a devout Catholic family but she has 'turned' and the young couple are moving into the Long Row. Her family threw her out for becoming a Protestant, wee soul she is staying with Mrs Cumming's sister and her man in the North Square until after the wedding.

We are all proud fit to burst at everything you have achieved so far in your new country. Don't ever doubt emigrating was the right decision, after hearing the Cumming story you know it was for the best.

With all our love
Ma and Pa

* * *

Cape Town

My dear Sam and Maria

Christmas and New Year festivities for 1919 seem very far away. Remember how we all saw 1918 in at the cottage and you all teased me for bringing a fruit cake from Scotland. Well I made a dumpling this year, Sophie was fascinated and apparently her 'man' and her friends all thoroughly enjoyed the half I gave to her.

Everyone has been really kind and welcoming from the church but I must admit my best friend here is Sophie, she is a terrible gossip and I hear all these fascinating stories about folks in District 6, people I'll probably never meet, but she has a wise head and we laugh together, which in these times is essential.

We all thought life would be wonderful after the war. Not a bit of it, with this flu epidemic life is very uncertain. Robert is extremely busy at the church supporting the congregation. He will not get a church of his own until after the flu epidemic is over, to be honest I'm quite happy to stay on at the cottage in Cape Town. Both Robert and I can speak a bit of Afrikaans now, if I'm truthful he is much better than me but I've been taught the language by Sophie and I think my version is definitely more colourful.

My part time job at the hospital has turned into full time, hence the reason I've not put pen to paper for ages. I now realise that being a ministers wife was a wonderful training in administration. Please don't laugh, Ishbel Stewart is now the Somerset Hospital's almoner.

The very first lady almoner was called Mary Stewart, she worked at the Royal Free Hospital in London and since my middle name is Mary, well Mhairi, in the Gaelic, it's obviously meant to be. And I would be lying if I didn't say it's very nice getting a salary envelope full of rand every month. I've never had so much money in my entire life!

Go well my dears.

Your forever friend

Ishbel.

* * *

Cape Town

Dear Sam and Maria

My mother usually corresponds and gives me all your news but I thought it was high time that I put pen to paper.

Firstly, congratulation on all your achievements during your first year in Australia, you must both be very proud. Your wee boy, Alexander Robert must be nearly a year old. I was very honoured that you included my name and I want you to know I think of him as my Godchild.

Our beautiful city of Cape Town has been badly stricken with the Spanish flu, the numbers are still going up daily. This was due to over 2,000 soldiers returning from France on two troopships which had a stopover at Sierra Leone. Some soldiers became ill and were treated in Cape Town, however after cursory examinations the other soldiers were allowed to travel, taking the disease all over the country.

As you know my mother is working at the Somerset hospital, my friends she is worn out working long hours day after day, she never complains.

When we first arrived she so enjoyed her time with Sophie learning Afrikaans and the local recipes and I suspect blethering. A number of the church ladies invited her for tea and lunches she was really starting to enjoy her life here on the Cape.

That has all changed, she hardly leaves the hospital now. Last Sunday she did not even come to church, in my entire life I have never known my mother not to worship on the sabbath.

I sincerely hope the infection rate is not too bad in Melbourne. Here it now seems out of control. My main task seems to be burying victims and trying as best I can to give comfort to the families. At the present time there is no possibility of me going to serve at a church in any other part of the country. Apart from anything else there is now a travel ban in place.

I am very worried about my mother working in the infirmary but you know what Ishbel is like, I am afraid all I can do is pray, please pray for us here on the Cape.

Hopefully my next letter will be more joyful and the plague will have abated.

Sending you my very best wishes.

Your friend

Robert

Glenboig

Dear Sis and Sam

Thank you for your letters, good to know Alexander is thriving and you Sam are getting a promotion with the new unit opening. Work situation not great here, all the works are laying men off. I'm ok at the moment and so is Paw but who knows.

Maureen always likes to read your letters when she comes to visit. Now a bit of gossip, Maureen has a young man. As usual the auld man disapproves, this time it's because he came back from the war quite badly injured. The lad's name is Neil Kelly, he lost his right leg from the knee down and an injury to his arm means his right hand doesn't work properly. It happened in the last weeks of the fighting, the poor lad was really unlucky. He only came back to the village about three months ago as he was taken to a surgical unit then a convalescent hospital.

Neil attends the same chapel as us and the priest has set up a club for returning servicemen, our Maureen is one of the volunteers making tea and suchlike, that is how they met. Neil seems a decent enough lad but the way jobs are here and with his injuries I don't hold out much hope of him getting work. That's why the auld man disapproves, you can just imagine him girning on. 'No girl of mine will marry a man who can't provide for her'. That's about the gist of his argument, but if he is not careful he will lose our Maureen the same as he did you.

The three young ones, Frank, Rose and Martha are all doing fine but they are fast growing up. Rose has left school and has been lucky enough to get a job serving in the Co-operative as a trainee. Frank leaves school this summer and that will just leave wee Martha. At the moment Martha wants to give herself to the church. Paw is encouraging her but my ma and the rest of us think she only wants to go into a convent to run away. There are few decent job prospects in the village, the whole of Coatbridge for that matter. The Spanish flu epidemic is taking hold now, and it's not just hitting the working class nobody rich or poor is safe. Martha has also seen the grief Paw has given you and our Maureen, I can't really blame her for wanting to run away to the peace and quiet of a nunnery.

My wee family are fine, I got a good one when I married

Clare and the weans are great, Veronica is two, nearly three now and baby Peter six months old.

Maw sends her love. Maureen fair misses you Maria, especially just now with this Neil business. Personally I think they should get on a boat same as you two did and build a life away from Coatbridge.

Wishing you well in your new country

Your brother

Dan

* * *

Gartsherrie

Our dear family

Firstly Sam, your pa said to mind and tell you they are fairly getting on with building the new football stadium at Cliftonhill, Albion Rovers should have a new home by the end of the year. After the war years it will be good for them to move from Meadow Park, a new beginning for your club. Pa says, 'Do you still have your supporter's scarf'? Memories, I knitted it for your birthday one year, can't remember which, I must be getting auld.

Bit of sad news, mind in my last letter I told you about the Cummings lad getting married. Well, didn't he get the Spanish flu and him a big strapping lad. One day he was fine, then dead two days later. The wee lassie has gone back to her parents, the Cummings family were not especially kind, they took over all the funeral arrangements and she had no say in anything. Poor soul she will surely end up an auld maid, no decent Catholic lad will ever marry her with that history.

Remember I told you in one of my earlier letters about the Battle of George Square, fighting for shorter working hours. Well the communists are really getting a hold in Glasgow the shipyards are known as Red Clydeside now. Your father says women are not getting the vote because the government are terrified they will all vote communist. Well I for one would not vote for Bolsheviks that killed a royal family and five youngsters at that.

Our wee Emily is fair coming along, pretty as a picture. Sometimes I look at her and imagine your Alexander, our hearts would love you all to be with us but our heads know you will have a much better life in Australia.

Our Agnes and Tom dote on their wee one, they did a lovely Sunday afternoon tea for her first birthday. As well as us they invited the Law family, Tom's maw and paw and his sister Catherine we all had a really lovely time, Agnes Law's wee Robert is a right warmer, that lad could eat for Scotland.

Our Agnes made sandwiches, sausage rolls and a big cake, Agnes Law made pancakes and those wee tatty cakes she aye makes for a celebration. I did a selection of scones and Tom's ma did a tray of iced gingerbread, she also gave our Agnes half a pound of tea which was very welcome, can you believe there are still food shortages.

Sadly Tom is very concerned for the future, he might be a manager at Gartsherrie Works but even that is no guarantee of job security in these strange times.

Our love to you all

Ma and Pa

CHAPTER 8
The Partnership

"Right lad, that's the garden all tidied now and ready for the winter coming in, mind you I bet Melbourne at it's coldest is nothing like a Scottish winter. Over there the frost covers the windows like white lace curtains. Now we had better stop blethering and go indoors and see if Maria will let us have a wee cuppa before dinner time."

"Great idea Sam," agreed Walter. "I think she has been baking, there's a lovely smell coming through the kitchen window whatever it is she's cooking.

"Sam, you know I really love the weekends I spend here with you Maria and baby Alexander. Maria and I work together all week and then you teach me stuff at weekends like gardening or how to sole a pair of shoes and we painted my room together last weekend. I reckon I was real lucky finding friends like you two.

"Maria is quite different at work you know. I have to toe the line, no shirking. She is very organised, not only has she kept all Mrs H's clients she has found some new ones. Next week when we have our meeting with Mr Green she is going to ask him if we can employ a junior lad under me. I'll be able to teach him what's what, good isn't it?"

"Well good Walter, well good! Now let's see about that cuppa, and if our luck is in perhaps a slice of cake."

Everyone now called Mrs Harris's house H.Q. it started one weekend at Northcote when Walter happened to say, 'when we are back at H.Q'. Somehow it stuck and even Mrs Wilson and Alice now referred to their place of employment as the H.Q.

Since the end of January occasional cases of the Spanish flu had been reported in the press. However, the authorities had been very strict about people wearing face masks and placing restrictions on the ports to try and minimise infections. As a result of the precautions taken by the government in Victoria, Melbourne did not suffer as badly as Sydney, and Australia did not fare nearly as badly as many other countries throughout the world.

Monday morning dawned and Maria was feeling very apprehensive about the impending meeting with the solicitor. After arriving at H.Q. the first thing she did was issue instructions.

"Walter, remember the meeting with Mr Green is this afternoon at four o'clock so we're going to have a right busy day if we want to get everything cleared for about half past three.

"I'll take the trap and collect the work from Mrs Broom and Mrs Myles. You return the gloves to Mr Pettifer and on your way back pick up the evening bags from Kramer's and the pearl and diamanté buttons I've ordered at the Stein Workshops. By that time we should both be back at H.Q. We can then sort out tomorrow's client returns and I'll make a start on this months invoices. And, can you tell Alice to expect Violet and Annie to call into the shop to collect their work, I'll leave the parcels labelled on the counter. Oh can you please also ask Mrs Wilson to make us a sandwich and a pot of tea at around one o'clock.

"Sorry to be sounding like a sergeant major Walter, but I'm so nervous about this meeting today. We agreed Mr Green would assess the business, and us for that matter, on a six monthly basis until you are twenty one. Walter, I so want all to be well and I'm not entirely sure what he expects. Now let's crack on."

The busy day flew past in the blink of an eye. Suddenly it was half past three, Maria ran upstairs and changed into her good green costume that she used to wear to chapel in Scotland and Walter went off to change into his Sunday best. 'Count to ten' and they headed off to the offices of Mr Green.

After the usual formalities Mr Green opened the meeting by saying, "Well Mrs Johnstone, Walter, I have to say I'm most impressed as to how you have managed Harris Finishings over the past months, particularly with all the flu that's been about. On the financial side the sales initially remained at the same level despite the death of Mrs Harris and for the last three months they have been showing a small steady growth, I'm extremely pleased with you both. Also Mr Goldberg has advised me that all the paperwork submitted to him has been maintained in good order.

"However my job is considerably more than just supervising company accounts. Tell me Master Walter are you happy with the present arrangement of having Mr an Mrs Johnstone act as your guardians?"

"Yes sir," replied Walter. "Mr and Mrs Johnstone have been

wonderful, Maria organises the business and I really enjoy going to Northcote at the weekend. Sam is great, he has taught me loads of things and sometimes Maria lets me help her bake and she showed me how to make puff candy. Quite often we all go out for a picnic and we have a book on birds, Sam and I try to see how many we can identify. Alexander is …"

"Walter, Walter, it's not you having fun at Northcote I'm interested in, it's how you feel you are progressing with regard to the business. The firm of Harris Finishings is your legacy from your grandmother, it's your future, not making puff candy, do I make myself perfectly clear? Now tell me what you have learned in the past six months."

Walter suddenly felt very naive he quickly realised Mr Green wasn't in the least interested in how happy he was. He was only interested in ensuring that he was carrying out his obligations diligently as a trustee.

"Mr Green, when Maria and I first took over the business we realised just how much we both had to learn. We spent the first few days clearing out the stock room and the shop, getting everything in apple pie order.

"A clerk from Mr Goldberg's company came in and showed us how to write up the ledgers and prepare the invoices. I usually prepare the banking and Maria does the invoicing and pays the bills as she has a much neater hand than me. Although we both know how to do all the paperwork. Maria said, 'if we want to make a success of the business we must both know absolutely everything about running Harris Finishings', she has even learned how to drive the trap.

"Mr Goldberg's office prepare the wages and check our accounts every month, they will also deal with taxation matters when the time comes. That's about the only things we don't see to ourselves."

"Good Walter! That's what I want to hear that you are buckling down and learning the business. Mrs Johnstone do you have anything else you wish to discuss with me?"

Maria took a deep breath before saying, "Actually Mr Green there are several things I'd like to discuss. Firstly can we employ a young lad to help with deliveries? I would like Walter and myself to be able to spend more time developing the business. I think it would also boost Walter's confidence if he had a young lad to train.

"I would also like your permission for Walter to move into Mrs Harris's bedroom upstairs and turn his present room into a second storeroom come workspace. It seems sensible to have the whole of the ground floor used for the business."

Mr Green smiled, "Mrs Johnstone, young Walter is indeed lucky to have found a mentor such as you. Yes, go ahead with your ideas with my blessing and I have no doubt when we meet again in six months time you will have more entrepreneurial ideas to discuss with me.

"Meantime if you want to develop any other innovations please make an appointment to come and see me. Now the formalities are over would you care to join me in a cup of tea?"

Maria inwardly breathed a sigh of relief as she answered, "That would be very nice thank you Mr Green."

They walked back to the office on cloud nine. Six months operating the business and Mr Green was pleased with them both. Walter was delighted that there was no further talk of boarding school and Maria relieved that her position, and excellent salary were safe.

Back at H.Q. Mrs Wilson and Alice were also anxiously awaiting the outcome of the meeting to decide the future of Harris Finishings. If the business was sold they would have to look for other work. Although their jobs had changed dramatically since Mrs Harris died, they both enjoyed working with Maria and young Walter, thoroughly spoiling wee Alexander was just a bonus.

Maria and Walter breezed into H.Q. excited beyond words. Walter grabbed Mrs Wilson and spun her round singing, "We've done it, we've done it, we've done it! We can all carry on working together. Harris Finishings is not finished, it's just begun."

After a celebration cup of tea with one of Mrs Wilson's famous Lamington cakes Maria set off home with Alexander. On the train while the baby slept Maria allowed her thoughts a free rein. Now that she felt confident that she could continue earning a salary of twenty pounds a month, together with Sam's wages there was no reason why they couldn't buy a small house rather than renting. She remembered Sam telling her how delighted his mother and father had been when his sister Agnes and her husband Tom had bought their own house in Drumpellier. 'It gives them a wonderful sense of freedom knowing their home is not tied to their employer'.

Maria had never forgotten that sentence, Sam might have a good job, and his new promoted position was starting soon but at the end of the day they were living in a tied works house, what if Sam was to take ill, they wouldn't have a home.

Once the seed was sown it took root and over the next few months Maria set to work. Firstly, she discussed her idea with Sam, his initial reaction was caution. "Maria lass we are scarcely settled here, and we are happy in this grand wee house the company are renting to us. I agree it would be a great idea to buy our own place but don't you think it's a wee bit soon to make such a huge commitment? Besides as well as a deposit we would also need money for more furniture, most of the furniture we have here belongs to the company."

"That's just it Sam, we are beholden to the company. If we manage to get a loan to buy a place we could live off your money and pay all of my salary towards clearing the loan. It shouldn't take more than maybe five years, now is the time to do it while I'm earning good money at Harris Finishings. Sam, would you mind if I investigate the possibility of buying our own place?"

Sam could refuse his Maria nothing, "All right Maria you can start investigating but as my ma would say 'let's caw canny.' "

Maria laughed, "Samuel Johnstone have you ever known me to be anything else but a good manager of money? The Riley family might have had a different religion from the Johnstone family but as far as money is concerned we all 'sing from the same hymn sheet.' "

Over the next few weeks Maria perused the houses for sale column in the Northcote Leader. Eventually she thought that the financial compromise might be to purchase a building plot and then they could build a house whenever they felt more secure. Maria talked her idea over with Sam and he was one hundred percent in agreement with his wife and encouraged her to go ahead and find a suitable piece of land.

Maria was desperately anxious not to make a wrong move so she decided to talk to Mr Goldberg in order to find out the best way to get a loan and what would be a sensible amount to borrow. Without giving away why she was going to see Mr Goldberg, one afternoon Maria announced to Walter that she was popping out to the accountant's office. Fortunately young Alexander was happy to be left with Alice, Mrs Wilson or Walter so Maria never worried that he was neglected, if anything the opposite, with his sunny nature and ready smile he was thoroughly spoiled.

Mr Goldberg greeted Maria, "Well my dear this is an unexpected pleasure, you are not due to hand in the monthly accounts or collect the salary payments. So, what is the purpose of your visit today?"

Maria nervously started on her prepared speech, "Mr Goldberg this meeting is not about Harris Finishings so you should not charge your services today to their account, I will pay you privately. My husband Sam and I would like to purchase a house instead of renting in Northcote. We have talked things over and I have spent hours pouring over properties and we think it might be wise to purchase a plot of land, try and pay it off as quickly as ever we can and then build a property on land we already own. Mr Goldberg do you think it's possible and how would we set about getting a loan? Phew, that's it said."

Over the months Harold Goldberg had come to respect Maria. Not only had she taken on the running of a business without a great deal of formal education but her sales figures had overtaken Lavinia Harris after around three or four months and she was ensuring that young Walter received a good business training.

"Don't look so scared my dear, you have come on a perfectly sensible errand. Firstly, I think it is a very good idea to purchase a property, most people rent nowadays but the problems with renting start to arise in later years when you have to leave work, then you lose your company house and are at the mercy of the commercial rental market, at a time when you have least money. Another thing in favour of purchasing is appreciation of your asset. I'll give you an example, Mrs Harris bought her property for two hundred and twenty pounds. It's now worth well in excess of three hundred, probably nearer four. Now that is a considerably higher return than could be expected from interest on a savings account.

"Mrs Johnstone, please arrange to supply me with details of your husband's salary and your outgoings, also anything else that you think is in any way relevant."

Maria went into her handbag and removed several sheets of notepaper detailing everything Mr Goldberg had asked her to submit.

As he accepted the papers he thought, 'this young lady could indeed go far.'

—

CHAPTER 9
Cape Town

Once again Robert arrived home to an empty cottage. He went into the kitchen and found a freshly made Malay chicken curry and some roti bread, the kitchen table was set, there was even jars of Sophie's homemade pickles and chutney laid out for him. Robert sent up a prayer of thanks for his wonderful housekeeper.

Since the flu pandemic started Sophie had become the rock of the household. Ishbel spent long tiring hours working at the Somerset hospital and Robert's pastoral duties seemed never ending. Sophie kept the household running, laundry washed and ironed, delicious and sustaining food prepared and the cottage kept spotlessly clean. Mr April no longer came three days a week, the church had seconded him to the cemetery service where he was working as a grave digger. As well as her household duties Sophie now kept the garden tidy.

Robert changed into his nightshirt and dressing gown while his food was heating. After eating his meal he decided to read the Cape Argos, as he read the newspaper he could feel his head drooping. He was just about to go to bed when he heard his mother arrive home. Ishbel looked exhausted, Robert immediately offered to heat her some food. She just sat down on the sofa saying, "No food Robert but I'd love a cup of tea and a plain biscuit." By the time Robert returned from the kitchen his mother was sound asleep. He gently woke her up and helped her into her bedroom, he put the tea on her bedside table but it was left untouched. Ishbel Stewart who had cared for so many over the years was now another victim of the Spanish flu.

The following morning Sophie arrived while Robert was in the kitchen preparing his breakfast, he told her of his mother's exhaustion the previous evening and his idea that she should have a complete rest.

"Sophie, I've let my mother sleep on, whether she likes it or not I think she needs a few days of recovery time. Can I ask you to look after her for me? I've got three funerals today but I'll try and get home early for a change, to be honest I also need an early night, the flu epidemic is taking its toll on all of us."

"Don't you worry reverend Robert, I'll look after your mother. You know Ishbel Stewart is a saint, she has been working non stop at that hospital and not just in her office let me tell you, did you know she has been nursing in the wards as well?"

Robert looked blank, "Indeed I did not Sophie, I thought she was just working in the office. Well it's all the more reason for her to take a little break." He finished his tea then said, "Sorry Sophie, I've got to go now. Let her sleep on a bit then give her a light breakfast in bed."

Sophie got on with her work then set a tray for Ishbel's nutritious breakfast of toast and a boiled egg, fresh from their own hens. Around ten o'clock she opened Ishbel's bedroom door and was horrified to find her sweating and delirious. It didn't need a doctor to confirm Sophie's immediate thought, Ishbel was suffering from Spanish flu.

Without hesitating Sophie put down the tray and rushed over to her bedside. Ishbel was still partially dressed in her clothes from the previous day and was drifting in and out of consciousness. Sophie removed her outdoor clothes and put on her nightdress, she managed to get her patient onto the bedroom chair to allow her to make up the bed with clean linen. Once she was settled back into bed Sophie quickly wrote a note and rushed over to a nearby cottage. She knocked the neighbour's door then swiftly moved back to the garden gate. The maid answered the door and Sophie shouted to her, "I won't come near you because Mistress Stewart has got the flu, I've left a note on your doorstep. I saw your houseboy Abbie working in the garden today, please ask your madam if he can run down to the Somerset hospital and give it to someone in authority telling them what has happened. The reverend is doing funerals today, I reckons he can't help in any case, so I'll wait until he gets home to tell him the bad news."

The maid swiftly lifted the note and closed the door, a few minutes later Sophie was relieved to see young Abbie running down the street clutching the letter.

Sophie spent the entire day doing everything she could to make Ishbel comfortable. However, when Robert returned home around five o'clock she wouldn't allow him to enter the cottage and had to break the bad news to him on the doorstep.

"Reverend, your mother has the Spanish flu. I'll look after her but I think you should stay away otherwise you really risk getting infected. Young Abbie who works next door has told the hospital of your mother's illness. He has also been up to District 6 and told my man that I'm going to stay here and look after the mistress. Why don't you go and speak to your superior and see if he can give you a bed until your mother recovers or perhaps one of the congregation would kindly oblige and take you in.

"Your mother would not want you to risk infection, besides you have a minister's work to do. My work is here to nurse one of the finest ladies I've ever met. Now please go I've packed a bag for you, leave as quickly as ever you can."

Robert tried to argue but Sophie was adamant, "I'll need to sleep in your room so you must go, besides it's what your mother would want, you know it is." Reluctantly Robert lifted the valise Sophie had packed and left the cottage, he would not return home for many weeks.

Exhausted Sophie eventually sat down with a cheese and pickle sandwich and a mug of bovril around eight o'clock. Just as she was about to take her first sip of the warming drink there was a knock on the door.

Sophie opened the door to a tall middle aged man carrying a brown leather Gladstone bag. Without preamble he said, "Are you Sophie David who sent the note to the hospital saying Mistress Stewart was suffering from the flu?"

Sophie answered the gentleman, "Yes sir, my mistress is in the bedroom. I have changed the linen twice today, I managed to get her to drink some plain weak tea but that's all I could get into her. Madam is in a broken sleep just now, I've been putting cold flannels over her forehead to try and lower the fever."

The gentleman said, "I'm Doctor Hofmyer. This is the first opportunity I've had to call, please let me see the patient."

Sophie showed him into the bedroom and his practiced eye immediately told him Ishbel was in safe hands with Sophie David nursing her. After carefully examining Ishbel he indicated to Sophie he wished to wash his hands and she showed him to the bathroom.

The doctor then came through to the sitting room where Sophie offered him a cup of tea and asked if he would like something to eat. "Mrs David, I would love something light to eat and a cup of tea."

Sophie disappeared into the kitchen and returned a few minutes later saying, "Sir, I can make you some nice scrambled eggs, the eggs are fresh from our own hens, with a bit of boiled ham and some home made bread, will that do?"

"Mrs David that sounds wonderful" was his reply. Sophie prepared the simple meal and set a place at the dining room table. When she returned to the sitting room to tell the doctor his food was ready she found him fast asleep in the chair.

"Sir, sir, your supper is ready for you, all set out in the dining room. Please come through sir."

Dr Hofmyer roused himself and followed Sophie. He sat down and thoroughly enjoyed the carefully prepared meal, which was the first decent food he had eaten in days. After he had finished he found Sophie clearing up in the kitchen.

"Thank you very much for the sustaining food Mrs David it was just what I needed. There is very little I can offer you by way of medical advice to alleviate the symptoms of this terrible influenza. Give Mrs Stewart aspirin and kindly nursing, there is no rhyme or reason as to the outcome for people infected in this epidemic, some live some die, regardless of age or any other factors. We must just pray your mistress is one of the lucky ones. Is her son aware of her illness?"

Sophie replied, "Yes sir, as soon as he came home this evening I sent him packing to stay elsewhere, I know the flu is highly infectious. I'll stay here and nurse Ish..., Mistress Stewart."

Doctor Hofmyer had not missed Sophie's slip up and somehow his heart gladdened to know of the attachment between madam and maid.

He bid Sophie good evening returned to his car and drove to his home in Rondebosch.

Over the following days a routine developed, Sophie cared for Ishbel and slept in Robert's bedroom. Every morning Robert would call at the cottage and Sophie would give him a list of everything she required. In the afternoon or evening, whenever he managed to get some free time, he would deliver all that was needed. Sophie gave him a daily update but she would not allow him into the cottage, although he often wrote a letter for his mother which Sophie would read to her. Later in the evening Dr Hofmyer would call in on his way home. Sophie always had a nice meal ready for him and he greatly looked forward to this oasis of peace in his harrowing day.

Each day before eating he would check on his patient and was greatly relieved that after the first forty eight hours she seemed to have weathered the initial crisis and very slowly started to recover under the ministrations of Sophie.

One evening after Sophie had served the doctor babotie with her home made mango chutney and wholemeal bread he said, "Tell me Mrs David how long have you worked for Mistress Stewart?"

"Sir, I first met her the day they arrived from Scotland, new year's eve 1917. I can honestly say I've never worked for anyone quite like her, I'm not her servant, I'm her friend. Mistress Stewart treats everyone the same, she is so very kind."

"That explains why you have looked after her so wonderfully, I have seldom encountered a home nurse as competent as you. And, I do understand your loyalty, I have got to know Mistress Stewart since she has been working at the hospital. Not only is she a wonderful administrator but she truly cares. I too have great admiration for the lady."

The first forty eight hours had been touch and go for Ishbel but then almost imperceptibly she started to slowly recover. One day about ten days into the illness Ishbel said, "Sophie, I've been in a nightmare somewhere between heaven and earth, today I'm starting to feel that I'm at last coming to the surface. Please tell me what has been happening?"

"I'm so pleased to hear you say those words," said Sophie. "We have all been terribly worried. Ishbel, I threw reverend Robert out and took over his bedroom. He has been staying with a family called Pretorius who attend the church. Mind you half the congregation are probably called Pretorius so I've no idea where he is actually staying. Your Robert has been wonderful, every morning he collects my list and brings me whatever I ask for. I've had him bringing everything from prime steak for your beef tea to niceties for the doctor's supper. The doctor from the hospital comes every night on his way home to see you and afterwards I give him supper."

Confused, Ishbel asked, "Is it doctor Hofmyer you are talking about, I vaguely remember him being here at different times. And Sophie, you say you have been making supper for him? He is a very senior doctor, I used to have to deal with him in my administration role, he was always very gentlemanly but truth to tell I was a wee bit in awe of him.

"Sophie I'm feeling confused and tired again, do you mind if I have a little rest?"

"Just you close your eyes and I'll read you the letter your Robert left this morning…"

> *Dearest Mother*
> *I've been so worried about you and I'm much relieved to hear from Sophie that you are starting to rally, be it ever so slowly. Prayer must be working!*
> *I have now written to the boys with details of your illness, I held back for a few days until the worst of the crisis was over but now you seem a little better I thought I had better get word to them.*

Sophie then muttered, "No need to read the next bit, just you have a little rest and I'll waken you for something to eat later. You must eat, you have got so thin, besides good nourishing food fights illness."

What Sophie did not read aloud was;

> *Sophie has been truly wonderful, if she was your sister she could not have done more. We will never be able to repay her for all her kindness and superb nursing.*

Slowly, unlike many others, Ishbel regained her strength. It was a long progress and Sophie banned Robert for another month while she stayed on at the cottage.

The routine established in the early days of Ishbel's illness continued, every evening around eight o'clock doctor Hofmyer would arrive and have supper before going home to his house in Rondebosch. As Ishbel improved she joined him for supper in the dining room and they both enjoyed the companionship of two friends fighting the same battle. As the weeks passed Ishbel found herself looking forward to Charles's visits. Sophie, who missed nothing, quietly teased her about her 'gentleman caller'.

They did not always talk about the pandemic, Ishbel shared stories of her childhood in the Western Isles and as a minister's wife in Perthshire. She also explained the reasons why she wanted to travel to Africa rather than living a sedate life as the widow of a man of the cloth in Scotland. "Charles, I really wanted to have an adventure to be my own person, I had always been a daughter, a wife, a mother, never Ishbel Mhairi Macleod, and this was my opportunity. I know there will be plenty of folks who will think I couldn't let my youngest son go and make a life for himself that I am an interfering mother who followed him all the way to Africa. Robert knows the truth and he has been a wonderful son letting me do whatever I wanted without ever trying to stop me from being Ishbel. I knew full well that he was not happy about me working at the hospital but not once did he try to stop me doing what I felt was right."

Charles Hofmyer told her that he had been born in Grahamstown and his father had worked for the Cape Government Railway. "I suppose you could say we were solid middle class, my mother was from an English family and a practicing Anglican, father was an Afrikaner. Hence the name, Charles, very English and Hofmyer very Afrikaner. Nothing remarkable about us, my elder brother became an engineer like my father, his name is Johannes or John, he settled in Durban with his wife and family. My younger sister Arabella lives on a cattle farm outside Durban happily married with three children.

"I was always interested in science subjects at school and as far back as I can remember I wanted to be a doctor. My parents sent me to London where I trained at St Bartholomew's Hospital, it's known to everyone as Barts. Fortunately my mother had a sister, Aunt Charlotte, living in Maida Vale, she kindly gave me a room in her large Victorian house. I think she had a soft spot for me because of my name.

"After I qualified I couldn't wait to get on a ship and sail home to Africa. I landed back in Cape Town and I've never had any inclination to leave."

One evening after supper when they were comfortably settled in the sitting room drinking a cup of coffee Charles Hofmyer summoned all his courage and initiated a conversation that would drastically change the life path for them both.

"Ishbel my dear, unlike you I was not lucky in love. I fell head over heels in love with a girl I met on the ship coming home, as with most shipboard romances it quickly ended when we reached dry land.

"After I arrived on the Cape I secured a post as an assistant to a G.P. and my medical career became paramount. Gradually I worked my way up the ladder eventually gaining my present position at the Somerset hospital.

"Yes, there have been a few ladies over the years but my career always came first, I'd be off to Jo'burg or Durban lecturing, working on research papers, taking clinics. Suddenly it's another Christmas, or another birthday and then one day realisation dawned that I was no longer a young man, I was becoming an old bachelor.

"When my Aunt Charlotte died I inherited her entire estate, I bought a nice property in Rondebosch and I'm now secure financially but other than work I've got very little in my life.

"Ishbel when you were ill and I came to see you of an evening Sophie always had a nice meal ready for me and a kind word. I realised that status, qualifications, money for that matter mean nothing unless you have someone to share your achievements with. I know we are friends but I feel a lot more for you than friendship. I wonder, oh Ishbel I'm not at all good at this, can we become sweethearts, no what I'm really trying to say is, Ishbel will you marry me?"

The proposal was unexpected and yet strangely expected. Ishbel took Charles by the hand, "What a huge compliment, I know we are both well into our forties but it's not too late to have a loving life together. Charles, my two sons in Scotland will be shocked at their mother getting married again. They will probably blame poor Robert for my disgraceful behaviour. However, Charles my dear, I would be honoured to change my name from Mistress Ishbel Stewart to Frau Ishbel Hofmyer."

Charles kissed his love for the first time and they both knew all would be well.

And it was, as soon as Ishbel was fully recovered they were quietly married by Dr Hausman in the Dutch Reformed Church.

Ishbel moved into Charles's house in Rondebosh and naturally Sophie came too, although she insisted on returning to the cottage in Oranjezicht one day a week to ensure Robert was being properly looked after.

Ishbel happily settled into her married life with Charles and thoroughly enjoyed turning the house into a happy home. Within her first year of marriage Ishbel thought that the menopause was upon her. However, to her surprise and delight she was in fact pregnant. Charles was over the moon that after all these years he was going to become a father.

He decided that after a lifetime of working in the medical profession he was going to take a sabbatical for a year and support Ishbel through the birth of their baby. As a doctor he was concerned about Ishbel's health, given that she was well into her forties and that she had suffered badly from the Spanish flu.

However, all was well and she was safely delivered of a little girl. Sophie supported Ishbel through her pregnancy and assisted at the birth of her longed for daughter. They decided to call the baby Elize Mhairi, and she was christened by her half brother Robert who was totally besotted with his new little sister.

Charles spent his sabbatical from medicine with his wife and child, the couple also enjoyed a trip to Natal in order to meet with Charles's brother and sister and introduce them to Ishbel and their new baby. Although baby Elize's cousins were all teenagers they thoroughly enjoyed having a new baby in the family to spoil.

At the end of his sabbatical year Charles returned to work at the Somerset hospital, however now he had a family he never again worked ridiculously long hours. His priority in life changed from work to family.

⁓

CHAPTER 10
Sad News

Glenboig

Dear Maria and Sam

I've been putting off writing this letter for weeks but Clare made me sit down and put pen to paper.

Sis there is no easy way of telling you this news, our Maureen has passed away. Her and Neil eventually eloped, our pa was so against them getting married, according to him a cripple who couldn't work wasn't good enough for a Riley girl.

They had a simple Catholic marriage service at the parish in Glasgow where they were staying with his aunt and uncle. Shortly afterwards Maureen was expecting and they decided that after their baby was born they would go to Canada. Neil's brother emigrated to Canada just after the war and he was doing quite well for himself.

Apparently it was a breach birth and Maureen died, her wee girl only lived a few hours before she too died. They were buried under the rites of the church but Clare and I were the only members of the Riley family that attended the Requiem Mass, the Virgil was held in the aunt and uncle's house.

Neil is inconsolable. He is still living with his family in Glasgow, they have been very good to him and helped him get some work. I don't know yet if he will go to Canada, return to Glenboig or make a home with his aunt and uncle in Glasgow.

As you can imagine my ma and the others are all completely distraught, first our Michael being killed in the war, then losing you then our Maureen. Pa is being his usual self, he was so against their marriage, even though they got wed in the chapel in Glasgow, and God forgive me I honestly think he regards what happened as a kind of punishment. He is incapable of giving in and saying he was wrong.

I'm sorry I can't write any more, it's all too raw.

I hope life in Australia continues well for you both and wee Alexander.

God bless

Dan

* * *

Cape Town

Dear Sam and Maria

I thought I had better put pen to paper and update you as to my life in Cape Town. My experiences dealing with the effects of the Spanish flu have been like living in a nightmare from which I could not awaken, so much sorrow. However, life is slowly returning to normal, but for so many it will never be 'normal' again, the plague has left thousands of families to mourn their loved ones.

Mother's brush with the flu was terrifying, as you can imagine Sophie was wonderful, if Ishbel had been family she could not have looked after her in a kindlier fashion. I will be forever grateful to Sophie, she most certainly saved my mother's life.

You will probably be rather shocked but after much thought and prayer I have now made a life changing decision. I am leaving the ministry and have accepted a position at Cape Town University as a lecturer. This is not a reflection on the congregation of the Dutch Reformed kirk in Cape Town where I have been treated with the utmost kindness and met some wonderful people. Neither is it the language, during the epidemic my Afrikaans improved in leaps and bounds and I'm now quite a confident speaker. I just don't feel I have the call to be a country minister, after having made a number of visits to congregations in the Klein Karoo I honestly don't think it is the right place for me.

Being brought up in the countryside in Perthshire I thought I would fit easily into life on the platteland but I just don't think I could do it justice. The scenery is breathtaking and the farmers, the boers, have a quiet strength but I've come to realise I'm more of an academic, a teacher, it doesn't mean I don't want to live a worthwhile Christian life, I just don't think I am the right person to preach in a small Karoo town. Looking back I think my 'call' was probably more a call to leave Scotland than to be a minister.

My mother has been very supportive and just wants me to be happy. My brothers, well from the tone of their letters I think they are thoroughly exasperated with me, they think I can't stick to anything, perhaps they are right.

Mother has her own news and she is writing to you separately, needless to say I am supporting her in her life changes in the same way as she has always been my strength.

I hope wee Alexander is continuing to do well, I'm so very pleased that you honoured me by giving him Robert as a middle name.

You have both packed so much into your short time in Australia you must be very proud. Perhaps one day we will be able to meet again, what a great pleasure that would be.

Sending you my very best wishes
Your friend
Robert

* * *

Cape Town

My dearest friends

What a lot I have to tell you. I know Robert has written separately telling you that he has resigned from the ministry. They are extremely sorry to lose him and have been very understanding. He was quite wonderful to the congregation during the Spanish flu epidemic.

Sophie is well, although there have been many deaths in her community from the flu, including Mr Adams the photographer who took the lovely photographs at your blessing.

Now for my news and I think you had both better sit down before reading this. You may remember I have mentioned Doctor Charles Hofmyer in previous letters. Well, Charles proposed and I accepted, we decided at our age a long engagement wasn't necessary so we had a lovely quiet wedding and I am now living with Charles in an elegant home in a Cape Town suburb called Rondebosch, as Mrs, or is it Frau Hofmyer - no longer Mistress Stewart.

Robert is moving out of the cottage in Oranjezicht and will be staying with us meantime but he has been looking for a small cottage somewhere near the university. I hope he finds something suitable as I think it would be good for him to be independent. We will certainly miss him and I think he will miss all the good home cooking.

Sophie is now living with us permanently, she has her own little self contained unit which she loves, she has her privacy and can invite her friends over for tea, she does like to keep up with the District 6 gossip.

Her husband passed away, not the flu, sadly drink. Sophie never complained but I think she did not have an easy time with him. Her son moved to Jo'burg as a teenager and has done quite well for himself but she rarely hears from him.

Sophie living in Rondebosch has worked out well for us all, except Robert, who constantly teases her that she has a double bedroom, living room and bathroom and he has only been assigned a single bedroom.

Now for the really _big_ news, I'm going to have a baby. Yes, nearer fifty than forty and with child. Charles is delighted, but concerned for my health, especially after having the flu, but we girls from the Western Isles are made of stern stuff. Robert and Sophie are beside themselves and looking forward to baby Hofmyer's arrival.

I have written to both Archie and Euan, you can imagine how hard those letters were to write. Both boys found their calling early in life and married women who have both make exemplary minister's wives. I am afraid they can't quite understand Robert changing his career and as for me, marrying Charles and now about to have his baby, that's not going to be easy for my boys to accept. I haven't received a reply yet but I can just imagine them struggling to try and write letters somewhere between disapproval and their ministerial duty to be kind and supportive to their mother.

I wish you could meet Charles, he is such a fine man. We are so suited and terribly happy together, be pleased for me my friends.

He is going to take a sabbatical from work to be with me when the baby arrives.

This is not at all how I envisaged my life in Africa but God has a plan.

Robert and I are so proud of all your achievements in your new land. Keep well dear friends.

God bless

Ishbel

CHAPTER 11
The House

Happy birthday to you
Happy birthday to you
Happy birthday dear Alexander
Happy birthday to you
Hurrah, Hurrah, Hurrah

It was Alexander Robert Johnstone's third birthday. His parents and Walter had arranged a small celebration. Maria baked sausage rolls and an iced fruit cake, and prepared a selection of gammon, egg and cheese sandwiches. Putting his arm around Maria's waist Sam said, "Maria, does this spread not remind you of Reid's and the Mount Nelson? Now they served truly spectacular afternoon teas."

Walter piped up, "What spectacular afternoon teas? You haven't told me about this, come on Sam get a telling."

The Walter McDonald at seventeen was very different from the young lad of fifteen who had inherited a business. He was almost as tall as Sam and handsome enough to melt the hearts of the girls at the weekly dances he attended. Walter was now a fixture in the Johnstone family and Sam and Maria thought of him as a young brother. Alexander adored him and his favourite cry was 'Walter play wiff me, let's play wiff my ball'.

Nearly two years previously Sam and Maria, with practical assistance from Mr Goldberg, had purchased a plot of land on a new development reasonably close to the brickworks where Sam worked using a loan from the Commercial Bank of Australia. Although it was more expensive, the accountant had advised them to purchase a larger corner plot which would give them better options when it came to building and would always be more saleable. A loan of one hundred and sixty pounds plus interest seemed an enormous amount of money but they took a leap of faith and signed the paperwork.

Just over three years after arriving in Australia from Scotland the building plot was now paid and Sam and Maria were contemplating building a home of their own.

Sam answered Walter's question, "Our posh afternoon teas were with our friends Robert and Ishbel Stewart, we met them on our journey by ship from Liverpool to Melbourne. Reid's Hotel was in Funchal on the island of Madeira and the Mount Nelson is in Cape Town, we went there for tea after Robert, who is an ordained minister, blessed our marriage at his cottage. Honestly Walter lad you have never seen spreads like it, we were so spoiled, wonderful memories of time spent with exceptional people. Happy memories are one of life's great blessings."

After Alexander's birthday tea Walter said his farewells and headed back into the city, conscious that sharing family celebrations with Sam and Maria was one of the blessings bestowed on him .

Once Alexander was in bed Maria made her and Sam a pot of tea, they sat sipping cups of the brew in front of the small fire Sam had lit as the winter nights in Melbourne could be quite chilly.

"Can you really believe the loan is cleared and we now own a little bit of Australia?" Sam said to Maria, "It's all down to you my love, between the salary you earn working with Walter and your money management skills, we have managed to live well and still clear the loan. A ten year loan paid in well, less than two. Now that's a truly amazing achievement!"

Maria replied, "Sam, that's only phase one complete. Now we have to decide what we're going to do about building a house. I want to make sure we have a secure home, fully paid, before Walter reaches twenty one. The way things are going at present all is well at Harris Finishings. The first young lad we brought in, James, is now full time and he is training up young Harry. The sales have increased beyond my wildest expectations and our profit margins are excellent, but as Mrs Harris would have said, 'always fair, always fair'. Sam who knows what the future holds after Walter reaches twenty one and receives his inheritance, he may marry and want to run the company with his wife or he may just outgrow my being around like a big sister. In any event I think we should plan that I might not have a position in four or five years time."

Sam looked shocked, "Maria do you really think after all you have done for Walter he would simply discard you when he has control of his inheritance? I can't believe the lad would do anything of the kind."

"No Sam I don't think for one minute that Walter would deliberately do anything nasty it's just you never know what will happen in life, the bottom line is, it's not my business and it's as well to be prepared. 'Hope for the best and prepare for the worst' as my mother would have said.

"I thought we could make an appointment with Mr Goldberg and ask him how much we can borrow from the bank before we start thinking about engaging a builder, in my head I know the house I would love but I think we need to be realistic."

"Oh Maria," said Sam. "You are so like my mother, always making a plan and having an ambition. Honestly you are more like her child than I am. Me, I'm like my father, I'm happy to work hard for my weekly wage and simply enjoy being able to spend time with my family at the end of the working day.

"You are right of course, arrange an appointment with Mr Goldberg and we will get a move on with our new home. A lot has already happened to us in the short time we've been in Australia. Maria, I often wonder what exciting things are yet to come for the Johnstone family."

Maria reached over and took Sam's hand, saying, "Sam, one of the best things about emigrating is how well your health has been since we arrived in Australia, away from the smogs in Glasgow and the terrible cold Scottish winters. The climate here seems to suit you and your new job is mainly office based which also helps. I know we ran away because of the whole Catholic and Protestant nonsense but life has been so much more living here in Australia. Alexander is thriving, we both have well paid jobs, the weather is lovely and we have a comfortable wee house to live in until we can build one of our own, now who would ever have believed that would be possible for an ordinary lad and lass from Coatbridge.

"The only sadness is missing family and friends from Glenboig and Gartsherrie. Do you know I have every letter we have received from home, and from Cape Town. I keep them in a biscuit tin in the kitchen cupboard. Sometimes I just like to look at them and think of home, family and friends."

The appointment with the accountant went well. The outcome was that the bank agreed to giving them a loan over ten years of up to four hundred pounds. This was considerably more money than either Sam or Maria had imagined they would be able to borrow. Swiftly the arrangements were made and the money for the new Johnstone family home was soon in place.

The following months seemed to fly past for Sam and Maria, between work, family life and the new house project. Eventually they were at the stage of engaging builders, after having completed planning applications and preparing budgets.

They learned new skills as they went along, Sam hands on practical and Maria financial. Maria was assisted through the house purchase finance by Mr Green and Mr Goldberg, who had both rather taken to the hard working Scottish lass.

Like his father, Sam was a member of the Freemasons and after arriving in Northcote he had regularly attended lodge meetings. Being a mason enabled Sam to make connections in the area and he was able to find an excellent group of tradesmen that he knew could be trusted to do a good job carrying out the building work.

After much discussion they opted to build a Federation style red brick bungalow with a tiled roof and wrap around veranda. The sitting room and dining room, which were facing to the front of the property would each have a bay window. There would be a kitchen, three bedrooms, plus a little box room and a bathroom.

Sam was particularly proud of the fact that the bricks used in the house would be made at the brickworks where he worked, now that would be something to tell his grandchildren one day.

Having taken advice to buy a larger plot they would now be able to build a home with good sized rooms and still have a large garden. Prior to dividing the land into plots all the native bush had been cleared making the ground a blank canvas. Sam spent many happy hours drawing up plans for the garden in which he intended to include a selection of fruit trees and a vegetable patch.

As the year wore on they watched the house take shape and grow and the pot of money allocated by the bank diminish.

In addition to seeing the house develop, Maria watched Harris Finishings thrive and prosper. Walter had long since moved into what had been Mrs Harris's bedroom and his old bedroom on the ground floor was invaluable for holding stock and separating the house into ground floor business and upstairs accommodation.

Maria spent most of her time in H.Q. while Walter was driven by James to the home workers all over the city, with young Harry making local deliveries and collections on his bike. However, Maria insisted that Walter spend one full day a week working in the office. Initially Walter had preferred to spend his time on the road but he recognised that Maria was right, he had to know the ins and outs of the business finances. Gradually he came to enjoy working with figures and seeing where the best profit margins lay.

Maria had left the local village school at fourteen, without any formal higher education. However, she somehow absorbed every piece of information given to her from Mr Goldberg and his staff like a sponge.

As she gained in business knowledge her other gift also came to the fore. Maria was a genuinely kind and likeable girl, both her clients and the home workers liked her, she had a smile that could light up a room. These were the qualities that Sam had so admired back in Glenboig when they had both worked in the brickworks together as youngsters. Although she never realised it Maria's pleasant manner and kind nature went a long way towards the success of Harris Finishings.

CHAPTER 12
The Passing Years

A lot happened in Northcote and Melbourne in the intervening years.

June 1924 and it was Alexander's birthday celebration, six years old and due to start school. The house seemed full of children, six of Alexander's friends had come to 'The Brig' for his party in addition his two year old sister Isabel Maureen had invited four of her friends. Twelve children were playing riotous games with Sam and Walter trying to keep some kind of order while Maria had taken herself off into the kitchen to finish preparing the birthday tea.

As she worked she thought about how life with Sam had changed from such humble beginnings to owning, well almost owning, their lovely home. They had named their house 'The Brig' after the affectionate nickname for Coatbridge where her and Sam had their roots.

As well as their son they now had a blond haired, blue eyed mischievous daughter who brought such fun into their lives, Isabel had the most infectious laugh imaginable and even at two years of age loved nothing better than playing tricks on her brother Alexander, and for that matter anyone who came into her orbit. Alice and Mrs Wilson adored her and she had Sam, Walter and Alexander firmly under her spell.

Maria loved her bairns to distraction but as well as play she made sure they both had an element of responsibility in their young lives. Perhaps Isabel would help Mrs Wilson make sandwiches or ice a cake, Alexander loved to go out in the trap with James and Harry and helped stable and feed the pony, Paddy. Maria was determined that her children would have a solid work ethic and not grow up spoiled.

'The Brig' was more than Maria's home, it was her relaxation and her hobby. It was decorated with beautiful curtains, made using the new Singer sewing machine bought for the business. The parquet floors in the bedrooms were adorned with Maria's home made rugs while the

wooden floors in the dining room and sitting room boasted Indian rugs
in rich colours. The hall, kitchen and bathroom floors were all tiled in a
rustic terracotta which was easy to keep clean. Over the years they had
gradually furnished their home with beautiful solid wood furniture,
chosen slowly and carefully, intended for a lifetime of use.

The kitchen boasted a lemon coloured kitchen cabinet and a white
wooden table and chairs, the walls were white and the material used for
drapes and cushions blue gingham. Maria had stencilled a pattern
around the walls in blue and lemon to tie the colour scheme together,
she loved her fresh modern kitchen with its up to the minute gas
cooker. A million miles away from the black leaded range she had
grown up with.

What made the house into a home was Maria had a way of
enhancing the rooms with flowers and plants she also had framed
photographs throughout her home, the wedding blessing, her children
and photographs sent from Ishbel in Cape Town.

Sadly there were no photographs from Scotland. Families like the
Riley's and Johnstone's had no extra money for luxuries like
photographs. However, Sam had drawn pencil sketches of his parents
and sisters from memory and they too were framed and a part of the
family home.

Sam, with help from Walter, had turned a bare plot into a
wonderful garden which gave them all so much pleasure and also kept
the kitchens well stocked with fruit and vegetables at both Northcote
and H.Q.

Party food ready Maria called all the children into the kitchen
where they enjoyed the birthday tea and peace reigned for a short time
before the games restarted.

At four o'clock the parents started to arrive to collect their
offspring and Maria was kept busy handing out cups of tea and slices
of cake to the mums and dads who had enjoyed a quiet afternoon.

By seven o'clock Alexander and Isabel were ready for bed and the
house was back to rights, leaving the adults free to have a bite of
supper. Maria said, "I'm exhausted, I think I'll just make something
easy, what about some toasted cheese topped with the chutney I made
from the garden produce, the one I called 'Sam's Chutney'. How does
that sound?"

"Sounds fine to me," agreed Sam.

"I'll grate the cheese, Walter you make us a nice pot of tea."

They all sat down to enjoy the impromptu supper at the kitchen
table and most delicious it was. After clearing away the dishes Walter

said, "I've got something serious I'd like to discuss with you both, can we go into the living room and sit down?" Sam, somehow sensing this was going to be an important conversation got out the sherry bottle and poured three glasses.

Sam and Maria looked at Walter expectantly. He sipped the sherry, the warming liquid gave him courage. "Maria, Sam you have been like my parents or a big brother and sister to me, not at all like guardians, which sounds more akin to prison wardens. I really don't want to let you down after everything you've done but well you know I shortly turn twenty one and I'll then receive my inheritance from my grandmother Mrs Harris. Well, when I formally inherit Harris Finishings I'd like to do something quite different from anything you could possibly imagine."

Maria thought, 'Oh no my worst fears realised. The lad wants to sell the business. Thank goodness the bank loan is nearly paid, the house will be safe.'

Walter continued, "Maria you have been incredible. The business is running tip top and going from strength to strength but..."

Sam interrupted, "Walter lad, we've always known that you would inherit the business and that very likely one day you'd want to make your own decisions and move on from our care ..."

"No, no, I think you've got it all wrong Sam, I don't want to move on, well actually I do. Please just listen and then you can tell me what you both think.

"Since finding out Vicky Harris was my mother and Lavinia my grandmother I have lost everyone on my mother's side of my family but I was given the name McDonald, my father's name and I have no idea what happened to him. Sam, you have been like a father to me but I have this ache to find my blood father, the man who deserted my mother. I want to know why. The only clue I have is some correspondence. Maria, do you remember when I moved into Mrs Harris's old bedroom? Well, I found a glove box with letters between Vicky and John McDonald, actually John Walter McDonald. Most of them are from their time in England but the last two are from the Union of South Africa. The letters do not sound like somebody who intended to jilt Vicky, in fact the exact opposite. They appeared to be very much in love.

"Maria I'd like to travel to the Transvaal and see if I can track my father down. Would you run the business on your own while I'm away? I realise it would be asking a lot of you and in return it's only fair that you have a real share in the profits, not just a salary. I'm going to ask

Mr Green to draw up documents assigning you twenty five percent of Harris Finishings. I've no idea how long I'll be away, I intend to follow in his tracks and goodness knows where they will lead."

Both Sam and Maria were astounded at this quite extraordinary ending to what had been a very ordinary family day. Maria was aware that tears were falling from her eyes, her first reaction was not I am about to receive twenty five percent of a successful business, it was, Walter we will miss you terribly and I really don't want you to spend your life chasing a dream.

Maria wasn't the only one shedding tears, Walter too was emotional, "I know you must think I'm mad but it's something I've got to do, or I'll spend the rest of my life regretting not being brave enough to try and find the answers."

The ever practical Sam said, "Walter lad we understand you want to find your roots and you are obviously trying to do the right thing by Maria. I won't lie, we will miss you. The bairns will miss you and the business will certainly miss you but if you feel this is your path we have to respect your wishes, wish you God speed, and do all we can to help you on your way.

"Maria and I followed our hearts coming to Australia, two young people from Scotland with hardly a penny to bless ourselves with travelling to the other side of the world, plenty folks must have thought that we were mad. We chose our path and it has led to a wonderful life, I would be lying if I didn't say we often miss family members but that is the price we have to pay for our life here in Northcote.

"Walter, where we lived we had an outside toilet and washhouse, water came from standpipes, we lived in tied houses without there ever being an opportunity for folks like us to buy our own place. The winters were bitterly cold and rain, lad we even have an assortment of words for rain like pelting, lashing, a plump, drizzle or a smir, there is so much of the stuff.

"However, the main reason we left was religion, Maria was bought up Catholic and I was a Protestant lad. Can you believe our wanting to marry was considered a sin of such epic proportions that Maria was thrown out of her home. If anyone understands why you need answers we do. Now drink up your sherry and then I'll go and make us a pot of coffee, as a wee treat."

While Sam ground the beans and put the percolator on Maria and Walter sat quietly talking.

"Maria, it's such a relief to have told you and Sam what I want to do. I know it will mean you have to do all the accounts and business planning but perhaps James could take on some of my duties and you could employ another young trainee. And now that the wee ones are growing up perhaps Alice and Mrs Wilson could give you more help with the business side."

"Before we start making a plan Walter you need to speak with Mr Green. It's only a few weeks until your birthday, rather than complicate things why don't you wait until you are twenty one and then go and see him and explain your wishes. Here comes Sam with the coffee pot, now let's enjoy a cup, what a treat. I'll away into the kitchen and get some of the shortbread that is left over from the party, now that will go well with the coffee."

Over the next few weeks Walter's impending trip was often discussed at 'The Brig'. Maria was well aware of the annual profits made by Harris Finishings, twenty five percent less tax would be a substantial sum of money for the Johnstone family. On the other hand Maria realised that without Walter she would have to shoulder one hundred percent of the responsibility to ensure that there was enough profit to pay the wages every week. Maria realised just how important the piecework money was to the many women outworkers they employed, and the thought that the livelihoods of so many people would be on her shoulders alone was rather frightening.

Whenever Maria had a 'wobble' Sam encouraged her, pointing out just how much she had already accomplished in business as well as bringing up two fine children.

At last the day of Walter's twenty first birthday arrived. Maria cooked a delicious Sunday lunch of roast beef with all the trimmings. They finished the meal and then toasted the birthday boy with coffee and chocolate cake, Alexander and Isabel clinked their glasses of milk shouting 'happy birthday Walter', then they insisted on singing 'Happy Birthday To You', not once but several times.

Maria had ensured that Walter was well prepared for his appointment with Mr Green, but now was the time for her to take a back seat. This would be the first appointment with the solicitor that Walter would attend alone.

Mr Green, who had been such a support to both him and Maria, sat quietly and listened to all Walter had to say about his plans to travel to the Union of South Africa and gifting part of his business to Maria.

When Walter had finished Mr Green paused for a few minutes to gather his thoughts before saying;

"Well Walter, you have done what very few people do, shocked me.

First a question, are Mr and Johnstone, who have been such admirable guardians to you for the past five years aware of your plans?"

Walter answered, "Yes sir, I told them a few weeks ago. In truth they are not exactly happy but as Sam said, they made a decision which their families did not agree with, a decision that led them from Scotland to Australia, so they understand and will support me with my plans."

"Well that's something at any rate," continued Mr Green. "I do agree with your decision to gift twenty five percent of your business to Mrs Johnstone, you can hardly expect her to put one hundred percent effort into running your business unless she has a stake in the enterprise.

"The letters you have from Mr McDonald written in the Transvaal over twenty one years ago provide a very tenuous link to encourage you to go on this foolhardy adventure, one letter from a hotel in Johannesburg and the other from a private house in Pretoria. Firstly, have you written to the owners of the house in Pretoria making enquiries?"

"Yes, Maria suggested I write to them, I sent a letter about three weeks ago. We thought that after all these years to write to the hotel would prove fruitless."

Trying not to show any emotion Mr Green continued, "Even if the people in Pretoria reply immediately it will be quite some weeks before you can realistically expect a reply.

"Walter McDonald we have gone completely off the agenda for this meeting. I think we need to get back on track and address the purpose for which you are here. We will look at the other issues you have brought up with me today at a later date.

"As you are aware Mistress Lavinia Harris, your maternal grandmother left you her entire estate to be held in trust until your twenty first birthday which has recently passed. I will now furnish you with a list of all the assets you have inherited."

The list seemed never ending and Walter, who had thought his inheritance would consist of the house and the business known as Harris Finishings was utterly amazed.

"So you see Master Walter McDonald you are now an extremely wealthy young man. You were not privy to this information before you concocted your scheme to travel to Africa, perhaps in the light of your new knowledge you may wish to reconsider your plans.

"My next question is, do you still wish me to draw up the papers to transfer a quarter of the business known as Harris Finishings to Mrs

Johnstone, remembering you are only transferring a share of the business, not the premises or any of your other assets."

Walter confirmed he wanted the documents prepared as soon as possible and he also instructed Mr Green that he wanted to gift five hundred pounds to Sam and Maria in gratitude for all they had done for him over the past five years. And, as a fair reflection of the accumulated profits from the business over the preceding years.

The meeting ended. Overall Mr Green was pleased by Walter's generosity to Maria and Sam but he was extremely doubtful about what he considered Walter's harebrained scheme of travelling to Africa for an indeterminate amount of time.

About two weeks after Walter's meeting with Mr Green Maria received a telephone call asking for her, Sam and Walter to attend a meeting at the solicitor's office for which a time and date was duly arranged.

Sam could not imagine why he too had been summoned by the solicitor however he agreed to attend with his wife and Walter.

The first part of the meeting was as expected with Walter assigning a quarter of the business to Maria, when this was completed Mr Green handed an envelope to Sam saying, "Young Mr McDonald has requested I present you with the enclosed cheque in gratitude of all you and your wife have done for him during your time as his guardians."

Sam opened the envelope and was astounded to find a cheque for five hundred pounds, together with a letter in Walter's hand...

Dear Sam and Maria

Please accept the enclosed money as a thank you gift for all you have both done for me over the past years, your kindness and warmth was way above anything that could be expected from guardians. You always treated me as part of the Johnstone family.

Maria, I'm so grateful that you have agreed to look after the business in my absence and I know Harris Finishings will be in good hands.

I know that you both think I'm slightly mad to be journeying to the Transvaal on what may very well be a wild goose chase (even if you don't actually say so) but I think you understand it's something I just have to do.

With my ever grateful thanks

Affectionately

Walter

* * *

Sam and Maria banked the cheque and at the same time made the final payment on their home, 'The Brig', this was the security they had both craved for. They also opened bank accounts in the name of both Alexander and Isabel, and deposited the sum of fifty pounds in each.

Over the following weeks Walter had several more meetings with Mr Green and Mr Goldberg ensuring everything was legally in place to allow Maria to run the business in his absence and that he would have access to funds during his travels.

It was now almost three months since Walter had sent the letter to Pretoria. One Saturday evening in spring he was sitting on the stoop with Sam and Maria enjoying a cool drink before supper when Walter made his announcement.

"Still no reply from Pretoria so I've decided to just get on with it and sail to the Union of South Africa. There is a ship leaving Melbourne bound for London via Cape Town in ten days time, I've booked my passage. I think I'll be able to get a train from the Cape to Jo'burg. Maria, will you tell Alexander and Isabel, I'll tell Mrs Wilson and Alice on Monday, and of course the disapproving Mr Green."

Maria took his hand, "I'm sorry Walter but I think you must tell the bairns yourself, they adore you and you can't just leave their life without a single word. You must talk to them tomorrow and assure them that one day you will return."

Sam was glad Maria had taken this stance as he too thought the children should hear the news from Walter himself.

As expected the children were upset at Walter's imminent departure, however he promised to write regularly and send them gifts.

The following days were busy and suddenly it was the night before the sailing, rather than come out to Northcote Walter had invited the Johnstone family to come into town and have a farewell dinner with him at the Alexander Hotel, near Spencer Street station. Alexander was thrilled at the idea of having dinner at a hotel with his name and Isabel was quite put out that they were not going to the Isabel Hotel.

This was the first time the Johnstone family had eaten dinner in a grand hotel, for the special occasion Maria treated herself to a new gown in pale green with the latest handkerchief hemline.

Looking at his Maria in the glamorous setting of the hotel Sam again thought how blessed he was to have married this incredibly beautiful and clever woman.

Everyone enjoyed the meal, even Isabel had got over the name of the hotel, the food was delicious and the service impeccable. After finishing the meal with their choice from the magnificent sweet trolly the waiter asked if the party would like to retire to the lounge for coffee.

Settling down on the comfy sofas Sam said to Walter, "As soon as we heard your travel arrangements we wrote to our friends Robert and Ishbel in Cape Town telling them of your arrival details, you might arrive before the letter so I've written two letters of introduction one to Robert and one to Charles and Ishbel.

"After the long sea voyage it might be a good idea for you to spend some time on the Cape to adjust to being on dry land and to get a feel for the country before heading up to the Transvaal.

"And now, there is something that I've waited a long number of years to do but first I'd like to tell you all a story. At the word 'story' Alexander and Isabel's interest perked up and they sat quietly listening to the tale;

"In 1917 Maria and I set out for Australia with very little to our name. On Hogmanay 1917, we spent the day in Cape Town sightseeing before seeing in the new year with our dear friends Robert and Ishbel at the cottage in Oranjezicht which the church had allocated for their use.

"We were walking up Adderley Street when we looked in the window of a beautiful jewellery shop. I asked Maria what ring she would choose, if she could have any one in the entire shop. Now remember we didn't have a spare penny to bless ourselves with. My darling wife chose a sapphire with a diamond at each side to represent us, Sam and Maria, and the sapphire in the middle to represent the oceans we had to sail across in order to reach our new life in Australia. There and then I made a promise that one day I would buy her a ring exactly like the one in the shop. Maria Johnstone, the ring!"

With that Sam went into his pocket and produced a small black leather box, he opened it and presented the contents to his wife.

As he slipped the ring onto her finger Maria kissed him saying, "Och my darling Sam, never for one minute did I imagine that you would be able to buy me such a beautiful and symbolic gift. Thank you Sam from the bottom of my heart."

The party drank their coffee, ate petit fours, and admired the ring and all too soon it was time for the Johnstone family to get the train back to Northcote and Walter to carry out the final preparations for his journey to Cape Town.

After Alexander and Isabel had gone off to bed Sam and Maria sat together on the sofa holding hands like two teenagers. They talked about their life together and the journey that commenced in Glenboig Brickworks in Scotland and had led them all the way to Northcote

Brickworks in Australia interspersed with the ocean voyage the blessing of their union by Robert in Cape Town, their two children and Harris Finishings.

Maria sat admiring her ring, "Sam, never in my wildest dreams did I ever imagine wearing an expensive ring like this on my finger. You have more than kept your promise made in Adderley Street on Hogmanay 1917. Thank you for everything my darling, not many husbands would be happy to have their wife going out working every day. You have always been my strength and support."

Sam smiled, "Maria, you should be glad I'm my father's son, he always encouraged my mother to do what she felt was right, I had a good role model. Most of the Gartsherrie men would have gone mad if their wives had joined the suffragettes but not Alex Johnstone. My Aunt Agnes Law never joined the organisation, Uncle Rab would have gone completely doolally.

Now let's get to bed, tomorrow is another day and your first day in sole charge of Harris Finishings. I just hope all goes well for young Walter and he does not return too disappointed."

CHAPTER 13
Walter's Journey

On the morning of his departure Walter at long last received word from Pretoria. It was not what he hoped for but at least he now had a direct connection to his father.

Pretoria

Dear Mr McDonald

Firstly, apologies for the delay in replying, I have been away on business.

In response to your letter from Melbourne enquiring about a Mr John McDonald who stayed in my family home over two decades ago, I am afraid I have very little information about him.

My twin sister and I were around eleven or twelve years of age when Mr McDonald stayed at our home. I have spoken to my sister Annabelle and we both remember him as a charming man who was always very kind to us as children.

I am unaware as to the reason for his stay, however I suspect he was a business colleague of my father. Our family business was in surveying and civil engineering, it was sold on the sudden death of my father five years ago.

Apologies that I can be of no further assistance to you in this matter.

Yours sincerely
Paul Kessall

* * *

There was also a postal delivery that morning in Northcote. Maria gathered up the mail to read on the train as she travelled into town.

Airdrie

My dear Sam and Maria

I thought I would write and let you know all is well with your wee sister Mary.

As well as carrying out secretarial work I also run the household for Liz, she has never fully regained her health and strength after suffering that bout of the Spanish flu after the war. However, she still works incredibly hard, writing and campaigning.

Liz is losing her sight, as you know I accompanied her to Europe so that she could enjoy the sights she had enjoyed in her youth once more. Hope you received the postcards and wee mindings we sent. I am now staying in Airdrie on a permanent basis.

Only women over thirty getting the vote was such an insult after all we endured during the war years, hopefully our campaigning will be successful and we will get the full franchise within the next few years. Equal rights for women is quite another matter and is still a long way off, sadly I don't think it will happen in my lifetime, certainly not in Great Britain, and as far as Gartsherrie is concerned, sometime never!!!!

Maria we are all so very proud of you doing so well in a man's world of business in Australia, an example to us all.

Some good news, Jessie Law is no longer working in the sweetie shop, she is now managing a drysalters shop in Bank Street. Quite a step up for her, she is loving the challenge. As you can imagine Uncle Rab is none too happy that Jessie is earning more than his lads. However, ma was furious with Aunt Agnes because she has not been at all encouraging of Jessie, although she is quite happy to snaffle the extra money Jessie brings into the house.

I've had my hair cut into a bob. I don't think pa was all that happy but ma said, 'Mary, you might as well be oot the world as oot the fashion'. Honestly, she has a saying for absolutely everything.

You will have heard Ramsay MacDonald is now the first labour prime minister. And, him a Scot from Lossiemouth, michty me!

I went to see a film on Saturday evening with Mary Law called The Navigator, it starred Buster Keaton. It was quite good escapism. Poor Mary her mother gives her a hard time and she is not in great health. Sometimes Mary comes down to the Long Row for a cup of tea and a blether, just to escape!

We do so love your letters and hearing all about the exploits of Alexander and Isabel. The family photograph you sent with your last letter is absolutely beautiful and sending it in a silver frame, well, there aren't many silver photograph frames in the Rows of Gartsherrie I can tell you. Ma and pa are so proud of you both and their Australian grandchildren.

With much love, your sister
Mary

* * *

Cape Town

My dear friends

I have enclosed a photograph of our darling daughter Elize, she is the apple of Charles's eye. Our children would play so beautifully together, Alexander the eldest, Elize second in command and little Isabel, who I'm quite sure with my name could hold her own with the other two. Part of me still wishes you had settled in the Cape, however I must console myself that you have both done so well in Australia.

Charles is planning a second sabbatical, he feels that the years are winging past so quickly and he wants to spend some time with me and our little daughter. We have been making plans for changes in the house but we are also intending to take a trip. We have not finalised our plans yet but we will travel to Durban and spend time with Charles's brother and sister, and also travel up the escarpment and into the Transvaal. Apparently great things are happening at Wits University (Witwatersrand, Johannesburg) and Charles has a number of friends who lecture there. He has also promised me that we will visit Pretoria, it's nickname is Jacaranda City, because of all the jacaranda trees which bloom every spring and are covered in purple flowers. Apparently it's a beautiful city but I can't honestly imagine anywhere being more beautiful than Cape Town.

Robert is well and now for some gossip, gosh I'm starting to sound like Sophie. Well, remember I told you he was stepping out with a young lady called Anna Badenhorst, they are getting engaged on her birthday. Elize is over the moon as she is desperate to *be a bridesmaid. Anna is very enthusiastic about the suffrage movement and Robert is supportive of her ideas, he couldn't be anything else with me as a mother. Her family are very conservative Afrikaners, which makes the future family dynamics look very interesting. However, both Charles and I think she is charming.*

My boys at home are both well as are their wives and my grandchildren who are all older than Elize, I can still detect an undercurrent of disapproval in their letters, even after all these years. After Fraser died we seemed to split into two families, Archie and Euan, Robert and me. It's rather sad and I wish my boys felt differently but such is life.

Sophie is keeping well and is very much an integral part of our family. She insists on working at Robert's wee cottage one day a week and leaving him some of her home cooking. However, Robert and Anna are presently looking to purchase a larger house to move into after they get married. I've told Sophie that she must find them a lady to help run their home from her network of contacts in District 6.

Our pathways are not at all what we imagined they would be when we were talking and planning on the good ship Trojan. However, I feel we are all following God's plan and I so hope that one day the plan includes us all meeting again.

With my very best wishes, your friend
Ishbel

* * *

As he was now an extremely wealthy young man Walter decided to travel first class as he set off on his mission to find his father, John Walter McDonald. Making this expensive decision had not been at all easy for him.

Until he was fifteen Walter had been raised by Mrs Wilson, who wasted nothing and made sure he knew the value of money, education, respectability and wholesome food. Mrs Harris had ensured that as soon as he was old enough he was expected to work for his keep.

Growing up, Walter had reckoned he was well lucky to be brought up in the security of Mrs Harris's home, he had a clean and comfortable room of his own, quality food and clothing, good schooling until he was fourteen and then a steady job. A great deal more than most orphans could expect from life.

After Mrs Harris died and Sam and Maria became his guardians Walter's life changed insomuch as he became part of a happy young family but the values instilled by Mrs Wilson and Mrs Harris were already ingrained. Maria reinforced the work ethic even though he was working for a wage, not pocket money.

Over the five years until his twenty first birthday Walter's weekly wage increased from three to five pounds, a heady sum for a boy of his age. Encouraged by Maria not a week passed that Walter did not make a deposit into his bank account, never for one minute imagining that one day the sum of money he had so carefully accrued over the years would seem so incredibly tiny when compared to his inheritance.

Mr Green, while thoroughly disapproving of Walter's jaunt to Africa, took his duties as a trustee very seriously and made sure that his charge was leaving well equipped. He arranged to make a line of credit available to him for the trip, and ensured that he had sufficient cash funds available for the first part of his journey. The solicitor also advised him to purchase a wardrobe of good quality clothing, a cabin trunk and suitable gentleman's accessories. Having done his duty Mr Green, solicitor and notary public, could now put the appropriate notations on the Harris file and consider his work well done.

Although travelling first class Walter did not carry the luxury to the height of a suite, he was shown to a very acceptable single cabin by a steward wearing the smart uniform of the Cunard Line.

Sitting alone in his cabin Walter entertained his first doubts as to the wisdom of his decision to sail to Africa on the slender chance that he could trace his birth father.

On the previous evening at the Alexander Hotel as well as being given the two letters of introduction a third envelope had also been given to Walter. On opening it he found a card with a ship drawn on it, on the reverse written in a childish hand were the words:

God speed Walter
Love, Alexander and Isabel

On seeing the card it made him realise the enormity of his decision, he was running away from, his business, his home, his friendships and his Johnstone family.

Walter spent his first day at sea reading in his cabin, he tried to lose his apprehension about his trip by reading an H.G Wells novel, 'Men Like Gods'. He could identify with the main character Mr Barnstable feeling he needed to go off on holiday alone but he certainly didn't want to end up in Barnstable's utopia.

As the day turned into evening Walter was starting to feel nervous about going into the formal first class dining room wearing his new dinner suit. After shaving he dabbed his face with eau de cologne and then massaged some brilliantine into his hair. Dressing formally all seemed such a performance and it took several attempts to tie his bow tie correctly but at last he looked, even if he did not necessarily feel, the part of a successful young businessman. Big deep breath and Walter McDonald was confident enough to face the luxurious first class dining room.

He was seated at a table between two young cousins, Miss Evelyn Walker and Miss Joslyn Graham, who were heading back to England after visiting family in Australia. Also sharing the table was an elderly doctor who had recently retired and decided to return to his home town in England. A middle aged couple called Daniel and Margaret Perriman with their two children, Laurel and Matthew completed the group.

There was an initial awkwardness at the table, eight people unknown to each other who were expected to become acquainted over the following weeks, perhaps even friendly, and then at the end of the voyage say goodbye never to meet again.

Walter decided to let the others do most of the talking while he got the measure of his companions. Years working at Harris Finishings had made Walter an excellent judge of character. By the end of the evening he had worked out that Doctor Chalmers was a bachelor who wanted someone to care for him in his old age, hence his return to Bournemouth where he had two spinster sisters.

The two young ladies were dressed in the latest flapper fashions and their conversation was very superficial; fashion, dancing and the functions they had attended while in Australia. They obviously came from monied backgrounds and had no need to work or take life too seriously.

The enigma at the table was the Perriman family, Mr Perriman was correctly dressed in a dinner suit, however to Walter's practiced eye it seemed rather tight and had a touch of shine about it, that made him think it was rather old. His wife was also dressed smartly but her gown was certainly not at the cutting edge of fashion and her jewellery was very modest. The children too were tidily but not expensively dressed. Walter wondered why, if you were not very comfortably off, would you choose to pay for four first class passages.

As well as making sure Walter was dressed correctly and had sufficient funds for the trip Mr Green had insisted that he have some French lessons, just enough to enable him to read a menu without feeling intimidated. Walter had not been keen at the time but he now sent up a silent prayer of thanks to Mr Green when he saw the elaborate a la carte menu the waiter had presented to him with a flourish. The lessons, which he had not particularly enjoyed, enabled him to navigate the French menu with a degree of confidence.

During the meal the good doctor in an avuncular fashion led the conversation and encouraged the two young ladies to talk about their Australian vacation. Trapped between the girls Walter had no alternative but to join their conversation. By the time they had given their orders to the attentive waiter Walter had decided that young Evelyn and Joslyn while pleasant were not particularly interesting, their lives seemed to centre entirely on material values. Who owned what, who went where and what they were wearing.

It would have dumbfounded Walter to know that both girls thought he was extremely handsome and quite a catch, they were both very disappointed to learn that he would be leaving the ship at Cape Town.

Walter tried hard to bring the Perriman family into the general conversation, while they were all very polite they were not chatty or particularly forthcoming.

The good doctor was quite the opposite. It turned out he had been an eminent surgeon but one who also had eclectic interests from antiques to fishing and who enjoyed the finer things of life, good food, wine, cigars and conversation.

At the end of the meal Walter declined an invitation from Evelyn and Joslyn to join them for dancing in the ballroom and retreated towards his cabin. A voice behind him called out, "Young man, would you care to join me for a nightcap in the bar?"

Walter turned and saw the doctor. On the spur of the moment he found himself saying, "Delighted, thank you Doctor Chalmers that would be an agreeable end to the evening." Walter had little experience of drinking alcohol, an occasional sherry with Sam and Maria and an even more occasional medicinal hot toddy. He thought, there has to be a first time drinking alcohol and it might as well be now.

The young and the elderly man found a comfortable corner in the opulent Wheelhouse Bar. When the waiter approached them and asked for their order the doctor replied, "I think I'll have a malt with a small jug of water on the side. Do you have Glenlivet by any chance?"

"Certainly sir, would you prefer twelve or fifteen year old?"

"First night out on the high seas young man, let's have the fifteen, is that all right with you Mr McDonald?"

Walter agreed that fifteen year old would be just fine, while wondering what on earth the spirit was going to taste like.

The doctor lit a cigar and settled himself into the comfortable leather chair before starting the conversation. "The young ladies are very pretty don't you think? I'm sure they were very disappointed that they couldn't persuade a handsome young man like yourself to go dancing with them.

"However, that Perriman is a right rum chappie. The entire family have no interesting conversation whatsoever, and evasive. I asked him outright what his profession was and he simply replied, 'I'm a man of business sir.' What is your opinion of them McDonald?"

The waiter arrived with the drinks giving Walter a moment of thinking time. He quickly decided, I'll never see these people or the doctor again after the voyage, I might as well just say what I think.

As he topped his malt up with water Walter said, "Yes doctor, I found the family a little odd, well perhaps unusual, they seemed awkward and didn't have a great deal of conversation. I also wondered why they had bought four first class tickets. They were dressed smartly enough but certainly not the clothes you'd expect people to wear while travelling first class on a liner."

"Ah me lad, you noticed that too!"

Walter replied, "I work in the clothing industry sir, Harris Finishings which I inherited from my grandmother. I could look at any lady in the dining room and know exactly how much her outfit cost, almost to the penny. Another thing was his accent, the children and Mrs Perriman have Australian accents but his speech is somewhere between Australian and British and he is constantly trying to speak correctly. Did you notice he always speaks slowly and with thought?"

"So young man, we have a mystery to interest us during the voyage. Can't spend every moment eating, drinking or playing bridge. What say we try and find out the story behind the Perriman family. It will probably be like them, extremely pedestrian, however it will keep us entertained until Cape Town."

Sipping his drink, which took him back to when Mrs Wilson nursed him with hot toddy when he had flu, Walter replied, "It's a deal sir. By the time we sail round the Cape we will have solved the Perriman mystery. I'll be Hastings to your Hercule Poirot."

They sipped their malt and chatted for a good hour before Walter excused himself and headed to his cabin. He slept like the proverbial log, having suffered broken sleep over the preceding weeks in anticipation of his trip.

The following day while walking on deck Walter saw an opportunity to play Hastings. The two Perriman children were walking towards him. He engaged them in conversation, "Good morning Laurel, Matthew. Enjoying a stroll or are you going to play deck quoits this morning? It's very exciting being aboard ship, this is my first experience of sailing. Have you been on a ship before?"

Matthew answered for them both, "Yes Mr McDonald, this is our first time onboard a ship."

He made to walk on but Walter simply walked beside them and kept up the conversation, "Are you travelling on vacation or are you relocating?"

Neither of the children seemed comfortable with Walter's innocent questions and made a ploy to get away from him as quickly as possible. Matthew said, "Laurel and I are just going off to play a game of table tennis, have a nice day Mr McDonald, goodbye."

Walter took himself off to the reading lounge and ruminated on his encounter with the young Perrimans'. Polite but definitely evasive, that was something to report to Poirot.

Daniel Perriman Esq was in fact Danny Percy from Belfast, Dublin, Liverpool, London, and Southampton, in Australia he had lived in places too numerous to remember but his step into respectability came when he started working as a clerk for Matthew Gregg & Son, Wholesale Provision Merchants in Sydney.

One day the owner, Mr Duncan Gregg sent him to his home on an errand to collect some papers he had inadvertently left in his study, an oversight he would later greatly regret. The maid showed Danny Percy's latest incarnation, Daniel Perriman into the morning room. A few minutes later a woman came into the room and introduced herself as Mr Gregg's daughter Miss Margaret. Danny immediately started to look for an angle as to how this encounter could be profitable to him.

By the age of thirty five Danny Percy, David Perry, Donald Pierce, Dave Paton and now Daniel Perriman had left a trail of broken hearts and fraudulent schemes over Ireland, England and Australia.

His practiced eye immediately noticed, no wedding ring and a plain woman about his own age, not ugly in any way, just somewhat undistinguished.

He explained his errand and the woman went off to retrieve the papers. On her return he politely asked if he could have a glass of water. Margaret offered him a cup of tea which he gratefully accepted.

When he was growing up in Belfast as the youngest of seven children the cry could often be heard, 'see that wee blighter Danny he has surely kissed the Blarney Stone'. Danny certainly knew how to tell a tale, when it suited him.

He engaged Margaret in conversation and he quickly realised that there had not been much romance in her life an omission that he had every intention of rectifying. Daniel was charming, amusing, polite and by the time he left his employer's house poor Margaret was somewhat smitten.

He subtly changed his job title from clerk to accountant and set out to win Margaret's hand and her inheritance.

This made life difficult for Duncan Gregg, the business was third generation and he had always hoped for a son to carry on the family name, however he was a widower with only one daughter, as the years passed it seemed unlikely that Margaret would marry as she was now in her mid thirties.

One evening after dinner Margaret announced that she wanted to wed his jumped up clerk, Daniel Perriman. Duncan Gregg found himself in a quandary, socially it was downright embarrassing for his daughter to wed Perriman but on the positive side he might gain a grandson.

Eventually worn down by Margaret's pleading he gave his permission for them to marry, but only on the condition Perriman change his name to Gregg. Margaret and Danny duly became Mr and Mrs Daniel Gregg.

As they say in Ireland, Danny Percy was no eejit, and he knew full well that Duncan Gregg would not be easily fooled, if he was going to get control of Margaret's inheritance he would have to play the long game. And play it he did!

After the wedding he moved into the family home, acquired new clothes and a promoted position in the business. A year after Margaret had changed her name from Miss Gregg to Mrs Gregg she became the mother of a healthy son.

Again Danny Percy was manipulative, the boy was given the family name of Matthew. His grandfather Duncan was delighted with the new addition to the family and spent many happy hours envisaging the day when another Matthew Gregg would take over and even grow the family business.

Duncan Gregg was not blind to Danny's faults and although he had no idea as to his background he was always wary of his son in law, the phrase 'too sweet to be wholesome' often entered his thoughts.

Eighteen months later a daughter, Laurel, was born. This further ingratiated Danny into the family. His real work could now begin.

Initially he was quite proud of himself, he had given Margaret what she wanted, marriage and children. Her father had received his heart's desire, two grandchildren including a boy, the eventual heir.

However, this was all in line with Danny's long term plan.

The next ten years passed, the business prospered, friends and business associates of the Gregg family accepted Danny and on the surface life appeared good. Now was the time for Danny to put his carefully thought out plan into action.

At the age of seventy Duncan Gregg was still a very fit man, Danny had been hoping that a heart attack or a bout of pneumonia would do his work for him but Duncan seemed fitter than ever. It was now time.

For a number of years Danny had been regularly skimming money out of the business, not large sums but he had been carefully amassing funds into a secret bank account. Over the years the embezzled funds had accumulated into a large sum of money. However, what Danny really wanted was everything, the house, it's contents, the business, and control of the Gregg family finances.

One Sunday afternoon Danny went into the garden shed and checked through the insecticides and other gardening necessities, to his delight he found several packets containing arsenic among the proprietary gardening products the gardener had left on the shelves. Danny was clever enough never to risk buying a product containing arsenic himself.

He removed a small amount of the grey powder and placed it in an envelope. Having acquired a quantity of poison that would never be missed and was untraceable to him the next phase was to administer the drug.

Every evening around ten o'clock Duncan was in the habit of having a nightcap, always the same, malt whisky with a small splash of soda water, accompanied by two little shortbread biscuits. Before retiring for the night Margaret would set a little silver tray with her father's nightcap.

It was simplicity itself for Danny to add a pinch of arsenic to the whisky each evening, a pinch, never more. Initially Duncan seemed unaffected and it was quite some months before he started complaining of stomach cramps and vomiting. Danny immediately suggested he go to see his doctor and meantime take a few days off work. Doctor Kerr found nothing suspicious but the symptoms, together with other disparate symptoms continued. Sometimes Danny would leave off doctoring the whisky for a few weeks, just to further confuse any diagnosis.

The weeks and months passed, gradually Duncan Gregg's health began to fail, in line with Danny's visits to the garden shed. Margaret did all she could to support her father and nurse him through his mystery illness. Danny used his father-in-law's declining health to take over some of the day to day running of the business, not for the better. The other senior staff constantly complained to each other about his arrogance and inefficiency but there was nothing they could do, he appeared to have inveigled himself into a position of trust, besides he was part of the Gregg family.

Sadly the inevitable happened. One day Duncan Gregg died of a massive heart attack, no suspicious circumstances were noted and a grand funeral was arranged by Margaret and Danny, known as Daniel in Sydney business circles.

After the funeral the family solicitor, Mr Cuthbertson came to the house to read the Last Will and Testament of Duncan Gregg. Danny sat beside Margaret trying to look concerned at the loss of his father-in-law while the solicitor read out various bequests to servants, employees and charities.

However, Danny was shocked to the core as he heard the lawyer continue.

> *'The remainder of my estate I leave to my grandson Matthew Gregg, to be held in trust until he is twenty one years of age. Until such time as he inherits the business is to be managed by my friend and current Accounting Director, Percy Smallman together with the existing Board. I appoint my solicitor, Mr Cuthbertson and my accountant, Mr Robson as trustees.*
>
> *I leave my daughter Margaret an annuity of five hundred pounds per annum.*
>
> *I leave my granddaughter Laurel Gregg the sum of five thousand pounds to be held in trust until her twenty first birthday.*
>
> *The Gregg family can continue to reside at my home, Glencraig, until Matthew reaches his majority, thereafter he can decide if he wishes his parents and sister to remain in his home.*
>
> *Finally, I instruct that my son-in-law Perriman, now known as Daniel Gregg, shall receive <u>nothing</u> from my estate whatsoever. However, he can continue working in the business as a salaried employee. If at any time, with good cause, Mr Smallman wishes to dismiss him he may do so'.*

Danny was angry beyond angry, he had assumed Duncan would leave his entire estate to Margaret. He stormed out of the room, shouting, "After all Margaret and I did for that ungrateful old man, we will contest the will, it's not over yet, not by a long chalk."

Mr Cuthbertson spoke quietly to Margaret and the children, "Your father's will has been very carefully written, taking into account the current law in the State of New South Wales, any challenge will not succeed."

Danny stormed into the sitting room and poured himself a large whisky, not seeing the irony.

Over the following weeks a number of events started to unfold. Danny stepped up his embezzling scams from the business. One evening Duncan Gregg's physician, Dr Kerr called at the home of Mr Cuthbertson the solicitor, to hand in some medication for his son.

The two men shared a brandy and the conversation got around to Duncan Gregg. Doctor Kerr said, "You know Duncan was a very healthy man, then he suddenly started to develop an assortment of disparate symptoms. If I hadn't known the man I would have said he was a hypochondriac, then he suddenly died with a massive heart attack. I tell you Cuthbertson, his death was a real surprise to me, and I was his doctor for well over twenty years."

"The whole circumstances also seem very odd to me," agreed Cuthbertson. "You should have seen the tantrum thrown by that ghastly son-in-law when I read the will. He was absolutely ropeable. As for Margaret, she seems to be totally under the man's thrall."

The doctor then articulated what he hardly dared to think, "Cuthbertson, do you think it's remotely possible that Duncan was murdered? His symptoms were varied and intermittent but, and I can barely believe that I'm actually saying this to you, but his symptoms were in line with arsenic poisoning."

"Is there any way, even at this stage we could find proof, that the son-in-law or Margaret for that matter, did indeed administer poison?" Cuthbertson asked the doctor.

"Actually there is, if we could get hold of Duncan's hairbrush we could have his hair analysed to check the arsenic content."

"Leave it with me," said Cuthbertson. "I'll see if I can come up with something." They finished their drinks and the doctor set off for home.

The solicitor turned the conversation with Duncan Gregg's doctor over and over in his head. He made up his mind that if Perriman had in fact been up to any sculduggery he would make it his business to find out exactly what mischief he had been about.

The following day when Danny was at work and the children at school he called into Glencraig to see Margaret. The maid brought them coffee and he opened the conversation, "Margaret I've known you and your father for a great many years and I want to ask you a question. Were you surprised at the content of your father's will?"

"Yes I was, I always knew he didn't particularly care for Daniel and favoured the children, particularly Matthew, however he effectively disinherited me, his daughter. I did everything I could to care for him and maintain a peaceful household and now all I have is five hundred pounds a year."

Cuthbertson thought the use of the word 'peaceful' telling. In his profession random words were often the key and he held great store by them.

"Margaret, have you changed your father's room in any way?"

"No I haven't, it's just as it always was. I know at some point I'll have to go through his things but the time isn't right, I've simply locked the door. Why do you ask?"

"I ask because I wonder if you would give me access to the room, I'd like to look through any papers he might have left in his desk."

"What exactly are you looking for? Another will perhaps?"

"To be honest I really don't know but I think a professional man should check the entire contents of his room before it is cleared."

"In that case, I'll show you upstairs."

If Daniel had known how easily the solicitor had gained access to Duncan Gregg's bedroom he would have been furious. After the undertakers had removed Duncan's body Margaret locked the bedroom door and steadfastly refused to allow her husband access. Margaret was normally very compliant, 'peace at any price' but on this one matter she had stood firm.

Margaret disappeared for a few minutes then returned with the key. On opening the door the drawn blinds and curtains made the room gloomy and it had a fusty sad smell.

Firstly Cuthbertson opened the window drapes to let in some light, he then sat down at the bureau and proceeded to look through his client's paperwork. He found some things of professional interest but in the main it was household accounts and personal letters. However, he did find a diary which he did not openly acknowledge.

All the while he was working, Margaret stood in the doorway watching him. After a time he said, "Margaret my dear, I wonder if you would be kind enough to get me a glass of water. It's very stuffy in here."

As soon as Margaret left, the solicitor slipped the diary into his briefcase. He then went over to the dressing table where he saw a number of tortoiseshell handled brushes and combs. Into the briefcase went a hairbrush completing Cuthbertson's mission, just in the nick of time, as a few seconds later Margaret returned.

Cuthbertson spent another good hour meticulously going through the contents of the writing bureau and the bedside drawers. He divided the paperwork into two piles, one he gave to Margaret telling her that she might want to keep some for sentimental reasons but the majority were simply household accounts.

"However, I have unearthed a number of things which are relevant to winding up the estate, I'll take these back to the office and return them to you in due course."

Before Margaret had too much time to think Mr Cuthbertson scooped the papers into his briefcase and made his farewell.

That evening he took his briefcase to the home of Dr Kerr. The two men settled themselves in the doctor's study and set about thoroughly examining the contents of the briefcase. As soon as the brush was produced the doctor put it into a clean paper bag and affixed a label. Next came the diary, carefully perusing the contents they discovered that Duncan had methodically noted all his symptoms on a daily basis.

He had also written extracts on the daily life within the house. It had annoyed him that Margaret was so subservient to her husband, that was the reason he had decided to leave her an annuity rather than a lump sum, which he felt sure Daniel would appropriate.

The children he obviously loved very much, having high hopes for Matthew who was doing very well at school and was an amiable lad who was very fond of his younger sister. According to the diary neither of the children seemed to have much affection for their father. Daniel did not appear to have been physically cruel to either of the children or Margaret, his cruelty seemed to lie in total indifference.

Much of the diary was about business or social events, however there was one telling entry about four weeks before Duncan's death;

'I've not been well for a long time now and tonight I saw a look in the face of that scoundrel who is married to my daughter. His expression said, 'get on with it, die'. I swear that man would love to kill me, perhaps he is killing me.'

Both men took the diary entries seriously. Dr Kerr promised to spend some time analysing the medical entries and to pass the brush on to a friend who was a police inspector. "Alan Smith is a good man, he will arrange for Duncan's hair to be analysed and we can then be pretty certain whether or not he was given arsenic. If he was the next step will be to exhume his body."

Danny's fury about the terms of the will knew no bounds and

simply stealing money from the business was not enough to extract revenge. He started to remove items from the house and sell them to further enhance his secret money stash.

Margaret noticed the missing items, initially she said nothing but as more and more items disappeared she made up her mind that she had to be brave and question Danny. The day she noticed that some of her jewellery, most of which had been left to her by her mother, disappeared was the day she finally challenged Danny.

Initially he denied taking the gems but eventually his real self shone through.

"Yes, you stupid, ugly woman, yes, yes, yes. I've been taking things and selling them, what else did you expect me to do? Your father treated us both like dirt in his will, it's time to line our pockets before the whole lot goes to your pasty faced son. The old fool deserved to die and I saw to it that he did.

"Don't question me Margaret, this is how it is, I'm the man of the house now and I'll do what I damn well please and you will do exactly what I tell you."

Unfortunately for Danny his son Matthew had overheard every single word.

The same evening Doctor Kerr received a telephone call from Inspector Smith, "I've just received the findings of the hair analysis taken from the brush belonging to Duncan Gregg, you were right old boy, arsenic. He was either dosing himself with the stuff or he was poisoned. Gregg was a respected stalwart of the business community in Sydney and I somehow don't think he was deliberately taking arsenic. I suspect you are definitely on to something, besides you said you had some other evidence. Can I make an appointment to see you tomorrow to discuss matters?"

A time was arranged and the doctor immediately called his solicitor friend to update him. Mr Cuthbertson agreed to join the meeting. The conclusion was Inspector Smith immediately applied to the courts to have Duncan Gregg's body exhumed.

By a strange coincidence while the meeting about the possibility that Duncan Gregg was murdered was taking place, Mr Smallman summoned Danny into his office.

"Mr Gregg, although it pains me to use the good name of Gregg when speaking to you. I have spoken with the other members of the Board and I hereby advise you that your employment is terminated forthwith. You are incompetent and a thief. Mr Gregg was well aware you were embezzling from the company, however providing it was within certain limits he was willing to overlook your crime, purely for the sake of his daughter and grandchildren. Since the death of Mr Gregg your stealing has been blatant. Mr Ross here will escort you from the premises. Mr Ross please take this person from my sight."

Standing outside the Gregg building and feeling angry and humiliated Danny checked his bank book, it contained over two thousand pounds, a heady sum. He walked into the bank and closed his account, this together with the money he had secreted away gave him considerably over three thousand pounds in cash.

His initial plan was to leave with the money and move on to pastures new, this time with well lined pockets. However, greed drove him back to Glencraig. The thought of all the easily transportable valuables was just too much of a temptation.

Danny stormed into the house and raged at Margaret, "Get me your father's gold watch and the collection of antique snuff boxes from his room and anything else of value that is easily portable you can lay your hands on, I'm going to pack my bags."

Not only did he pack his clothes he threw into his case anything of worth that he could find.

In the midst of all the upheaval the doorbell rang. The maid answered the ring and let Inspector Smith into the hall. Margaret went downstairs, she was shocked when the police inspector introduced himself and inquired, "Mrs Gregg is your husband available I would like to have a word with him on a very urgent matter?"

Margaret enquired as to what the matter was that was so important he required to see her husband.

Danny, who was hiding behind the open bedroom door heard the inspector say, "Mrs Gregg it is regarding the death of your father, we suspect he may have been poisoned and we urgently need to ask your husband some questions."

Danny thought the game was up but surprisingly Margaret said, "My husband is presently at business in the city. He will not be home until this evening, perhaps you could return later if you want to speak with him."

To Danny's amazement the inspector left saying he would return at seven o'clock. 'Five hours start', he thought, 'I've got to make the most of it.'

"Margaret, I've decided you must get packed too, we are going to travel together as a family. While you are at it pack cases for the children."

Margaret tried to argue but she was too used to agreeing with Danny, besides she always felt that there was an undercurrent of violence in him and it wouldn't take much for it to tip over.

As soon as Matthew and Laurel returned from school Danny instructed them to get ready for a trip and informed his children that they would be leaving within the hour. As soon as they were ready he herded his family into his father-in-law's car and drove straight towards the docks. Questions from the family were met with, "You will all do exactly as I say, do you understand? There will be no arguments, no discussion, you will all simply obey me."

Danny pulled up outside a reputable shipping office and sauntered in, he enquired of the clerk, "Tell me, have you any passenger vessels sailing within the next day or two for Great Britain?"

The clerk checked the schedules, "We have a few cabins still available on a liner called *Stella*. It's leaving tonight at ten o'clock, sailing to Melbourne then Southampton via Cape Town." Danny immediately bought four first class berths to Southampton, which he paid for in cash.

He returned to the car and then drove back towards town until he saw a motor garage. Danny drove past the garage until he reached a row of shops. He dropped Margaret and the children, instructing Margaret to purchase any toiletries they were likely to need on the liner and drove back to the garage where he sold the Gregg family car. He walked back to the shops to meet his family with another large injection of money in his wallet. Next he engaged a taxi to take them to the Central Railway Station where Danny paid off the driver.

The family then headed into the station where Danny bought four first class tickets for Newcastle, a town to the north of Sydney, making a point of requesting information on train times and how long the journey would take so that if he was later questioned the counter clerk would certainly remember him.

The family returned to the taxi rank where they boarded yet another cab and this time Danny instructed the driver to take them back to the docks. A false trail having now been laid they boarded the liner and were shown to their luxurious cabins.

When the ship finally weighed anchor at ten o'clock that evening Danny breathed a sigh of relief. The world would now see a respectable businessman with his respectable wife and children, travelling in some style to London where he and his family would start a respectable new life.

Danny set out the ground rules for his wife and children in no uncertain terms. They had to be polite and well mannered at all times, the name of Gregg was never to be mentioned, they were now the

Perriman family. Finally, under no circumstances were they to draw attention to themselves. What Danny failed to realise was that being reclusive was exactly what did draw attention to them.

During the following days a pattern started to develop, much to the disappointment of Evelyn and Joslyn, after dinner Walter rounded off his evening by enjoying a nightcap with Dr Chalmers.

They didn't just play Poirot and Hastings, they talked about all manner of things. Walter confided his family background and his reason for travelling to Africa, he also told the doctor about the Johnstone family and the large part they had played in his life over the past six years. Walter thought it was just conversation but Edward Chalmers realised it was also a form of therapy, Walter was opening himself up to a complete stranger, a stranger whom he would likely never see again after the ship docked in Cape Town.

In his capacity as Hastings, Walter concentrated on talking to the children and the doctor kept a weather eye on Danny and Margaret.

"Remember the first night you were in the dining room and you commented on their dress Walter?" said the doctor. "Well, I have never been a man to take a great deal of notice of what a woman wears, as long as she looks pretty, but Margaret Perriman looks as though she hurriedly packed for a weekend away, and then quite by accident found herself travelling first class on a long sea voyage. Today I saw them in the shop, she was purchasing several scarfs and a fur wrap, perhaps to ring the changes. Interestingly, I did notice he had a very full wallet, now isn't that a turn up for the books."

Walter updated the doctor on his efforts to gain the confidence of Matthew and Laurel. "I really feel sorry for those two children. Laurel looks as though she's a rabbit caught in a trap. However, I'm starting to get a tentative relationship going with Matthew. We've played table tennis and quoits together several times and we have plans to play deck draughts and some other games together. If we are going to find out anything at all I'm sure it will be through Matthew."

The friendship between Walter and Matthew developed slowly. Walter thought about the way Sam had helped and encouraged him through a traumatic time in his own life and in the same kindly way he tried to be a mentor to Matthew.

One day when Walter and Matthew were playing deck draughts on their own without Laurel, Walter said, "Exceptionally well done Matthew! You've beaten me three games straight. Come on let me buy you a lemonade to celebrate."

They went down to the family lounge and Walter ordered their drinks. This was the opportunity Walter had been waiting for but he did not want to overplay his hand. He started off chatting very generally, "I come from the city of Melbourne, whereabouts in Australia do you live? I'm travelling to Cape Town, are you going to Africa or are you sailing on to Southampton?"

Matthew answered briefly, "Sydney and Southampton." At last he was getting somewhere. Walter then kept the conversation general, discussing the various sports facilities on the ship, how good the food was in the dining room, nothing contentious whatsoever.

Their drinks arrived and as they sipped them Walter stunned Matthew by saying, "Matthew, how on earth did you and Laurel manage to get the time off school to go on a long trip at this time of the year?"

Matthew's face drained of colour, he muttered, "I'm sorry Walter I can't talk about why we had to leave so quickly. If I could believe me I would, but my father doesn't like us to talk to anyone."

Walter decided to gently question the lad further, "Matthew are you frightened of your father for some reason? Would it help you to talk? I'll be leaving the ship in Cape Town but if I can help you in any way I'm happy to do so."

Matthew was struggling. He so wanted to tell Walter his side of the story but he was also frightened of his father who lectured him and Laurel every day about being discrete. Suddenly he became aware that he was being very unmanly, tears were involuntarily streaming down his face, there was no sound just the wetness.

Walter had not missed the emotion, "Look Matthew I will be honest, I'm really worried about you and Laurel. There's obviously something troubling you both. Can I do anything to help you, even if it's just sitting here listening?"

Matthew sat silent for a few minutes. Walter thought the moment had gone, when the boy suddenly blurted, "We're running away, my father made us all pack very quickly then he drove us into the city, he laid a kind of false trail, making us move from our car to taxis, then we boarded this ship and he told us we were going to live in London.

"He's always been his own person, he was never much interested in my mother or Laurel and me, well he positively disliked me. He disliked me because my grandfather loved me. My grandfather died recently and I miss him very much. From bits and pieces I've overheard and things my grandfather said I think my father has been stealing from the family business. I don't know for sure but I'm absolutely sure he had something to do with my grandfather's death.

"I think the only reason we're with him is to create a false family image but he isn't a family man he's a selfish loner. And another thing, we're using the name Perriman, our real name is Gregg. My grandfather insisted he change his name to Gregg when he married my mother. Not only have Laurel and I lost our grandfather, our home and our friends but we've lost our name."

Whatever Walter had expected to hear it wasn't that Mr Perriman was a potential murderer. His first thought was to keep Matthew safe.

"Matthew, I think you should keep our conversation quiet for the moment. Don't tell your parents or Laurel that we've had this conversation. I need time to think. Just try and carry on as normal for the time being. I'd like to ask you just one more question. What would you like me to do to help you and Laurel?"

Matthew thought for a moment then replied, "To be honest I wouldn't care if I never saw my father again. I just want to go back home with my mother and Laurel, go to school and eventually inherit my family, the Gregg family, business."

Dinner that evening was tense for Walter, he tried his best to appear normal, chatting to Joslyn and Evelyn, he also mentioned how good Matthew was at deck games. The doctor sensed that there was an undercurrent and he too tried to keep things normal while noting that Mrs Perriman was wearing a taupe silk scarf over her tan coloured evening gown.

As soon as they could decently do so, Poirot and Hastings headed for the bar, although their little detective game now seemed very serious indeed.

Walter updated the doctor on his conversation with Matthew that afternoon. "We have moved into very different territory doctor. I found Matthew very credible today. I'm sure he's telling the truth. Do you think the captain would be able to use the 'ship to shore' to relay a message to Sydney police to enquire if they really are looking for Perriman, Gregg or whatever name he is using?"

Dr Chalmers considered a moment, "I think it's too early to go to the captain. I think we need to speak to Matthew together and then perhaps with Laurel before we launch into something quite so serious, after all we are just a couple of amateur sleuths."

The following day Walter managed to get Matthew alone and immediately suggested they go down to the family bar. As soon as they sat down he wrote a note to Doctor Chalmers and gave it to the waiter with instructions to find the doctor and give it to him urgently, giving the man a half crown to encourage him to be speedy.

"Matthew I've been thinking about what you said yesterday. In truth I've thought of little else. I've asked Doctor Chalmers to join us, he too has been very suspicious about your father and we want to help in whatever way we can."

The doctor bustled into the lounge and quickly joined Walter and Matthew. He placed an order for two coffees and a lemonade. Walter decided to waste no time and asked Matthew to tell the doctor everything he had told him the previous day and anything else that he felt they should know.

Matthew had also had some thinking time and he had decided that his best chance of getting home to Sydney was to confide in Walter and Doctor Chalmers. He started off by telling them about the argument he had overheard between his parents, and the phrase he would never forget. 'The old fool deserved to die, and I saw to it that he did.'

"He has also been stealing, he has taken my mother's jewellery and he has packed all sorts of small valuables in the suitcases. My father looks and sounds as though butter wouldn't melt in his mouth but behind that exterior he is a ruthless man. I fear for what he will do to us when we get to London and we are no longer useful in his grand plan."

Doctor Chalmers spoke directly to Walter, "This cannot go on any longer. You are absolutely right the captain must contact Sydney police via the ship to shore and see if they are indeed pursuing Matthew's father. Secondly, Daniel Perriman mustn't get an inkling of what we are doing until we get word from Sydney.

"I suggest we finish our drinks and then Walter, you take Matthew to the sports room or the deck sports, just do something normal anything that will not raise suspicion. I'll speak to the captain. Now Matthew, I can't emphasise this enough. Do not give your father any grounds for suspicion that we are on to him."

They went their separate ways. Laurel joined Matthew and Walter playing various deck games until their mother appeared and took them off for a light lunch.

Walter immediately headed for the bridge where he was told that the captain and the doctor were in the captain's office. A young officer took Walter to join them.

The doctor greeted him, "Come in Walter, I have just been updating our good captain on the Perriman situation. Do you have anything you want to add?"

"I'm sure you have covered everything but I just want to say Matthew is a good lad and he is genuinely scared. I believe everything he has told us."

"One thing already checks out," Captain Lewis advised. "Perriman booked passage just a few hours before we sailed, and paid in cash. I've just confirmed this with my purser. Now I'm going to speak to my wireless operator and see what we can do about checking the other accusations. "Meantime I suggest we all act normally. I have no idea how long it'll take to get word back from Sydney and we don't want to spook Perriman."

Walter and Doctor Chalmers headed down to the Wheelhouse Bar, where they ordered club sandwiches with whisky and soda. "It's out of our hands now my boy, it's just a waiting game. I never for one minute imagined when we jokingly took on the roles of Hastings and Poirot that our little diversion would turn out to be such a serious matter. I'm now worried that young Matthew puts the blighter on alert."

"Let's just hope we can keep it all under wraps until the captain gets a reply," agreed Walter.

The afternoon seemed to pass very slowly and as Walter got ready for dinner he was dreading how difficult it was going to be giving an impression of normality while knowing that it was possible they were eating their meal with a murderer.

The soup course had just been served when a young officer approached Daniel Perriman and said quietly, "Good evening sir, I wonder if I could ask you to accompany me? The captain would like a word with you."

Such was Perriman's feeling of security that he immediately assumed the captain wished to see him to invite him to join his table or attend a function. He walked out of the dining room looking rather smug.

By the time the sweet trolly arrived Perriman had not returned and a feeling of tension had developed around the table.

Once again the young officer discretely appeared. This time he spoke to Doctor Chalmers. "Doctor, can I ask you and Mr McDonald to accompany me? The captain would like a word with you both."

The men followed the officer to the captain's private office where he greeted them. "Sit down gentleman and I will update you on the happenings of the past few hours.

"A message was sent to Sydney as we discussed. I'll give you the reply, in brief. The police had been alerted by Mr Gregg's doctor and solicitor as to the possibility of arsenic poisoning. Perriman had somehow managed to slip through their net, which confirms everything the boy told you.

"The police have asked that I hold Perriman in custody until we reach Cape Town. Arrangements will then be made to return him to Sydney. So instead of enjoying life in first class your erstwhile table companion is now confined to the brig.

"I'll speak with the family and advise them what is happening. They will also be required to return to Sydney as they will be called upon to give evidence.

"Gentleman, for whatever reason you decided to carry out this investigation I must congratulate you. An inspector from Sydney police called Alan Smith has also requested I convey his thanks to you both."

Walter and Doctor Chalmers headed straight for the bar where they ordered a reviving scotch and water.

The story of the amateur sleuthing and Perriman being held in the brig went round the ship like wildfire. Both Walter and the doctor felt immensely sorry for Margaret and the children, who scarcely left their cabins. However, Walter would sometimes join the children and play cards or board games with them.

On the evening before he was due to leave the ship in Cape Town, Walter received a letter from the steward, it read.

Dear Walter

Before you disembark at Cape Town I wanted to write and thank you for everything you and Doctor Chalmers have done for both Laurel and I. It might sound odd to thank you for imprisoning my father but he richly deserves everything that is coming to him.

My mother is still crying, but I think she will eventually accept it's for the best that he is out of our lives.

I'm dreading the trial and I think we will be in for a difficult time. I have decided that it would be best to engage a tutor for both Laurel and myself for a year or so until all the talk dies down and then for us to register at a different school. I don't really want to return to our old house but that is all in the future, I'll need permission to sell from the trustees and I'm not sure whether or not my mother will want to move.

When you return to Australia we would love to hear from you, perhaps visit you in Melbourne and meet the Johnstone family who you talk about with such affection.

Once again our thanks.

Matthew and Laurel

* * *

Walter greatly appreciated the letter, and the doctor was also very

touched when Walter showed it to him in the bar that evening.
The doctor was sad to be losing his companion, his Hastings. "I'll miss you my boy. I'll need to find some keen bridge players to amuse myself with until the ship reaches Southampton. I'm also going to ask to be moved to another dinner table, I couldn't abide those two girls twittering on all the way to England.

"Then I'll settle down to a quiet life in Bournemouth. Initially I'll stay with my sisters in the family home, that is the contact address I have given you, eventually I intend to purchase a flat or a cottage and engage a housekeeper. Besides, I'm not entirely sure when my furniture will arrive, and that will take a bit of sorting out. I'll really miss our nightly malt my boy."

Walter replied, "Doctor, I'll miss our nightcap in the bar but most of all I'll miss our talks. You've taught me a great deal and I'm very grateful. Tomorrow starts a new chapter for me, but whether or not I find my father I intend to eventually return to Melbourne and make a success of Harris Finishings, the business I inherited from my grandmother. Goodnight sir, my mentor."

The doctor ordered another scotch and thought, 'I wish that boy was turning up at my door.'

CHAPTER 14
The Adventure Begins

As the liner sailed into Cape Town the following morning, Walter could now understand exactly what Sam and Maria had meant when they talked about their first impression of this beautiful city.

Table mountain was wearing its white table cover of cloud as they docked near the 17th century Castle of Good Hope. Walter felt butterflies in his stomach, the adventure proper had now begun.

Walter had booked a room at the Mount Nelson, the hotel which held such wonderful memories of their blessing day for Sam and Maria.

As his taxi approached the hotel through the impressive white column entrance, Walter was saluted by a man dressed in a smart khaki uniform topped with a topi hat and wearing white gloves. The long driveway led through manicured gardens set against the majestic backdrop of the mountain. Walter could immediately see why Sam and Maria had been so awestruck by the hotel.

He checked in at the reception desk and was shown to his bedroom, which had a magnificent view over the gardens and across the city bowl to the ocean. Before unpacking Walter sat down at the mahogany writing desk and penned a letter on the hotel's headed notepaper to Charles and Ishbel. He felt he had to offer quite a long explanation as he was unsure if the letter sent by Maria explaining his quest would have arrived in Cape Town.

Walter took the letter to reception where they arranged postage and then he took himself out onto the terrace. Over a light lunch of tea and ham sandwiches he read the local paper the Cape Argos.

After lunch he decided to go out for a walk and explore the city. Following the directions Maria had given him he found the cottage in Oranjezicht where Ishbel and Robert had first lived, it hardly seemed to have changed since the blessing photographs. He then spent a delightful afternoon walking through the Company Gardens then down Long Street and exploring the city centre.

After returning to the hotel and having a much needed rest Walter was changing for dinner when there was a knock on the door, "Letter for you sir," said the young bellhop. Walter gave him a few coins and excitedly opened the envelope.

Rondebosh

Dear Walter

I've taken the liberty of using your Christian name as I feel I already know you from Maria's letters. I received her letter from Melbourne some days ago saying to expect you and that you wanted to try and investigate the whereabouts of your father, a Mr John McDonald.

We would love to meet you, if you are free tomorrow evening please come to our home in Rondebosch for dinner. If you arrive at around six o'clock we could have a drink on the stoop and you can tell us how we can help in your enterprise before we eat. My son Robert and his fiancé Anna will join us.

With kindest regards

Ishbel

* * *

Robert immediately penned a reply saying he would be delighted to accept the invitation.

As the liner was going to be docked in Cape Town for several days Walter had invited Dr Chalmers to join him on his first evening in Cape Town for dinner at the Mount Nelson.

Walter met the good doctor at reception and they made their way into the bar for a drink before dinner.

"I think this calls for a glass of champagne by way of a celebration," said the doctor. "After you left this morning the South African police took that scoundrel Perriman into custody. He will be returned to Sydney on the first available ship and I guarantee he won't be residing in a first class cabin this time. His wife and the children will return on the same ship, meantime Captain Lewis has arranged for them to stay in a local hotel. The bit I can't understand is why Margaret helped him cover up his crimes. Perhaps she loved him, love makes people do strange things."

They discussed their exploits on the liner and the exposing of Daniel Perriman. "I still can't believe that what started as a bit of fun to pass the time on the journey turned into a real life investigation. Well my boy, I've given our signed statements to the South African police force, I expect they will assign someone to accompany that scoundrel Perriman back to Sydney.

"You know I think Matthew has got the makings of turning into a fine young man. When you get back to Australia Walter perhaps you could get in touch with the lad, I'm sure he would appreciate hearing from you."

"Yes I will sir, he said as much in his letter that he'd like to hear from me. I'll keep you informed as to what happens to the family, I also intend to write to Sam and Maria and ask them to obtain copies of any Sydney newspapers covering the case. Hopefully I'll be able to forward a full report to you when I get back home to Melbourne."

"Walter, I've enjoyed your company and our adventure but before we say our final goodbyes I just wanted to wish you well in your quest. If I had a fine young man like you turn up at my door and say he was my son I'd welcome him with open arms."

A smartly uniformed waiter directed them to their table in the restaurant where they would enjoy their final meal together.

"Ah, here comes the chateaubriand! Is that not a fine piece of meat and accompanied by a good Cape red wine, what could be finer? Delicious! I only hope Perriman enjoys his bread and water. You know Walter, I'll dine out for years on the Daniel Perriman story."

The elderly and the young man spent a memorable evening together. Two unlikely people brought together for a short time like characters in a play but the memories they had created together neither would ever forget.

Sadly the evening ended and Walter bid farewell to his friend 'Poirot' with a hearty handshake and a promise to write to him in Bournemouth and let him know the outcome of his search for his father together with Sydney newspaper reports on the Perriman trial.

The following morning Walter spent a considerable time writing a long letter to Sam and Maria telling them of his adventures onboard the ship and his arrangement to visit the home of Charles and Ishbel that evening.

Walter took a hotel car to Rondebosch to meet up with Sam and Maria's friends. As the car drew up outside the house Ishbel, Charles and little Elize came down the driveway, accompanied by Emmy their Jack Russell to welcome Walter into their home.

Soon they were joined by Robert and Anna, everyone sat on comfortable Lloyd Loom chairs around a matching table on the stoop while Charles opened a bottle of white Constantia wine. Walter immediately felt he was among friends which was very reassuring. After saying his farewells to Doctor Chalmers the previous evening he had felt very alone, not knowing another soul on the entire continent of Africa.

Walter had brought beautiful bunches of flowers for his hostess and Anna, his next duty was to give Elize a special present from Maria. Elize was incredibly excited at being presented with a beautifully wrapped box. After undoing the ribbon and taking off the paper she carefully opened the box where she found, resting on a bed of pink tissue paper, with her head supported on a silken pillow a beautiful porcelain doll with soft blond curling hair. Maria had dressed the doll in a glamorous outfit which she had made, using her trusty Singer sewing machine. Inside the pillow was the dolly's sleeping attire of a fine cotton nightdress and dressing gown, both exquisitely hand embroidered and as a finishing touch, little matching slippers.

Elize was absolutely ecstatic and then totally absorbed in what name she was going to give her new friend. Eventually she decided on Sylvia, just because she liked the name.

Walter felt he hardly needed to give Robert and Ishbel the letters of introduction so warm was their welcome. He was bombarded with questions, Robert and Ishbel wanted to know everything that had happened in the lives of their friends in the intervening years since they said farewell to them in January 1918.

Eventually Charles said, "Dinner will be ready soon, it was prepared by Sophie but Ishbel has arranged for our daily help Eve to come in and serve. Now, before we start our meal Walter, how can we help you in your quest to find your father or to discover what happened to him? You have the floor, please tell us your story."

Walter told his tale, he also allowed Ishbel to read the letters John McDonald had sent to Vicky from Africa. Ishbel agreed with Walter that the sentiments recorded did not sound like somebody who had no intention of returning to his loved one.

Ishbel said, "Walter, in the first letter your father states that he travelled out on a ship called the Morgana. Maritime records are excellent, as a starting point why don't you try to find confirmation of the ship's exact arrival date in Cape Town also the passenger list. You already know the date of the Johannesburg letter so you can then calculate if he stayed in Cape Town for any length of time. If so, you might be lucky and find hotel records of his stay. Just because Vicky didn't receive a letter from Cape Town it doesn't mean he didn't post one, you know what the posts can be like even now, and the letter would have been posted over twenty years ago."

Suddenly it all seemed obvious to Walter, "Thank you so much Ishbel, I'll get on to researching the shipping records tomorrow. Actually I'm not a bad sleuth, together with another passenger, a Dr Chalmers, we uncovered a mystery on the ship while we were sailing to Cape Town and a suspected murderer is now being sent back to Sydney."

Everyone clamoured for an explanation but Charles said, "There goes the dinner gong, let's settle ourselves at the table then we can all listen to Walter's exciting tale over our meal."

Walter had a really enjoyable evening, spending time with the people he had heard so much about. After dinner Sophie joined the party in the lounge for coffee. Anna made no comment but she found this familiarity very strange indeed. While her parents had always been kind to their employees, the idea of a member of staff sitting chatting and having coffee with the family was totally unthinkable. Having been brought up in the Union of South Africa she rather suspected Charles must also have found it decidedly odd. However, she loved Robert and he loved Ishbel so they simply accepted their strange Scottish ways.

In fact Anna was totally wrong. Charles was well aware that without Sophie in all probability he would not have a wife and daughter, his gratitude to Sophie was unbounded.

Riding back to the Mount Nelson in a taxi Walter planned his research project, at last he was taking his first positive steps towards finding his father.

Straight after breakfast Walter headed to the Maritime Archive Office. Searching the records was slow and Walter was immensely grateful to a young man called Eugene who helped him plough through the ledgers. Eventually he found details of a ship called SS Morgana landing in Cape Town and on the manifest was the name John W. McDonald Esq., first class passenger.

It was a strange emotional feeling for Walter actually seeing his father's name written in ink. Eugene wrote down all the details for him and he headed back to the hotel to carry out some calculations. Taking into account the date of the letter from the hotel in Jo'burg and assuming his father had written the day after arriving and the journey had taken approximately three days, it looked as though his father had spent several weeks in Cape Town.

He enquired at the reception desk regarding old guest records. The receptionist proudly told him that they had an archive dating back to when the hotel opened in 1899. The helpful fairy dust had certainly been liberally sprinkled that day. The receptionist offered to visit the archive room later in the afternoon when more staff would be on duty.

Walter ordered some lunch but he could hardly eat anything, he was so excited at the possibility that he was walking in the footsteps of his father.

He was busy writing a long letter to Sam and Maria updating them on his visit to see their old friends in Rondebosch. Just as he was starting to explain his shipping research at the maritime offices a young man approached him carrying a silver tray.

"Sir, it was quite extraordinary, I actually found some details of your Mr John W. McDonald. He stayed at the hotel for fifteen nights from the date he landed in Cape Town on the SS Morgana. Another relevant piece of information which may be of assistance, he gave his profession as civil engineer. Twenty years ago the country was awash with engineers working on the mines and the infrastructure to give access to them. That would explain why a civil engineer would leave England to come all the way to Africa. It's amazing how much I managed to find in the records. His bill was paid by Nederlandsche Bank voor Zuid-Afrika, that is the Dutch Bank. Perhaps he was going to work for them but I think its more likely they were just acting as intermediaries for a mining or construction company.

"He signed for his meals and I thought I would bring you the chitties with his signature on them, you can look through them and see if there is anything else you find of interest. I've also taken the liberty of bringing a piece of tracing paper as I thought it would be useful for you to have a copy of his signature."

Walter thanked the man profusely for his efforts, he could scarcely believe that in one day with the help of the hotel receptionist and Eugene at the mercantile offices he had gleaned so much information.

He carefully went through the pile of signed chitties, his father had mainly eaten alone but there were a number of dinners for three or five, and he did not dine in the hotel on several evenings. The activity suggested he had been staying in Cape Town specifically to do business and not just for a rest period after the voyage.

Maria had taught Walter to be methodical. As far as he could he plotted his father's movements on a day by day basis to see if he could find any pattern.

After he had done as much as he could with the information available, on the spur of the moment he decided to take the hotel car to Rondebosh and see if Ishbel was free to discuss the information he had found out so far.

Ishbel was delighted to welcome her unexpected guest, they sat out on the stoop and Eve brought them iced tea. Ishbel read all the information carefully.

"Well Walter you have certainly discovered a lot within a remarkably short time. If you tie the engineering connection of Mr Kessall with your father's profession as a civil engineer it looks as though he was possibly engaged by Mr Kessall as an employee or perhaps he was a self employed private contractor working for the company.

"I think the next move is to find out if Mr Kessall's family business used the Dutch bank, that would be another connection. I would also try and find people who worked for the Kessall family over twenty years ago. That might be an ask, but I can't see any other obvious route.

"I think you have probably now done as much as you can in Cape Town, it's next stop Johannesburg on the remote chance you might find something out at the hotel. Then it's Pretoria, that's definitely your best bet. A visit to the Kessall family might elicit far more information than you could possibly receive in a letter. Often it's not just what people say it's how they say it, you have to read folks you know Walter."

They sat and chatted about a number of things. Walter told Ishbel about the influence Sam and Maria had been on him.

"You know Ishbel without Maria I would have been packed off to a boarding school and the business and house sold. Yes, at twenty one I would have inherited a great deal of money from my grandmother's estate but I wouldn't have inherited any purpose in life. Maria taught me so much and she never let me forget that one day I would inherit a business and with it all the responsibilities that it entails. Maria would say things like, 'You know Walter there are ladies out there working on our projects who depend on the money we pay them to provide for their children, to put food on the table'.

"And Sam, well Sam has been the father figure I never had, he's taught me so many things from painting a room to planting potatoes. I can put up shelves and we made a swing for the wee ones. Every week we worked on a new project, I can now turn my hand to most practical things.

"Ishbel, having the Johnstons' as my guardians wasn't just about learning skills, we had so much fun together. Picnics, making tablet and puff candy, being an uncle to Alexander and Isabel, fishing with Sam, cooking with Maria, going to the beach for the day and having fish and chips before catching the train home. So many wonderful memories, memories that I'll carry with me all my life.

"As to the business of tracking down my birth father, Sam and

Maria have been very supportive, but I'm not stupid, I know perfectly well they didn't want me to go off on a mission which might well lead to great sadness or simply to nothingness, a series of dead ends. "Mr Green, our solicitor and the trustee of my inheritance from my grandmother was absolutely furious with me. To be fair he ensured I was well equipped for the journey, he even made me learn a bit of French so that I could read a menu, but I think he sort of feels I'm letting Maria down by leaving Melbourne after all her hard work in developing the business."

Ishbel gently said, "Walter, for what it's worth I think you've made the right decision whatever you find, even if it is absolutely nothing. Firstly, the timing is right, you are young and single, without family responsibilities. And, dear Maria will look after your business for the time being. Harris Finishings is in safe hands with her at the helm! Secondly, you don't want to carry important questions around with you for your entire life. What if ...?, should I...?, I wonder...? You could spend your life haunted by these questions. Better to grip the issue now, and when you return to Melbourne you will be able to move forward unencumbered by regrets.

"Now my dear, Eve will be back shortly with Elize from school and Charles will be home around six o'clock. Why don't you stay and have a family supper with us. Then tomorrow you can start to make your plans for your journey up north."

After another delightful evening at the home of Charles and Ishbel, Walter returned to the hotel where he asked reception to book rail travel for him to Johannesburg, and to make a reservation at the Potsdam Hotel.

Before going into breakfast the following morning Walter checked in with the reception desk. Tickets had been acquired for him on the overnight train leaving Cape Town for Pretoria that evening at five o'clock, stopping at Johannesburg. Apparently there was no hotel by the name of Potsdam in Johannesburg, the Johannesburg hotel from where John McDonald had sent the letter to Vicky. The reception staff had booked him into the Carlton Hotel instead.

Walter was disappointed at this news but not greatly surprised, he knew that his best chance of tracking down information was definitely from the Kessall connection.

After a hearty breakfast and having packed his cases Walter decided to follow in the footsteps of Sam and Maria and visit Camps Bay before taking the train north.

Driven by a chauffeur called Ralph in one of the Mount Nelson's guest cars he was able to drink in the magnificent scenery and he could absolutely understand why Sam and Maria would have liked to settle on the Cape. Ralph was a fund of information and Walter could sense the pride he had in his city from the enthusiasm with which he spoke.

Ralph dropped him in the village of Camps Bay and Walter enjoyed a relaxing walk alongside the beach, where he contemplated the next part of his journey before returning to the car, carrying two large ice cream cones.

Laughing, Ralph said, "Never in all my years of driving has a passenger bought me an ice cream cone, Mr McDonald I'll certainly remember you and our drive today. Now would you like me to take you to Hout Bay? It's just a small fishing village but the scenery is beautiful and sometimes you can get a trip on a boat out to Seal Island."

Walter enjoyed the remainder of the day, including a boat trip to see the seals. Ralph drove him back to the Mount Nelson to collect his bags and then on to the railway station in plenty of time to catch the Union Express, the new service running from Cape Town to Pretoria. through the Klein Karoo from the Cape then up the escarpment into the Transvaal.

The Union Express was like no other train Walter had ever seen. From the moment he was dropped off by Ralph he was cocooned in luxurious service. His luggage was whisked away and his overnight portmanteau taken to his cabin.

As the steam train left the station Walter took himself into the lounge car where he sipped a glass of white wine while drinking in the dramatic scenery as it unfolded.

When darkness fell Walter returned to his cabin to change for dinner. Like the rest of the train the dining room was luxurious, the tables set with crisp white monogrammed linen, crystal glassware and fresh flowers.

Walter ordered Franschhoek smoked trout followed by springbok as he was determined to enjoy the whole South African experience. The food was superb, he enjoyed a glass of sparkling wine with his trout, followed by a deep Vergelegen red with the meat, showcasing South African wine at its finest.

Sadly, for the first time since leaving Melbourne Walter felt lonely, travelling on the Union Express was the kind of luxurious experience that was best shared.

Back in his compartment Walter slept to the rhythm of the train, he was barely awake when there was a tap on the door. A smartly uniformed waiter entered with a wake-up tea tray and opened the blind. "Good morning Sir! Breakfast is served in the dining room up until ten o'clock, can I recommend you enjoy a Karoo lamb chop as part of your breakfast? It's a real South African treat!" And he was gone.

Walter drank his tea but refrained from eating the accompanying biscuits. Another fourteen hours, three delicious meals and he would arrive at the railway station in Johannesburg.

———

CHAPTER 15
Life Without Walter

After the first full week of being solely responsible for Harris Finishings Maria realised exactly how much work Walter had carried out. Over the years they had developed a routine and the routine worked. Now everything seemed to rest firmly on her shoulders, looking after both Harris Finishings and 'The Brig'. As the weeks rolled past Maria felt that there never seemed to be enough hours in the day.

Alexander had been enrolled into a school near H.Q. this meant Alice was able to do the school run as well as looking after Isabel. Maria found the return train journey to Northcote was a good time for Alexander to do his school homework. This effectively removed the little bit of relaxation she had enjoyed each evening on the train when she had some thinking time or could simply relax by reading a magazine or newspaper.

Maria was trying to be all things to all people and Sam decided that this state of affairs could not continue much longer so he took matters into his own hands. One evening after they had finished dinner and the children were tucked up in bed Maria announced, "I'll just away and make a pot of soup now before I get the clothes ready for the morning."

Sam sat her back down in the chair. "Indeed you will not young lady! This endless activity is simply not sustainable, you are wearing yourself out. If we go on like this you're going to make yourself ill Maria! You are spreading yourself far too thin."

"What else can I do Sam? We now own twenty five percent of the business so we have a real stake in making Harris Finishings successful."

"Yes Maria we do have to make the business profitable but not by sacrificing your health and our family time together. Please listen to what I have to say carefully and really think about it before we discuss it any further.

"Firstly, I want you to employ a lady to come to 'The Brig' every day during the week and do the housework and laundry while you are working in Melbourne. Perhaps she could also prepare vegetables which would make the cooking easier in the evening. There's no need for you to bake, just get Mrs Wilson to make some scones or a fruit loaf for you to bring home from time to time.

"You should be concentrating your energy on the business and the family not on things that you can pay someone else to do. Maria, you also need a bit of time for yourself to do the things you really enjoy like arranging flowers and reading. You haven't picked up a book or even a magazine since Walter left.

"This isn't strictly my territory but I think you could get Alice to help more in the business. Alexander is at school now and Isabel is well past the baby stage. She is a bright wee lass and she loves helping Mrs Wilson.

"The boys who are working for you are fine lads but they are too young for any of the responsible book work. Why don't you train up Alice? Not only would you gain from it but it would be good for her to learn another skill.

"I'll help out at weekends but remember, Walter used to contribute here in Northcote too. He often did wee jobs like cutting the grass or hedges and he was always playing with the bairns. Do you know I might even get somebody in to help me with the garden, if my health goes then where would we be?

"Now Maria Johnstone, just you sit there quietly and have a serious think about what I've said, I'll away and put the kettle on for a nice wee cup of tea."

When Sam returned with the tea tray and some home made shortbread he found Maria in tears. "Darling girl, don't take on so. I didn't mean to upset you, but it had to be said, you are doing far too much."

Maria took her husband's hand, "Sam, I know you are right but it's so difficult, can you imagine your mother having someone coming in to clean her house for her. My ma worked all hours to keep us bairns well fed and the house clean, but she still managed to take in laundry for a wee bit extra money. I can remember her heating the irons on a metal plate clipped on to the front of the coal range, as one iron cooled she swopped it for another. Ma even had a contraption called a goffering iron which she heated by filling it with hot coals and then used it to make perfect frills, I think she was able to charge more money for the fancy finish.

"Because of the way we were both brought up it seems wrong somehow to have a servant. I know we have staff at H.Q. but somehow that's business and it's acceptable. Oh Sam, I don't know if I'm explaining myself very well. You are right, of course you are, but somehow it goes against the grain for people like us to employ help in the house."

Sam poured the tea, "Maria, think of it this way, if we employ extra help we will be providing employment for somebody, giving them a weekly wage. Remember how happy you were when Mrs Harris employed you and enabled you to earn extra money, money that helped us get on our feet. You are now financially in a position to help someone else onto the ladder.

"Promise me that tomorrow you will make a start on reorganising your priorities at H.Q. Perhaps we can write an advert tonight and I'll put it in the window of Mack's Store on my way to work. We can advertise for a local woman to come in from Monday to Friday. Agreed?"

Maria picked up her teacup, looked at her husband and said, "Yes Sam, I'll write a card tonight before we go to bed but I tell you this, it's a piece of information I'll never write home about. This is our secret and it stays in Australia. Go on bossy boots pass me a wee bit of shortbread."

The following weeks seemed even busier for Maria organising major changes at home and in the business but it was time well spent. The lady they engaged as a housekeeper for 'The Brig' was called Mrs Rogers, a widow in her forties with grown up children. Mrs Rogers slipped seamlessly into life at 'The Brig' and after a few weeks it seemed that she had always been part of their lives. Not only did Ella Rogers become the Johnstone's housekeeper she arranged for her father to come in one day a week and help with the gardening and other odd jobs.

Alice was delighted to be offered full time work in the clothing business, and she proved to have a real aptitude for figure work. The extra ten shillings a week in her pay packet was also very welcome.

Maria employed a young girl of fifteen called Jean for Mrs Wilson to train and to take on some of the heavier work, sadly this was not a success. However, Mrs Wilson managed to find a suitable girl through her local connections and Faye joined the team at H.Q. Maria had been doubtful at first as she was only fourteen however from day one wee Isabel adored her. Between Faye and Mrs Wilson Maria never had to worry about her daughter Isabel's welfare while she was working.

Walter's eagerly awaited letter arrived from Cape Town. Sam and Maria sat on the sofa reading it together, they were enthralled to hear about the Perriman adventure. It seemed more like reading a detective story than something that had happened to young Walter, their part was now to gather as much information as they could about the case ready for Walter when he returned home.

They were delighted to hear about the welcome and help he had received from Ishbel and Robert, also about their new partners Charles and Anna. Maria was particularly happy to hear that Elize had loved the doll she had dressed with such loving care and that Elize had named her Sylvia.

In fact the Perriman trial garnered interest throughout Australia and Maria would put together a fat file of press cuttings for Walter.

The changes instigated by Sam ensured that although Maria was running the business on her own she still had time to spend with her husband and the children. Weekends were always sacrosanct, 'Johnstone' time.

CHAPTER 16
The Transvaal

By the time the Union Express steamed into Johannesburg railway station it was almost nine o'clock in the evening. Helped by a porter Walter managed to find a taxi and headed straight to the Carlton Hotel.

Walter had enjoyed his sojourn on the train, it had given him some quiet thinking time, and he felt that he was at last travelling in his father's footsteps.

After checking into the Carlton Walter went straight to his bedroom and slept soundly.

The following morning after eating a good breakfast Walter suddenly felt unsure as to what exactly he should do next. He returned to his bedroom and prepared an action list:

- *contact the Dutch bank*
- *find out what happened to the Potsdam Hotel*
- *write to Mr Kessall*
- *put an advertisement in the local newspaper asking if anybody knows anything about both the current or previous whereabouts of Mr John Walter McDonald.*

Now that he had a plan on paper Walter sprung into action, firstly he wrote to Mr Kessall advising he was staying in Johannesburg and asking if he could meet with him at a convenient time.

Then, he prepared the advertisement for insertion in the Rand Daily Mail. Thinking that he had perhaps missed an opportunity while in Cape Town, he also wrote an advert to have inserted in The Cape Argus.

Walter penned short letters to Sam and Maria and Doctor Chalmers letting them know of his progress so far and that he was now staying at the Carlton Hotel in Johannesburg.

After paying a visit to the hotel reception where he gave instructions to have his letters posted and the adverts inserted in the newspapers Walter then ordered a taxi to take him to the railway station and caught the first train to Pretoria.

The Nederlandsche Bank voor Zuid-Afrika, was situated in Church Square, Pretoria, it was a long shot that they would help him but Walter knew he had to try. This journey to Africa was his one and only opportunity to trace his father and he had to follow every single clue available.

The cashier at the bank made it clear that he would not release any information on any client transactions, regardless of when the transactions had been carried out. However, he did offer to pass a letter on to Mr John Walter McDonald if he was indeed a current customer of the bank.

Walter was allowed access to a private room where he penned his letter. It took him quite a time to compose a document that he felt was suitable.

Pretoria

Dear Mr McDonald

The contents of this letter will no doubt come as a shock to you. However, I will try and keep it succinct. My name is Walter McDonald and I am the son of Victoria Harris (Vicky).

I was brought up by my grandmother Lavinia Harris, as my mother died in childbirth. Sadly, I only found out Lavinia Harris was my grandmother shortly before she died.

Mrs Harris left most of her estate, including a successful business, Harris Finishings, to me; my inheritance was held in trust until I was twenty one years of age.

For the past five years I have been under the guardianship of a wonderful Scottish couple, Sam and Maria Johnstone who have ensured I inherited a thriving business and given me a happy family life. I owe them more than I can ever repay.

I am now over twenty one and I have decided to try and trace my birth father before settling into a life of business in Melbourne and have too many responsibilities to spend time away from home.

I found letters sent to my mother from John McDonald and I do not think they were from an uncaring man. In fact the opposite, they seemed to be written by someone who loved Vicky very much.

I understand you may very well not wish to have anything to do with me. However, if you do wish to contact me I am currently

staying at the Carlton Hotel in Johannesburg. I also attach
details of my business address in Melbourne and the Johnstone's
address in Northcote (a suburb of Melbourne).

Please be assured I do not wish to bring disruption to your life
I simply want to know what happened over twenty years ago that
caused you to disappear from my mother's life.

Hopefully
Walter McDonald

* * *

When Walter left the bank he felt drained, writing the letter had
been very emotional. He found a comfortable hotel where he had a
cup of coffee and gathered his thoughts before catching a train and
returning to his hotel in Johannesburg.

Walter felt the atmosphere in Pretoria and Johannesburg was very
different from the relaxed attitudes back in Cape Town. Even in the
hotel restaurant the clientele seemed to be predominantly men
discussing business and politics. Sitting alone Walter did not linger over
dinner, he ate his meal, returned to his room and wondered what the
following day would bring.

After breakfast Walter was delighted to receive a communication
from Mr Kessall. He found a quiet corner and a comfortable leather
chair before opening the letter.

Pretoria

Dear Mr McDonald

Thank you for your letter and I hope you are comfortable
staying at the Carlton.

Unfortunately I will be away from home on business for a few
days. However, if you would like to join with me and my wife
Hannalie on Saturday for lunch we would be pleased to welcome you.

If I do not hear to the contrary we will expect you around one
o'clock.

Best regards
Paul Kessall

* * *

While delighted with the invitation Walter wondered what he was
going to do for the next three days.

Walter spent his time tracking down where the Potsdam Hotel had been located and discovered it had been demolished fifteen years previously. He also found out where the offices of the Kessall civil engineering company were located. However, he felt that he could not visit them until after the lunch arranged with Paul Kessall on the following Saturday.

As there was very little Walter could do in the quest to find his father, over the next few days he decided to do a little sightseeing. He visited the new Union Building in Pretoria, the Parliament of the Union of South Africa on its wonderful sight atop the highest point in Pretoria, a truly impressive building.

Kruger, Rhodes and Marks had all now passed into history and the new brigade of politicians was led by Hertzog and Smuts.

Walter could feel the excitement of growth in the Transvaal and throughout the Union, there seemed to be no end of possibilities for enterprising men, but only if you were from European stock.

The days passed and at last Saturday dawned and Walter set out for his luncheon in Pretoria.

He was welcomed by Paul Kessall and his wife Hannalie and introduced to Paul's sister Annabelle and her husband Jan.

As it was a beautiful day Hannalie had arranged for the lunch to be served outdoors on the stoop. Before lunch was served the company were offered a glass of Cape wine and the maid offered little dishes of biltong, olives and salted almonds. Walter had got used to biltong since arriving in Africa and now really enjoyed the dried beef snack.

Initially the conversation was general, how had Walter enjoyed Cape Town, the weather and his journey from Australia. Eventually Paul Kessall brought up the subject of John McDonald.

"Walter, Annabelle and I were quite young when John McDonald stayed with us, and as I said in my letter he was a delightful young man, probably in his early twenties. The war, although in its last days, was still being fought, but we were living through strange times. Although the Boer war was still going on there was a will to get things moving, infrastructure was all; roads, bridges, mines, railways.

"Our father was an engineer and his business was booming, he desperately needed more qualified staff. John McDonald was from a Scottish family but his mother was from the Netherlands so he had a good command of the Dutch language and he didn't stand out as an Englishman.

"As I said we were children so I've no idea as to how John was recruited, I only know he stayed with us for about a month, perhaps more, while working for my father. Then one day we came home from school and he had disappeared. My father did not offer an explantation and we knew better than to ask questions out of turn.

"Years later I happened to mention John McDonald and his stay at our home. Father told me he thought that he had got involved in the fighting, remember the war didn't finish until the end of May 1902, and he had no idea what eventually happened to him. The only other thing of any interest he said was that John had a fiancé back in England.

"I'm sorry Walter but that's everything Annabelle and I know about John's whereabouts. Although I would say this, he was an extremely nice person! He used to play games with us and he often came to watch me play cricket.

"When my father passed away the business was sold. I am a lawyer and Annabelle's husband is also in the legal profession, so it seemed the sensible thing to do.

"Our mother is still alive, she lives happily in Port Elizabeth with her sister in their old family home."

Having got the business conversation out of the way Paul Kessall went on to host a delicious and entertaining luncheon.

Travelling back to the Carlton on the train Walter thought that he had gleaned very little new information.

Having ascertained from Paul Kessall that he had no objection to him contacting the new owners of the family engineering business, come Monday that was going to be Walter's next move.

Having been alerted by Paul Kessall the Administration Manager was very helpful and gave him the names of a number of former employees from 1900 to 1905. There were two employees still with the company who had been there since 1900. Once again interviews with them led to nothing, they had been young trainees at the time John McDonald was in Pretoria and neither of them remembered him.

It took Walter several weeks to track down everyone on the list he had been given. Each day started with hope and ended with disappointment. Several former employees had died, one was suffering from dementia, of the others only two remembered John McDonald and they both confirmed that he had been working with Mr Kessall and then he just seemed to disappear and they never heard any more about him.

As each day passed Walter became more despondent, clues were fast running out. He eventually decided that he had no option but to return to Cape Town and board a ship bound for Melbourne. However, before leaving the Transvaal he thought that he should return the kindness of the Kessall family by inviting them to lunch at the Carlton.

He sent an invitation to Pretoria and was pleased to receive a reply saying that Paul, Hannalie, Annabelle and Jan would be delighted to lunch with him the following Saturday. Meantime, Walter booked a ticket on a train back to the Cape for the Monday.

The luncheon went extremely well although everyone was sorry that Walter's investigations had not been more successful. Shortly before the party broke up Annabelle said, "Walter, this might be a very slim hope but we would be happy to give you our mother's address in Port Elizabeth, you could write to her and see if she remembers anything about your father."

Walter gratefully accepted the piece of paper and the slim hope it offered.

Back in his room Walter was busy composing a letter to Mrs Kessall Snr when he suddenly thought, 'there is nothing left for me to do now in the Transvaal, why don't I go down to Port Elizabeth and see Mrs Kessall in person'.

Walter quickly changed his travel arrangements, he cancelled his train ticket to Cape Town and rebooked for Durban. The concierge suggested that if Walter was not in a great hurry to reach Durban he might like to stop off in the Drakensberg mountain range as the scenery was a sight to behold.

Walter spent the afternoon planning his schedule to ensure that his trip to Port Elizabeth and from there to Cape Town would take in a lot of the sights of southern Africa as this would be his one and only chance to explore the country. He also decided that unless something extraordinary was uncovered in P.E. that would be an end to his adventure and on his arrival in Cape Town he would book a berth on the next liner leaving for Melbourne.

After departing from the Carlton in Johannesburg Walter spent three weeks sightseeing as he progressed to Port Elizabeth where he booked into the Palmerston Hotel and immediately wrote to Mrs Kessall Snr.

He spent the first few days in P.E. catching up on mail and sending presents to Alexander and Isabel, he also bought a special gift for Elize as he intended to meet with the Hofmyer family prior to sailing back home to Australia. On his third day in P.E. Walter received a reply from Mrs Kessall Snr.

Port Elizabeth

Dear Mr McDonald

Thank you for your letter, I would be pleased to invite you for morning coffee tomorrow, Thursday, at eleven o'clock.

Annabelle wrote to me regarding your quest to find your father John McDonald so I was not surprised to receive your note. I look forward to meeting you.

Regards

Annalise Kessall

* * *

Travelling to Mrs Kessall's home Walter was rather nervous, he felt that this was probably his last opportunity to glean any information about his father.

The taxi stopped outside a substantial Victorian house in Richmond Hill. Walter was shown into the morning room and a few minutes later Mrs Kessall arrived. For some reason Walter expected a wrinkled elderly lady dressed in black. To his surprise Annalise Kessall was a beautiful woman in her mid to late fifties, most elegantly dressed.

"Welcome Mr McDonald, you are indeed lucky to catch me in P.E. My sister is presently on a trip to Cape Town, I was supposed to accompany her but I'm involved with a number of charities and I'm afraid work called. However, I'm leaving on Saturday to join Rose.

"Ah the coffee, thank you Dora, I'll pour. Now Mr McDonald how can I help you? But firstly do you take your coffee with cream and sugar?"

They settled down with their coffee and a slice of fruit bread. Once again Walter repeated his story only this time he gave a fuller version, there was something about the kindly Annalise Kessall that made him open up to her.

After Walter had finished speaking and she had topped up the coffee Mrs Kessall told him what she knew.

"Mr McDonald, John McDonald came to stay at our home in Pretoria in 1902 a few months before the end of the war. My husband had recruited him as a civil engineer to work on a number of infrastructure projects in the Witwatersrand. Apparently John's mother was Dutch so the Afrikaans language was not a major problem. His father was Scottish and I think he was partly brought up in Edinburgh so he spoke English with a Scottish accent. John was fresh from university, a clever boy and my husband took a shine to him, hence the reason he came to stay with us. The twins were about eleven at the time and he seemed to bridge the gap between the adults and the children, he taught Paul how to play chess and he would help them with maths homework or play cards of an evening. Yes, John was a popular addition to the household.

"He stayed with us for around six weeks, and then one night the house was broken into and John was kidnapped. There was a note left on his bed, 'The traitor will fight for his own side'. Nothing was stolen or damaged, apart from the kitchen window.

"Our maid found the note in the morning when she was taking in the morning tea, she immediately told my husband. Then we found the broken glass in the back door vestibule and realised that was how the person or persons had entered the house.

"My husband, asked the maid to clean up the broken glass and arrange for our odd job man to replace the glass pane as quickly as possible. We checked John's bedroom, some of his clothes were still in the wardrobe and personal belongings like a hair brush and cufflinks were still in his room. To be honest I can't remember exactly what we found.

"I helped pack everything into a suitcase and my husband put it into the loft, in the hope that one day John would return. We decided that it would be best for everyone if we pretended nothing had happened and said as little as possible. We didn't know if our family would be targeted or the business would be at risk, the best course of action seemed to be to keep our heads below the parapet.

"Obviously Paul and Annabelle did not tell you about John's disappearance as they did not, and still to this day, do not know what happened. However, I felt you have the right to know the fate of your father. Although I'm truly sorry to have created another cul de sac for you.

"Mr McDonald if you had written to me rather than visiting I would still have told you as much as I know. Unfortunately we never heard any more from John, the matter was closed in the Kessall home. We could only presume John had ended up embroiled in the fighting."

Walter finished his coffee but he felt absolutely flat, it looked like he would never find his father because in all likelihood his father was dead. He thanked Mrs Kessall for her kindness and honesty and returned to his hotel.

The remainder of the journey to Cape Town took several weeks, partly due to trying to dovetailing transport and partly because Walter wanted to spend some time coming to terms with what had happened to his father. In one sense he was relieved to know that John had not purposely jilted Vicky and that by all accounts his father had been a good, decent, well educated, man. However, that did not assuage the knowledge that he would not see his father in this world.

Eventually the train rolled into Cape Town, where his long journey had started. Once again Walter had booked accommodation in the Mount Nelson and his spirits lifted when he saw that Ralph had been sent to collect him.

After settling into his room he wrote to Charles and Ishbel but he did not give them the result of his investigations as he wanted to tell them face to face. He invited all the family to the Mount Nelson for Sunday lunch, which he intended to be his farewell, as by that time he hoped to have made his arrangements to return home to Melbourne.

On his travels Walter had been keen to buy Alexander, Isabel and Elize gifts but he did not wish to have to carry large boxes around with him. Elize's gift was a gold bangle with her name, Elize Mhairi, inscribed in copperplate writing, which he intended to give her at the farewell lunch.

Sunday dawned a beautiful morning and Walter took a walk through the hotel gardens before his guests arrived. In a sudden moment of clarity Walter realised he had left Melbourne a youth and he was returning as a man.

Gathered around the lunch table everyone in the party was anxious to hear the outcome of Walter's investigations. There was great disappointment when Walter relayed Mrs Kessell Snr's tale, everything pointed to the likelihood that John McDonald had died towards the end of the Boer war.

As always the food at the Mount Nelson was delicious and Walter tried to keep up everyone's spirits. He had now come to terms with the fact that he was going to return to Melbourne without succeeding in his quest.

When Walter presented Elize with her gift, she was delighted at being given such a beautiful gold bracelet, which everyone admired. Quite the little star of the show.

Ishbel steered the conversation away from Walter's impending return to Australia and they talked of Robert and Anna's forthcoming wedding, Sam and Maria and the family in Melbourne and the places in the Union of South Africa which Walter had visited.

They said their final farewells in the grounds of the Mount Nelson. Walter was sad to say goodbye, he had immediately warmed to the Stewart and Hofmyer clan and could fully understand why Sam,

Maria, Robert and Ishbel had been drawn to each other during their voyage to the Southern Hemisphere.

Everyone said their goodbyes but as they walked away Elize ran back and threw her arms around Walter saying, "Thank you so much for my grown up bracelet, I'll always treasure it! And please remember and thank Auntie Maria for Sylvia. Tell her I love her!" Tears in her eyes she ran off to join her family.

The next few days were busy for Walter, eventually he decided to sail back to Sydney and get a train from there back home to Melbourne.

Now that he had made his decision Walter was anxious to get home and immerse himself into his business. He wrote to Sam and Maria outlining his travel arrangements, he also penned letters to Dr Chalmers and Matthew Gregg who had recently been on his mind. The African chapter was now firmly closed.

CHAPTER 17
Letters and Repercussions

One evening Sam returned from work and found a pile of mail in the box, firstly he opened the top letter with the ever welcome Scottish postmark.

Coatbridge

Dear Wee Brother and Maria

We do so love your letters and descriptions of life in Australia. All your letters to ma and pa are passed around the family.

Our Emily is coming on a treat as I am sure is your Alexander and Isabel, I have enclosed a recent photograph of her, together with one taken of her entire class at school. Sam, remember when we went to the school held in the Gartsherrie Institute and Jennie and Margaret Mathieson were our teachers, we loved them so much.

It's hard to believe that through the suffragette movement Jennie and ma are now such great friends. Still no sign of the equal franchise here - Liz writes articles and booklets, she even lobbies politicians, I believe quite a number actually support the cause. All with the help of our Mary who is her stalwart, her sight isn't great now.

My Tom continues to worry about work, since the war the tonnage has dropped significantly at the works. Isn't it dreadful that a war which brought so much misery was the source of full employment and a bit of prosperity for a time here in Lanarkshire.

Tom's sister Catherine, my friend and bridesmaid married recently. Her first fiancé was killed in the war, you would remember him from Gartsherrie Primary days Sam, big Alan Watson. Poor Catherine was distraught and I worried that she would never find love like so many lasses left bereft after the war. Well, she was promoted from the Co-operative offices in Coatbridge to supervisor of the typing pool in Morrison Street, Glasgow. It's the headquarters of the Co-op in Scotland and quite a place, absolutely magnificent building. Anyway, while working in Glasgow she met a very nice gentleman who had been widowed, the wedding was held at Gartsherrie Parish Church, or as we always called it, The Hill Kirk, in Church Street. Wee Emily was the bridesmaid and Tom gave her away, sad that her mum and dad were not with us to enjoy the happy day.

Dad Coats passed away two years ago. As you know after his death Catherine and mum Coats came to stay with us in Drumpellier. Sadly Tom's mother died from a stroke a few months past. Catherine was going to postpone the wedding but we encouraged her to go ahead and I think it was the right thing to do.

Do you know what our ma said? Honestly, she is a one, 'Agnes, you make sure Catherine gets married without delay she is no getting any younger and if she wants a bairn she better get a move on'. The gospel according to Mistress Johnstone, ever practical is our ma.

Catherine is now living in quite a posh red sandstone flat in the west end of Glasgow, the ones with oriel windows and high ceilings with ornate coving. We visited for tea one Sunday, it was quite a journey but we had a really lovely time.

Catherine has a husband and beautiful home of her own now. I'm really happy for her but we all miss her so much. Letters are not the same as a blether over a cup of tea and a home made scone.

I have also enclosed a wee drawing for Alexander and Isabel from Emily. While we are all glad that you are making such a success of life in Australia we miss our family. You know what Coatbridge districts are like, everyone supports their family, friends and neighbours, they might have wee fall oots but when it's needed support (and a wee cuppa) are always on hand.

We have yet another election in October, after a no confidence vote for Ramsay MacDonald, that will be the third election in two years.

You will probably have heard there is a big empire exhibition on at Wembley Park in London this year. Last time Liz and Mary were in the capital they visited the exhibition. Mary was most impressed, she brought back some presents for Emily, including souvenir *Pears* soaps from the *Pears Palace of Beauty* and a postcard of *Bubbles*. When they go to *London* they always bring back lots of presents for us, particularly *Emily*, they spoil her no end. *Ma* and pa also receive little niceties which ma always shares with the *Law* family. *Incidentally, Uncle Rab* is still a right auld grump.

Must go now as *I*'ve got to collect *Emily* from school and then make the dinner. *Honestly Maria I* don't know how you manage to work full time and look after the house and family.

Much love

Agnes, your <u>big</u> sister, (even if *I*'m only five foot nothing)

* * *

Next to be opened was an expensive looking cream envelope in an unknown hand. It was addressed to Mr and Mrs Samuel Johnstone with an Edinburgh postmark. Sam carefully opened it and found inside a letter to him and Maria, together with a sealed envelope addressed to Walter. The letter addressed to them read.

Edinburgh

Dear Mr and Mrs Johnstone

Via my bank in the Union of South Africa I received a letter from Walter McDonald who I understand was your ward for some years.

Please be kind enough to ensure that he receives the enclosed letter. At the time of his writing to me I understand he was in Johannesburg. However, I have no means of knowing where he is at the present time.

Your assistance in this matter would be greatly appreciated.

Yours sincerely

John McDonald

* * *

Sam was amazed, stunned, excited and couldn't wait for Maria and the children to arrive home so that he could share the news with them.

Next came a routine electricity bill and finally another letter addressed to Walter, the sender's name was Matthew Gregg, the boy in the Perriman case. After much thought Sam decided to open the letter.

Sydney, New South Wales

Dear Walter

I don't know your present whereabouts so I have written to you care of Mr and Mrs Johnstone at your Northcote address.

You will probably know by now, Mr Perriman, I can't think of him as father, has been charged with the murder of my grandfather. The publicity has brought many other things out of the woodwork, mainly embezzlement. However, it turns out he also ran away with the life savings of several women after promising marriage to them, he really is a despicable man.

My mother has been taken into a sanitarium, she just can't deal with his actions. I think the final straw was the way he had robbed the other women, she realised he would have robbed her and run off if it hadn't been for my grandfather's fortune. Mother thought he loved her but he never did, he certainly never loved me or Laurel.

The trial is due to start January next year. Remember you said if you could ever help me you would, well I'd like to take you up on your offer, well not exactly you. I was wondering if you would ask Mr and Mrs Johnstone if Laurel could stay with them during the trial. I will be called as a witness so obviously I need to be in Sydney. Laurel and I are presently staying at the home of a Mr and Mrs Smallman, a director in grandfather's business.

The Smallmans have been very kind to me and my sister, as has my trustee, a Mr Cuthbertson, who was grandfather's solicitor and friend. However, I'd like to get Laurel away from Sydney altogether, you can imagine what the N.S.W. newspaper headlines will be like during the trial. It was bad enough when he was first arrested.

If she could attend school or have a private tutor in Melbourne so much the better, money isn't a problem, I'll be able to pay Mr and Mrs Johnstone. I ask for their help because you always spoke of them with such warmth and they sound decent people. Since the shipboard experience Laurel has become very introverted, she badly needs kindly company.

I hope all is going well for you Walter in your quest to find your missing father. I am the exact opposite, I just want to see the back of mine.

Don't worry about me, Mr Smallman and his wife have been

very supportive, he was a great friend of my grandfather. I have told him how you started working in your grandmother's business when you were just fourteen years old and how it's stood you in great stead. I previously enjoyed school but now I'm never going to be anonymous at any school in Sydney and I don't relish the idea of having a tutor. What better than to emulate you and start work in the business as soon as ever I can.

With my very best wishes
Matthew

* * *

Sam had just finished reading the letter from Matthew when Maria and the children arrived.

After welcoming his family home Sam excitedly said, "Maria, we have quite a mail today, you will never believe the contents of our posy, just sit quietly and read them all, I'll away and start the dinner."

While Sam was cooking, Alexander and Isabel set the table. The meal was easy to cook, thanks to Mrs Rogers preparation. Maria came into the kitchen, saying.

"Sam, I can scarcely believe the content of the letters, I don't know whether I'm relieved, shocked or overawed. What a responsibility for us, taking on Laurel. And, Walter's father making contact, what a mail. And, a letter from your sister Agnes to take us right back to Coatbridge and keep our feet firmly on the ground.

"After the children go to bed we will have to sit down quietly and decide what to do next."

The family ate dinner but the adults thoughts were not on their food, they couldn't wait to get the evening routine finished and sit down and talk.

Story time seemed to take forever, but at last the children were settled. Maria made a pot of tea and they settled down in the sitting room with the letters.

"Sam, let's start with the easy one," said Maria. "Of course we'll welcome Laurel! I'll write to Matthew, apologise for opening the letter addressed to Walter and let him know we'd be delighted to have Laurel stay with us. Do you agree?"

"Of course I do sweetheart! Sounds like that wee lass needs some ordinary family life, mind you I think the newspapers in Melbourne will also carry reports of the trial. We must just do our best to protect her.

"Now to the big decision, do you think we should open the letter from John McDonald to Walter? It could contain the answer to Walter's quest."

Maria replied, "It's so difficult to know what's the right thing to do. Can I make a suggestion? Before deciding what to do why don't we send an urgent telegram to Ishbel, she might know Walter's present whereabouts. I'm pretty sure that when he decides to return to Cape Town he'll make contact with her and Charles. If we manage to get in touch with him we can ask him if he wants us to open the letter. Sam, will I go ahead and send a telegram from the Post Office tomorrow?"

"Of course, that's got to be our first move," agreed Sam. "Now while we're about it, why don't you get your writing pad out and send a letter to Matthew?"

Northcote

Dear Matthew

We just wanted you to know immediately that we have received your letter addressed to Walter. As you know Walter is travelling and we are unsure where he is at present.

Matthew, under the circumstances we took the liberty of opening your letter. Naturally we would be delighted to have Laurel come to stay with us for as long as necessary. We were thinking it might be a good idea for you both to come in December and spend Christmas and Hogmanay with us, that would settle Laurel into our home and you could return to Sydney early in January.

For a young man you must be going through a terrible time at present but rest assured bad times do not last forever, the wheel of life will turn and bring you better days.

Just let us know when you will be arriving and we will meet you at the railway station in Melbourne.

Can I suggest you only tell the people that you really must of your destination. Even then, ask them to be very discrete, we don't want Laurel to be accosted by journalists looking for a story.

We look forward to welcoming you and your sister to our home and be assured we will do all that we can to help her through these troubled days.

With our very best wishes

Sam and Maria (Johnstone)

* * *

The letter was posted the following morning at the post office in Bourke Street and a telegraph sent to Ishbel in Cape Town.

Urgent we contact Walter STOP Good news STOP
Do you know his whereabouts STOP Sam and Maria STOP

The following day there was a telephone call at H.Q. for Maria. Alice called from the stockroom, "Maria, there is an urgent telephone call from Mrs Rogers at your house." Maria rushed to the telephone.

"Mrs Johnstone, it's Ella Rogers here, I wouldn't normally telephone you at the office but the boy from the postal service has arrived with a telegram so it must be urgent. What should I do?"

Maria, knowing it must be from Ishbel asked, "Mrs Rogers please open the telegraph and read it to me. I expect it has come from my friend in Africa."

There was a thump as the handset was put down and then a crackling noise. Maria could barely contain herself. At last Mrs Rogers came back on the line, "Here goes Mrs Johnstone..."

Received yours STOP Walter has reserved berth to return Australia STOP
He is at Mount Nelson STOP I have left a message for him to contact you urgently
STOP Ishbel STOP

Maria's voice was shaking as she responded, "Thank you so much for letting me know. If another telegraph arrives please telephone me immediately Mrs Rogers. Thank you ever so much, bye for now."

Maria scarcely slept that night. The following day at H.Q. was tense, every time the shop door opened or the telephone rang Maria's heart was in her mouth. At lunchtime when she sat down to have sandwiches and a cup of tea with Alice, Mrs Wilson, Faye and Isabel, she could hardly eat such were the butterflies in her tummy. Maria would have loved to share the story but it was not her secret to share.

Somehow Maria managed to keep working through the afternoon, just as she was giving up hope a lad wearing a blue uniform and a jaunty cap came into the shop, he cried, "Telegraph for Johnstone!"

Maria took the telegram with trembling hands and said to the boy. "Can you wait a moment please I may have a reply. The telegram read;

Passage booked home STOP Staying Mount Nelson STOP I've written, think
father killed Boer War STOP I'll await your response STOP Walter STOP

Maria got a form from the boy and quickly wrote;

Received letter from John McDonald in Edinburgh Scotland STOP Response to your bank letter STOP Can I open letter addressed to you STOP Maria STOP

The telegraph boy calculated a charge of two shillings and sixpence for sending the reply. Maria gave him three shillings saying, "Sixpence for yourself lad if you send this reply urgently."

The boy who considered twopence an excellent tip said, "Certainly mam! I'll take your reply straight back to the office." And he was gone.

When Sam returned from work he was desperate for the return of his family to find out the next instalment. At last they arrived, Maria threw her arms around her husband as she entered the hallway of 'The Brig'. "Oh Sam, we have made contact. Walter is at the Mount Nelson and I've sent a telegraph asking if we can open the letter."

For Maria the evening seemed never ending, as did the train journey into Melbourne and the morning working on the accounts. At last, just before lunch the telegraph boy made a welcome return. Maria almost snatched the buff envelope from his hands.

Thank you STOP Open envelope STOP I will not sail to Australia until I hear from you STOP Walter

Once again Maria gave the lad a good tip however she was extremely annoyed with herself for not thinking to bring the letter from John McDonald with her to H.Q. as this would have enabled her to send an immediate reply to Walter. At last the working day ended and Maria travelled home to Northcote with the children.

As they entered the hall they could smell stewed sausage and Sam was just mashing the potatoes. Maria rushed into the kitchen and showed Sam the telegraph. "I can't wait any longer Sam. Put the dinner on at a peep to keep warm. We can read the letter then write a reply to Walter and telephone it through to the telegraph office."

Maria instructed Alexander and Isabel to change into their play clothes and then set the dinner table, something in the tone of her voice told the children not to argue but to do exactly as they were told.

Sam and Maria went into the sitting room and sat down on the sofa, they gingerly opened the letter addressed to Walter. Sam carefully read it aloud.

30 Cadogan Crescent
Edinburgh, Scotland

Dear Walter
As you can imagine your letter, forwarded by my bank in the Union of South Africa, has come like a bolt from the blue. Yes, I loved your mother with all my heart, you were certainly right

about that.

I have sent this letter c/o your guardians in Northcote, also a copy to your business address. Hopefully, one or the other will eventually reach you, because of the time lapse I have not sent anything to the Carlton Hotel in Jo'burg.

Firstly, I will try and give you a brief synopsis about what happened at the turn of the century.

Vicky and I desperately wanted to marry, sadly two things stood in the way, firstly I am not Jewish and while they were not particularly religious the Harris family had no wish for their beloved only child to marry a goy. Secondly, I had recently left university and had not yet made my mark on the world. The Harris family were very well to do, they wanted a husband for Vicky who was wealthy and successful.

Vicky and I decided that the quickest way for me to get my career on the move and make some serious money was to go to the Boer Republic in southern Africa where they were crying out for Civil Engineers and my Scottish/Dutch background would be an asset.

The following part of my life is fairly complicated but in brief I got caught up in the Boer War that ended in May 1902. I was wounded, luckily for me I was found alive but badly injured on the velt by a Boer officer who took me to his farm where his wife and three daughters nursed me back to health. After I was sufficiently recovered Meneer Van Wyk arranged to exchange me for an Afrikaans prisoner, the army then sent me back to Great Britain.

As soon as I arrived in England and was demobbed I tried to make contact with Vicky, I discovered her father had died and Vicky and her mother had simply disappeared. I tried everything I could to trace them but to no avail. Eventually I decided to return to Africa and try and make contact with the Van Wyk family. Again a long story but only the youngest daughter Sybella had survived the war. We eventually married and set up home in Bloemfontein. Tragically my wife Sybella and our two children all died from the Spanish flu in 1915.

As you an imagine I was completely distraught, first I lost Vicky and then my dear African family.

I'd had enough of life in Africa, I returned to England, eventually moved to Scotland and settled in Edinburgh, it's a

*beautiful city and I have established a successful engineering
practice.*

*I will be honest with you Walter, while my business life is
busy and interesting privately I am very lonely and often think of
'what might have been'.*

*If you have a mind to hear more of my story please contact me,
I would be honoured to eventually meet with you and talk further
about the paths our lives have taken.*

With my very best wishes
John

* * *

Maria started to cry and when the tears started she couldn't stop
them. Sam put his arms around her, "There, there, my darling girl,
don't take on so, it's wonderful news!"

Between her sobs Maria said, "I know it's wonderful and I'm so
happy for Walter and John sounds such a nice person. Oh Sam, it's
been so tense since the letters arrived I just feel so incredibly relieved.
I'm sorry but the floodgates have just opened."

Hearing their mother cry, Alexander and Isabel came running into
the sitting room saying, "What's wrong Mummy, why are you crying?"
Maria and Sam had to try and explain that they had received some very
good news and Mummy was crying because she was relieved and happy.

Sam took charge, "Right littlies, come into the kitchen and we'll
finish getting the meal ready while your mummy washes her face. A
delicious dinner cooked by Mrs Rogers will soon stop her crying.
Besides we have rice pudding with fruit for afters." A cheer went up
from Alexander and Isabel.

After dinner Maria wrote another telegram.

*John McDonald sounds very decent STOP 30 Cadogan Crescent, Edinburgh,
Scotland STOP Suggest change ticket, go to Scotland STOP Maria STOP*

Walter read the telegram over and over again. Desperately wanting
to know the whole story but for now he had to settle for knowing that
his father was alive and living in Scotland.

After many months in Africa, and having reconciled himself to
returning home with the mystery only partly resolved, Walter's life was
now taking another sharp turn away from Australia and Harris Finishings.

The news called for another visit to reception at the Mount
Nelson, where he gave instructions for his revised travel arrangements

and posted letters to Ishbel, Sam and Maria, Matthew and Dr
Chalmers, giving Maria and Mathew in Australia Dr Chalmers' address
in Bournemouth as a contact point.

Later that afternoon Walter received a reply from Ishbel.

Rondebosch

Dear Walter

What an amazing turn of events.

*Please come for supper this evening, it will only be Charles and
Elize, very homely. After our lovely lunch in the Mount Nelson
we thought we had said our farewells and your quest was over. Now
it looks like you have an opportunity to see your dream come true.*

*We feel so privileged to have been included in your search and
somehow it brings us closer to Sam and Maria.*

Your friend

Ishbel

* * *

Walter had just finished reading the letter when there was a knock
on his door. It was the duty concierge who confirmed his new travel
arrangements. "Mr McDonald we have changed your booking, the
passage to Sydney is cancelled and I have managed to get you a first
class cabin on the SS Caledonia to Southampton, it's sailing the day
after tomorrow. I trust that gives you enough time to complete your
business in Cape Town?" Walter assured him that the arrangement was
perfect and asked for a driver to take him to Rondebosch that evening.

Once again Walter arrived at the Hofmyer home and as always he
received a warm welcome.

Walter presented Charles with a bottle of Vin de Constance, that
very special Cape wine from Groote Constantia. For Ishbel there was a
beautiful bouquet of roses arranged by the Mount Nelson florist. He
also asked the florist to make up a little posy for Elize. Sophie was not
forgotten, she was given a box of imported Belgium chocolates, in a
round box tied with a big pink bow.

Over a superb glass of wine they discussed the telegrams that had
been winging back and forth from Melbourne. "To think," exclaimed
Ishbel, "you could have saved yourself all that time and money by
asking the Cape Town branch of the Dutch Bank to send a letter to
their client John W McDonald. Mind you, what an adventure and the
chance to see a bit of Africa you would have missed out on if you had

sent the letter from Cape Town, perhaps it was all meant to be."

Sophie came out to the stoop. "Dinner is ready, very simple tonight, grilled kingklip with sauté potatoes, mind you kingklip is definitely the king of fish. However, pudding is a real treat, Ishbel and I made a trifle this afternoon, using cherries marinated in Cape brandy. Elize, I've made a little chocolate cup for you, so it's treats all round."

The food was delicious and the conversation fun and entertaining. They talked of Robert and Anna's forthcoming marriage and the wedding date which was set for two months time. The marriage was going to be conducted by Rev. Dr. Hausman in Cape Town and Ishbel was delighted that they had found a perfect house in Constantia.

The reason they were not in Rondebosch to greet Walter was that they were visiting Anna's parents up in Paarl. Elize piped up, "I'm going to be a bridesmaid at my Uncle Robert's wedding, Mummy and Sophie are making me a beautiful dress, it's cream with a sash of Stewart tartan and I'm going to have cream flowers in my hair. Auntie Anna has a nephew who is going to wear a sailor suit, I'm glad I'm not a boy, imagine having to wear a sailor suit. I've no idea what Auntie Anna's dress will look like, it's all a BIG BIG secret."

After dinner Sophie joined them in the sitting room for coffee and her home made koeksisters. While Ishbel and Charles were upstairs saying goodnight to Elize, Walter questioned Sophie, "Well Sophie have you got a glamorous outfit made for the Cape Town wedding of the year?"

Sophie replied, "Indeed no Mr Walter! Not glamorous, discrete! I'll sit in the back of the church and watch Mr Robert's wedding to Miss Anna but I won't attend as a guest. Can you imagine the shock if I sat with the Hofmyer family, the Badenhorst family would be absolutely horrified at the very idea of the coloured hired help attending a family wedding. Mr Walter, my position here is unique, partly because I nursed Ishbel through the Spanish flu and helped at the birth of Elize and partly because Ishbel is a very special person and she is my friend, There are no other servants that I know of who call their employer by her Christian name. Mr Charles and Ishbel feel I should attend Mr Robert's wedding to Miss Anna but I have made it very clear to them all that it's not appropriate. I'll wish the young couple luck in my own way."

Walter took his leave shortly after Ishbel and Charles returned, as he had a lot to arrange prior to boarding the ship heading for Southampton and the next part of his adventure in Scotland.

The following day Walter tied up all the loose ends, including sending a wedding present to the Hofmyer home for Robert and Anna and a warm letter thanking Charles and Ishbel for all their hospitality. He also sent a separate letter to Sophie;

Dear Sophie

I just wanted to thank you for all your wonderful cooking which I've enjoyed on my visits to Rondebosch, you are indeed a very talented chef.

However, the main reason I am writing is that I was very touched by our conversation regarding your not attending Robert's wedding, I found it so sad, you are such an integral part of the Hofmyer family and I know they would want you to be a part of Robert and Anna's special day.

Having spent some time in Africa I can also understand why you have decided not to attend as a guest.

In Australian society class is much more fluid and having met Ishbel and Robert I can see why they became friends with Sam and Maria, they are from the same mould, you would also have been Maria's friend had they settled in Cape Town instead of in Australia.

When I am travelling back to Australia I very much hope I can spend some time in beautiful Cape Town and meet up with you again.

With my best wishes

Walter

PS thank you for the box of your delicious home made koeksisters, I'll enjoy.

* * *

Walter boarded the SS Caledonia and was shown by a steward to his cabin. There were very few new passengers boarding in Cape Town for Southampton and routines and friendships were already set. This rather suited Walter as he badly wanted some quiet thinking time.

The journey back mirrored the journey of Sam and Maria, the SS Caledonia made scheduled stops at St Helena, Cape Verde and Madeira. On each occasion Walter took the opportunity to explore the port.

However, when the ship berthed in Madeira he felt it was a given that he must visit Reid's Hotel. After enjoying tea and sandwiches he paid a visit to the hotel reception where he bought two postcards showing Reid's Hotel in all it's splendour and sent them to Rondebosch and Northcote. A delightful memory to his friends of their journey to the Southern Hemisphere on the SS Trojan.

CHAPTER 18
Arrival in Bournemouth

On arriving in Southampton in the middle of a British winter Walter decided to book into a hotel for the night and then go shopping for a winter coat and hat before travelling to Bournemouth and then up to Scotland.

Also on the shopping list was some bottles of fine malt. While aboard the Caledonia Walter had decided to visit Dr Chalmers, aka Poirot, before travelling north to Edinburgh.

When Edward Chalmers first arrived in Bournemouth to the delight of his two sisters, Clarissa and Grace, he moved back into the family home. Chilton House had been the dwelling place for three generations of the Chalmers family, a house which had not changed a great deal since Queen Victoria was on the throne.

Five years at medical school, time spent working in London and over thirty years in Australia had made Dr Chalmers forget about the fussy oppressive furnishings in Chilton House. Heavy mahogany furniture, dado rails, elaborate swagged curtains, display cabinets full of bits and bobs, ornate plasterwork, absolutely everything in the house seemed to require frills and furbelows.

No doubt there were some beautiful pieces of furniture, art and porcelain in the family home but they were well hidden in the general clutter that was the Victorian style beloved by his sisters Clarissa and Grace.

The good doctor found his spinster sisters as fussy as the decor in their home. Within days he knew he had to escape before he drowned in a sea of ornamentation.

He quickly found a furnished flat to rent near Westbourne Village, not too far in distance from his sisters home but a million miles in style. The ground floor apartment was decorated in pale colours with light oak furniture in a nod to the Arts and Crafts movement, the

French doors led out onto a beautifully landscaped garden area. All in all it was a perfect retreat. Edward Chalmers had found a place to call home until his furniture arrived from Australia and he could purchase a suitable property.

Walter arrived at the contact address Dr Chalmers had given him in Cape Town, the ornate bell-pull was answered by an elderly maid dressed in black with a frilly white apron and mop cap. When Walter enquired after Dr Chalmers, the maid directed him to the morning room and scurried off to find Miss Clarissa.

Walter sat waiting for his friend. After a few minutes the maid returned and handed him a piece of paper. "I'm sorry sir but Dr Chalmers no longer resides here, this is his new address." Walter thanked the woman and promptly left the house which somehow felt stifling and not just because it was rather overheated.

As they drank their morning coffee Clarissa and Grace had yet another conversation about the cheek of their brother Edward, returning home from the colonies after years away and then complaining about their beautiful home. A conversation which would be repeated in many forms countless times over the years.

Walter took a taxi to Dr Chalmers new abode. The doctor answered his ring. On hearing Walter's voice on the intercom he said, "Come in, come in young man." Walter entered through the front door and the doctor greeted him, "I can't tell you how glad I am to see you my boy. Although I never expected you to arrive in Bournemouth quite so quickly. And bearing bottles of Scotland's finest product, a red letter day indeed!

"Sadly it's a bit too early in the day for a Scotch, come into the kitchen and I'll get a pot of coffee on the go."

While the doctor made the coffee Walter buttered some tasty scones that had been baked earlier in the morning by the doctor's housekeeper, Mrs Edgar.

"Walter my lad, I can't tell you what a relief it was to escape from Clarissa and Grace. They mean well but honestly the house is so old fashioned, full of clutter and dark colours. I've spent too many years in the light of Australia, Chilton House is too oppressive, I just couldn't stand it, so I found this delightful little berth. When my furniture arrives I will look to buy a place but meantime I'm quite well suited. The lounge has a lovely dining area looking out onto the gardens, cheerful kitchen and two bedrooms, what more do I need.

"Let's take the coffee into the lounge and you can update me on all that's been happening at your end." Walter followed Dr Chalmers into the lounge.

"Well Doctor I was all set to return to Australia, passage booked, when there was a flurry of telegrams between Maria, Ishbel and me. My father had apparently responded to a letter I sent to John Walter McDonald via the Dutch bank in Pretoria on the remote chance he was still a client. Obviously I don't know the full contents of his letter but Maria has sent me his contact address in Edinburgh.

"Before heading north I wanted to take stock for a few days and have a chinwag with you. I hope you don't mind me turning up out of the blue."

"Not at all, delighted to see you, why don't you drop anchor here, I've got a spare room and there is an excellent inn nearby where we can get a hearty dinner. I've got a wonderful housekeeper who comes in every weekday morning, she also takes away the laundry and returns it nicely washed and ironed. It's all the help I really need, I was extremely lucky to find her."

The two friends enjoyed their coffee while Walter updated the doctor on the latter part of his adventure, his earlier letters having already arrived in Bournemouth.

"So you see sir, I've no idea what is contained in the letter from John McDonald, only his address in Edinburgh, the only clue I have is that Maria said in her telegram, 'He sounds very decent.' "

"Very decent is certainly something positive to go on but I think you are quite right, spend some time here, it's only a few days until Christmas, you're welcome to stay over the festive season. New Year is the big holiday in Scotland, why don't you wait until early January before going north? Then if your father has another family you won't be turning up in the middle of their celebrations."

"I hadn't thought that one through. You're quite right sir, much better I turn up after the holidays."

Walter and Dr Chalmers had no idea that the Johnstone family in Northcote were also entertaining guests for the Christmas holidays.

CHAPTER 19

Christmas in Melbourne

From October to early December was a very busy time for Harris Finishings, all the suppliers were intent on getting completed goods into the shops in time for Christmas. It was all hands on deck at H.Q., Maria was also immensely grateful for Sam's foresight in encouraging her to bring Alice into the business proper, they made a good team.

Thankfully work started to wind down by mid December which was a great relief for Maria as Matthew and Laurel were due to arrive on the 20th of the month, Matthew was scheduled to return to Sydney on the 5th of January as his father's trial was due to start on Tuesday the 8th.

Since receiving the letter from Matthew asking if Laurel could stay with them, Sam and Maria had carried out a regular correspondence with Matthew. He informed them that Mr Smallman had insisted he have a tutor but since his fourteenth birthday he had allowed him to spend a little time working in the family business. Matthew seemed to be rising to the challenge of emulating Walter who was quite obviously his hero. Mr Smallman had also employed a governess for Laurel but worryingly she seemed to have lost interest in doing anything apart from reading Susan Coolidge or Louisa May Alcott novels.

Mrs Rogers had been kept busy organising the house in Northcote for the arrival of Matthew and Laurel, Matthew would have to share with Alexander and Laurel with Isabel.

As the school summer holidays for Alexander started on 18th December, Maria decided for the sake of her sanity she would close the office on the 20th when her young guests arrived and not reopen until the 27th of December when she would fit in a few days catch up. Work proper would recommence on 2nd January. All the H.Q. staff were delighted at this long paid Christmas holiday and Maria felt it was a small reward for all their hard work.

Before the holidays Maria also had an appointment with Mr Green.

Prior to starting on the business part of the meeting he enquired, "Well Mrs Johnstone where is that young rogue Walter at the moment while you are here in Melbourne working hard running the business?"

Maria explained that Walter had made contact with his father and was at present on his way to Great Britain she was aware of Mr Green's expression of disapproval. However, it became even more incredulous when she told him that it was Walter, together with a Doctor Chalmers who had been instrumental in the Daniel Perriman arrest.

"What next, Mrs Johnstone, what next? In many ways I'm very proud of Walter, with your guidance he has matured and worked hard but I wonder where all this delving into his father's past will lead. I know you might see me as disapproving but I would hate to see the boy hurt. As far as the Perriman affair is concerned, well I'm speechless."

Maria thought she might as well tell Mr Green about Matthew and Laurel and get it over with in one meeting. On hearing her latest news the solicitor was certainly not speechless.

"So not only are you running Harris Finishings you are now taking in waifs and strays sent by Walter. Mrs Johnstone you and your husband are exceptionally kind people but there is a limit. When young Walter returns I'm going to have a serious word with him about the debt he owes you.

"Now, to business, I am most impressed, as is Mr Goldberg, on how you have taken the business forward. In the future an annual financial report will suffice. However, please use me as a sounding board if you think I can be useful to you at any time.

"Over the holidays I wonder if you would like to think about the following suggestion. Instead of all the driving about why don't you employ some ladies to work from H.Q. on a full time basis, you certainly have the turnover to warrant two full time employees. Please give my idea some consideration and we'll talk about it again in the new year. I have a feeling next year will herald exciting times for Harris Finishings."

They talked about some other routine business matters before Maria left to return to H.Q. With everything else that was happening in Maria's world her head was in a spin at Mr Green's suggestion, however she decided to put it on hold until she had an opportunity to sit quietly and discuss the idea with Sam.

The opportunity to sit quietly and discuss anything about business did not come soon. The final few days at H.Q. were non stop, particularly since Alexander and Isabel were already high as kites on Christmas.

Mrs Wilson prepared a special celebration lunch for everyone to enjoy on the 20th before the holidays started. Afterwards Maria took the children to the railway station to meet Matthew and Laurel who were arriving by train from Sydney. Thankfully back in Northcote Mrs Rogers was holding the fort and all was prepared for Matthew and Laurel's arrival.

Maria found Matthew to be a handsome lad, tall for his age, articulate and well mannered. Laurel was petit and pretty but with almost a vacant stare, it was as though the world was revolving, people were interacting but she was simply an observing bystander.

Sam was home from work in time to greet his family and the two children from Sydney. Everyone enjoyed a homely supper after which Maria took the girls to their bedroom. Maria helped Laurel unpack and then she got the girls settled for the night, in keeping with the usual Johnstone routine Maria read to them. The book she chose was 'The Treasure Seekers' by E Nesbit. It was probably a little too old for Isabel and slightly too young for Laurel but Maria felt it bridged the gap, besides she enjoyed the book. She almost chose 'The Railway Children', her particular favourite, but decided a story where the children's father was in prison was not at all appropriate.

Meantime Sam and Matthew were drinking hot chocolate in the sitting room. Sounding older than his years Matthew addressed Sam.

"Mr Johnstone, I really appreciate you and Mrs Johnstone allowing Laurel to live with you until the court case is over, and for inviting me to stay during the holidays. Walter often talked about you and how you were like a father to him and how Maria made sure he worked hard but she also made delicious cakes, arranged fun days out and knitted him winter jumpers.

"You know I'm so worried about Laurel. She was always quite a reserved girl but now she hardly speaks at all. I'm also concerned about my mother, as I told you in my letters she is now in a sanatorium. Mother has been called to be a witness at the trial, I'm not sure if she is capable. Like Laurel she barely speaks and when she does it's about ordinary matters, silly things like what brand of tea she prefers, never about 'him' or what happened to my grandfather."

"Matthew, I'm no medical man but it sounds to me that both your mother and Laurel are just blocking out the pain of the past months. And, I also think you are dealing with the situation like an adult not a teenager. A lad of your age should be playing sport, climbing trees with his pals, fishing, getting up to mischief. In a nutshell you should not have the cares of the world on your shoulders.

"How on earth does anyone deal with their father murdering their grandfather and numerous other crimes to boot? I can't possibly imagine your pain.

"I was brought up in a wee works house in an area of Coatbridge called Gartsherrie. We had very little money and I suppose you could say we lived in great poverty. However, my father worked hard and my mother was a wonderful manager, we always had nourishing food on the table and clean clothes. I never felt poor because my parents loved each other and they loved me and my two sisters. You and Laurel might have had material comforts but money doesn't necessarily make for a happy home.

"Rest assured Maria and I will do our best to make Laurel feel safe and valued during her time with us. There's no need to worry about your wee sister! Sadly for a young lad you have plenty of other worries.

"Now Matthew I think you should go to bed. Alexander will be asleep, I doubt he will waken when you go into his room. Settle yourself down for the night and we can talk more over the next few days."

Matthew went to his room and got ready for bed. As he lay down to sleep the tears came, slowly at first then rolling down in a cascade of relief. He put the sheet into his mouth and sobbed, sobbed for himself, sobbed for Laurel and sobbed for his mother.

Before the children arrived Sam and Maria had decided that the best thing to do was to keep Matthew and Laurel busy with ordinary life. The next few days were spent shopping, cooking, gardening, playing with Alexander and Isabel, just living a normal family life.

Christmas came and went, there were presents and a roast chicken dinner followed by an exciting new pudding that was all the rage, called a Pavlova. It consisted of meringue topped with whipped cream and fresh fruit. Maria thought it was very exotic, how she would have loved to make it for her family in Glenboig and for the Johnstone clan in Gartsherrie.

Christmas afternoon was spent in the garden and in the evening everyone played various games like tiddlywinks and snap.

Sam, who was a good observer, thought, 'if anybody is going to bring Laurel out of herself it's not going to be me or Maria, it's wee Isabel'. From the time Laurel arrived at 'The Brig' Isabel seemed to decide that Laurel was going to be her special friend, poor Laurel, when a three year old decides you are her special friend, special friend you have to be.

On Hogmanay while the womenfolk were in the kitchen, Sam, Matthew and Alexander decided to go for a walk, a walk which led to

Alexander's favourite place, the swing park. While Alexander was enjoying himself Matthew said to Sam, "Have you noticed Laurel is much better already and it's all down to little Isabel. In just over a week your daughter has done what the doctors, the Smallman family and I could not achieve. Laurel is smiling again! I even saw her laughing when Isabel was singing, 'Yes We Have No Bananas'.

"Sam, I can leave on the 5th in the knowledge that Laurel will be safe with you, Maria and Doctor Isabel."

Reluctantly Sam felt he had some information he had to tell Matthew.

"Matthew lad, since you arrived we've not had any newspapers in the house. The other day at work I read a copy of The Herald and I'm sorry to say there was a long article about the upcoming trial. Sadly I think the press are going to have a feeding frenzy, Laurel is going to be most vulnerable to seeing newspapers when she is travelling up to town every day with Maria and the children. Lad I can't promise we can hide every mention of the trial, we will do our best but I think there will be a lot of publicity.

"On another matter Maria had a meeting with our lawyer, Mr Green, recently and he is going to arrange for a tutor to come to H.Q every working day. As well as it being important that she continues her education we think keeping Laurel busy with the minimum of thinking time is probably the best way to go."

"Sam I don't expect you to hide everything. She knows when the trial starts and that it's bound to be reported in the papers. It's more I don't want her accosted by the press. Hopefully Laurel can be anonymous here in Melbourne."

"Can I make a suggestion?" asked Sam. "I don't think we should use her given name outside the house. Laurel is a very unusual name, it wouldn't take much for a smart person to put two and two together."

As they headed for home both Sam and Matthew were thinking about the name, Laurel Gregg.

Everyone stayed up to see in the bells and welcome in the new year. As always Maria with help from Mrs Wilson had baked a good selection of traditional Scottish cakes, shortbread, sultana cake, cherry cake and black bun for Hogmanay and the steak pie and trifle was prepared for the New Year's Day dinner.

On the other side of the world Jessie Johnstone and Annie Riley were carrying out the same rituals in Scotland. Ishbel, Robert and all their family in Cape Town, with the help of Sophie, were also celebrating a Scottish Hogmanay. Scots in every outpost on the planet we're cleaning, cooking and preparing to welcome first foots over the door, carrying a piece of coal, to bring in the new year.

All too soon it was the 5th of January and Matthew accompanied Maria and the children into Melbourne from where he caught a train to Sydney, clutching a pack of sandwiches prepared by Maria. His nightmare was just beginning.

Back in Northcote just as he was leaving to go to work the postman handed Sam a letter. Seeing his mother's handwriting he put it into his pocket to read during his break.

Gartsherrie

My dearest Sam, Maria, Alexander and Isabel

I have sent this letter early in the hope it reaches you before Christmas and the New Year.

As usual Christmas will be a working day here but I'll make a nice steak pie for our dinner and perhaps a pudding. I still have some of the apples that your Uncle Rab gave me wrapped in newspaper in a box in the coal shed, maybe I'll make an apple sponge.

Your Uncle Rab looks after the garden of two spinster ladies, they are very good to him and let him have any extra vegetables and fruit. Agnes always passes some down to me which is a great help. That's one thing about the Gartsherrie folks, if they have they share.

We send our love and hope you all have a wonderful Christmas and I know Maria keeps a good Scottish table for Hogmanay and New Year. As always we will see the auld year oot and the new year in with the Laws up in the Herriot Row. They like your paw to go outside just before midnight so that he can be their first foot after the bells ring, a tall dark and handsome man, that's who you want first over the threshold, preferably carrying a piece of coal and some shortbread or cake. My Alex is certainly handsome, perhaps that is why I fell in love with him all those years ago.

No doubt Agnes will make her special tattie cakes that everyone loves so much, to her secret recipe. She won't even tell me how she makes them.

Mary Law still doesn't keep in great health but she never complains. Mary makes a bit of extra money helping Mrs Millar laying folks out and at births or miscarriages, I don't know what the folks hereabouts would do without Mrs Millar to help with their passing and everyday medical needs. The doctor is very expensive and to be honest I think Mrs Millar does a much better job.

Since the war ended and with it full employment there is always an underlying worry about work, will the men still have a job. So far our Agnes's man Tom, your pa and Uncle Rab are still in employment so is their eldest, James Law, he is an apprentice joiner. Young Robert Law, (the red haired one) finishes school this year, hopefully he will get a job in the Gartsherrie works.

We are very proud of you all, our family in Australia.

With our love and very best wishes for 1924.

All the Johnstone family

* * *

Sam walked out of the canteen and had a short walk before starting back to work. He always had a lump in his throat when mail arrived from Scotland but his mother's homely letter coming just after the holiday reinforced the miles that separated him from his kith and kin.

CHAPTER 20
Christmas in Bournemouth

Dr Chalmers thoroughly enjoyed spending Christmas and New Year in the company of Walter. His sisters called a truce and invited them to the family home for Christmas lunch, together with some other friends and family, it would have seemed churlish to refuse.

In the event Walter and his mentor had a very pleasant day and enjoyed a good old fashioned Christmas celebration. The meal started with the finest Scottish smoked salmon followed by roast turkey, cranberry sauce, bread sauce, roast potatoes, vegetables and chipolata sausages. Walter had never seen a Christmas meal like it, this was celebration food designed for the cold British climate.

After lunch the younger members of the party decided to go out for a walk before starting on the Christmas pudding and Stilton while the older folks snoozed or played bridge.

The young people decided to walk along the promenade and then down to the end of the pier. The wind was blowing and it was bracing to say the least but it was a wonderful way to walk off the hearty meal.

Walter got into conversation with a young man about his own age who was studying to be a veterinary surgeon at Edinburgh university and was spending the holidays with his parents in Bournemouth before returning to Edinburgh for his final year. As soon as the young man, whose name was Andrew Brown, said the magic word, 'Edinburgh' Walter bombarded him with questions about the city.

"Well it's either called Auld Reekie or The Athens of the North, take your pick. Beautiful architecture from the Middle Ages through to Georgian, a castle on an extinct volcano. Yes, it's a really interesting historical city. And, it has great pubs! Students always like great pubs, Deacon Brodie's, Sheep's Heid Inn, Bennets Bar the Oxford Bar in Young Street and if you go down to the port of Leith, well the choice is endless. Incidentally Walter, I don't think you should mention to my parents my encyclopaedic knowledge of Edinburgh watering holes, or for that matter enlighten my Uncle Edward. They think my allowance all goes on textbooks and extra tutorials. As the Scots say, 'aye, that will be right'.

"However, if you are seriously thinking of travelling to Edinburgh pack plenty of warm clothes. It's cold beyond cold! Bournemouth on a winter day is tropical compared to Edinburgh in June. The icy winds blow down the North Sea from the artic circle. Saying that, I've loved my time in Edinburgh studying at the Dick Vet, that is what everyone calls our college. It's also great to be able to take a train up north or down into the borders and go hill walking at the weekends.

"I used to play cricket at school but I've really got into rugby since moving to Edinburgh. When I qualify, hopefully next year, I intend to settle in the borders, where I can combine work and rugby beautifully. That is if I can find a job."

Andrew then asked Walter what type of work he was involved with. Walter felt Harris Finishings suddenly seemed very tame when set against attending university in Scotland.

The group returned to Chilton House where they enjoyed plum pudding which was served on a generous blue willow pattern platter. The lights were turned off then the pudding was doused in warm brandy and set alight, illuminating the dining room in a blue glow. A choice of brandy butter or custard was served with the pudding, traditional and absolutely delicious. The meal was rounded off with Stilton cheese, walnuts, figs and port.

Walter and Dr Chalmers were full to bursting when they returned to his flat. They mutually agreed that on Boxing Day they would eat very lightly indeed.

Over the next few days Walter tried to prepare himself for meeting his father and spent time rehearsing in his head any number of scenarios. Thankfully he also had the kindly doctor to use as a sounding board.

Up north in Edinburgh John McDonald was playing a similar game of mental scenarios, however on Boxing Day he received a very welcome letter from Melbourne.

Northcote

Dear Mr McDonald

I am writing to confirm that your letter did arrive in Northcote and a few days later the copy sent to the Melbourne office also arrived. There was a flurry of telegrams sent between Australia and Africa, the upshot being Walter has sailed to Great Britain and

intends to visit you.
Walter has not seen your letter, he simply has your address in
Edinburgh.
I thought I should let you know Walter is on his way to
Scotland.
With our best wishes that the meeting goes well. Walter is a
good lad and my wife and I are extremely fond of him.
Kindest regards
Sam Johnstone

* * *

John McDonald was overjoyed when he received Sam's letter. Overjoyed but also very apprehensive.

On New Year's Day Dr Chalmers and Walter were once again invited to Chilton House for lunch. No traditional Scottish steak pie with mashed potatoes was served in this part of the country. After the hors d'oeuvres the star of the menu was rare roast beef served with Yorkshire pudding, horseradish sauce and all the trimmings. This was followed by a choice from a selection of sweets, jellies, queen of puddings or lemon tart.

This was a more intimate family meal than Christmas dinner had been. Apart from Walter, the doctor and his two spinster sisters Clarissa and Grace the only other people in attendance was their other sister Rosalind, her husband George Brown and their son Andrew.

After the meal Andrew and Walter decided to go out for a walk while the senior members of the company settled down to a game of bridge.

Andrew joked, "Well Walter I hope you didn't say too much about my knowledge of pubs to Uncle Edward, although I bet the old fellow visited his fair share of them when he was a lad in medical school.

"My mother, Rosalind, is his favourite sister and he has always been very kind to me and my older brother, giving us both a decent allowance while at university. My older brother is a doctor in London now but I thought about the damage I could reek on the human race if I joined the medical profession so I decided I was safer ministering to cows and sheep.

"Bit of an exaggeration, I actually enjoy working with animals and I always tease my brother with, 'you only had to learn one set of anatomy, I have had to learn the anatomy of everything from a cat to a cow'.

"Tell me Walter, why are you so interested in Edinburgh, are you thinking of enrolling at the university?"

The whole story was far too complex for Walter to confide to a young man he hardly knew. At the same time he didn't want to tell a downright lie, he simply said, "My father now lives in Edinburgh. After the holidays I am going up to visit him. I've never been to Scotland before so it's all very new and exciting."

"Great!" replied Andrew. "I'll give you a note of my address. I share a flat with three chaps on the south side of the city near the Dick Vet in Summerhall. When you need a bit of young company contact me and I'll introduce you to some of the best beer and fish and chips in the city.

"Truth to tell, I'll be glad to get back to the flat. It's great when I first arrive home for the holidays, my father gives me a vacation allowance and my mother makes sure our cook puts all my favourite meals on the table and I don't need to worry about washing my clothes or money for the gas meter, pure bliss.

"I also work as a student at a veterinary practice in Christchurch when I'm in Bournemouth, it's mainly small animal work. You can just imagine the clientele; old dears bringing Tiddles in to have her nails cut or stitching up Jack Russell terriers who have been in fights. I tell you Walter that's where the money is to be made, small animals. You can wrap the owners around your fingers."

Walter and Andrew enjoyed their long walk, by the time they returned to Chilton House the oldies had all given up on bridge, the three sisters were chatting over a cup of tea and the two men were snoozing.

The following morning over breakfast Dr Chalmers spoke quite seriously to Walter.

"Walter I have thoroughly enjoyed your company, also that of my reprobate nephew over the holiday period. Does Andrew seriously think I don't know what he gets up to in Edinburgh, I was a student at one time too you know, although my student days now seem a million years away.

"Anyway to important matters. I think it's now time for you to start planning your journey north. Perhaps you could leave all your light clothing in a case here and return to collect it and say goodbye to me before you travel back to Australia. I would love to hear all about your meeting with John McDonald first hand.

"You will have to arrange rail tickets, accommodation and suitable clothing. However, before you do anything else I think you should write to your father, tell him you are presently in Bournemouth and ask him to give you a date when it would be suitable to meet with him, you don't just want to knock on his door out of the blue."

Walter agreed with the good doctor and while Mrs Edgar was busy in the kitchen he took himself off to his bedroom and got out his writing pad.

Bournemouth

The hardest bit of this letter is knowing how to address you, Mr McDonald, John, Father, I really don't know.

After searching Africa for you to no avail I was fully intending to return to Melbourne and take up the reins of my life, my passage was in fact booked, when I received a telegram informing me you were alive and living in Edinburgh. I immediately changed my passage to Southampton and arrived in England shortly before Christmas.

On the ship from Australia to the Union of South Africa I formed a friendship with a retired doctor who lives in Bournemouth. I decided to visit Dr Chalmers before heading north to Edinburgh.

As I have not seen the letter you sent to Melbourne I am unaware of your present circumstances and do not wish to cause you or your family any embarrassment.

Can you please write to me c /o Dr E Chalmers in Bournemouth and give me a time and place where we could meet.

I await your reply prior to booking rail travel and hotel accommodation.

Kindest regards
Walter

* * *

For the next few days Walter was on tenterhooks awaiting a reply, at last the awaited letter arrived. Mrs Edgar brought the mail through to the dining table where Dr Chalmers and Walter were eating breakfast.

"That's the morning mail doctor, and there is also a letter here for you, Mr McDonald."

Walter accepted the letter and was surprised to find his hand was shaking.

As soon as Mrs Edgar left the room Walter said, "It's from him sir, my father John McDonald. After all this time searching, following clues, travelling from Australia to Africa and then on to England. So many hopes then having them dashed, I'm almost frightened to open his letter."

Dr Chalmers stood up saying, "I'll leave you my boy, give you some privacy to digest what he says."

Walter responded, "No please stay sir. I'll read it aloud, you and my Johnstone family have been in this with me from the beginning you deserve to hear the outcome first hand."

Edinburgh

My dear Walter

I cannot begin to tell you the joy I felt when I read your letter forwarded by my bank. It was such a surprise and stirred in me so many emotions. This was followed by a letter from your guardian Mr Johnstone, he advised me you were travelling to Scotland. Since then I have eagerly awaited every post hoping to hear from you.

I am not sure how much of my story you have uncovered. In brief, when I returned to England and couldn't trace Vicky, I eventually returned to the the Union of South Africa and married the daughter of an Afrikaans family who saved my life. We were happy and had two beautiful daughters. Sadly my wife and girls died in the Spanish flu epidemic.

Since returning to Edinburgh, the city of my birth, I have opened another civil engineering practice. However, I have purposely kept the practice small and easily manageable.

Walter, I live alone I would be honoured to welcome you to my home at any time.

Looking forward to hearing from you.

Your father, John

* * *

When Walter had finished reading both men had a tear in their eye.

Dr Chalmers spoke first, "Walter, the letter confirms the telegram you received from Mrs Johnstone, he does sound a decent man.

"Well my boy, much as I will miss your company you had better start planning your journey."

Walter went off to the train station and booked his journey to Edinburgh, via London. By the time he returned to the flat, Dr Chalmers had telephoned his sister Rosalind for information on Edinburgh hotels. "I've just spoken to Rosalind, apparently the North British in Princes Street is your best bet. It's near Waverley Station and central for most things in the city. Rosalind gave me their telephone number, you can give them a call after lunch. Mrs Edgar has made us a fine bacon and egg tart, and set the table with various condiments and brown bread. I think she has decided to keep us off the rich food for a while."

After lunch Walter had all his arrangements in place and was ready to write to his father.

Bournemouth

Dear John

Thank you for your letter inviting me to Edinburgh.

I have now made my travel arrangements and will be staying in the North British Station Hotel, which I understand is very central.

I wonder if you would like to have dinner with me at the hotel on 10th January. If that date is convenient I will book a table in the restaurant for eight o'clock and perhaps we could meet in the lounge bar around seven.

Please leave a message at the hotel.

I greatly look forward to meeting with you.

My best wishes

Walter

* * *

Taking Andrew's advice Walter went out shopping that afternoon and bought some warm clothes for protection against the Scottish climate. On his return he was greeted by an excited doctor.

"Walter my lad, mail for you from Australia. Perhaps this letter will throw more light on the telegrams.

Northcote

My dear Walter

Phew, what a time it's been with telegrams flying to and from Africa. Thankfully it looks as though your quest has succeeded.

I have enclosed a typed copy of John McDonald's letter, I did not send the original just in case it goes missing and I think it's something precious you will want to keep. It's safely in Northcote and awaits your return.

The business is going very well. The first months were difficult, not so much difficult as really busy - I was exhausted. Alice working full time in the business has been wonderful, Sam's brilliant idea. We really work well together, Mrs Wilson now has a new girl to help her called Faye, she is a real hit with Isabel. I am not pushing any major expansion until you return, I think this is probably a time to consolidate, saying that, Harris Finishings is in a good place.

Mrs Rogers is a treasure at 'The Brig' and her father continues to come in and help with the garden and other odd jobs this takes the strain away from Sam. While the Australian climate has been good for him he has to take care of himself, his lungs were so badly damaged during the war.

We have the two Perriman children coming to stay with us for Christmas and the New Year, Matthew will return to Sydney for the trial in early January and Laurel will stay with us until after it is all over.

Details of the trial have already hit the newspapers and it looks set to garner a lot of publicity. I wouldn't be surprised if the British papers don't cover the case, I really hope not as I'm sure you and Dr Chalmers won't want your names in the press.

As you can imagine Mr Green was not best pleased at you changing your berth to travel to Great Britain. However, he knows your inheritance is being looked after, it is the least we can do, it was working with you that gave Sam and I the opportunity to buy 'The Brig'.

Can I ask you to do something for us while you are in Scotland? Please make contact with Sam's parents and my brother Dan. We would be so very grateful if you would give them a lovely gift and a decent amount of money. I will repay you when you return to Melbourne.

The bairns have enclosed a little letter, they really miss you.

Go well on your travels and our very best wishes that you and Mr McDonald have a successful meeting.

Sending our love

Maria, Sam, Alexander and Isabel

* * *

'The Brig'

Dear Walter

We both miss you _lots and lots_. Thank you for all the presents you have sent. Isabel loved the locket best and I love the gun, all my pals think it's the best best best present anyone has ever had.

Come home _soon_

Love

Alexander and Isabel

* * *

Walter read the three letters aloud. The one from John McDonald explained a lot, and Walter was glad it had arrived before he travelled north.

Dr Chalmers too was pleased to hear the contents of the letter as it bode well for a good reunion between father and son.

It was with mixed feelings Edward Chalmers bid farewell to Walter. On the one hand he was delighted the boy had been successful in his mission, and John McDonald did sound like a decent man. However, over the past weeks he had thoroughly enjoyed the company of Walter and that of his young nephew, Andrew.

As he waved Walter off, Doctor Edward Chalmers decided that he was not quite ready for retirement just yet, he needed another little interest in his life.

CHAPTER 21
The Search is Over

The journey from Bournemouth to Scotland seemed never ending for Walter. After travelling many thousands of miles by sea, rail and road he was at last on the final leg of his mission to find his father.

Walter alighted the train in Scotland's capital city on a cold dreich January night. A porter helped him transport his luggage the short distance to number 1 Princes Street and the comfort of the North British Hotel. As he left the station the word that came into Walter's head was 'grey'. He seemed to be surrounded by the dark drab colour and he was very glad he had followed Andrew and the doctor's advice and purchased galoshes, warm sweaters and shirts, a fedora hat and a tweed jacket in readiness for the Scottish winter. He already had a long winter coat which he had bought when he first landed in Southampton.

The following morning when Walter drew his bedroom curtains it was still raining. He had a wonderful view of the castle and the medieval part of the city from his room, but the view was shrouded in mist and rain.

If the outside of the hotel seemed bleak and uninviting the dining room was not, the breakfast offerings all sounded delicious, however Walter decided to opt for the traditional Scottish, which included a potato scone. The name evoked happy memories of Maria and her delicious 'tattie scones'.

Walter had intended to explore the city before meeting his father. However, the hotel proved more inviting and he settled down in the lounge with a copy of The Scotsman.

The rain did not halt all day, and the weather forecast in the newspaper predicted rain for the next three days. Edinburgh did not seem a very cheerful city and Walter couldn't imagine why Andrew Brown was so enraptured with 'Auld Reekie'.

That evening as he was changing for dinner Walter's heart was pounding, the letters from his father and conversations with the Kessell family seemed to indicate that John McDonald was a good man but what if they didn't get along, so many 'what ifs' eventually Walter had to give himself a shake and hear Sam's voice in his head saying, 'what's for you won't go past you' and 'just take life as it comes my lad.' At six fifty five Walter headed downstairs to the lounge to await the arrival of his father. He did not have long to wait before John McDonald arrived.

Walter saw a tall, distinguished, middle aged man with greying hair and a slight limp enter the lounge, he knew immediately, beyond any doubt he was looking at his father, John Walter McDonald.

John saw Walter rise and like Walter he too instantly felt the connection. The two men walked towards each other. "Walter? John?" They shook hands and sat down, thankfully just at that moment a waiter approached and asked them what they would like to drink. Well tutored by Dr Chalmers, Walter ordered a Glenfiddich, no ice, with water on the side. John ordered the same.

While they were waiting for their order Walter went into his pocket and produced the photograph of Vicky he had found in Mrs Harris's bedroom with the inscription to her mother. John in turn produced the same photograph inscribed, 'To my darling John, love Vicky'. The connection was made.

"I honestly don't know where we start Walter. I know you are my son, I just need to look at you and acknowledge you as such. I'm also frightened that you think I did not do the right thing by your mother. When I left for Africa I had no idea Vicky was pregnant, in fact I doubt if she knew.

"I'll tell you later about all my adventures in Africa but for now I just want you to know how much I loved your mother.

"When I eventually returned to England from Africa after the war my biggest fear was that Vicky would have married someone else. Nothing could have prepared me for her complete disappearance.

"Vicky and her parents lived in Windsor. When I arrived at their house I found that her father had died and the house had been sold. The neighbours and some friends told me Lavinia or, as I knew her May, couldn't settle in the house after her husband died and had moved with Vicky to London. Further enquiries with friends and at local shops gave me the same story. I contacted Vicky's father's business partner, apparently May had accepted a substantial payment for her inherited share of the firm and had given him the same story, that she was moving to London.

"Unfortunately nobody seemed to have knowledge of a forwarding address or a specific area in London, just London. I remembered that initially May had come from the Highgate area so after exhausting my enquiries in Windsor I headed for London. My first foray was Highgate, I managed to find some far out relations of May's family but they had not heard anything about her in years. Apparently her husband Elisha Harris came from a very well to do family in the clothing manufacturing business and May had married above herself so she wanted to keep her family well in the background.

"The folks in Highgate suggested I try Hendon and Golders Green. I spent months investigating not only in Hendon and Golders Green but in other areas where there was a Jewish population. The Harris family were not particularly religious but nonetheless I thought May might prefer to settle in an area where they weren't the only Jews. I checked Kelly's Directory. I checked marriage registers, synagogues, but every single avenue led to a dead end.

"I couldn't expect my parents to keep financing me so eventually I had no option but to stop searching. Africa beckoned, I sailed to Durban and travelled north in search of the Van Wyk family who had saved my life during the Boer war. Again, a long story which I'll tell you in the fullness of time but the only person left was the youngest Van Wyk daughter, Sybella.

"Sybella had lost her fiancé during the final days of the Boer war at a skirmish near Bloemfontein, and I had lost my Vicky. To be honest we were two lost souls brought together, we married and slowly fell in love. I had a good marriage and together we had two beautiful daughters. Tragedy struck again, my wife and daughters died in the flu epidemic. Honestly Walter, it was like losing Vicky all over again, I was devastated!

"I just couldn't continue to live in Bloemfontein without my family so I came back home to Scotland. My father had passed away while I was in Africa, I lived with my mother for a time until she too passed away. Then I bought a house in Cadogan Crescent and started up a small business in Edinburgh. I'm financially independent but I couldn't just sit around doing nothing. However, I've purposely kept the business small, I've a staff of four and we just take on small interesting projects."

At this moment a waiter approached them, "Mr McDonald, your eight o'clock table is ready, would you care to follow me through to the dining room?"

They were both glad of the interruption and followed the waiter through to the dining room. As they perused the menu John said, "Game birds are still in season, I would imagine the grouse would be good here and you can't go wrong with an Aberdeen Angus steak. What do you fancy to eat Walter?"

"I'm going to have the steak pie and think of Maria, if it wasn't for her and Sam my life would be very different. Firstly, I wouldn't have a business. Mr Green, my trustee would have packed me off to boarding school and liquidated all my assets. Secondly, Maria took on the running of Harris Finishings single handed while I went off searching for you. We could never have sat here having dinner if it wasn't for the kindness and generosity of the Johnstone family."

"In that case I'll join you, steak pie for two, and how about we share a nice bottle of claret to celebrate finding each other?"

They enjoyed their food and talked about many different things, there seemed to be almost too many things to say and discuss, there were no awkward silences, it seemed as though they had always known each other.

They finished off the evening with another whisky in the lounge. It was almost midnight when John said, "I really must ask reception to call me a taxi, it's high time I returned home. Walter, this has been such a wonderful evening, never in my wildest dreams did I imagine I had a son!

"Will you visit Cadogan Crescent tomorrow? There are so many more things I want to discuss with you but it's impossible to condense over twenty years into a few hours."

Walter promised he would visit his father the following day and they took their leave.

Back in his bedroom Walter couldn't get to sleep his brain was whirring, eventually he got out of bed and wrote a long letter to Sam and Maria, he also wrote to Dr Chalmers and Ishbel and Charles in Cape Town. He then settled down to sleep, the sleep of the exhausted. At last his quest was over.

CHAPTER 22
Melbourne and Sydney

After waving Matthew off on the train to Sydney, life settled into a new routine at H.Q.

Maria and Sam had been concerned that if anybody heard the name Laurel they might connect it with the Perriman case and contact the press. Maria decided to take Laurel aside and make an important suggestion to her. However she was concerned that Laurel would find their idea difficult to accept. Surprisingly it turned out to be easy.

"Laurel, I've been thinking you have a very unusual name perhaps when we are outside it might be better to call you Laura. Also, I think I should introduce you to your new tutor as Laura and I'll also have a word with Alice, Mrs Wilson and Faye and ask them to call you Laura until after the trial. If James and young Harry have heard the name Laurel they will think they have misheard. Alexander will be fine, the only difficult one will be Isabel, she is rather young to understand the idea of using a different name for you. I'll try and get her to see it as a game. We would hate a reporter to find you, it's much better if you are kept anonymous. It's bad enough that Matthew has to be a witness at the trial without you getting dragged into all the sordid publicity."

"Maria, I don't mind in the least being called Laura, anything that distances me from the trial is absolutely fine. I'm so sorry for Matthew having to give evidence but at least when the trial is over we will be free. If Walter and Dr Chalmers hadn't rescued us Matthew thinks we would be dead by now and so do I." Maria was horrified at Laurel's opinion of her father but relieved that she had so easily accepted her idea of using the name Laura meantime.

Laurel's tutor was a young man called Alfred Williams, he had just finished his degree at Melbourne University and a few months tutoring a young pupil was an easy way to make some money while he was looking for a permanent post. Every morning he arrived about ten o'clock spending the morning working with Laura on English, mathematics, history and geography. At one o'clock they had a break for lunch, which they enjoyed with the rest of the workers at H.Q. in Mrs Wilson's kitchen. In the afternoon Alfred tutored Laura on art, he always included Isabel in this lesson. Isabel looked forward to her art class and felt very grown up sitting beside her special friend Laura.

All the H.Q. women were very supportive of Laura and they wrapped a blanket of kindness around her as the trial progressed.

After Alfred had left for the day Alice often gave her simple tasks on the finishing side to keep her busy or Mrs Wilson would get the girls to help peel the vegetables for soup or prepare fruit for jam, any wee task that would keep them occupied. Sometimes Faye took them out shopping, which Isabel particularly loved, going out with her two favourite people in the whole wide world.

Mrs Wilson had now taken over a lot of the cooking for 'The Brig' and kept the Johnstone family supplied with home baking, jams, marmalade and all the other niceties that Maria had made for the family when she had more time.

The Johnstone family simply included Laura in their family life and after a short time adjusting to the new routine it seemed as though she had always been a part of the family. What particularly pleased Sam and Maria was that Laurel or Laura was now slowly coming out of her shell, Isabel's adoration being one of the main factors. For the first time in her life Laurel felt she was important, well if not actually important, special in somebody's world. Laurel had become a big sister figure and revelled in the feeling.

One morning before going to work Sam opened a letter from Matthew.

Sydney

Dear Sam and Maria

Firstly my thanks to both of you and everyone at H.Q. for what you have done for Laurel, or should I now say Laura. From her letters she seems to like her tutor, if not the mathematics lessons. It is such a relief not to have to worry about her.

Isabel seems to give her a lot of comfort and joy. Also Alexander, she really enjoys spending the last hours of the day in H.Q. Rather more than her lessons!

My mother has suffered a complete nervous breakdown. The doctors have signed papers advising that she should not be called as a witness, another relief.

It looks as though I will have to give my testimony on Monday or Tuesday of next week. I am not too worried about giving evidence, my fear is of actually seeing him again. I have nightmares about looking into his face. I'm also frightened that he will be acquitted, I know there is a stack of evidence against him but I have grown up watching him manipulate people. He could talk his way out of anything while seeming to be the injured party.

I hope all is going well with Walter's search for his father. I've written to him at Dr Chalmers address in Bournemouth.

I cannot go into the Gregg office meantime as the press are camped outside. Mr Smallman and the staff have been wonderful keeping everything going, strangely we have had an upsurge of business.

I'll write to you after I've given my testimony.

Thank you again.

Matthew

* * *

One evening after the children were all settled for the night and Sam and Maria had cooried doon to enjoy a hot chocolate together before bedtime Maria said, "Sam, do you remember just before the holidays I mentioned that Mr Green had suggested we take on two full time ladies to work at H.Q. which would cut out a lot of the driving time? Well, I've been thinking about it and the more I think the more it seems an excellent idea. We could convert Walter's old bedroom on the ground floor into a workroom and the materials currently stored there can be moved upstairs. Sam, what do you think?"

"I think it makes a lot of sense, particularly if you can recruit two ladies from your existing homeworkers, or perhaps four working part time. They all know your standards and wouldn't be phased by being expected to do many different types of work. Can I also make another suggestion, put Alice in charge of the workroom. You should spend your time managing the whole operation."

"I hadn't thought about promoting Alice," said Maria. "But you're absolutely right, it's a brilliant idea! I'll set up an office upstairs where I can do all the paperwork and planning. I'll speak to Alice on Monday but I don't think it's a good idea to carry out the actual move until Laurel or should I say Laura moves back home to Sydney. Although we can start on the preparation, I think I'll make an appointment with Mr

Green after I've got the details clear in my head."

"Yes my sweet, I agree one hundred percent. Start planning by all means, but don't think about starting on major changes while we are still responsible for young Laurel, one thing at a time."

In Sydney, Matthew was preparing to give evidence at his father's trial. Thankfully the court had accepted a written affidavit from his mother because of her health and Laurel because of her age. Affidavits had also been submitted from Walter, Dr Chalmers and the Captain of the Stella.

At last the morning arrived, Matthew could scarcely eat any breakfast. Mrs Smallman tried to encourage him to at least have some toast, but it seemed to turn into cardboard in his mouth.

As they were leaving the house Mr Smallman, who would also have to give evidence regarding the embezzlement, put his hand on Matthew's shoulder saying, "Your grandfather would be so proud of you Matthew, just answer the questions honestly and look at the judge, don't look in the direction of that man."

The case was going to be heard in the new high court building in Taylor Street, adjacent to the magnificent Greek revival courts in Darlinghurst Hill. As the car approached the building and Mr Smallman and Matthew alighted, he just wanted to run, run as fast and as far as he could from the court. Matthew felt the weight of Mr Smallman's hand on his shoulder and he knew he had no option but to walk inside the imposing building.

It was after the lunch recess before Matthew was eventually called. Taking the advice given to him by Mr Smallman, he took the oath and kept his eyes firmly fixed on the judge. Firstly he was questioned by the prosecution, the questions were much as he expected and he gave truthful answers to everything he was asked. Then came the defence barrister, he did his best to cast doubts on Matthew's evidence. Matthew did not deviate from his story, his evidence was simple and truthful and he had no intention of allowing the barrister to make him say anything otherwise.

Eventually it was all over and he was sitting on a bench outside the courtroom. After a time Mr Cuthbertson, his grandfather's solicitor, joined him. "Well done my lad, you spoke well. It will be finished very soon now. We all owe a huge debt to your friend Walter and the old doctor on the ship for bringing Perriman to justice.

"I hear Laurel is living with Walter McDonald's guardians in Melbourne at present, that was an excellent idea getting her away from this circus.

"After the verdict I want you to ask Mr Smallman to make an appointment to bring you to my office, we need to have a discussion and make plans for the future of you and Laurel.

"I understand your mother is very poorly. That's another crime that can be laid firmly at Daniel Perriman's door. Before she met him your mother was a kindly sensible woman who efficiently managed your family home. Dr Kerr tells me that she is presently in a sanitarium suffering from a nervous breakdown, it's all so tragic."

As he left the building Mr Cuthbertson said, "Remember Matthew, soon as the trial is over I want to see you."

The remainder of the week Matthew stayed indoors at the Smallman's home, the trial continued and the press continued to report the details with great gusto.

The following Monday the judge summed up the case and instructed the jury to carefully consider their verdict.

This was the worst time for Matthew, he couldn't sleep such was his fear that his father would be acquitted.

Thankfully the verdict was unanimous, guilty on all counts. In a hushed court the judge sentenced Daniel Perriman to death by hanging. A sentence which was eventually commuted to life imprisonment.

The newspapers carried detailed reports of the trial and the verdict details. Thankfully Matthew was protected by Mr and Mrs Smallman and Sam and Maria did their best to ensure young Laurel was also surrounded by loving support. Sam wrote to Matthew.

Northcote

Dear Matthew

You must be so relieved the trial is over, although I understand Perriman is appealing the sentence. Whatever happens he will be out of your life and very soon you can start to live again. Your life, and Laurel's have been on hold for many months now, it's time to get back to some sort of normality.

Maria and I were wondering if you would like to come down to Melbourne for a few weeks before you decide what you are going to do next. It might be good to put some space behind the trial before you move on.

Let me know if you think this is a good idea and when we receive your arrival details Maria will meet you at the railway station.

Laurel is obviously relieved that the trial is over but I think she very much wants to push it to the back of her mind. She seems perfectly happy at her lessons (although she moans about maths) and she has fitted in well, both into our family life and the work at H.Q.

Looking forward to hearing from you.

Sam

* * *

Matthew showed the letter to Mr Smallman who agreed that it would be a good idea for him to spend some time in Melbourne. "Yes Matthew, I do indeed think you should take up Mr Johnstone's kind invitation. Then you can bring Laurel back home with you. However, I think you should have your meeting with Mr Cuthbertson before you go to Melbourne. I'll telephone him and arrange an appointment.

A few days later Mr Smallman accompanied Matthew to Mr Cuthbertson's office.

The solicitor made them welcome before getting to the point of the meeting.

"Firstly, I would like to say how relieved I am that Perriman has been convicted and we can all now move forward. Matthew, as you already know you are your grandfather's principal heir. Under normal circumstances your mother would have guided you through your education until your majority. I am sure Mr Smallman here would also have given you a insight into your family business.

"But these are not normal circumstances. I have spoken with the chief medical officer at the sanatorium where your mother is presently a patient. Sadly, he cannot see her being released for some considerable time. The allowance provided to her by your grandfather will more than cover medical fees, meantime we simply have to trust that the doctors will look after her and bring her back to health and strength.

"Matthew I need to know what you think we should do about your family home. Ddo you want to return to live at Glencraig one day? I can arrange to let it out or put it up for sale. There is also the contents, you will have to make decisions regarding your grandfather's possessions.

"As far as your education is concerned, I have investigated a number of excellent boarding schools for you and Laurel. Yet another important decision to be made."

From this point on Matthew couldn't actually understand what Mr Cuthbertson was saying it was just a noise and he could see his future running away from him.

Eventually he interrupted the stream of words, "Mr Cuthbertson, I know you mean well but I'm not ready to be rushed into anything at the moment. Mr and Mrs Johnstone have invited me down to their home in Melbourne where Laurel is staying. I would like to have a few weeks with them to clear my head before I make any decisions."

Thankfully, Mr Smallman who was very fond of Matthew backed him up, saying, "Mr Cuthbertson, I think the boy needs time away from Sydney. I'll arrange a rail ticket and send a telegram to Mr Johnstone with his arrival details. Matthew can go to Melbourne almost immediately."

True to his word Mr Smallman made the arrangements and two days later Matthew and his case arrived at Flinders Railway Station where he was met by Maria, Laurel, Alexander and Isabel. Alexander was delighted to have Matthew back with them, he missed Walter, and he had enjoyed having the older boy spending Christmas with the family at Northcote.

Maria welcomed Matthew and shepherded her flock to catch the Northcote train home.

When they arrived at 'The Brig' dinner was already prepared by Sam. As an after dinner treat Maria had brought home a tin of jam doughnuts courtesy of Mrs Wilson.

After the girls and Alexander had gone to bed, Sam and Maria were able to talk to Matthew about his experiences over the past weeks.

Matthew accepted a cup of hot chocolate from Maria saying, "You have no idea how glad I am to be here in Northcote with you both. Thank you so much for inviting me back to 'The Brig'. It was hell in Sydney, absolute hell! Sorry to use that language but it was, I thought the nightmare would never end and then when the trial finished and he was found guilty my relief didn't last long. Grandfather's solicitor sent for me, he wants to pack me and Laurel off to boarding school.

"Sam, I want to be like Walter and start working in my business rather than going to school. Mr Smallman bought me some time sending me down here to Melbourne but I need to figure out what I'm going to do."

Sam replied, "We have been through this with Walter lad, different circumstances but essentially the same script. Tell me Matthew, how do you get on with Mr and Mrs Smallman?"

"Quite well actually, they are a lot older and not as much fun as you two but they are kind. I guess they are well into their fifties with a grown up family."

"This might be a long shot lad and I might be taking things for granted but why don't you ask Mr Smallman if he will become your guardian and train you in the business. You could also say that you would study with a tutor part time, say two days a week, whatever works for you. Then by the time you are twenty one you really would be well qualified to take over Matthew Gregg & Son.

"If you think you would be happy with my suggestion you could write to Mr Smallman while you are here, sometimes it's easier to set things out on paper."

Matthew looked relieved, "To be honest Sam, I'd rather you and Maria were my guardians but your idea makes a lot of sense. Mr and Mrs Smallman might not want their life disrupted by being guardian to two youngsters but I'll take your advice and write to him over the next few days."

Maria chipped in, "I agree with Sam, it could be a very good solution but before you write I think you need to talk to Laurel. It's only fair that she has her say. You don't know how she feels about living with the Smallmans', perhaps she would rather go to a boarding school with other girls of her own age."

"I hadn't thought of that," said Matthew. "I'll speak to Laurel, she has certainly come out her shell since staying with you."

Maria laughed, "Don't blame me, it's Isabel who is mostly responsible, you also have to thank Alice, Faye and Mrs Wilson, they have all played a part in boosting her confidence."

Over the following days Matthew drafted the letter to Mr Smallman, a letter he considered the most important of his life. When he felt happy with his composition he decided now was the time to ask Laurel for her opinion.

Saturday came and the children were out playing ball in the garden. Maria spotted them and called Alexander and Isabel into the house, thinking this might be a good opportunity for the brother and sister to have a talk.

Matthew used the moment, "Laurel, before I came back down to Melbourne Mr Cuthbertson, you know grandfather's solicitor, called me into his office. He wants us to go to boarding school and for me to decide about what should happen to the house and the contents.

"I've spoken to Sam about the conversation and he suggested that I should ask Mr Smallman to be our guardian and that he allows me to learn the business from the inside. Before I finalise my letter to him I want to know how you feel. Would you rather go to a boarding school which would probably be more fun than spending all your time with

Mrs Smallman and a tutor, what do you want to do?"

Laurel listened to her brother with mounting horror. "Matthew Gregg! I don't want to go to a boarding school! I don't want to live with Mr and Mrs Smallman and I certainly do not want to go back to Sydney! I want to stay here, this is where I belong. For the first time in my life I feel happy. You remember what it was like at home Mummy skirting around him all the time, trying to keep the peace, Grandpa disapproving or being ill, and you and me trying to be invisible.

"Matthew this is a real family and I want to be part of it. Will you ask Sam and Maria if I can stay here and have them as my guardians?"

This was not the answer Matthew expected, and yet, all Laurel said was perfectly true. "Laurel, the Johnstones' have done so much for us already, it's a lot to ask that they virtually adopt you. I can't imagine how we are going to ask them."

Matthew answered her brother with a positivity that he had never seen in her before. "Maria says, we should always be honest and truthful. It would be a lie if I said I wanted to go back to Sydney. I'm going to tell her the truth, I want to stay here. I just hope Maria and Sam will agree. Another thing, you want to learn the Gregg business, but Matthew, I really want to learn about the clothing industry in Harris Finishings."

That evening when Maria was making supper Laurel went into the kitchen. "Isabel, can you please go and play with Alexander for a wee while? I'd like to talk to your mummy." Isabel didn't look entirely happy but she went off to find Alexander.

Laurel took a deep breath and said, "Maria, Matthew has been telling me that Grandpa's solicitor wants us to go to boarding school and Sam suggested that he ask Mr Smallman to become our guardian. You always say, 'tell the truth and shame the devil,' well the truth is I would love to stay here with you. I promise I will behave myself and not be any trouble. Can I stay please?"

Maria was not entirely surprised by this turn in events but nonetheless agreeing to taking another child into their family home on a permanent basis was quite a decision.

"Laurel pet, you are a good girl and we love having you stay with us but becoming your guardians is a big step. I will have to speak to Sam. If he agrees we will then have to make it right with the solicitor in Sydney. Leave it with me and we will talk to you and Matthew tomorrow. Now Miss please slice the tomatoes and finish off making the salad."

Maria waited until they were going to bed before telling Sam about her conversation with Laurel. "What do you think Sam? I doubt it will be that straightforward. After all we have no connection with the family other than the man that got her father arrested for murder was our ward young Walter. Put like that would you allow her to stay with us?"

"Put all the admin aside Maria, would you like Laurel to stay on with us? I have no objection, she is no bother and our wee Isabel dotes on her."

Maria agreed, "I'm very fond of her, besides Isabel would be distraught if Laurel was sent away somewhere she didn't want to be. Tomorrow we will tell Matthew that if Mr Cuthbertson is in agreement Laurel can make her home with us. However, I think we should get Mr Green to act on our behalf rather than us dealing with a solicitor."

Mr Green's reaction was predictable. "So, not only is there no sign of young Walter returning to take up his responsibilities, it looks like you are going to gain even more. This at a time when you are planning changes within the business.

"Mrs Johnstone I know you well enough not to try and dissuade you, however I'm greatly relieved that you have asked me to act on your behalf rather than entering into some informal arrangement. I'll contact Mr Cuthbertson with your suggestion. Has this Mr Smallman agreed to take the boy?"

Maria replied, "Thankfully yes. He sent a telegram in response to Matthew's letter, I'll let you read it.

"I think he is quite warm to the idea, apparently he was a great friend of Matthew's grandfather and both him and his wife are very fond of the lad.

Mr Green read the telegram. "Well that sounds positive. I'll get a letter off to Cuthbertson. I have his details, he has been sending the funds to pay for Laurel's tutor. As soon as he gets back to me I'll advise you."

Before leaving Maria thought she had better keep Mr Green up to date with the goings on in Scotland.

"Before I leave I just thought you might like an update on what is going on in Scotland. Walter appears to be getting on well with his father John McDonald."

Mr Green turned his eyes heavenwards, "And you Mrs Johnstone are becoming a guardian yet again to a young lady he sent you while you are continuing to build his business.

"I have always liked young Walter he is a good lad but he has a reckless streak. If something seems right to him he acts without weighing the repercussions."

"Mr Green, you called Walter a 'good lad' and he is. Sam and I are pleased to be able to help young Laurel, she has been put into our lives for a reason.

"As you know I am now ready to make the staffing changes. I've written to Walter with the details, he's up to date with what's happening in the business. Incidentally, he's helping in his father's engineering business, administration I think. I'm jolly glad as I think he needs to be working."

Mr Green showed Maria out, "As I've always thought you are a remarkable woman, go well my dear."

Thankfully the formalities for the children were completed without incident. Matthew returned to Sydney refreshed from his stay at Northcote. As far as Laurel was concerned, life in Sydney was over.

Matthew settled into life with Mr and Mrs Smallman and his job working at Matthew Gregg & Son. He also had private tuition Tuesday morning and all day Friday, Saturday was cricket and swimming. After church on a Sunday there were family visits and he enjoyed getting to know Mr Smallman's three children and their families.

Matthew was determined that his grandfather would have been proud of him. He worked hard and did his best to shut out memories of the trial and his life at Glencraig. After some thought he instructed Mr Cuthbertson to sell the property. He wrote to Laurel and asked her if there was anything in the house she would like. They agreed on some pieces of furniture and personal items that they wanted kept, these they had put into storage. The majority of the contents of Glencraig were consigned to auction, another chapter closed.

—

CHAPTER 23
Edinburgh

Walter stayed in the North British for several weeks while seeing his father most days. Gradually they became more and more comfortable in each other's company, and they openly shared their stories.

Walter told John about growing up under the care of his grandmother Lavinia Harris and how eventually he found out that he was in fact her grandson. He related the happy years spent as part of the Johnstone family and then at twenty one finding out that he was an extremely wealthy young man.

John in his turn told him how he had been kidnapped in Pretoria and forced into the army and the trauma of being injured. "The only reason I survived was the Van Wyk family found me on the velt and took me into their farm and nursed me back to health. When I was able to travel they returned me to the British lines in exchange for a Boer soldier.

"Near the end of the war, Sybella's father was killed in the same skirmish that took her fiancé."

He told Walter the heartbreaking story of how Boer women and children had been forced into British concentration camps. Sybella's mother and two sisters died from typhoid in one of the camps, Sybella, the only survivor of the family returned home only to find the Van Wyk farm totally destroyed by the British during Lord Kitchener's 'scorched earth policy', the British even killed all the animals. Fortunately her aunt gave her a home and helped her recover from the horrors of the concentration camp.

Walter was horrified at this story as he had no idea that the British had waged such cruelty on the Boer women and children.

Eventually Sybella sold the land where the Van Wyk farm had once stood. This was the money that helped John start his business in Bloemfontein.

Every day there was a new revelation as the picture on the jigsaw of their lives slowly become clear.

As well as building a relationship with his father Walter was aware of his responsibilities to Maria and Sam. He wrote to Dan Riley and Mr and Mrs Johnstone asking if he could meet with them in Coatbridge. Although still awaiting replies he had raided Jenners and purchased gifts, a bottle of malt for each of the men, together with a warm cashmere scarf.

For Dan's wife Clare and Sam's mother and sisters he bought beautiful silk scarves. Knowing how much Sophie had appreciated his gift of confectionary he also bought presentation boxes of chocolates for each of the ladies.

One morning as he was sitting at breakfast the receptionist approached him, "Good morning sir, three letters for you today."

Walter finished his breakfast then took his letters and a cup of coffee into the lounge.

Gartsherrie

Dear Walter

Thank you so much for your kind letter from Edinburgh. Of course we would be delighted to meet you. A Saturday afternoon or a Sunday is best for us, Alex is working all week.

Over the years we have heard so much about you, from the very first day in Northcote when you put Maria right on pricing her work from Mrs Harris.

Sam and Maria both think the world of you and the thought of meeting with you is so exciting.

Please tell us when is good for you, Alex will meet you at Sunnyside Station. We would gladly welcome you into our wee house in Gartsherrie.

With all good wishes
Jessie Johnstone

* * *

Glenboig

Dear Mr McDonald
Thank you for your letter from Edinburgh.
Clare and I would be really pleased to see you. A Sunday would be best as I work all week. You can get a train to the

village and I will meet you at Glenboig station.

I would also love for my mother, two sisters and brother to meet you so they can hear first hand how our Maria is doing in Australia. I'll see what I can arrange once I know what day you are coming.

Looking forward to meeting you.

Dan Riley

* * *

                                                   Edinburgh

Dear Walter

I have just returned to Auld Reekie, this is my final year so sadly no slacking. I'll have to work really hard, this is the nose to the grindstone year. However, it would be great if we could meet up in town and I'll introduce you to one of the fine hostelries in the city.

I'll collect you at the North British on Saturday first at around 7.00pm, if I don't hear otherwise.

Your hard working friend.

Andrew

* * *

Pleased with his mail Walter paid a visit to Waverley Station to check train times. He had decided to visit Coatbridge on two consecutive Sundays as he didn't want his visit to be rushed with either family.

He wrote to Dan with details of the train he intended catching to Glenboig and to Jessie saying he would arrive at Sunnyside station the following Sunday at 12.15pm.

Later that day when they were having lunch John said, "Walter, I was wondering if you would like to move into Cadogan Crescent, I have plenty of empty rooms and after spending months on ships and in hotel rooms I am sure it would be good for you to have a comfortable home to come back to. I don't want to push things and if you prefer to stay at the hotel I'll completely understand."

The offer was not completely unexpected and Walter had thought about what he would do if asked the question.

"John, that's a very generous offer and I would be happy to accept. I'm going out with a friend from Bournemouth on Saturday and I'm visiting Sam's family on Sunday. Perhaps I could move in next week, say Tuesday?"

"Excellent," said John, "that will give my housekeeper time to get everything prepared for your arrival."

Walter thought this was the time to bring up another subject. "John, I'll enjoy spending some time with you in Cadogan Crescent but I also need to start thinking about travelling back to Australia. I can't expect Maria to look after Harris Finishings indefinitely. Maria and Sam have been incredibly supportive but I really do have to return to Australia and take up the reins of my life."

John poured himself a glass of water to give him a moment before asking the question that had been in his mind almost from the first evening he had met his son. "Walter, I wonder would you consider settling in Edinburgh. Perhaps you might start a business called McDonald Finishings.

"I know your grandmother left you very comfortable financially. However, I have consulted with my lawyer and I have now willed you my entire estate, less a few bequests. As well as owning this house I own a number in Fife which I rent out. Walter, you will be an extremely wealthy man one day. I'm telling you this now but I also want you to understand that it's not subject to you staying in Scotland. Whatever you decide to do with your life and wherever you locate you will inherit your due from your father."

Walter was completely taken aback with this revelation. "John, I didn't trace you in the hope of an inheritance, I did it because I wanted to understand why my mother did not have your support when I was born. I could clearly see from your letters that you loved her. I now know the reasons and understand the series of events that led to you missing each other.

"Please don't think I need an inheritance to accept you as my father, I appreciate your kindness but an inheritance isn't conditional on us being father and son."

"I know you aren't out for money Walter, but can you imagine the pleasure it gives me to be able to will my estate to my son, not to a list of charities. Now let's change the subject, the will is a fait accompli.

"Where are you going on Saturday with Dr Chalmers nephew?"

Walter replied, "I have absolutely no idea. We're meeting at the hotel and then a pub crawl by the sounds of it. Although I can't have too much to drink as I'm off on Sunday to see Sam's family in Coatbridge."

Saturday evening saw Walter sitting in the lounge awaiting the arrival of Andrew. Walter had almost given up on him when he arrived, accompanied by two pretty girls.

"Fiona, Janet, this is Walter, he is paying us a visit from the colonies, Australia no less. Walter, Janet is studying European languages and Fiona mathematics. Now I know I promised you a visit to a fine Edinburgh hostelry but the ladies want to go to the flicks. How about we have a small libation here then we could head off to see a film? There's a Harold Lloyd and a Charlie Chaplin which both look good. Or, in this fine Presbyterian city we could go and see The Ten Commandments, directed by Cecil B DeMille."

This was not at all what Walter had imagined his evening would be, however he indicated to a waiter and they placed an order. The girls ordered Dubonnet and lemonade, Andrew ordered a pint of Youngers Pale Ale, Walter decided that as he was drinking with a younger set he should try the beer. "Just give me a half pint of the Youngers, I've not tried your Scottish beer yet."

Andrew opened the conversation, "Janet and I have known each other for years. Her brother John is also training to be a vet and he is in my year at the Dick, we are both cramming like mad.

"Janet and I have been walking out for the past year. The attraction is I'm too lazy to learn another language, when we are qualified and go off on exotic trips she will be able to look after me and order my beer.

"Now Walter, don't be put off by young Fiona studying mathematics, bless her she inherited the gene. Her father is head of the maths department at a posh school and her brother Graham has graduated with a joint maths and physics degree. But outside the library and the lecture theatre she is quite nice, passably normal really."

Everyone laughed, the drinks arrived and the evening began. After a second round of drinks amid hilarious banter they headed out into the cold night and ended up going to see the Harold Lloyd film, Safety Last. The final scenes were quite scary shot on the side of a skyscraper. Fiona grabbed Walter's hand and he continued to hold it until they left the cinema.

Walter invited everyone back to the hotel to have a coffee. Andrew thanked him, "Jolly kind Walter, but I have to get the young ladies back to their residence. Curfew is ten thirty on a Saturday and we don't want another carry on like last week. We had to throw stones at the window of Janet's room and waken her flat mate, then she had to come downstairs and distract the gorgon who rules over the young ladies while Janet slipped inside."

The two couples walked hand in hand to the tram stop. Walter whispered to Fiona, "Do you think I could see you again, perhaps we could have dinner together one evening?"

Fiona smiled, "Thought you'd never ask! Look our tram is coming. Thursday at the North British, seven o' clock. Is that alright with you?"

"Perfect, see you then."

Walter walked back to the hotel on cloud nine. Not only was Fiona extremely pretty but she was good company. It was as though the fun door had opened again in his life after so many months of serious pursuits.

Sunday morning Walter checked he had everything ready to take on his trip. Remembering how thrilled Elize had been with a piece of jewellery he had also bought a small gold locket as a gift for Emily.

The train pulled into Sunnyside railway station promptly at 12.15pm. As he walked out of the station Walter was greeted by a man who looked like an older version of Sam.

"Hello young man, are you Walter McDonald?" Alex extended his hand and Walter shook it warmly, saying, "Mr Johnstone, I'm very pleased to meet you! I've heard so much about you and your wife from Sam and Maria."

"I'm pleased to meet you too lad. Jessie has made a pot of soup and she has some sandwiches and home baking on the go. It's not too long a walk to oor wee hoose in Gartsherrie, everyone is eagerly waiting in the Long Row to meet you. They're fair excited, so they are!"

They walked along Sunnyside Road, past the Gartsherrie Institute and up the Long Row, all places Walter had heard about but never imagined he would ever see.

After about a fifteen minute walk they entered the Johnstone's modest home where Sam's sisters Agnes and Mary were waiting to welcome Walter. Agnes's husband Tom and their daughter Emily were also in the welcoming committee. The entire Johnstone family were awaiting expectantly to hear news of their family in Melbourne.

After taking off his coat Walter distributed the gifts saying he had bought them on Maria's instructions. Everyone was delighted, Emily was especially thrilled to receive a gold locket, Walter was greatly pleased that his last minute purchase had brought so much joy.

Walter had a wonderful day, the people who he had heard so much about suddenly became real, he felt as though he had always known them.

The Johnstone clan revelled in the stories of Australian life and we're pleased to hear that Sam was secure in his job. Their favourite topic, which created much laughter, was Alexander and Isabel, Walter told them many anecdotes and tried to paint the personalities of the children. As he spoke he thought, Alexander is definitely his father's son and Isabel her mother's daughter.

He thoroughly enjoyed the meal Jessie's prepared and he could now appreciate all Sam's tales of his mother's wonderful cooking and hospitality.

The time seemed to pass in an instant but eventually Walter had to leave to catch the train to Glasgow from where he would get a connection to Edinburgh Waverley.

After the farewells, and as he was going out the door, Jessie handed Walter a parcel wrapped in greaseproof paper, saying, "Just a couple of slices of my iced gingerbread. Enjoy it with a wee cup of tea tonight!"

As they walked back to the railway station Walter handed Alex an envelope, it contained twenty one pound notes. "Alex, Sam and Maria asked me to give you this and to thank you for all the support you and Jessie gave them when they most needed help. Be proud of your son and his lovely wife and my thanks to you and your family for making me so welcome today. Perhaps we can meet up again before I return to Australia."

Realising there was money in the envelope Alex started to protest but Walter stopped him. "Please Alex, allow me to carry out Sam and Maria's wishes."

Walter quickly shook hands with Alex and hurried into the station to catch the train to Glasgow.

When Alex arrived back home Tom, Agnes and Emily had already left for their bungalow in Drumpellier and Jessie was preparing scrambled eggs for tea. Mary and her parents sat around the table to enjoy the simple meal. Jessie said, "Alex you've hardly said a word since you took Walter back to the railway station is there anything wrong?"

"Jessie, the lad gave me an envelope from Sam and Maria there is a gift of money inside." He handed Jessie the envelope, she opened it and counted the pound notes.

"Twenty pounds, Alex! I never thought to see that amount of money in my whole life. It was right good of Sam and Maria to think of us. I think we should accept the money in the spirit in which it has been given, love. It would be churlish to refuse and it will give us a bit of security. Mary, will you come with me to the Airdrie Savings Bank tomorrow and help me open an account, we can deposit the money against a rainy day."

On the Monday morning Jessie Johnstone opened a bank account with a credit of eighteen pounds. Two pounds were kept back and they were carefully hidden inside the velvet backing of the silver photograph frame sent to Gartsherrie by her Australian family. Never had Alex and Jessie known such security.

On the return journey from Glasgow to Edinburgh Walter allowed his thoughts to drift to the coming Thursday night and his dinner date with Fiona. Although they had only spent one evening together he had rather taken to her and was looking forward to spending an entire evening in her company without Andrew and Janet.

Monday was spent preparing his move and on Tuesday morning Walter moved his possessions into Cadogan Crescent. He had been allocated a bedroom, sitting room and a bathroom. John gave him a set of house keys as he was aware that Walter should feel independent to come and go as he wanted.

Thursday evening Walter went into town in his best bib and tucker to meet Fiona at his old stomping ground, the North British Hotel.

He had booked a table for dinner at seven thirty and was thrilled to see her arrive promptly at seven o'clock wearing a beautiful blue dress under her heavy winter coat. The colour of the dress set off her blue eyes and soft brown hair, which was cut in the latest bob style.

Walter ordered a Dubonnet and lemonade for Fiona and a Glenfiddich for himself. They settled down with their drinks and suddenly Walter felt a contentedness wash over him. Here he was in an excellent hotel enjoying a drink with a beautiful girl with his quest to find his father complete. He had visited Sam's family, next Sunday he would visit Maria's folks then all he had to do was visit Dr Chalmers to collect his case and say his farewells in Bournemouth before finding a berth back to his home in Australia. He had come full circle.

"Tell me Fiona, why did you decide to study mathematics? And, what is your eventual career plan?"

"Mathematics was the only thing I was any good at, it's as simple as that. My father is head of mathematics at a very academic boarding school so my curiosity was always encouraged. I was never actually pushed but I did get superb tuition.

"Strangely enough my mother can scarcely balance the household accounts, her talent is art. My mum is a wonderful artist, she also has a beautiful singing voice, she speaks Gaelic and has won a medal at the Mod. That's a very big thing in Scotland to win a Mod medal. Sadly, I have not inherited my mother's artistic genes, I can't hold a tune and I certainly can't draw or paint.

"My career choice is therefore down to inheriting dad's genes like my brother. I'm not a mathematical genius, and I'm quite aware of that. I'll never write a brilliant original doctorate, no I expect to get a mid range degree, complete my teaching certification and spend my life teaching spotty children fractions and long division. What a terrible waste of an education is it not?

"I hear from Andrew that you are a successful self made businessman in Australia. Now that is impressive!"

Walter burst out laughing, "I left school at fourteen and I used to drive my grandmother's pony and trap, very entrepreneurial don't you know. My career is a long story but I'll tell you over dinner if you really want to know."

"Of course I want to know. Life in Australia sounds so, so exciting. Sheep sheering, kangaroos, koala bears, deserts, coral reefs, incredibly exotic."

"Fiona, I live in Melbourne. I've only seen a kangaroo and a koala bear in the zoo. I've never seen an Australian desert or coral reef and I've never been sheep sheering. I guess Melbourne is pretty much like Edinburgh but with no castle and much better weather."

"You are shattering my dreams Walter McDonald. Let's go into dinner and you can tell me your path from driving a pony and trap to staying in the North British."

Walter and Fiona had a wonderful evening, that special evening when two people first meet and they can't stop talking so anxious are they to know each other and the more they talk the more they realise that they like each other and want to spend more time in each other's company. The special evening they recall on their silver wedding anniversary.

After dinner Walter asked reception to call a taxi and he took Fiona back to her halls of residence.

As the cab pulled up she said, "Walter it's almost curfew I've got to go in now."

Walter gave her a quick kiss saying, "Fiona, can I see you on Saturday? Perhaps I could pick you up in the morning and we could spend the day together?"

As she ran towards the halls Fiona turned and called out "Course you can! I'll meet you here at ten o'clock. Thanks for a magical evening Walter. Night night."

Walter got back into the cab and gave the driver his address in Cadogan Crescent. He opened the door and went straight up to his room. Tonight he did not want to talk to John he didn't want to speak to anyone he just wanted to keep the magic of the evening alive.

The next morning when Walter went down to breakfast John greeted him with, "Well Walter, you have made it to the Scotsman.

There is an article about you and Dr Chalmers investigating Perriman on the ship saying it's all due to you both that he's on trial." Walter immediately read the report. Thankfully there were no names 'an elderly English doctor' and 'a young Australian businessman' were the descriptions given.

There were also several letters beside his place at the breakfast table, the first one was from Dr Chalmers:

Bournemouth

Dear Walter

I enclose a cutting from The Times, telling of our Hastings and Poirot adventure. An impressive article then appeared in the Bournemouth Daily Echo, I have become something of a local celebrity. They say everyone gets fifteen minutes of fame and this is mine.

Clarissa and Grace appear to have forgiven me for refusing to stay in Queen Victoria's boudoir. Rosalind and George are most impressed and this afternoon I'm giving an interview to a journalist. The local business group have asked me to give them a talk and the vicar has asked if I will address the church Men's Society. I've never been so popular.

You can tell young Andrew when you see him that his Uncle Edward is famous - don't worry my boy, you will get plenty of credit for your part in the investigation (which was most of it).

I was very pleased to hear that John McDonald is a good man so all your work to find him has been worthwhile.

Have you decided when you intend to return to the colonies yet? Your case awaits to be collected.

I have now purchased the delightful little flat I rented. My furniture has arrived from Australia and I have replaced some of the rented pieces with my own. However, I decided to sell a lot of the items, they made quite a bit of money at auction! I've decided that at my time in life it's better to keep things fairly simple.

Mrs Edgar asked me to send you her regards. I think you were quite a favourite with her the way you always appreciated her cooking.

Yesterday was something of a red letter day, I received a letter from Mrs Johnstone enclosing Australian press cuttings in the lead up to the trial and the news that she is going to care for Laurel

during the trial, apparently Matthew and Laurel were invited to
spend Christmas with them and then the poor boy will return to
Sydney to give evidence.
   Looking forward to seeing you before you head off to the land of
the kangaroo.
   My best wishes
   Poirot

* * *

Walter laughed on reading the letter and passed it to John to read.
He now knew what the fat letter from Australia contained. Maria had
also written to Walter enclosing clippings and updating him on the
Gregg children.

At last it was Saturday morning, thankfully cold, bright and dry.

Walter arrived outside the hall of residence heart beating faster
than he would have thought possible. Fiona came out of the building
wearing a long grey woollen coat with a red hat and black button boots
with a shaped heel.

He couldn't resist, Walter kissed her on the cheek, she took his arm
and they headed towards the train station. Walter had planned the day,
firstly they took the train to Musselburgh where they had a long walk
along the beach and the banks of the River Esk. The conversation just
seemed to continue from Thursday evening without interruption. It
was a beautiful, if cold, day. Although they had only met one week
before, Walter and Fiona both felt as though they had know each other
for ever.

Back in the village they found a family bakery shop with a small
tearoom where they each ordered tea and a bacon roll. There was only
four rickety tables and they could watch people queuing in the shop to
buy bread, rolls and cakes.

"Perhaps I should have found somewhere nicer to take you but I
quite like it here," said Walter. "It reminds me of the places I used to
go to with Sam and Maria, usually exhausted after running up and
down the beach with Alexander and Isabel.

Tomorrow I'm going to Glenboig to meet Maria's brother and, I
suppose, reassure him that Maria is well and happy in Australia.

Fiona, would you like to emigrate to Australia?"

"What a question Walter! To be honest I've never given the idea of
leaving Scotland a thought. My parents live in Bridge of Allan but I've
always fancied the idea of living in Edinburgh. My brother Graham

lives in the city and it's not too far to visit my parents."

The words just came to Walter from deep in his soul, as surely as he knew his name he knew he had to say them. "Fiona, I know we have only known each other a week and you still have to finish at university and I haven't met your family and as for me, I've only known my father for a few weeks. Fiona, will you marry me?"

In the background were east coast voices buying bread, treacle scones, shortbread and pies. Fiona and Walter were half way through eating their rolls and drinking mugs of tea. It was certainly not the most romantic place for a proposal. Fiona laughed, "Walter McDonald, get down on your knees and ask me again." He did, she threw her arms around him and said, "Yes of course I'll marry you and one day we can tell our children about this wee bakery in Musselburgh."

They finished their lunch and left to the applause of the customers and the ladies working in the shop. The wife of the owner put two slices of cake into a paper bag, she handed it to Fiona, saying, "One of our specialities, a couple of slices of paradise cake, it tastes right like wedding cake. You two enjoy!"

They walked hand in hand back to the railway station where they caught a train to Edinburgh.

On the journey back into town Walter said, "Fiona, I know I haven't completed the formalities with your parents yet but will you let me buy you a ring this afternoon?"

"Of course you can buy me a ring. There are lots of jewellery shops in town. Walter, is this not quite quite mad, and yet it seems perfectly sane."

Walter insisted they go into the North British and have a glass of champagne to celebrate before going shopping.

Hand in hand they walked into the new town. They found a beautiful old fashioned jewellers shop in Rose Street and went inside.

Walter, with a confidence he would never have had when he first left Australia said, "We would like to see a selection of engagement rings please. The shop owner brought out several trays, Walter immediately dismissed the one containing rings with small stones.

Fiona tried on a number of rings but none seemed exactly right. The jeweller said, "You have very delicate hands miss, I have a ring which I think might suit you." He disappeared into the back shop and returned with a beautiful ring, a central diamond surrounded with smaller diamonds which gave the impression of a flower. Fiona tried it on and they both knew 'that was the one'.

The ring was beautifully boxed and presented to Walter, the

assistant said, "I'm sure you will have a special moment when you will want to present your fiancé with the ring sir."

By the time they left the shop it was getting dark. However, dusk seems to enhance Edinburgh. Walter said, "Would you like to come back to Cadogan Crescent and meet my father? Then I'll take you out for dinner."

"Sounds wonderful, but I'm a bit nervous about meeting John McDonald, after all you have known him such a short time."

"Don't worry, he's a very nice man. Life hasn't treated him kindly, losing my mother and then Sandette and his two daughters, but he still has a pleasing way with him."

They arrived at Walter's new home where John was delighted to welcome Fiona. He immediately rang for his housekeeper Mrs McKenzie and asked her to arrange some tea.

Fiona produced the now somewhat squashed bag containing the paradise cakes from her handbag and looked at Walter, they both laughed.

"John, we've got quite a story to tell you. Meet Fiona, my fiancé."

He produced the ring from his pocket and presented it to her.

"I know this must come as quite a shock but we both know it's the right thing to do, we are in love and intend to marry, just as soon as Fiona graduates."

Mrs McKenzie came in with the tea and some shortbread, they also ate bits of the paradise cake with the welcome tea, while the young couple discussed their plans with Walter's father.

They didn't go out to dinner but shared a simple meal with John instead.

Walter made sure Fiona was back at the halls of residence before curfew. As they parted they kissed passionately and arranged to meet during the week.

The following morning Walter was up in good time for his visit to Glenboig. He hadn't heard any more from Dan as to who he would meet so he just took the gifts for Dan and Clare, he was not entirely sure of the age of their children so he thought he couldn't go wrong with a big selection of sweets and chocolate.

Dan was at the station to meet him. He shook Walter by the hand saying, "My sister has written about you Walter. We are right looking forward to hearing all about how her and her man Sam are doing in Northcote."

They walked towards Dan's small cottage, owned by the Bedlay Colliery where he worked as an electrician. Clare was waiting to welcome them but there was no sign of the children.

Dan explained, "After Mass this morning our bairns went off to spend the day with Clare's sister and play with her brood. My mother is coming over later and we thought it best that the bairns didn't meet you as they would probably tell their grandfather about the man with the funny accent and he would put two and two together and know that you had something to do with our Maria.

"It's terribly sad, we haven't even told my other sisters and brother about your visit. Clare and I wanted my ma to meet you and the fewer people who know you're here the better. No doubt Maria will have told you what a difficult auld sod my da is."

Dan and Clare accepted the gifts from Walter but while they really appreciated the thought behind them they were thinking, how on earth could we explain wearing a cashmere and a silk scarf in Glenboig, although the whisky was appreciated. Clare hid the stash of sweets and chocolate saying she would give it to the children as wee treats over the coming weeks while thinking, 'all those sweets will last for months and months'.

Walter had also brought photographs of the children. He had packed photographs of Alexander and Isabel to take on his adventure and it was a simple matter to get copies made to bring with him to Glenboig. Dan and Clare were thrilled to see photographs of the children. "My isn't Isabel like my side," said Dan, "and Alexander, well he is the spit of his father. We really appreciate you taking the trouble to bring photographs of the wee ones."

Clare served a nice meal which the three of them enjoyed together while Walter told them stories of Maria's life in Australia. They were all sitting laughing when there was a knock on the door and a small middle aged lady came in carrying scones wrapped in a spotlessly clean tea towel.

Dan introduced his mother, "Walter, this is my mother, Annie Riley." Walter shook the lady's hand, he felt as though he was towering over the tiny woman.

After looking at the photographs with tears in her eyes Mrs Riley said to Walter, "It was right good of you to bring photographs son, I can't take them home but the image of those two beautiful bairns, my grandchildren in Australia, will be burned into my soul."

Walter was very moved, he took her hand and said, "Maria is a wonderful woman and she is happy in her life with Sam in Australia. They have come through some hard times but they are thriving and Mrs Riley I want you to know Maria thinks of you often, when she is cooking she will often say things like, 'my ma always made it like this' or she comes away with Scottish sayings like, 'as my ma used to say, this place is like Annaker's midden' or if somebody sneezed she would say, 'as my mother used to say, God bless you and the devil miss you'. You are still in her life and the values you taught her live on in Australia."

While Clare and Dan were busy making tea and buttering scones in the scullery, in her homely kitchen warmed from the fire blazing in the black leaded range, Annie Riley shed years of pent up tears. Walter gave her his handkerchief, gently saying, "I'm sorry I didn't mean to make you cry, I just wanted you to know what a truly fine daughter you have raised."

Clare brought in the tea and scones and once again Walter told tales of life in Australia.

After drinking their tea Mrs Riley rose to go. "I'd better be getting back now, Patrick will think I've run away with a soldier. Mr McDonald, if I live to be a hundred I'll never forget your kindness. Please give Maria my love and tell her I pray for her and her family every single day.

"That's me away Dan, Clare thanks for the tea. Cheerio, see you efter." There was a silence after she left with so much left unsaid.

Eventually Dan broke the silence, "You know Walter it's not just about religion with my pa. It's more he's got to control, he knows best. Sam was a Protestant, he would never have been acceptable. Neil was a Catholic but he wouldn't be able to find a decent job because of his injuries, not acceptable, do you see what I mean. What makes it all so sad is he's not a happy man in himself and he has pulled my ma down to a shadow of herself.

"Occasionally, like today, you can see a glimpse of Annie O'Connor - that was her maiden name. My pa has ground down her personality.

"My oldest brother Michael was killed in the war, I got out early and married Clare, Maria met Sam, poor Maureen died. The other three are still at home. I hope they find the gumption to get out and find happiness like Maria and I have done."

When it was time for Walter to leave, he thanked Clare for the lovely food she had prepared and put on his coat and hat. Before leaving he handed Dan an envelope saying, "Maria and Sam asked me to give you this, please use it to help your family. I was so sad not to be able to give your mother a gift but under the circumstances it was impossible."

"You are wrong Walter. You gave her a wonderful gift! Ma now knows that Maria has not forgotten her and that she's included in the life of her grandchildren. You could not have given her a better present."

Walter caught his train but this time he felt a sadness as he travelled to Glasgow, because Patrick Riley was such a thrawn man his family were deprived of so many joys.

Once he was settled into the train from Glasgow to Edinburgh Walter started to think about Fiona, counting the hours until Tuesday when he was due to see her again. He had asked her to write to her parents and arrange a time to visit them as he was anxious to formally ask her father for her hand in marriage, even though he had preempted things by giving her a ring.

He had just arrived home and John was pouring him a drink while he related the events of the day when the doorbell rang.

John answered the door and showed Andrew into the sitting room. Walter quickly introduced him to his father and John offered him a drink.

Andrew eagerly accepted, "A highland malt! Thank you sir, not the normal drink of impecunious students, I'll thoroughly savour the treat.

"Walter I just had to come and see you, what's all this about you getting engaged to Fiona after only meeting her last Saturday? Have you any idea of the earache I'm now getting from Janet?"

John rose to leave, "I'll away and leave you lads to sort this one out. Goodnight, and please feel free to help yourselves to the whisky. I find it cures most problems."

"Excellent malt by the way," enthused Andrew. "Your father certainly has good taste in whisky Walter. I expect my Uncle Edward introduced you to Scotland's finest. I always enjoy it when he breaks out a bottle, he says it encourages good conversation.

"Anyway, to more important matters. Are you really engaged to be married?"

"Yes Andrew, I am going to wed Fiona. We both just knew it was right for us and we are going to get married as soon as she graduates."

"Right, so you are going to get married, what then? Do you settle in Edinburgh or do you carry her off to the colonies?

"And, if you don't go back to Australia what happens to your business back in Melbourne? I know everyone thinks I'm a bit devil may care but even I can see that you two have a lot to figure out.

"Janet and I have been going out together for quite a while. Can you imagine the grief I'm now going to get? Fiona going about with rocks on her finger and I haven't even done the down on one knee bit.

"Back to my question, where are you and the lovely Fiona going to put down roots Walter?"

"I had thought to stay here until Fiona finishes university and we can get married, then go back to Australia together as husband and wife. In fact I've been bracing myself to write to Maria and ask her if she would carry on running the business for another year."

Andrew laughed, "Well Walter McDonald I'll say this, you have the cheek of the devil. You go off looking for your father, track him down and come to Scotland, via Africa and Bournemouth. Now you're going to write to your business partner Maria and say, 'I have just met a beautiful girl and fallen head over heels in love, please look after my business for another year'. I can't imagine you are going to be very popular back in Melbourne."

"Put like that it does sound unreasonable. Somehow I just fell so completely in love with Fiona that I assumed all would be well back at H.Q.

"I'm seeing Fiona on Tuesday. I promise you, I'll address the question of the business. You're absolutely right Andrew, I am being selfish. After I've spoken to Fiona I'll write to Maria."

"Good that's settled," agreed Andrew. "Now you can pour me another glass of that exceptionally fine malt and I rather think you could do with another too."

Tuesday evening Fiona and Walter enjoyed a Scottish high tea in Jenners. After they had finished their fish and chips the waitress brought them a fresh pot of tea to enjoy with the scones and cakes.

"That was absolutely delicious," exclaimed Fiona. "You really are spoiling me. By the way Walter, I've written to my parents and asked them if I can take you to meet them on Sunday. The sooner you do the 'Mr Macpherson sir, may I have the hand in marriage of your daughter Fiona' the better. I'd hate them to find out I'm sporting a ring before the formalities. I've given you a glowing reference so hopefully my mother and father will just be jolly glad that I'm not going to end up as their spinster daughter."

Thinking about his conversation with Andrew, Walter said, "Fiona, after we get married how do you feel about living in Australia? H.Q. has evolved from a home into business premises, although I still have a bedroom there. We could buy a nice house in the suburbs and like Maria I could travel into town every day."

"I honestly don't know Walter, one part of me finds the whole idea of travelling to Australia and starting a new life incredibly exciting and I expect Australia has schools full of snotty nosed sprogs who need to learn fractions. But it's such a daunting prospect leaving behind family, friends and everything I've ever known.

"Walter, how do you feel about settling in Scotland?"

"It's not so much how I feel about staying here as the responsibilities I've left behind. We can arrange the wedding date as soon as you finish your course and get your degree in September. I will stay here until then. For me to travel back and forth to Australia would be pointless. Besides, I don't want to leave you Miss Macpheson, soon to be Mrs McDonald."

"Well that's settled then, we can decide over the next few months where we will settle after we get married. Do you want to half that wee fern cake sitting all on its lonesome?"

After he arrived home Walter took himself off to his bedroom and penned a letter to Australia.

Edinburgh

Dear Sam and Maria

Firstly, I have visited both Gartsherrie and Glenboig and was wonderfully welcomed. Both families were delighted to hear your news and were thrilled that Alexander and Isabel are doing so well.

As well as gifts I gave Alex and Dan £20 each. Maria, I was so sad not to be able to give your mother a gift, she is a lovely lady and you are in her thoughts I told her how much you mean to her and I think it brought comfort. I will visit again before I return home.

Now for my truly amazing news, I'm engaged to be married to a lovely girl called Fiona. Fiona is studying for a mathematics degree at Edinburgh university. I know it's all very quick but we both just feel it's right for us, now I really know how you two feel about each other.

Maria, I know this is a frightful cheek and I know Mr Green is going to be absolutely furious but I would like to stay here until October. We plan to get married after Fiona qualifies in September. Would you hold the fort until then? All going well we will be back in Melbourne by Christmas and we can start the new year with you having a long holiday. I promise to bring you a seriously good present, bribery…. Maria you have been wonderful and I don't want to abuse your kindness but will you please let me stay in Scotland for the time being, as well as being with Fiona it will give me time to develop a relationship with my father.

Please give my love to the children. I have posted a doll in Scottish national dress to Isabel and a Meccano set to Alexander.

Fiona and I are going to have a studio photograph taken on Saturday, I'll send you a copy then you will see why I've fallen for her. She is also very clever kind and funny, it's not just her looks I've fallen in love with.

Keep well my family in Australia
Walter

* * *

Walter realised that he had been a bit economical with the truth in his letter to Sam and Maria but he felt sure that Fiona would agree to their setting up home in Australia.

The weeks and months passed, Walter had never been so happy. He built a relationship with his father, to the extent that he got involved in the management side of John's business. It helped Walter realise that good management skills could be transferred across any number of professions and it wasn't only the clothing industry where he could earn his money.

His romance with Fiona blossomed. Thankfully her parents and brother approved of Walter and her father gave permission for them to marry at the Church of Scotland kirk in Bridge of Allan on 4th October.

It was a great relief to Walter when he received a letter from Maria in which she agreed to carry on looking after the business until he returned in December.

Walter and Fiona often talked about their eventual home and Walter felt that the prospect of choosing a house in a beautiful city where the weather was kind would be tempting. Besides, there was also the adventure of the journey to the Southern Hemisphere and a chance to visit many new and interesting places including his beloved Cape Town.

Fiona spent the summer vacation working with her mother on the wedding plans as she knew her studies during her final months at university would not allow time to choose dresses and flowers.

One Saturday the young lovers had taken the train through to St Andrew's for the day. It was a beautiful sunny blue sky day the heavens decorated with an occasional puff of white cloud but as always on the east coast there was a breeze.

Walking along the beach Walter brought up the subject of Australia. "Fiona, on a day like this it really reminds me of Melbourne, except we get lots of days like this, not just about five a year.

"Can I book passage for us to travel out to Australia after the wedding? I promise you, if you are really unhappy we will return to Scotland but I need to make decisions about the business. Maria has been marvellous but it's not right for me to take advantage of her."

Fiona gripped his hand, saying, "Walter I know you must go back, at least for a time, and it would be such an amazing adventure. Go ahead and book our berths and we will sail off into the sunset together."

With relief Walter booked a first class cabin on a ship leaving Southampton on 10th October. He wanted to have a few days with Dr Chambers in Bournemouth before they departed Great Britain, not just to collect his case. He was keen to introduce his new bride to Poirot.

Fiona worked hard during her final term at university and gained a 2:1 degree.

Just weeks before the wedding, Walter and Fiona were out with their friends Andrew and Janet, who were going to be their best man and bridesmaid. Walking along Princes Street Gardens the foursome were laughing and joking when suddenly Andrew took Janet's hands, he got down on his knees and proposed. "Janet my beautiful and incredibly long suffering girlfriend will you marry me next year after you graduate and I complete my probationary year. We can't let these two lovebirds have the only wedding on the campus."

Janet laughed, "Get up off your knees you mad Englishman. Of course I'll marry you! Does this mean we are now officially engaged?"

Andrew went into his pocket and produced a small worn black leather box, saying, "Unlike our friend from the colonies I'm merely an impecunious student. However my mother has sent me Grandma's ring to convince you that I'm serious." Inside the box was nestled a beautiful sapphire and diamond ring.

"Wow!" exclaimed Janet. "Well I did say 'yes' before you produced the ring. It's beautiful, more than beautiful."

Fiona and Walter offered their hearty congratulations with Walter insisting the party share a bottle of champagne, his treat.

They had a wonderful congratulatory evening and Walter managed to find an opportunity to tell Janet what a good family Andrew was part off and how she would love his mother Rosalind.

Autumn was particularly beautiful that year the changing colours of nature was joyous, the Virginia creeper on the back of the house in Cadogan Gardens was a glorious red and life was good.

Fiona had gone off to stay at her parents home in Bridge of Allen for the fortnight before the wedding, Janet had accompanied her leaving Walter and Andrew free to have some time together before they went their separate ways. On a number of evenings they sampled John's malt collection and John enjoyed spending time with the two young men as they discussed their life plans.

John had accepted that Walter was going to return to Australia with his bride, however he appreciated the months they had spent together and he had privately resolved that once the young couple had settled he would go out and visit them. Besides, he was also keen to meet Sam and Maria Johnstone.

Walter also used the time to meet up again with Alex and Jessie Johnstone, having heard about the last meeting Sam and Maria had with his parents in Sloan's Pub in Glasgow, he arranged to meet them there on a Saturday afternoon.

They all enjoyed the famous steak pie and being able to relax and blether together The men shared a pint in the old Victorian pub while Jessie enjoyed a sherry and thought of the last time she had seen her son back in 1917. Walter told them of his impending marriage and his arrangements to return to Australia. They all had plenty to say and the conversation flowed.

Before they left to go their separate ways Alex said, "Give the family all our love. Yes we miss them but we know they have made the right decision. Jessie and me are so grateful you contacted us, so we are. Walter it's been grand to put a face to you. We both wish you every happiness with Fiona, she sounds a grand lass. Safe journey lad." The men shook hands, Walter kissed Jessie and they parted.

In order to meet Maria's mother again Walter formed a plan with Dan. Clare brought Mrs Riley into Glasgow and they had afternoon tea at Pettigrew & Stephens in Sauchiehall Street. Mrs Riley was more relaxed in the city far away from her home in Glenboig and enjoyed telling Walter about her firstborn daughter Maria. They had a lovely afternoon together and before they left to go their separate ways Walter presented Mrs Riley with a locket, inside was two photographs, one of Maria and Sam and another of Alexander and Isabel, saying, "Mrs Riley, I realise you won't be able to wear the locket but I thought it would be small enough to hide away and you could look at it whenever you want."

Annie Riley thanked Walter profusely, "Walter lad, you have no idea how happy you made me after your last visit to Glenboig. Just knowing Maria has not forgotten me is everything to me. I'll treasure your gift and I now include you in my daily prayers."

As Mrs Riley and Clare headed towards Queen Street station the older woman said, "Clare pet, I think it would be better if you kept the locket, I can see it at your place."

Clare accepted the locket and assured her mother in law it would be safe with her.

At last the wedding day dawned and it was just as special as they imagined it would be. Fiona wore a ivory dress in the handkerchief style, with shaped heel shoes in a matching shade, her veil was held in place by a pearl cluster clip and she wore a pearl necklace, both presents from her parents. Her chosen flowers was a fall of white lilies.

Standing beside his beautiful bride, Walter felt he was the luckiest man in Scotland.

Sitting in the congregation, John too felt he was the luckiest man in Scotland, not only was he united with his son he now had a lovely daughter in law.

After the wedding breakfast the young couple headed south, first to Edinburgh then an overnight train to London.

As a honeymoon treat they spent a day in London with a luxury night at the Ritz, travelling on to Bournemouth the following day.

Walter had booked them into an old coach house hotel in Bournemouth, with antique furniture and a four poster bed. After breakfast they set out to visit Dr Chalmers. They were joined by Andrew's parents who were delighted to hear all about the wedding and talk about the impending marriage of Andrew and Janet.

Each day Walter and Fiona spent time with the doctor as well as enjoying their honeymoon.

On their final visit there were three beautifully wrapped parcels on the dining room table. The doctor asked Fiona to open them.

"My dear, I hope you will accept a small wedding gift from me as a token of my great esteem for you both. The small parcel is from Rosalind and George." It contained an elegant art nouveau silver clock. Fiona then opened the larger of the packages from Dr Chalmers, a Lalique vase and the final box contained - what else but a bottle of old malt.

After thanking the elderly man for his generosity, a quick toast with a glass of sherry and the taxi arrived to take Fiona and Walter to the railway station.

As they said their goodbyes Edward Chalmers knew it was very unlikely that he would ever see Walter again but he would be eternally thankful to whatever power had put Hastings into his life.

Dr Chalmers was feeling rather down after the youngsters had left so he decided to go out and treat himself to a decent lunch. The Red Lion's steak and kidney pudding was appealing, besides he could accompany the meal with a glass of fine claret and toast the young couple.

He returned home sporting a rosy glow from drinking a half bottle of claret which had perfectly accompanied the pudding. A telegraph boy was standing at his front door. The lad said, "I've got a telegraph for a Mr McDonald at this address but I see the name on the door says Chalmers, have I come to the right place?"

Dr Chalmers accepted the telegram. "Yes my lad, Mr McDonald is a guest. Wait here and I'll see if there is a reply, give me a form."

Opening the telegram in trepidation Dr Chalmers read;

Mr Walter, can you return to Edinburgh STOP
Mr McDonald has had a stroke STOP
Please contact me immediately STOP
Mrs McKenzie Housekeeper STOP

Knowing that Walter would now be well on his way to Southampton the doctor quickly wrote a telegram to Walter McDonald, c/o the purser on the liner Endeavour berthed at Southampton.

Walter, most urgent you contact me immediately STOP
do not sail STOP Edward Chalmers STOP

The doctor handed the telegraph boy the reply and gave him a sixpence tip asking him to have it sent as quickly as possible. The boy left with a spring in his step.

⁓

CHAPTER 24
A Change of Plan

From the heights of happiness Walter was plunged into the depth of despair. The purser on the liner arranged for their luggage to be unloaded, porters loaded a taxi to take them and all their belongings to the railway station.

The train journey back to Scotland was very different from the exciting journey south. They were unable to book a sleeper from London and spent the night propping each other up while wishing the nightmare journey would soon be over.

Mrs McKenzie started to cry with relief when Walter and Fiona finally arrived at Cadogan Crescent. "Thank goodness I caught you in time, Mr McDonald is in the Royal Hospital, he is a poor soul. I found him in the sitting room, paralysed down the left side and he couldn't speak properly. I phoned the doctor immediately and he had him hospitalised."

Surrounded by cases and boxes Walter said, "I'll get our luggage indoors. Can you make us some tea please and something to eat then we will get a taxi to the hospital."

After getting all their belongings upstairs, Fiona and Walter washed and changed before going downstairs to eat poached egg on toast and drink some welcome tea.

Fiona insisted on accompanying Walter to the hospital where they found John asleep. A discussion with the duty doctor confirmed he had indeed suffered a major stroke. However, his condition now seemed to be stable.

Back in the ward Walter tried to communicate with his father. John opened his eyes and Walter had the good sense to ask him closed questions. "John, if you can hear me blink." John blinked. "If you are in pain blink." No blink. "Can you move your right arm?" He moved his right hand. "Can you move your left arm?" No movement.

"At least we have communication John. You are in good hands here meantime, but as soon as you are able we will arrange for you to come home. We will leave now, try and get some sleep and we will come back to see you this evening."

Walter reported his experiment to the doctor and promised to be back that evening.

"Fiona, I can't leave him, I just can't. We should have been enjoying our honeymoon travelling to Melbourne and instead we're back in Edinburgh and having to care for a very sick man. You didn't sign up for this."

"Oh yes I did," declared Fiona. "I promised in sickness and in health and it's not just your health, it's family. Let's get back to the house and send some telegrams and make phone calls. We have a fair bit of admin to get on with."

The hardest telegram for Walter to send was to Sam and Maria;

At Southampton when John took a stroke STOP
returned to Edinburgh STOP
he is very poorly we will have to care for him STOP
I'll keep you informed of our plans STOP
Sorry STOP Walter STOP

The following days were full, visiting John and dealing with the repercussions of his illness, both in the business and informing friends and family of the change in circumstances. Walter and Fiona decided there was no option but to set up home temporarily in Cadogan Crescent.

Walter was very relieved when he received a telegram from Maria;

Do what you have to STOP
hope John makes a good recovery STOP
don't worry about business STOP
keep me informed STOP love Maria STOP

After two weeks in hospital John arrived home. Walter had rearranged the house turning the dining room into a downstairs bedroom and sitting room where John would be comfortable and still a part of day to day life rather than being confined upstairs.

Fiona found herself some work tutoring students in mathematics. It wasn't particularly demanding but under the present circumstances it was suitable and gave her some independence and confidence that she was using her education.

The days shortened and they entered a cold Edinburgh winter.

Suddenly it was almost Christmas and it would soon be time to bring in 1925. Walter and Fiona would never forget 1924 for many reasons and although he never spoke of it Walter was disappointed that he had not been able to show his bride the delights of Madeira and introduce her to Ishbel and Charles and the newly wed Robert and Anna, as well as the sights and sounds of the Far East. Instead of a summer Christmas in Melbourne with his Johnstone family they would be celebrating in cold grey Edinburgh. Walter thought he would never get used to the biting cold but under no circumstances did he intend to desert his father.

CHAPTER 25
Changes in Melbourne

Maria and Sam and the children were looking forward to welcoming Walter and Fiona back to Australia. The business of Harris Finishings had moved on under the guidance of Maria with the encouragement of Sam and Mr Green. In addition to the homeworkers they now had two full time and two part time ladies working from H.Q. together with the two boys James and Harry doing the deliveries and collections. Alice supervised all the day to day work and Maria carried out the business side from her upstairs office.

As well as ensuring everything was running smoothly Maria spent time each week looking for new avenues of business. Much to her delight she found a lucrative source of sales making uniforms for factory workers, they were straightforward to make and if personalised with the client's name or emblem attracted a good price.

When she received Walter's telegram Maria's heart went to her boots, not only had she been looking forward to their arrival but the children, including Matthew, were excited at the prospect of welcoming Walter and Fiona from Scotland. However, she did not show her disappointment when replying.

At her next meeting with Mr Green she let him see the telegram from Walter.

"Mrs Johnstone, while sympathising with Walter and his father I am most concerned about you and the business. You must have a proper holiday soon, also thinking time. The business is doing extremely well thanks to your efforts but I think now is the time to restructure and look closely at your business plan. I was very much hoping we could work on that with Walter, who is after all the principal shareholder. Reading this telegram I don't so much think, when will he be back, but if. What are your feelings?"

"Sadly, I think you are probably right. Walter has been away now for well over a year and as you know changes have happened. I feel I can't make any more changes without consulting him, after all it's Walter's property we work from and he owns 75 percent of the business. I can't imagine circumstances are going to change soon. There is another piece of information I think you should know. John McDonald is a man of substance and he has willed most of his estate to Walter. That could be another reason for him to stay in Scotland.

"On a personal level, we are so disappointed Walter and Fiona won't be with us for Christmas, the children are all very upset. Matthew too, is coming down to spend the holidays with us. Sam takes a real interest in Matthew and writes to him regularly. I'm pleased to say he is doing well and Mr Smallman has been a wonderful mentor to him. You will have heard his father's sentence has been commuted to life imprisonment, Sam and I are glad because we don't think it would have been good for Matthew to think he was in any way instrumental in his father being hanged.

"Laurel is coming on a treat and after the holidays we're sending her to school. Now that she is more confident I think she needs the company of other youngsters her own age."

Mr Green spoke very seriously to Maria, "Keep me informed regarding any communications from Walter. In the new year I may well write to him, I need clarification of his intentions.

"Mrs Johnstone I am now going to ask you a personal question. Are you in a financial position to buy Walter out of the business and then rent the premises from him?"

The colour drained from Maria's face, "Mr Green not for one minute have I ever considered buying Walter out of Harris Finishings as a possibility. Sam and I do have some savings. Coming from a background like ours we have always been careful with our finances. The land and the house in Northcote are paid and we have no debts. Mind you, I doubt if we have anything like the amount we would need to buy seventy five percent of the business."

Mr Green replied, "We are nowhere near that stage yet but I always think it's best to be prepared for all eventualities. Have a discussion with your husband over the holidays and we'll be led by the actions of Walter.

"Now go and enjoy the holidays and we'll see what 1925 brings."

Travelling home on the train Maria blocked out the chatter of the children. Mr Green had certainly given her something to think about.

On the last working day before the holidays everyone was delighted to meet Matthew off the Sydney train. He was due to stay at

'The Brig' for just three weeks and he had been counting the days. Over the holidays Sam and Maria arranged a lot of treats; a visit to see the fairy penguins at Philips Bay, a day at the zoo, picnics on the beach, sausages and damper bread in the garden. The days that Sam and Maria had to work, Mrs Rogers helped out while Matthew and Laurel amused the younger children.

Sam took Matthew and Alexander fishing one day giving Sam an opportunity to talk to Matthew alone.

"Well lad, how are you enjoying working in your family business and staying with Mr and Mrs Smallman?"

"I'm learning an amazing amount. Mr Smallman expects me to spend time in each department learning every aspect of the business. My two tutors are both fine, Mr Smallman says he wants me to have the option of going to university rather than just moving straight into the business. Actually I'm starting to think he might be right. Initially I just wanted to work in the business but I think it might be enjoyable to study and get some life experience, perhaps in another city or abroad.

"As far as staying with the Smallmans' well obviously Laurel got lucky staying with you and Maria. But I realise I could so easily have been packed off to boarding school and they are kind. They have three grown up children and we often visit one of them on a Sunday or the family come over for Sunday lunch with their parents. It's nice to be able to enjoy younger company with the grandchildren but at the same time after all I've been through I feel years older than people of my own age.

"I'm really grateful that you let Laurel stay, she is adamant she will never return to Sydney and I can't really blame her.

"Mother is not keeping any better, I visit once a month but I might as well not bother, apparently she is of an age when a nervous disposition is not unusual in women. The doctors have tried a number of treatments including electric therapy. It sounds dreadful but I am assured it offers a good chance of improvement.

"The house is now sold, it made a good price and the ghouls bought lots of stuff at the auction. Furniture, rugs, even bits and pieces like garden tools, crockery and cutlery. Apparently it was the notoriety of the Perriman's trial that got people out to bid for a piece of the man that committed such a heinous crime.

"Financially everything is fine. Sam, as well as the tutoring and school fees for Laurel, it's only fair that you and Maria are not out of pocket. Mr Cuthbertson has asked that we agree on a fair amount and he will arrange to send you a cheque every month, you can let me know before I leave what I should tell him and he will backdate the money to when Laurel first arrived in Melbourne.

"Sam, what do you really think Walter is going to do?"

"Well Matthew, Walter spent a lot of time with us and I know the lad well. He will never walk out on his father while the man needs him. If John McDonald passes away I think Walter will follow his original plan and bring Fiona to Australia, but without question, while John is poorly he will stay in Edinburgh."

After the holidays were over and Matthew returned to Sydney, Maria made another appointment with Mr Green.

As always she was warmly welcomed, "Good morning Mrs Johnstone and how can I be of help to you today?"

"Mr Green I've received another telegram from Walter;

Christmas greetings STOP Letter on its way STOP
John is now home STOP
I'm dealing with his affairs and caring for him with nursing help STOP
make whatever business decisions you feel necessary STOP Walter STOP

Maria confided in Mr Green, "Sam thinks Walter will stay in Scotland as long as John needs him, he is a loyal lad and I think Sam is right.

"I've prepared a plan to take the business forward. I'll await Walter's letter before taking any action, meantime I would be obliged if you would read through my plan and let me know what you think."

"Certainly Mrs Johnstone. No business can stand still for years awaiting the owner's decision as to which country he would like to live in."

A few weeks later Walter's long awaited letter arrived;

Edinburgh

My dear Sam and Maria

Where to start? We had actually boarded the liner when we received a telegram from John's housekeeper. We contacted Edinburgh and heard the terrible news that John had suffered a stroke. There was no option but to return swiftly to Scotland.

John is now home from hospital, I have set up a room for him downstairs and engaged a nurse. He is progressing slowly, I doubt he will make a full recovery but we can see a definite improvement already.

I have also organised daily massage therapy. The therapist was blinded in the war and retrained to carry out massage, he is excellent and John enjoys his daily visit.

Thankfully I knew a bit about his business before John's

stroke. Very briefly, two of the employees are going to buy the business and rent the premises from John. Quite a relief that I don't have to worry about a business where I know nothing of the profession. The paperwork should be complete by the time you get this letter.

Fiona has been absolutely wonderful, my strength and a ray of joy. She is working as a private mathematics tutor, mainly preparing youngsters for university. Financially it's not necessary for her to work but she wants to use her education.

Maria, I realise things are changing and you need to make decisions regarding the business. I imagined we would be together by now, once again planning and plotting but we have to be realistic. I can't see my being able to leave John for at least another year, perhaps longer.

If Harris Finishings requires a capital investment I am in a position to finance changes, just send me details.

Please give my best wishes to everyone at H.Q. also Sam, Alexander, Isabel and Laurel, I'll write to young Matthew separately.

I have reached a point where I need to decide what I am going to do with myself in Scotland now everything is organised for John's care. It's not an easy one, I've no professional qualification (In my letter to Matthew I'll advise him to get a formal education). I do have business skills, I just need to work out a project in which I can use them.

Maria, I'm so sorry we didn't return as promised but I know you understand it was out of my hands.

With all my best wishes and thanks for holding the fort. I miss you all, my dear family.

Walter

* * *

Maria read the letter several times before giving it to Sam. "Isn't that strange John and Walter have done in Scotland exactly what Mr Green suggested we do here, allowed the management to buy out the firm. I can hardly believe what I'm reading."

After reading the letter carefully Sam said, "Maria, take the letter to Mr Green and get his opinion. If you want to use our savings to buy a bigger stake in the business I'll back you all the way."

Armed with Sam's support, once again Maria had a meeting with Mr Green. He wasted no time, without preamble he said,"Mrs Johnstone I have carefully read your business plan and it definitely has merit.

"It's ironic Walter fought me tooth and nail not to sell the business and now he appears to be walking away from his grandmother's inheritance.

"Do you want me to write to him with a proposal to purchase an increased stake in the business? If so I'll ask Mr Goldberg to crunch the numbers and calculate the worth of the business, then you will be able to work out how much you can comfortably afford."

Scarcely believing what she was saying, Maria instructed Mr Green to go ahead and get a figure from Mr Goldberg as the first step to her acquiring an enhanced share of Harris Finishings.

Six months later Maria and Sam owned fifty percent of the business and Walter had agreed that for the next two years the business would not require to pay him rent.

By Christmas 1925 the turnover had doubled from the time when Walter had set off in his quest. The business was now less reliant on finishings and was concentrating on producing simple uniforms in quantity.

Once again Matthew joined the Johnstone family for the Christmas holidays. He was now almost sixteen and turning into a very handsome young man. During the holiday he confided in Sam, "I've been talking with Mr Smallman and next year I'm going to spend two terms at college and then university for three years. Mr Smallman has made it clear that as soon as I complete my education he intends to retire. I think he sees himself as a safe pair of hands until I join the business, it's really quite a responsibility, I'll go from being a student to running my own business.

"Incidentally, Laurel loves helping at H.Q. after school and during holidays. She tells me Maria has been teaching her dressmaking and she has notebooks full of designs, apparently she wants to be a dress designer and have her own salon."

"I already know," said Sam. "Laurel is very talented, Maria really enjoys teaching her dressmaking and they spend time together pouring through magazines. Maria thinks Laurel would enjoy art school, perhaps some sort of textiles or design course. But that is all in the future, meantime we just want her to be happy, and I think she is quite settled here in Northcote."

CHAPTER 26
A New Beginning

Back in Edinburgh 1925 was also a year of change, John had been making a steady recovery. While he was grateful to Walter and Fiona for all their support he also felt that now life had settled into a routine it was time for Walter to do more than simply running the household. John was acutely aware that had it not been for his sudden illness Walter would now be in Melbourne managing his own business. Instead of which he had recently sold a further twenty five percent to his business partner.

One morning as his masseur was leaving John slowly said, "Ask Walter to come and see me. Thanks."

Walter came to see his father followed by Mrs McKenzie carrying a tea tray. Walter greeted John, "How are you this morning. Is there anything I can get for you?"

John was able to write with his right hand which was an easier way to communicate than speaking which was still slow. He handed Walter a piece of paper, it read, *'Walter, I appreciate you looking after me but you should be in Melbourne working. You need a career'.*

Walter read the note which mirrored what he had been thinking for some months. He badly wanted to work but the only thing he knew was the clothing industry and he had no network of contacts in Edinburgh.

"I know John, it's something that has been worrying me," agreed Walter. "I don't have any formal qualifications, I just learned on the job. When my grandmother died all her customers gave us a chance to produce the goods and when we did they stuck by us. Harris Finishings has an extensive network both of workers and clients. The majority of our clients are Jewish and it would be impossible for me as an outsider to break into that market in Scotland. In fact I'm even in the wrong city, I would need to be in Glasgow to have any hope of setting up in the clothing trade. John, I just don't know what career move to make."

Slowly and carefully John spoke, "My boy your talent is management. Fiona is working as a tutor, how did she get clients?"

"Initially we placed several small advertisements in The Scotsman. To be honest she has never advertised again, after the first few jobs it's been word of mouth."

John explained his idea, "Why don't you set up an agency offering tuition, bring together compatible students and tutors. Fiona must have plenty of contacts through the university. People often can't handle fees directly or have difficulty finding a suitable tutor. You could bring the right people together and do the invoicing and payments for a commission.

"It wouldn't be a big capital outlay, you can use my old office upstairs, just get another phone line in for the business. Fiona will be a good sounding board, discuss the idea with her."

Walter felt that a light had been switched on. He had not looked further than the clothing trade but his negotiating and management skills were transferable.

"What a great idea John! I can't wait to get started."

"In that case Walter, go upstairs and clear out my office, it's yours now."

Walter with help from Fiona set up a business called, M.T.S. (McDonald Tutoring Services). It worked surprisingly well, as after a few months Fiona gave up giving tuition in order to interview prospective tutors and clients and assist with the administration.

Walter was delighted with his new project as it gave him back his self respect and confidence. John was also delighted as he felt a successful business might encourage Walter to stay in Edinburgh.

One day just a few weeks before Christmas Fiona said to Walter, "Let's go out for dinner tonight to the North British like we used to when you first arrived from Australia. I think we deserve a treat."

Walter agreed, "Yes we do. We've been working hard for weeks now. I'll phone and book a table for seven o'clock."

They decided to have a drink in the lounge before their meal. Walter ordered a whisky and soda and asked Fiona if she would like her favourite Dubonnet and lemonade. "No thanks Walter, I think I'll just have a lemonade tonight."

They chatted for a time about how well the business had taken off and the forthcoming marriage of Andrew and Janet which was going to be held in Edinburgh. Walter was particularly looking forward to the wedding as Dr Chalmers was accompanying Andrew's parents Rosalind and George from Bournemouth.

Out of the blue Fiona said, "Walter darling, I've got some news for you. How do you feel about a new little person entering our lives? I'm in the family way." Walter almost dropped his glass.

"When? Oh Fiona! Delighted does not cover how I feel. I don't think any adjective fits the bill. I'm over the moon. Are you well?"

"Yes, I'm fine, I've been to see the doctor and it looks like an early June baby. I didn't want to say anything until I was absolutely sure and I don't want to tell anyone until after Andrew and Janet's wedding, that's their special day."

They ordered their meal, which was no doubt delicious but Walter could only concentrate on one thing, he was going to be a father. Funnily enough, although he had found his birth father in John, Walter thought he wanted to be a father just like Sam. Sam was his father figure without a doubt.

The Bournemouth contingent arrived on the Thursday before the Saturday wedding. As well as Andrew's parents, Dr Chalmers, Clarissa and Grace, various other cousins and their grown up children travelled north. Andrew's brother and his wife and children arrived from London. Quite a gathering at the North British.

Walter and Fiona joined with Janet's immediate family to meet Andrew's family for a drinks reception on the Friday evening to allow the two sides of the family to be introduced.

Walter was delighted to see Dr Chalmers once again, so much had happened since they had said goodbye thinking he was taking his bride back to Australia.

Dr Chalmers greeted Walter. "We meet again Hastings, it's wonderful to see you looking so well."

"That's what marriage does Poirot," replied Walter. "Andrew is indeed a lucky man, Janet is a lovely girl and a clever one. As well as working as a freelance translator she sometimes gives tuition through our company. We are so looking forward to their wedding tomorrow at Morningside Parish Church."

The wedding was a wonderfully happy day and the two families got on well together.

After a short honeymoon the newlyweds travelled to the borders where Andrew had found a position in a veterinary practice. Their new home would be just a train ride to Edinburgh allowing Janet to continue to forge a worthwhile translating career.

Dr Chalmers stayed in Edinburgh for a week after the wedding, during which time he was able to meet John McDonald on a number of occasions as well as spending time with Walter and Fiona.

The evening before he left they were enjoying a farewell dinner at the North British when Walter couldn't keep the secret any longer. "Doctor, before you leave I want to share some wonderful news. Fiona is going to have a baby next year."

His mentor replied, "The clue is in the word, 'doctor'. I've known since shortly after I arrived, however I guessed you wanted to keep your news secret until after the wedding. Very commendable my boy.

"Let's have a bottle of champagne. I'm sure it won't hurt baby McDonald if Fiona has a small glass. Walter, I have every confidence that you and I will be able to finish the remainder of the bubbly between us."

CHAPTER 27
Time Does Not Stand Still

The years passed 1926, 1927, 1928.

Two businesses on different sides of the world were growing and two entrepreneurs were pleased that their hard work was paying off.

In Australia Maria had a third child in 1927, another wee boy which they named Samuel Riley Johnstone. Samuel after his father and Riley after Maria's family, Maria would have liked to call him after her brother Dan who faithfully corresponded and kept her informed about the goings on within the Riley family in Glenboig but she didn't want to use the name Daniel in case it hurt Matthew and Laurel by reminding them of their father.

As he grew, Samuel was much more of a mischief than either Alexander or Isabel had ever been. Young Faye was kept busy looking after the third Johnstone child who was totally fearless and always up to some nonsense.

Maria changed the company name to Harris Clothing and it was now generating more profit by making overalls and uniforms for corporates than ever they had on finishings. A number of the rooms in H.Q. we're utilised purely for manufacturing and Maria was employing eight full time machinists as well as a cutter, with the ever reliable Alice supervising the operation.

In Edinburgh, Walter and Fiona had been blessed with a baby girl who they called Alice Victoria after her grandmothers. This was followed in 1927 by a son, Samuel John.

M.T.S. was a great success, even John was amazed at how his idea to keep Walter busy had taken off. As well as offering private tuition the company now provided tutors for companies all over Scotland.

Although he had not made a full recovery John's health had greatly improved and he was now able to speak fairly clearly. His greatest joy in life was his grandchildren, Alice and Samuel.

In Australia Sam and Maria were preparing to bring in 1929. Alexander and Isabel were fast growing up, Matthew was at university and Laurel was finishing school and going into further education at art college. And, young Samuel, well he was being spoiled by everyone.

Sitting together and talking about their holiday plans Sam suddenly changed the subject, "Maria, I don't think Walter will ever come back to Australia, besides his new business seems to be really taking off.

"You know I never interfere in the day to day running of the company but I think it might be time for you to negotiate with Walter about buying him out of the business completely. We have replaced our savings and a good bit more besides. Why don't you speak to Mr Green about the whole situation? If you keep increasing the value of the business the way you are doing we'll never be able to buy Walter out."

Over the holiday period Maria often found herself thinking about Sam's idea and she knew he was right. In January 1929 when Matthew had returned to university, Laurel to college, and Alexander and Isabel were back at school, Maria did as Sam had suggested and had the conversations with Mr Green and Mr Goldberg.

The upshot was by June 1929 Maria and Sam were the sole owners of Harris Clothing and the building named H.Q. with the help of a loan from the Bank of Australia. Their wildest ambitions had been fulfilled. The Johnstone family were now really on the move.

Gartsherrie

Dearest family

Firstly apologies for being so tardy with my letter writing but what a time it's been. As you already know at last we have the franchise - <u>women over 21 can vote</u>. I never thought to write those words in my lifetime. Mary and Liz were in Parliament when the Representation of the People Act 1928 was passed. Millicent Fawcett also attended, what a crown to her life's work.

Agnes Law, her daughter Mary, Jennie and me toasted the victory in sherry.

We old stagers in the movement had all been going through a 'what now' moment <u>when</u>....

You will never believe this. Sam, you remember Mrs Millar she was the midwife and local wise woman who used to treat folks in the rows when they were ill. Well, Mrs Millar passed away and she has left me a huge amount of money which I am going to use to open a women's refuge. Mary Law, Jennie, Liz and our Mary are also involved. We call ourselves 'Ella's Friends.'

Your father has been incredibly supportive, it's not easy for him working in the Gartsherrie works with people whispering about me inheriting a fortune, actually it's not so much inheriting as being the custodian of her inheritance. What a responsibility I have taken on my shoulders.

I'm spending my days looking for a suitable property. It's just like the old suffragette days, back to Jennie's morning room for planning meetings.

Maria you have done so well with the business in Australia and you have given back by encouraging young Matthew and Laurel to fulfil their goals. I'm so proud of you both.

With love from our home in Scotland to your home in Australia.

All our love
Ma and Pa

CHAPTER 28
The End of the 1920's

After all the business excitement and optimism of 1928 and early 1929 in Melbourne and Edinburgh out of sight there was trouble lurking. Before 1929 was over the world would experience the unbelievable, the Wall Street crash.

Rumours and articles in the press started in September 1929, and as the weeks passed everyone was avidly reading the newspapers and knowing no good was going to come from the American news reports. Both Sam and Maria were worried as the bank loan to buy the H.Q. property was secured on 'The Brig'. Over the past decade the Johnstones had experienced their share of ups and downs but never anything like the present worry. However, the Wall Street Crash would become as nothing to a sadness that was about to engulf the family.

One evening the children were in bed, Laurel was sitting at the kitchen table sketching, Sam and Maria were in the sitting room once again talking about the economy in Australia when the front door bell rang. Sam got up to answer it wondering who on earth was calling at this time of night.

The telegraph boy handed him a brown envelope enquiring, "Will I wait for a reply sir?" Sam asked him to wait a few moments while he went back into the sitting room to open the envelope with Maria. As he read he turned white, without saying a word he handed the missive to Maria;

Terrible news STOP
your father has been killed at the Gartsherrie Works STOP
letter to follow STOP
so very sorry STOP Jennie STOP

Maria went out to the hall and asked the boy for a reply form. Which she completed;

Thank you for telegram STOP
will await letter with details STOP
look after ma and God Bless all the family STOP
Sam and Maria STOP

The boy left, once again knowing that his buff envelope had brought news of the worst kind. However, he did receive a good tip and would ensure the reply was sent posthaste.

When Maria returned to the sitting room she found Sam exactly how she had left him, sitting clutching the telegram. Laurel bounced in, asking, "Who was that at the door at this time of night?" Even as she was saying the words she could see the telegram and knew it heralded bad news.

Maria said gently, "Laurel pet, we have received some terrible news, Sam's father has been killed. Please go to bed and let us be on our own. We can talk tomorrow."

Laurel went into the kitchen made a pot of tea which she took into the living room, saying, "I'm so very sorry Sam, night night."

Maria poured the tea, Sam was still silent as though frozen in time. Eventually he broke the silence, "I want to go home Maria, I want to go home. I can't thole the idea of my ma trying to cope without my pa. They were two parts of a whole, always have been, even as weans we knew our parents loved each other to distraction."

Maria knelt down in front of her husband and held his hands. "My darling, I don't know what to say, I know how close you have always been to your father. Then a knock at the door and our lives are in pieces. Sam, if you want to go home, and your work will give you a leave of absence, somehow we'll get together the money for the fare."

"Maria lass, I can't think straight at the moment. It's just all too much of a shock. I'm away to bed, drink your tea, give me a little time before you come through."

Maria sat for a good hour before washing the teacups and going through to the bedroom. Sam was sitting on the bed still fully clothed. Maria sat beside him, she said nothing just held his hand. They sat in silence for a long time before Maria eventually whispered, "Sam we have to try and get some sleep, we both have to go to work tomorrow."

Almost like a child he got into his nightclothes and did as he was bid. Neither of them slept a great deal they just lay holding hands.

In the cold light of day they recognised that in the present climate it simply wasn't possible for Sam to take a long unpaid leave, he had no option but to grieve in Northcote.

By the time Christmas came around Sam and Maria were having crisis talks as to how they were going to keep the business going during what looked like being a long worldwide depression, also wondering how safe Sam's job at the brickworks would be.

All their savings had been sunk into purchasing the remaining fifty percent of the business from Walter but worse still, the loan from the Bank of Australia was secured against 'The Brig'. Ten years of work now hung precariously in the balance.

As always, Matthew returned to Northcote for Christmas. One evening after the three younger children were in bed Matthew, Laurel, Sam and Maria sat around the kitchen table and talked frankly about how they were all going to weather the storm.

Matthew started things off, "After I graduate Mr Smallman will retire and I'll find myself having to guide the business through a worldwide depression. I honestly can't believe how things have changed in a matter of months. Even the Christmas hamper trade has been hit, thousands of people send gifts of Australian produce to family abroad every year, you know dried fruits, honey, macadamia nuts, luxury items of that sort. This year we have sent hundreds, not thousands of hampers and boxes.

"Laurel, I know you are due to start art school after the Christmas holidays and yes there is money available to pay your fees but I'm going to have to make a lot of hard decisions in the business like laying off staff. I intend to buy a little property in Sydney using some of the capital from when we sold the house. Then it's baton down the hatches until better days."

"We are in much the same position," agreed Maria. "We must do what it takes to survive, for us the priority is earning enough to pay the loan instalments to the bank every month."

Laurel piped up, "Maria, if you're not going to be using all the rooms at H.Q. why don't you rent a couple out? That would bring in a bit of money. We have to think of every way possible to keep things going."

Hogmanay 1929 was not the joyful celebration of previous years, welcoming in the new decade did not promise great joy. However, the adults together with Matthew and Laurel did their best to make it a happy time for the three younger children.

The first few months of the 1930's were not easy. Maria spent her days trying to cut expenditure while still actively seeking new business. The hardest part was laying off some of the machinists and telling the homeworkers that their work was going to be considerably reduced.

Thankfully Harry had left Melbourne to go to work for his uncle in Sydney.

The staff at H.Q. was now cut back to James who drove the company van which was garaged where the horse and trap had once been housed. Mrs Wilson, two machinists along with Alice and Faye. The one thing that stood them in good stead was Maria acted early rather than see the business go down slowly. Taking up Laurel's suggestion she also rented out two of the rooms to small factory units who could no longer afford larger premises.

One Saturday morning the first letter of explanation regarding Alex's death arrived from Jennie.

Coatbridge

My dear Sam and Maria

This is such a hard letter to write, please forgive me if I can't express myself very well but losing Alex has been so difficult.

There is no soft or easy way to say this, a policeman arrived at the refuge and told Mary Law that your Pa had been killed in an accident at the Gartsherrie works, Sam, I'm so sorry, there is no body. We broke the news to your mother, as you can imagine she was devastated.

Your sister Mary and Liz returned from London where they were on holiday, Mary is taking it very hard indeed. Your sister Agnes, Tom, and all the Law family are supporting your mother, we are all doing our best under the tragic circumstances.

Rev. Maxwell conducted a remembrance service at your house in the Long Row at which your mother was very stoic. When the grief eventually broke Agnes Law was wonderful and looked after Jessie with great kindness and understanding.

Then, a letter was delivered from the Gartsherrie Works telling Jessie that as there was now nobody living in the house who was an employee of the company she would have to move out with very little notice.

We all gathered around and she had a number of options. Jessie is presently staying with Liz and Mary in Airdrie, she intends to move into a room at the refuge whenever she feels she can cope. Sam your mother is independent and I personally think she has made the right decision not to stay with me or either of her girls.

Agnes, Mary and your Ma will all write to you but I felt

you should know the circumstances as soon as possible.
  These are difficult times and we must just try and get through
them the best way we can.
  It breaks my heart to write this letter.
  Your friend always
  Jennie

* * *

Sam opened the letter when all the family were sitting around the breakfast table. Sam Johnstone, this normally easy going family man suddenly shouted, "Bastards! A shower of evil bloody bastards! My father loses his life working for the greedy swine and they throw my mother out on the street."

Sam never used bad language, Maria was absolutely horrified at his outburst, the children and Laurel looked terrified. Sam threw the letter at Maria and rushed out of the kitchen slamming the door behind him.

Maria smoothed the crumpled letter and read it aloud. Both Alexander and Laurel fully understood the contents and could understand why Sam had been so angry.

Deciding it was best to get the children out of the way Maria said, "Laurel, please take Alexander, Isabel and wee Samuel to the swing park and I'll give you some money to go to the ice cream shop afterwards. I need some time to talk to Sam, he's had a terrible shock."

After the children and Laurel left the house Maria went out to the garden and found Sam sitting in the shed crying his eyes out. Maria knew there was nothing she could say to give him comfort, she simply held his hands.

Eventually they returned to the house where Maria prepared lunch for the children returning. Sam reread the letter and realised that his feeling of loss had been replaced by anger. For the first time he fully realised that the decision to emigrate to Australia had removed them from a system where working men were still virtually slaves to the company they worked for, they were slaves as surely as any black African working on the cotton or sugar plantations had been.

It took a long time for Sam to deal with his loss. In due course his sisters and his mother wrote to him about the death of his father but nothing hurt as much as that first letter from Jennie.

Somehow during 1930, 1931 and 1932 Maria managed to pay the loan to the Bank of Australia, cover the school fees and keep the business afloat. Thankfully Sam retained his job, albeit at a reduced salary, and his income kept the home running.

After Laurel graduated she helped Maria in Harris Clothing, refusing any payment as she received a monthly allowance from Matthew.

When Maria protested that she should be paid Laurel argued, "Maria, it's my pleasure to be of help in the business. After everything you and Sam have done for me over the years this is my chance to repay some of your kindness."

The business of Matthew Gregg in Sydney was also struggling but like Maria he had taken steps early to protect the company. He was also fortunate in that he had a sizeable amount of money in reserve and no property loans.

Back in Scotland Walter's business also felt the pinch but having low overheads and other sources of income he was able to accept the loss in turnover and await better days.

The first small green shoots of recovery from the Great Depression started in Australia in late 1932.

Somehow Sam and Maria managed to stay afloat, pay the loan, pay the wages and run their home without incurring any additional debt. But the strain took its toll, Maria's strawberry blond hair now had threads of silver and no longer able to afford help at the house in Northcote Sam had to take on extra chores leaving him feeling permanently tired.

One evening in the comfort of 'The Brig' Laurel and Maria were sitting in the kitchen having a hot chocolate before bedtime when Laurel declared, "Maria I've had an idea! It's not new, I've been churning it over for ages, but the time to tell you never seemed right, we have all been working so hard just to keep our head above water.

"Since the Wall Street crash the world seems to have gone topsy turvey mad. Now this Emu War, who would have believed that what was once a protected species is now causing crop havoc and the Australian army is having to fight them.

"Then the poor wee Lindbergh baby was kidnapped and murdered in America.

"And, then there is the Nazi party growing in Germany. We are living in a world gone mad. Surely 1933 will start to see in better times.

"Anyway, I want to tell you my idea, I'd like to open a dress shop, where I would design exclusive clothes for rich clients. Maria, there are still plenty of monied people about who can afford a bespoke service, they want to look like movie stars, my challenge is finding them.

"I inherit five thousand pounds from my grandfather's estate when I'm twenty one. If Matthew loans me an advance would you consider

allowing me to rent part of H.Q. as a studio, you would also get the
business of making the garments, it would be a fifty fifty partnership
I've even thought of a name, Laurelei. What do you think?"

Taken aback Maria replied, "Laurel, obviously there is a lot to
process here but I think you have the making of a wonderful idea,
besides your talent needs to be used creatively, it's certainly a possibility.

"We have only ever used the shop entrance for deliveries and
collections. Perhaps we could revamp the entrance and you could use
Walter's old bedroom as a studio for private fittings and discussions
with clients. We could decorate the room and put in some dividing
screens, sofas, rugs, pictures on the walls, it needn't be too expensive.
We can buy from auctions and through the trade. Perhaps you could
get Faye to model for you, she is very pretty and has a lovely figure. All
we need for Harris Clothing is a discrete brass plaque on the side of
the door.

"When Matthew arrives for the Christmas holidays you can discuss
your idea with him and see if he'll give you an advance. If I had the
money I'd certainly invest in you! Laurel, you have the artistic talent,
I've an eye for a bargain and I'm good at administration but never in a
million years could I produce designs for haute couture.

"Tell you what, we'll get some ideas down on paper with costings
ready before Matthew arrives. You know the success of this venture
rests on getting a few well known people to use you, then you would
become almost a selective secret; special, exclusive and expensive.
Harris Finishings then Harris Clothing have depended on volume,
Laurelei Couturier will produce beautiful and expensive garments
selling a unique product to the wealthy."

Laurel laughed, "Maria, you are saying 'will' I think that means you
are behind the idea."

Maria agreed, "Actually I do think we should take it forward,
besides I think we all need something to lift our spirits instead of just
plodding on and hoping to pay the wages each week."

For the two weeks until Matthew was due to arrive from Sydney
Laurel and Maria worked hard on the business plan for Laurelei
Couturier.

Sam too was supportive, he agreed with Maria, since the start of
the depression all their lives seemed to be spent just keeping their
heads above water it would be exciting to start something new again.

Over the holidays they discussed the idea with Matthew. Soon after
his return to Sydney a cheque for one thousand pounds arrived in the
post. The money acted as a catalyst and Laurelei Couturier stared to

take shape.

Before spending a penny of the money Maria insisted that Laurel have a meeting with Mr Green to get his opinion on her plan and to have him initiate the appropriate legal papers.

When Laurel returned from the meeting she had a smile from ear to ear. "You will never believe me, Mr Green is all in favour of the downstairs conversion AND he thinks I'm very talented AND he thinks we will make a successful partnership, with you in charge of practical and me artistic he says the business cannot fail. Honestly Maria, I was speechless! We certainly have his blessing, let's press on."

After bleak years of simply trying to keep the wolf from the door, the next three months were not only busy they were exciting and enjoyable.

The day the signwriters erected the elegant new sign, in black and gold, *Laurelei Couturier*. Laurel felt her long held ambition was at last coming to pass.

Initially Laurel had thought about having a manakin in the window wearing a fabulous outfit but in the end she decided to take Maria's advice and dress the window quietly and elegantly, a backdrop of black velvet, an easel with a sketch pad, showing a beautiful outfit and a white silk flower arranged on crumpled black velvet.

A number of visits to auctions enabled them to acquire, at very reasonable cost, two chaise longes and screens for the salon, also a sofa and several chairs. The girls re-covered the furniture using remnants of quality fabric. These together with a selection of coffee tables, a full length mirror and rugs completed the furnishings. Maria suggested that they framed a number of Laurel's pencil sketches to decorate the walls, two jardinieres found in a junk shop and filled with ferns dressed the room, together with finishing touches of fashion magazines and bowls of flowers. The colour scheme was mainly cream and taupe with touches of black and gold. Maria suggested using neutrals as the coloured material of the outfits would be better set off against a quiet background.

By using trade discounts, picking up bargains, and the skills of the H.Q. staff Laurel was able to acquire a salon that looked as though it cost a fortune for less than two hundred pounds.

The only thing Laurelei Couturier required now was clients. Maria put out the word to many of her business associates about the new service, emphasising that the quality they had always known from the Harris Clothing business would translate into high end fashion.

One morning Laurel received a telephone call from a lady called

Mrs Amy Cohen. An appointment was arranged for two o'clock that afternoon. Laurel was so nervous she couldn't eat any lunch. "Maria do you think you could be with me when I meet Mrs Cohen?" she implored.

"Absolutely not," replied Maria. "This is your project, I can't hold your hand. Laurel you have an incredible talent, now you must learn to sell that talent, in the same way Walter and I were thrown into the deep end and had to learn how to run Harris Finishings. One day you will thank me but I'm now going to push you into the deep end of the swimming pool.

"I'm going out now, I've got an appointment with Mr Drummond at Bunnykins then I'll drop some paperwork into Mr Goldberg and collect Alexander and Isabel from school. Remember I'll always be in the background but if Laurelei is going to be successful you need to be it's face."

Mrs Cohen turned out to be an ideal client to design for, tall, slim with rich dark brown hair. Laurel listened carefully to the brief over a cup of coffee and Mrs Wilson's biscuits after which she promised Mrs Cohen that she would have sketches, material samples and a toile ready in two days time.

By the time Maria and the children returned, Laurel was sitting in the kitchen with Mrs Wilson, Alice and Faye telling them all about her first meeting with a paying client. Laurel was excited beyond excited and Maria was reminded of how nervous she had felt in the early days.

"Maria, Mrs Cohen wants a gown and co-ordinating evening coat for a big function next month, apparently her husband is a banker, and it's part of his image that she looks good. I've got an idea as to what she is looking for, I'll have the sketches and her toile ready for Thursday. I think I'm going to suggest using material from the sample books of Saunders & Winters.

"Incidentally, she loved the decor, said it was such a relief from salons which are all red velvet and heavy mahogany. If only she new it was economy that dictated our style of decor. And, wait until you hear this, her husband is a friend of Mr Green, HE recommended us."

Happily Mrs Cohen was delighted with Laurel's sketches and ordered her evening outfit in a colour somewhere between cream and mushroom with crystal trimming.

The finished outfit was stunningly beautiful and Maria was extremely proud that her girls had produced work of such quality. However, the real test was, would Mrs Cohen approve?

Mrs Cohen was delighted, the outfit fitted perfectly and she looked stunning.

Laurel who had created the design recognised that she had been very lucky, her first commission was for a woman with a model figure, and a model figure with many wealthy contacts.

Slowly the commission started to come in, bringing welcome extra work for the Harris Clothing side of the business.

Together the two businesses managed to come through the difficult years of the depression. Maria was again able to afford help at 'The Brig' and ensure that her three beloved children received the education she always wanted them to enjoy.

CHAPTER 29
War Clouds Gather

The mail arrived just as Maria and young Samuel were leaving to catch the train into Melbourne. Maria popped the treasured letters into her handbag to read on her way to H.Q.

Coatbridge

Dearest family in a far land

Looks like we are heading for yet another war, the second in my lifetime.

Mary Law and I have been stocking up on pulses, rice, sugar, tea, also any tinned goods that we can use to make the basis of a meal, things like corned beef and sardines, food to feed the women at the refuge. We have also been buying extras, mixed spice, cinnamon, ground ginger, coffee and suchlike.

Our Mary and Liz have even bought a case each of sherry, port, gin, whisky and brandy. A bit too extravagant for the refuge don't you think? We will make do with elderberry wine made from our own berries that will suffice for any celebrations at the refuge.

Thank goodness the garden keeps us supplied with fruit and vegetables or as I call them jam, soup and chutney. We have even planted different types of potatoes so that we will have a steady crop throughout the year.

Liz and our Mary have rented out their flat in London. I am very glad as I would be worried sick if they were travelling in wartime. They will baton down the hatches in Airdrie.

Maria I must thank you for sending that big parcel of dried fruits, beautiful quality, I'll treasure. Your sisters Agnes and Mary were both delighted with their parcels and Agnes Law, well she was over the moon, no doubt they will all write to thank you.

The treat was doubly special as the parcels were sent from your friend Matthew Gregg's company. It warms my heart the way you helped those children through the trial of their no good father and now they are both successful in the adult world.

I remember only too well what it was like in the last war. Honestly, those of us that lived through the 14 - 18 war and the Spanish flu afterwards can't believe how the politicians have taken their eye off the ball and allowed the Nazi party to take over Germany, that wee runt Adolf and the rest of his ugly crew won't be happy until the killing starts again.

Sadly I rather think war will be what brings a bit of prosperity back to Coatbridge, the whole of Lanarkshire and Clydeside for that matter. The heavy industry will be in big demand same as last time. It's already happening.

All that, peace in our time, nonsense. I think Chamberlain was just buying time so that we can get ready for the fight to come. Thank God you are in Australia although no doubt the Empire will get dragged in. Thankfully Sam you are too old now to be called up, even if it wasn't for your weak chest. My worry is for the boys Alexander and young Samuel. Amazing to think Alexander is studying to be a doctor at Otago Medical School in New Zealand - even further from Scotland. Your father would be so proud to know that his grandson, who carries his name, will become a professional man.

Refugees are starting to arrive from Germany. Mainly Jewish folks but anyone who does not agree politically with Hitler should think about leaving the Reich before it's too late.

I worry that when the war starts, for start it will, that we won't find it easy to communicate with you. Even if you don't hear from your family here in Scotland remember every day you will be in our thoughts and prayers.

God Bless and love to you all
Ma

* * *

Edinburgh

Dear Sam and Maria
I'm sorry my letters have been so sad of late.

John has now passed away. Such a long and protracted illness, if it hadn't been for the support and love of Fiona I just don't know how I would have coped. We had a lovely service for him and I have never regretted my quest to find my father. I think having his family around him made John's last years comfortable and happy.

I so wish you could meet my dear wife but now that we can get away from Edinburgh and travel to Australia I don't think it would be a good idea. Like most of the country I think a second war with Germany is not far away. The tension is almost touchable, I'm probably not describing it very well but it's like we are collectively drawing in our breath and making ready for who knows what.

I would love to bring my family out to meet you, I have told them so much about life in Australia. My Samuel wants to meet the man he was called after. I remember all the happy carefree times we shared with great affection. I fear for my own children's future.

Laurel and Matthew just seem to go from strength to strength. I am so grateful for everything you have both done for them, they are a credit to your guardianship. That makes three waifs you have looked after as your own, what incredible kindness.

My dear Doctor Chalmers, my Poirot, is getting a bit frail now. I went down with his nephew Andrew to visit him over Easter. He still enjoys his Scotch and we exchange letters most weeks. His two sisters, Clarissa and Grace passed away. The family home was inherited by him and his sister Rosalind (Andrew's mother). They sold the property and split the proceeds between Andrew and his older brother. I was so pleased for Andrew and Janet, they have now been able to clear their mortgage and Andrew has bought over the veterinary practice where he has been working since qualifying, the money has given them security. Poirot sent Fiona two pieces of Lalique from the house to add to her glass collection, it started with the vase he gave us as a wedding present. We hope to get down to Bournemouth to see him before hostilities start.

What memories your parcel brought, all that wonderful dried and crystallised fruit. Fiona was delighted and has asked me to convey her thanks. Maria, remember every Christmas you used to buy a box of crystallised fruits as a special treat. Alexander used to love the cherries and when we got to the second layer the cherries placed inside the pineapple rings were always gone, he always denied it was him. Can you believe the wee monkey is now studying medicine, how the years fly past.

Mail may be interrupted in the coming days but know as soon as ever we can the McDonald family will travel to Australia. I also want you to know John would love to have met you, he was always grateful that when I needed help you were both there for me. May God bless you both, also Alexander, Isobel and Samuel (I have written separately to Matthew and Laurel).

Thank you for everything.

Walter

* * *

Glenboig

Dear Maria and Sam

So proud to hear that young Alexander is doing well at his medical studies, first professional man in the Riley family.

Since our pa died ma has blossomed, it's the only word Maria. I think the mother we have now is the person she was when she was a girl before she was downtrodden. Clare said she reminds her of our Maureen and I think she is right. Thankfully none of us seem to have inherited pa's nature, it makes you wonder what happened to Patrick Riley as a child to make him the way he was.

You will probably have heard things are not good in Europe, we call Hitler Mr Schickelgruber here, it brings him down to size. Another war seems inevitable, my worry is for the youngsters. Plenty of work at the moment, the country is getting ready for the coming conflict. The women are turning the extra money into food, especially the older ones who remember the shortages of the last war.

I don't think the Americans will be much help, according to the papers in February they had a big Nazi rally in Madison Square Gardens. I'm no convinced about the French either, bunch of big lassies if you ask me.

I must not forget, Clare said to remember and thank you for the parcel of dried fruits, she was thrilled. So nice that you are now able to send presents to maw and the others, she has shared some with her pals Maisie and Teresa. I think she just enjoyed saying to them.

'These were sent by my daughter Maria who lives in Australia'. Your family photographs now take pride of place on the sideboard. And, she wears the locket Walter gave her, for years my Clare kept it hidden in her handkerchief box.

Remember when we thought Martha was going to go into holy orders, well that's her going to have a late in life baby. Her and Joe had a lovely wedding at the chapel, I gave her away and your wee sister looked a picture in the pale blue costume you sent over for her. That's the last of us married now, we all thought Martha was going to be a spinster but there you are you never know how your life will turn out.

We send our best wishes to all our Australian family.

I hope I'm wrong about hostilities, I really do.

With all our best wishes to all the family

Dan

* * *

Cape Town

My dearest Sam and Maria

I can scarcely write this letter for the tears in my eyes. We have lost our darling Sophie, my friend and companion since the day we landed in Africa.

It was all very sudden. Charles was playing chess with a friend down in Muizenberg. Sophie and I were in the kitchen making scrambled egg for our lunch when she said. "Ishbel I haven't felt great this morning, I've got a pain in my arm and I don't remember bumping into anything. I feel baie moeg." It means very tired, we have two comfy chairs and a low table in the kitchen where we often sit in the winter with a coffee or tea. I told her to sit down and said I'd finish the lunch. I heard a soft groan, turned round and she had passed to her maker. It would have made no difference if Charles had been here, there was nothing a doctor could have done, massive heart attack.

We are all bereft, it was so sudden. What a turnout at the funeral, all her friends from District 6 paid their respects. I organised a tea for everyone in a church hall. Sophie would have loved the celebration of her life, surrounded by all her friends.

When I was clearing out Sophie's rooms together with Elize, a very sad task, we found an envelope full of rand together with a beautiful letter leaving the money to Elize. Elize has decided that she will use it in some way to honour Sophie, we have not decided exactly what yet but I feel Elize will be guided. I also found a letter addressed to me, I cannot bring myself to repeat the contents, I was so very touched. Sam and Maria, I'll just say this, we do the best we can in life but we have no conception as to what a difference we can actually make to the lives of others.

Elize is going into her second year studying pharmacy. Although he has never actually said so I think Charles would have liked her to study medicine. However, Elize is also fascinated by plants and their healing properties, I think that was the reason for her career choice. My darling girl works hard but she is still a real personality, she was always full of stories and a bit of an actress as a child. Do you know she still has Sylvia sitting on her room, she so loved that doll you sent her, lots of her stories started, Sylvia and I... or Ek en Sylvie... if she was speaking in Afrikaans.

The political situation in Europe is not looking at all good. I fear for my grandsons in Scotland. People back home are worried about another war.

We have quite a sizeable Jewish population here in Cape Town. There is a movement to try and get German refugees resettled here. Charles has met a Jewish doctor from Berlin who managed to come here with assistance from one of Charles's old colleagues. Honestly, I can hardly write his story, apparently the Nazi party have enforced sterilisation on anyone they don't consider worthy of the German gene pool. They are also secretly killing people in mental homes and homosexuals are also persecuted. It's not just the Jew they want to eradicate it's everyone who does not conform to their Aryan ideals or they have decided will be of no use to the Reich.

Robert too has heard similar stories from Jewish academics who have managed to get out of Germany and settle here.

In all the years we have corresponded I think this is the saddest letter I have ever written. Our personal loss of Sophie and potentially the loss of millions should there be another war. So desperately sad.

We send our love and prayers to you both, also Alexander, Isobel, Samuel, Laurel, and Matthew in Sydney. My how the family has grown. And, a family to be proud of.
   God bless my dears
   Ishbel, Charles and Elize

* * *

Over the past few years life in Northcote had improved considerably from the early part of the nineteen thirties. Once again Mrs Rogers was the family housekeeper, her father no longer worked in the garden but one of her nephews helped out which was a great relief to Sam. Not having to worry about cutting grass or cleaning out gutters made his life considerably easier.

Harris Clothing was doing extremely well. Maria had considered opening a factory unit but after the Great Depression she decided to invest elsewhere. Travelling along the coast to visit clients she noticed that small villages and towns were starting to expand, she wondered if this might be an investment opportunity.

Once again Mr Green proved to be a great sounding board. Taking his advice Maria and Sam started to buy up small parcels of cheap land on the outskirts of towns and villages. The sections were carefully chosen with a view to their strategic positioning when development came, as it surely would, eventually the land would become prime real estate. Meantime some of the land was leased for agriculture which provided a small income. However, it was the long term value that the Johnstones' were interested in acquiring.

Laurel's couturier business had gone from strength to strength and Laurelei Couturier was now the 'go to' salon for the great and the good of Melbourne society.

Difficult to believe, but Laurel was now married and the mother of twin girls, Miriam and Sonja. Her husband was the son of one of her clients, Hermione Stern. The romance with Joshua had been fraught, while his family liked Laurel personally and respected her talent and business acumen, she was not Jewish and they were not at all happy about the idea of having non Jewish grandchildren.

Love will always find a way, Laurel converted to the Jewish faith and they were married at the East Melbourne Synagogue, the oldest shul in the city. Matthew gave her away and Isabel was her bridesmaid, while Sam and Maria sat in the front row beaming like proud parents, the only real parents Laurel and Matthew had ever known.

The circumstances of the wedding reminded Sam and Maria of the Catholic v Protestant conflict they had endured back in Scotland.

Reading the letters from Jessie, Walter, Dan and Ishbel made Maria realise that war really was imminent and she must position the business to cope with the coming crisis.

Hearing that Sophie had passed away physically hurt, Maria understood that Ishbel must be feeling totally bereft. Yes, Ishbel had friends in Cape Town but nobody would ever take the place of Sophie, soul sisters who were born into different worlds thousands of miles apart.

When the train steamed into Flinders station Samuel hurried off to school and Maria headed for H.Q. Laurel and Isabel were already at work while the twins were safely in the care of Faye. Isabel had stayed overnight with Laurel and Joshua as they were both working on a big society wedding project that included outfits for the bride, bridesmaids, bride's mother and two sisters.

Like Laurel before her, Isabel was studying art and design, majoring in textiles. However, during holidays and any free time she had available Isabel worked with Laurel.

Maria tried to concentrate on work but her mind kept drifting to the letters she had read on the train. The feeling that their lives were all about to change dramatically would not leave her.

That evening after dinner, while Isabel was working on the wedding project and Samuel was doing his homework Maria gave Sam the letters to read. After reading them he placed them down on the table saying, "They paint a disturbing picture for the future do they not? Maria, it's not our future, it's the young ones I am concerned about.

"I know what war is like on the front line. The politicians and generals in their comfortable offices well behind the lines, eating five course dinners at the end of the day, finished off with a bottle of port. These folk have no conception of the hell the men and junior officers are sent to endure in the trenches. They issue their stupid orders and the troops have to carry them out or be shot as cowards.

"After the mustard gas attack when I was repatriated from France I knew I could never discuss the war with you or my mother and sisters. One night I sat with my pa and talked for hours, I got it all out, we ended up in tears, two big men from Gartsherrie crying like bairns. I have never spoken of my experiences since, not even to you my darling. I never needed to speak of them, I shared them with my pa all those years ago.

"Reading the letters has kindled a fear in me. Even during the worst of the depression years I knew we would pull together as a family and see better times, and we have Maria another war, it frightens me, no family in the British Empire will be left untouched.

"And, hearing that Ishbel and Charles have lost Sophie. I fear Ishbel will be distraught, Sophie played such a big part in their lives. I know we only met her a few times but you could tell from Ishbel's letters she was a real character. Somehow you could imagine her in Glenboig or Gartsherrie, having a good blether as she was hanging out the washing."

Maria took her husband's hand, saying, "My Sam I've felt like you are saying all day. I can only describe it as a sadness in my soul. At lunchtime I went out and sat in the cathedral for half an hour, there was a lunchtime service on and the hymn they sang was 'The Day Thou Gavest, Lord, Has Ended'. I cried so much I had to go into a cafe have a cup of tea and pull myself together before going back to show my face at H.Q.

"Who knows what the coming years will bring but today I just thought, 'Maria, your family is now in the hands of God and he has been with us ever since we left the single end room in Glasgow'. Aye Sam, can you mind the shooglie bed with the feather mattress?"

They both laughed. Maria said, "I'll away and make us all a hot chocolate it's time the bairns put their books away. Sam, what will be will be, the coming years are out of our hands, they are in the hands of God."

—

CHAPTER 30
The War Years

War with Germany was declared by the Prime Minister of Great Britain, Mr Chamberlain in London on 1st September 1939. Sam took it very badly, his memories of the fighting in France had come back to haunt him.

Although he didn't articulate his thoughts to Maria he was terrified that his boys would eventually get caught up in the fighting.

On 3rd September 1939 the Australian Prime Minister, Robert Menzies announced on every radio channel Australia's forthcoming involvement in the war.

By the 15th of September Menzies had announced the formation of the Second Australian Imperial Force. War now seemed very real indeed. Strangely when she heard the announcement Maria's first thought was, I hope everyone received the second box of dried fruits and nuts I sent to them in Scotland before the war started, they were all so pleased with the first boxes I sent through Matthew.

At the outbreak of hostilities life seemed to change very quickly, Harris Clothing moved their production into making uniforms for the forces and ancillary services. Maria was busier than she had ever been.

The brickworks where Sam was a manager increased production and Sam too was busier than ever before. As in Glenboig and Gartsherrie the war brought an element of prosperity to Northcote. The principal employer, the brickworks, was offering plenty of overtime and taking on additional staff.

Sam and Maria had always enjoyed spending time together, with their children and extended family. Sadly the war seemed to fill their lives with work and they missed the companionship they had always enjoyed. When they did get time together it was cherished.

Financially Harris Clothing was in a very good place and the Johnstone family land portfolio was healthy. For a couple brought up in industrial Lanarkshire who had arrived in Australia with little more than the clothes they stood up in, they were now well placed. Sam and Maria now owned outright numerous tracts of land, 'The Brig' and H.Q. as well as having a substantial bank balance which was now measured in thousands of pounds the prosperity a reflection of all their hard work.

Despite the hostilities there was still a demand for Laurelei bespoke outfits. However, Laurel's designs had simplified to reflect the times they were living through.

Her husband Joshua was a lawyer in his father's firm, he enjoyed his life married to the woman he loved together with their two enchanting baby girls. He was about to be made a full partner in the family firm and he lived with his beloved family in a beautiful home in the suburbs. Joshua had a perfect life, perfect, but for the worry that one day, like so many other young Australians, he would eventually be conscripted to fight in a European war.

Initially life didn't change much for Alexander in Dunedin, he continued with his medical studies and longed for the day he could put his skills to good use.

Isabel finished her course at college and then went on to work full time in the family business. Sadly, her dreams of designing beautiful outfits were put on hold. Isabel's skills were required in the day to day running of the business. However, she still managed to enjoy life going dancing and having nights at the pictures with her friends.

Thankfully Samuel was still at school. His dream which he only shared with Isabel was to one day join the Royal Australian Air Force. His sister warned him, "Sam, on no account tell Mum and Dad that you would like to join up. Although daddy doesn't talk about it he went through a terrible time when he was fighting in France. It would worry them sick to know that you want to enlist. Keep your thoughts secret, hopefully it will all be over before you are old enough for the forces. If you still want to fly when you are older you can join the Air Force during peacetime, I think they could handle that."

In the Union of South Africa, Simon's Town, situated just down the coast from Cape Town, become a base for allied shipping, as it had been in the 14-18 conflict.

Ishbel joined an organisation to provide assistance to sailors who needed help in a strange land and Charles came out of retirement taking on part time work giving lectures to medical students.

After many years of marriage and having reconciled themselves to being childless, Anna became pregnant. The entire family were delighted, however a sadness would come over Ishbel as she sat knitting in the comfy chair in the kitchen looking at the empty chair opposite and thinking how happy Sophie would have been to know that she was going to be a grandmother to a child that she would be able to hold. Her Scottish grandchildren all having been born after she had sailed for Africa.

Matthew Gregg's business thrived, he was putting in long days at the office and was now living in a house at Potts Point, convenient for his business premises. He was handsome and popular but he had not yet met 'the one'. Matthew had seen the love between Maria and Sam, he had heard of Walter's almost instant engagement and wedding to Fiona, a partnership that had endured and brought great happiness. Even his sister Laurel had met her love match in Joshua. Matthew decided that unless he met someone who was truly his soulmate he would rather remain a bachelor.

His father was still in prison and his mother was in the prison that she had created in her mind. Matthew faithfully visited her every month and ensured that she was well cared for and had everything that she required. As time passed she seemed to regress more and more into her comfort world. A world that had no memory of her two children.

In Australia, although young men had gone off to fight, the population did not have to deal with severe food and fuel shortages. They did not dread the air raid siren, or hear the Nazi jackboot on their streets. They read about what was happening in Europe, they did not live it.

Suddenly the reality of war touched the country in an unexpected way. On 7th December 1941 Japanese fighter planes attacked the American base at Pearl Harbor. On 8th December President Roosevelt declared war on Japan. Three days later Germany and Italy declared war on the USA, it was now truly a world war.

The new year celebrations to bring in 1942 were muted in the Johnstone household and in many others throughout Australia. The war now seemed to be invading their personal world. On 19th February 1942 the Japanese Air Force attacked Darwin in two raids. The capital of the Northern Territory was a small town and Darwin was not heavily defended. The entire Australian nation were horrified at the loss of 250 lives, and the damage to infrastructure in their country. Sadly these attacks would not be the last, until November 1943 there would be nearly a hundred further raids.

Joshua received his dreaded call up papers and was due to report for officer training on 8th March 1942. Alexander like many of his year at medical school would be required to report for service in September 1942, after his final exams.

In spite of the war, life goes on. Maria just kept her head down and carried on working. Occasionally a letter would arrive from Scotland or Cape Town, thankfully so far all the family were safe and she felt America coming into the war could only be for the good in the long run.

After his initial eight weeks training, Joshua was transferred to the Officer Training College at Duntroon in Canberra. Laurel missed him to distraction, work was her saviour and she threw herself into designing for Laurelei.

One afternoon at H.Q. Laurel and Isabel were working together in the salon when Lauren asked, "Isabel whatever is wrong with you, you might as well tell me for as sure as eggs is eggs something is amiss. I'm surprised your mum hasn't noticed and got it out of you but I think Maria is so caught up with everything that's going on perhaps she hasn't noticed you are not your usual self."

Isabel thought about denying that anything was wrong but the need to tell someone her secret was too strong. "Oh Laurel, there is something wrong, you know I was going out with that chap from St Kilda, Alan Peebles, he passed out as a lieutenant. Well, Alan sailed with his regiment nearly six weeks ago, I've got no idea where he is, Laurel, I'm pregnant."

Whatever Laurel had expected to hear it wasn't that. "Oh Isabel, does he know?"

"No, it only happened the day before he embarked. Just the once, he was leaving and I thought I really loved him and it happened and I'm going to have a baby. Mum and Dad will be so disappointed, I can't find the words to tell them, I just can't. I was wondering, do you think Matthew could find me a job in Sydney and I could have the baby there?"

Laurel just didn't know what to think, "Isabel, I have honestly no idea what you should do. I'll need to think this through. First things first, have you been to see a doctor yet?"

"No, but I've missed my monthly twice."

Laurel went into practical mode, "Right, tomorrow I'll make an appointment for you with my gynaecologist. I'll get him to send his fee note to me, your mum doesn't need to know anything at this stage. Once we know what's what we can make a plan."

Laurel told Maria that she and Isobel were going out on an appointment, Maria was so busy she didn't even ask where. Before entering the surgery Laurel slipped a ring on Isabel's finger and introduced her as her friend, Mrs Johnstone. The doctor confirmed that Isabel was indeed in the early stages of pregnancy, congratulated her and confirmed that all was well.

They left his office in shock and headed to the Hotel Windsor where they ordered a pot of coffee. Isabel broke the silence, "Honestly Laurel I don't know how I didn't burst into tears when the doctor said 'congratulations', it's anything but congratulations. What on earth am I going to do, it's real now? I'm going to have a baby."

Laurel took her hand, saying, "Between Joshua getting called up and now your news, I can't sleep for worry. I don't think running away to Sydney is the answer. Remember Walter's story, it will all catch up with you eventually. I think you have to tell your mum then we can work it out as a family.

"If you want I'll speak to Matthew. You could perhaps go to Sydney for a breathing space to think things over but moving away and thinking you can have a child in secret is a complete non starter."

Isabel could feel the tears running down her face, "I was so stupid and I know if he had not been going to war it wouldn't have happened."

They sat talking in circles for some time. Laurel eventually declared, "We have to get back to H.Q. now. I need to collect the twins and take them home. Do you want me to tell Matthew the reason you want to spend some time in Sydney, or will we just keep your secret between us two meantime?"

"Just tell Matthew I need a bit of time away from Melbourne to have a rethink about work. Not exactly a lie, I really want to work in the creative design aspects of the clothing industry, not the administration. Did you know my dad's mother was a trained milliner, fashion must run in the family. I know the mantra at the moment is 'There's a war on', but it won't be forever and managing Harris Clothing is not my life's calling."

As they neared H.Q. Laurel promised to telephone Matthew that evening.

The following week Isabel headed north to Sydney and Joshua arrived in Melbourne from Canberra for a welcome short leave.

As the train took Isabel closer to Sydney she felt it was taking her away from her problem. It was almost possible to forget the real reason she was visiting Sydney, a city where she had long wanted to spend time.

Matthew met her at the Central Railway Station with a hug and a beautiful bunch of flowers, "Isabel Johnstone, I'm so glad to welcome you to Sydney, the first Johnstone to visit me and get to see the Gregg Empire. I've booked you into the Sir Stamford at Circular Quay, it's nice and central. I'll drop you off at the hotel and you can get a good nights sleep. Did you eat on the train?"

Isabel laughed, "Of course I ate on the train, breakfast, lunch and dinner. I'll be glad to just have a cup of tea and get to bed now. Thank you for the beautiful flowers, roses, my favourite! I'm so grateful to you Matthew for organising my trip, I just wanted a little break and thinking time away from Melbourne."

Matthew said, "We can talk properly tomorrow, I'm going to take the day off. I'll call for you around eleven o'clock, that will give you plenty of time to catch up on your beauty sleep after a long day today, not that you need beauty sleep."

Taking Matthew's arm as they headed to his car Isabel chuckled, "Away with you Matthew Gregg! You don't need to pay me compliments. We used to play snakes and ladders together. Remember the line up at all the games was you and me versus Alexander and Laurel. Shame, you got the dipsy child. Alexander was always the clever one. Can you believe he will become a qualified doctor this year? Ma and pa are proud of him, fit to bursting."

They gossiped until arriving at the hotel, then Matthew made sure Isabel was registered and being shown to her room before he took his leave.

Isabel had a good sleep, the first since the nightmare had begun. By the time Matthew arrived the following morning she had enjoyed a light breakfast and was dressed in a navy trouser suit with a crisp white blouse.

For the first time Matthew saw the girl he thought of as his little sister as a beautiful stylish woman. They settled themselves into his new beige Packard Convertible and set off.

"Nice car!" commented Isabel. "Very smart, I've been driving recently, my dad gave me some lessons and for some reason it seems to come easy to me. Mum hardly drives now, she prefers me to drive or to use the trains. I think with her, driving was always a necessity rather than enjoyment. Samuel is desperate to start learning to drive, he wants me to give him lessons but I said a definite NO. As well as being too young Dad thinks he is a bit too reckless and I think so too, I could easily see him driving much too fast. Can I have a shot driving your car?"

"What, you want to drive my little pride and joy? Alright, I'll let you but not in the city, when we go up the coast I'll give you a chance to drive.

"Today, I'm going to take you to see the office and then we can go on the ferry over to Manly, it's a spectacular sail and we can have fish and chips on the beach. What do you think?"

"I think that sounds fabulous, It's such an adventure coming all the way to Sydney."

Matthew had made plans, "I'm going to take a few days off while you're here. I thought we could take a trip up into the Blue Mountains, perhaps stay at Cooper's Grand Hotel. But first I'm going to take you to the nerve centre of Matthew Gregg & Son."

The offices were housed in a Victorian red brick building. Matthew raced Isabel upstairs to the third floor where the boardroom and his office were located. As they reached the top of the circular staircase he jocked, "We do have a lift but if we're going to have fish and chips later you need the exercise Miss Johnstone."

Isabel retorted, "Cheek of you Matthew Gregg! Just because you have your name above the front door. I must say this is a very grand boardroom with all these portraits of scary looking men overseeing all your decisions around the mahogany table. Gosh the nearest we have to a boardroom in Melbourne is Mrs Wilson's kitchen table."

"Maybe," laughed Matthew, "but I bet you get a better cup of tea and remember I've tasted Mrs Wilson's delicious scones and Lamington cake. We get tea in tiny China cups with wee posh biscuits at our board meetings."

"Well, I am impressed! It looks like the photographs of royal palaces I used to see in school books. Now let me inspect your office, the hub of the Gregg empire." Like the boardroom the office was decorated in a traditional style with midnight blue velvet curtains, there were no portraits hanging on the walls. There was however several framed watercolours. Isabel immediately recognised the style, saying, "I love your paintings and I know who painted them, Laurel really is incredibly talented. Can you paint, Matthew?"

"Heavens no! I have absolutely no artistic talent whatsoever. Don't you remember I was always good at maths? I used to teach you and Alexander your tables and get you to play mental arithmetic games. Although you preferred being with Laurel making dolls clothes or drawing. When young Samuel came along. He was the only one who really appreciated the maths tuition.

"Come downstairs and I'll show you the clerks rooms, and on the ground floor we have the reception area and a sales showroom. The warehouse is quite near here but it closes at noon on a Saturday, I'll take you to see the beating heart of the business another day."

After a tour of the offices and being introduced to a number of the staff Matthew kept his promise and they ended up on a ferry to Manly. Isabel was fascinated to see the new Sydney Harbour Bridge from the water and she found the whole idea of commuting by ferry to the city suburbs, around what must be the finest natural harbour in the world, thrilling beyond words.

"I can see why you love Sydney Matthew. It's so exciting! Whereabouts do you live?"

"It's nothing like the mansion I was brought up in," Matthew explained. "I've a relatively small house at Potts Point. After I sold the family home and left Mr Smallman's house I rented a small bungalow for a time, however I eventually decided that while property prices were still relatively low, due to the depression, it would be a good time to buy. There are some really lovely villas at The Rocks and Potts Point which have an easy commute to the business districts. I was tempted to buy a villa, but being on my own I didn't need anything too large, eventually I managed to find a property in a Victorian terrace which meets my needs. I have a housekeeper who comes in every day during the week and a lady who helps her with the heavy cleaning one day a week, that's all the help I really need. The garden is very small, I keep it tidy myself, it's my relaxing time. I always enjoyed helping your dad out in the garden at 'The Brig' you know.

"If you would like to see my house I'll ask Mrs Thomas if she'll organise lunch for us one day, perhaps on Tuesday."

They had a glorious afternoon in Manly, swopping childhood memories and catching up on each other's lives. They did not dwell too much on the war. Yes, it was affecting those they loved. Yes, with Japan in the conflict it was becoming too close to home for comfort, a boom net was even being constructed in the stunningly beautiful Sydney harbour. Yes, the world seemed to be changing at breakneck speed but they both wanted to step back, relax and muse on happier times.

Isabel was tempted to confide her secret to Matthew but she decided to put it into a box at the back of her mind and simply enjoy the day.

Before boarding the ferry back to Circular Quay they sat together on a bench near the wharf enjoying fish and chips and each other's company.

Sunday, they took a drive down the coast to Wollongong, or as Matthew called it 'the gong'. It was a wonderful day, the hood was down, the ocean views spectacular, and the conversation lively.

Monday, Matthew returned to work while Isabel did some shopping then visited the National Art Gallery of New South Wales. In the evening Matthew joined Isabel at the hotel. They enjoyed a glass of champagne in the lounge before dinner. As they sat eating their sole with shrimp sauce Isabel said, "Matthew when we enjoy a lovely meal like this I often think about my family back in Scotland and feel a bit guilty. Apparently there are lots of shortages in Britain. Not just food, coal, clothing, but everything. The only thing they seem to have in abundance is rain.

"Everyone was so thrilled to receive the boxes Mum arranged for you to send to the Scottish relatives just before the start of the war. Apparently the dried and crystallised fruits are considered a real luxury and when you included honey and nuts in the second consignments, well as my mum would say, 'they were all wasted'. Gosh we all grew up with all the old Scottish words and phrases, Laurel speaks Scottish as well, goodness knows what her new Jewish family think of her fluent command of Lanarkshire words and sayings."

Matthew laughed, "I'm not immune, sometimes no other word or expression will cut it. When you are scunnered or peeved no other word will do, usually prefixed with 'right'. Another thing that has stuck with me, if I hear anyone sneezing I desperately want to say, 'god bless you and the devil miss you'. You know Isabel, your parents saved my life and Laurel's. I'll never be able to repay them."

They enjoyed the remainder of the evening together, finishing with coffee and chocolates in the lounge. The following day Matthew picked up Isabel in his Packard and they drove to his home for lunch.

The meal Mrs Thomas prepared did them proud. It was a beautiful day, coming into the Australian autumn and the housekeeper had set up a table outside in the small, but delightful rear garden. Relaxed, they enjoyed chilled Chardonnay with a cold collation, served with home made bread, fruit and preserves.

Isabel loved the Victorian terrace house with its exterior wrought ironwork finishings, corniced ceilings and dado rail in the hall and stairway. Matthew had decorated the house in pale colours with voluptuous muslin curtains.

Matthew was delighted with Isabel's approval. "When I bought the house it was decorated like the boardroom times one hundred. I stripped everything back, and redecorated. First thing to go was the velvet curtains and dark colour scheme. Can you believe I did a lot of the work myself, your dad taught me well and to be honest I enjoy decorating and gardening, using my hands, it's very satisfying."

Wednesday, Matthew had to go into work, Isabel met him at lunchtime and they ate sandwiches in his office then he took her to visit the company warehouse.

Thursday Matthew had to work during the day giving Isabel time to visit the Royal Botanic Gardens. She took her sketch pad and spent some time drawing the exotic flowers and shrubs.

In the evening instead of eating at the hotel Matthew took Isabel to a little French restaurant where they dined on moules mariniere followed by quiche with a green salad.

Matthew asked his guest, "Would you like some cheese or pudding? They are famous here for chocolate pots, and I know what a chocoholic you are, or perhaps tarte tatin?"

Isabel replied, "It all sounds delicious but I'm full, really lovely supper. Matthew you've been so kind to me here in Sydney, I hope I haven't disrupted your life too much."

"Nonsense, I haven't had so much fun in ages. And, tomorrow we have our trip up to the Blue Mountains to look forward to.

"I think I'll get you back to the hotel at a reasonable time tonight and we can make an early start. Tell you what, I'll come over to the hotel and we can have breakfast together at around seven thirty and get on the road by eight o'clock. Is that alright by you?"

Isabel replied, "Perfect, I'm really looking forward to our trip to the Blue Mountains, quite an adventure."

On her shopping expedition in Sydney Isabel had treated herself to a new pastel pink dress for their trip which she wore with white accessories.

When Matthew saw her at breakfast once again he was stunned at just what a beautiful young woman Isabel had become.

They left the hotel promptly and were on the road heading north by eight o'clock. They intended to stop for coffee en route before arriving at the hotel in time for a late lunch. Blessed with a beautiful day the top was down on the Packard.

They were hardly on the road before Matthew and Isabel were once again reminiscing. Isabel started chatting about her background. "Isn't it strange none of us Johnstone kids have ever been to Scotland and yet the things we say are far more Scottish than Australian. Oh Matthew do you remember when Samuel was a baby and Mum used to say, 'Eye knows cheekie cheekie chin, cheekie cheekie chin knows eye' and she would point on his face and then we would all join in, and Alexander would pretend to be a Chinaman."

Matthew agreed, "Yes there was a lot of laughter at 'The Brig'. Laurel and I had never known such fun. Your mum worked so hard yet she would always find time to get us all in the kitchen baking or making sweets. Remember the tablet? We all had to take turns beating it, but the result was scrumptious, it's a wonder any of us still have our own teeth.

"You know the background with my parents, well there is a Scottish word that fits my father perfectly - sleekit. No English word works, he was sleekit. Walter and Dr Chalmers rescued us on the ship but it was your parents who gave us a family life and made us whole. When we first arrived at Northcote Laurel was very much a lost soul and it was you Miss Isabel Johnstone who initially brought her back. Look at her now married to Joshua, the mother of twins and a successful businesswoman.

"I hated going back to Sydney after the school holidays. Laurel just refused, she bunkered down with you all and thankfully your family took her to their hearts.

"Every time I left to return to Sydney your mum would give me a picnic to take on the train and a box with home made treats. In the box there would always be two letters, one each from your mum and dad encouraging me and reassuring me that 'The Brig' would always be my home and they loved me. Can you imagine how much that meant?"

Isabel just touched his hand, "We did have lots of laughs before this ghastly war started. It's been so wonderful to spend a little time with you away from all the sadness. I've purposely not read a newspaper since arriving in Sydney."

Travelling to the Blue Mountains and anticipating an exciting weekend all was well with Matthew and Isabel, except for the secret locked tightly in a corner of Isabel's brain.

It happened in moments, as most tragedies do, a car overtook a lorry on the other side of the road and ploughed into the shiny beige Packard. The driver of the overtaking car was killed instantly and Matthew and Isabel were rushed to the Penrith Hospital.

Most of Matthew's injuries were superficial, cuts and bruises, whiplash and two cracked ribs, however he also had a broken leg. Isabel's injuries were more serious, as well as the cuts and bruising she required surgery.

In bed after having his broken leg set and a collar fitted around his neck to relieve the pain, Matthew asked the nurse what had happened to Isabel, his passenger. The nurse promised to find out Isabel's condition and let him know.

A good hour later a doctor came into the room, using a sympathetic manner he spoke to Matthew, "Mr Gregg your wife has come through surgery safely but I am very sorry to tell you that she has lost the baby she was carrying. There was nothing we could do to save the foetus, unfortunately we also had to remove her spleen. Otherwise the young lady's injuries are similar to your own, although no broken leg bones in her case. I'll ask the nursing staff to wheel you down to see her this evening when she is fully conscious. Physically she is capable of having another child but losing her spleen means she will have to take great care of her health as she will be very prone to infections."

Matthew was dismayed, he wasn't sure if he was suffering from concussion or he was dreaming the words the doctor was saying. However he did manage to say, "Isabel isn't my wife, she's my sister, well not exactly my sister, her family looked after me and my real sister when we were young. Is she going to be alright?"

The doctor replied, "You are both going to be in hospital for some days but yes. I think all will be well. Is there anyone we can contact for you? Also, the police want to interview you both. I've told them to come tomorrow morning, tonight you both need a good rest.

"As I said someone will take you to see the young lady later, does she have family we should inform?"

Trying his best to concentrate through a terrible headache Matthew struggled to say, "Isabel's family live in Melbourne, she's up here on holiday. If you don't mind I would rather 'phone her parents after I've spoken to her, I don't want strangers to break the news."

In the evening a nurse came with a wheelchair and took Matthew down the corridor to visit Isabel. Before going into the room she said, "Mr Gregg, the young lady is still very poorly, you can only stay a few minutes."

Matthew was horrified to see her looking so pale and fragile.

"Isabel my dear girl, can you hear me?"

Isabel opened her eyes on seeing Matthew the tears formed, "I'm so sorry Matthew, they've told me you know about the baby. You must think I'm terrible but I just wanted to get things straight in my mind before I told my mum and dad, that's why I came to Sydney. Then, we had such a good time together and it was like the old days, I just wanted to be your wee Isabel again. Please don't tell Mum and Dad, they don't need to know, only Laurel knows. It's bad enough for them to hear we've been in a car crash."

Stroking her hand Matthew calmed her, "There, there, of course I won't tell your parents about the baby, it's our secret. We can talk later but I want you to go to sleep now, I'll ring your mum and dad and tell them about the accident. All will be well. Goodnight my little one."

The nurse returned and he kissed her gently before leaving to go to the ward sister's room where he could make the telephone calls.

First he called Laurel and gave her the full story, then he phoned 'The Brig'. Sam answered the phone, "Matthew lad it's great to hear from you, we had a letter from Isabel today, apparently you are giving her a great holiday."

Matthew interrupted him, "Sam, I'm telephoning with some bad news, we were in a car crash this morning. It's all right, we are both going to be fine. Apart from a broken leg and a couple of cracked ribs my injuries are superficial but Isabel had to have an operation to have her spleen removed, she also has cracked ribs, cuts and bruises. Sam will you tell Maria and young Samuel the news, also tell her mum I'll make sure Isabel gets the best treatment possible. I'll telephone you again tomorrow with an update, I'm using the ward sister's office so I can't stay on the line too long. Goodbye and don't worry."

Matthew then telephoned Mr Smallman who was still on Gregg's board and asked him to advise the staff about his accident and arrange for them to reschedule his appointments and take over the running of the business meantime. He also telephoned Mrs Thomas to put her in the picture.

A nurse helped him back into bed and Matthew slept the sleep of the exhausted.

The following morning the local police arrived to take statements. Fortunately both the lorry driver and several witnesses confirmed that the driver of the car had been responsible for the accident. They also advised him that the Packard had been taken to a local garage and was a write-off. Once he had been given the relevant paperwork Matthew was advised that he was unlikely to be called to an inquest as his statement would probably suffice.

After the police left Matthew asked the nursing staff if he could once again visit Isabel. This time she was fully conscious, as soon as she saw her visitor she started to cry, "Matthew I'm so sorry if you feel deceived by my coming up to Sydney but I just needed a bit of time to think things through before I told Mum and Dad. After I arrived surprisingly I started to enjoy myself, we had such fun together that I put everything to the back of my mind. Not very mature I know."

Isabel then repeated the full story as she had told it to Laurel. "Now there is no baby and I don't know whether I am glad or sad. When I go home Mum will spoil me and quite frankly I don't deserve to be spoiled."

Matthew held her hand, "Isabel, only Laurel and I know about the situation and I suggest it is never spoken of again, remember you were only a few weeks pregnant and at that stage there is no baby. I suggest that after we leave here, I book you into a convalescent hospital in Sydney and you get fully fit before you return home.

"Isabel, what happened to you was incredibly sad but you cannot allow it to define you. Are we agreed that it is never to be spoken of again?"

"Matthew Gregg, you always were bossy, but you are probably right. What good would come of upsetting my parents, the best mum and dad in Australia? In my heart I know you are right, the secret must remain between you, me and Laurel."

"Yes, that's me, bossy Matthew. This afternoon I'm going to make some phone calls. The doctor said we should be able to leave next week, I'll get the arrangements in Sydney organised and keep your folks up to date until they allow you up to telephone." He kissed her on the cheek and buzzed for the nurse to take him back to his room.

True to his word Matthew made the phone calls and five days later an ambulance took them back to Sydney, Isabel to the convalescent hospital and Matthew to his home at Pott's Point where Mrs Thomas had taken up residence in order to look after him until he was fully recovered.

During the following two weeks Isabel and Matthew spoke on the telephone each day and sent each other cards and letters. Isabel also sent him some delightful drawings which he arranged to have framed.

On leaving the hospital Isabel once again moved into the Sir Stamford at Circular Quay. Each day she took a taxi to visit Matthew until he was able to have the plaster on his leg removed and return to work full time.

One evening they were eating dinner in their favourite French restaurant when Isabel pondered, "I suppose I can't put it off indefinitely I'll have to return to Melbourne soon. Apart from anything else I need to help in the business. If it wasn't war work Mum would never have allowed us to get so busy, she likes her time at home with Dad. He's busy too, the war has brought on a need for building materials. I'm sure they too are looking back on the days when we were all children with fond memories, life seems so serious now."

"I know what you mean, my business has boomed since the start of the war, actually even before hostilities. Far sighted people like your mum were sending food all over Europe, believe it or not Gregg's sent tons of dried fruit parcels to Germany.

"Isabel, it seems like forever that we have been close. Yours was the kind of family I grew up longing for, then your parents accepted me, despite my truly wicked father. I've got to be truthful with you, over the past weeks I've come to see you differently. At the risk of you running for the hills or Melbourne I have to speak out. Isabel Johnstone I've fallen in love with you - I've always loved you but now I'm in love with you and I want to spend my life with you."

Isabel replied, "I've always loved you too, you numpty, but I know what you mean, the last weeks have changed everything. What are we going to do?"

"Isabel Jessie Johnstone, will you marry me?"

"Matthew, I don't know if you have a middle name, Gregg. Of course I will!"

They decided that it would be best to go to Melbourne and speak to the family directly rather than tell them on the telephone. Two days later they were sitting on a train taking the long journey south.

Maria had organised a homecoming dinner to include Laurel and the twins, Joshua was still at officer training college. The only other family member not attending was Alexander who was still in Dunedin.

The family welcomed back their bairns with kisses, cuddles and a flurry of questions. After making sure they were both well Maria announced, "I've made Isabel's favourite supper, shepherds pie followed by apple crumble with custard. If I remember correctly the four of you used to fight for the crispy bits."

Samuel piped up, "It's not fair, I'm too young to have been included in a lot of your adventures, you three must have been a right handful. We're they Dad?"

"Not at all, well perhaps a bit. Your mother and I are proud beyond measure of our five children and now we have the twins, our grandchildren."

Matthew felt he had to speak out before supper. He stood up to gain everyone's attention above the chatter. "The last weeks in Sydney have been a revelation for both Isabel and myself and things have changed. Mr Johnstone, Sam. I want to ask you for the hand in marriage of your beautiful daughter Isabel."

Sam was dismayed, Maria less so. Isabel's letters from Sydney contained more and more references to Matthew and she had started to think of them as a couple even before Matthew's announcement.

Laurel rose and kissed them both. Everyone was delighted, Sam told everyone to shoosh until he had formally given Matthew permission to wed his daughter.

"Matthew of course you can marry our wee Isabel. But I just want to say you won't soon be our son, you are our son. It's been our great gift to have you and Laurel join our family all those years ago. I know you lad and I know you will make Isabel a wonderful husband. As for Isabel, well, she will make you laugh, she will also be a great companion through life. And, you have to thank her mother for this, she is also a good wee cook and baker. Matthew, Isabel, God bless you both!"

Over the next few days Matthew bought Isabel a beautiful engagement ring and they organised a celebration dinner for all the family, this time Joshua was present as he had a few days leave.

Matthew couldn't stay away from the Gregg business indefinitely, he knew he had to leave Isabel and return to Sydney.

One evening after dinner when they were out in the garden Matthew turned to his fiancé, "Isabel I'd like us to get married soon. You know I need to return to Sydney and I can't be without you. It's not as if we've just met and don't know each other. When can we marry? Go on give me a date."

Isabel laughed, "Soon, let's keep it small, just the family and you can invite the Smallman family, after all they were very good to you. Say, four weeks from now. You can return to Sydney meantime, I do know you have to work. I'll make the plans here, you could also write to Alexander and ask him to be your best man, you were always thick as thieves. I'll have Mum and Laurel to help me and we can write and talk on the phone. I'm sure we could do the deed in four weeks."

Matthew kissed his future wife and knew he had found his soulmate.

A few days later Matthew returned to Sydney. Maria, Laurel and Isabel arranged the wedding while trying to keep up to date with work at H.Q. As well as the Johnstone and Smallman families Isabel invited, Alice, Faye, Mrs Wilson and Mrs Rogers. Also James and his wife Hannah. After leaving H.Q. James, encouraged by Maria, had opened a small business specialising in buttons and trims and he was now a trusted supplier to Harris Clothing and Laurelei.

Laurel designed a simple but stunning calf length dress for Isabel which could be worn with a fascinator rather than a traditional veil.

They decided to have the wedding breakfast at 'The Brig' where the guests would hopefully be able to spill into the garden. Melbourne weather being unpredictable Maria arranged to have a small marquee erected on the lawn.

Isabel insisted they employ caterers as she wanted to ensure that everyone would be able to enjoy the day without worrying about preparing and serving food and drinks.

As all the hectic preparations were going on Maria thought of her marriage to Sam in the Glasgow registry office, their celebration meal had been fish and chips eaten out of a newspaper. In her mind her real wedding would always be the blessing conducted by Robert in Cape Town.

Alexander and Matthew spent the two nights before the wedding staying with Laurel and Joshua while 'The Brig' descended into an organised chaos. Happily Joshua had managed to get some leave and Alexander had a few weeks free before starting a training course on treating wounds caused by warfare.

On the morning of the wedding everything fell into place, the florist arrived with the flower arrangements, bouquets and buttonholes, the caterers erected tables and took over the kitchen, Laurel arrived and helped Isabel into her dress.

Maria dressed in a beautiful powder blue outfit with cream trim and accessories, topped with a stunning cream and blue hat. When Sam saw her he felt a tear in his eye. "My darling girl you look every bit as beautiful as you did the day I met you outside Glenboig Brickworks when I had just returned from the war. We've travelled a long road and I don't just mean the miles. I'm so proud of you."

Maria smiled, "Oh Sam, we made the right decision travelling to the other side of the world. Three, no five bairns, a lovely home, fulfilling careers, money, investments. We loved each other when we had nothing and we love each other now. Not a bad recipe for marriage. I just hope Matthew and Isabel are as blessed as we have been."

With Samuel escorting his mother and Sam his daughter they left for the marriage ceremony at All Saints Anglican Church.

When Sam and Maria first arrived in Australia they decided on a religious compromise, the children would attend Sunday School at a church that neither had its roots in Scottish Presbyterianism nor Irish Catholicism. Anglican worship somehow worked for the family. Over the years the children were all told of their Protestant and Catholic background but both Sam and Maria's message to their children was one of Christian kindliness and tolerance.

After the service everyone returned to 'The Brig' where the guests enjoyed a beautiful buffet meal and sipped sparkling wine. Mrs Wilson had insisted on making the wedding cake which she had trimmed with pale pink sugar roses to echo Isabel's bouquet.

Everyone enjoyed a wonderful day filled with love and laughter. In the evening Joshua drove the happy couple into Melbourne where they spent the night at the Hotel Windsor. As they entered the foyer Isabel suddenly felt a cold sadness. Matthew obviously had no idea of the sad memory that the hotel evoked for her, she was whisked back to the day when she had sat with Laurel discussing her pregnancy. It had all happened just a few months previously but in Isabel's mind it happened in another world.

The following morning they caught the early train to Sydney. On the Monday morning Matthew was back at work and Isabel was trying to decide what she was going to do to fill her time, no Laurelei, no Harris Clothing, no camaraderie with her friends and family at H.Q., no Mum, no Dad, no Alexander, Samuel or Laurel and her girls. The tears started to fall and a wave of loneliness washed over her. Where it came from Isabel couldn't tell, she loved Matthew to distraction, Mrs Thomas had always been very nice to her, Sydney was a beautiful city, but still the tears came.

Isabel suddenly realised how lucky she had been to be brought up in a Scottish household. Her mother didn't react to drama, she could hear Maria saying, 'for goodness sake get a grip of yourself, don't you realise how lucky you are'. Mentally Isabel gave herself a good talking to, washed, dressed and went downstairs for some breakfast.

Over the next few weeks Isabel became familiar with the house and she spent some time getting to know the city, including taking ferry trips to the various suburbs.

Isabel found herself in a similar position to the one Walter had found himself in when he first arrived in Edinburgh. No existing business, no contacts in the clothing trade, where to start?

One evening at dinner Isabel and Matthew happened to be talking about how frustrating Maria was finding it not being able to send gifts to Scotland during the war.

Matthew explained, "Sending gifts for expats became quite a big part of the business and it started in a very small way. We had an inordinate amount of dried fruit in the warehouse one year. Someone, I can't remember who, remarked that, plenty of people in Europe would love to have such good quality produce in their kitchen. The thought germinated. I did the costings then put an advert in the papers of all the major cities for smart prepackaged gift boxes to be sent abroad with a gift card. The idea just took off, we were inundated with orders.

"Then we produced a catalogue and included other Australian products like ginger in syrup, honey, macadamia nuts, and crystallised fruits. It was incredibly successful, I had to open a new department to cope with the work. Obviously the overseas gift exports have all stopped since the war started but after it finishes I think it will quickly become extremely popular again after years of shortages in Europe.

"Thankfully I'm still supplying to the military, but as that business falls away I have the reinstating of the gift business firmly in mind."

Over the next few days Isabel mulled over the conversation about mail order. Eventually she had an idea, she waited until it was clear in her mind before telephoning H.Q. in Melbourne, "Laurel, I've got an idea and I want to run it past you and Mum. I'm thinking of doing a small mail order range. A target market to all the women who live out in the woop woops. I thought lingerie to start. Limited range, classy, not too expensive. If I send down a few sketches can you look over them and get Mum to do costings?"

Lingerie by Isabella took off like a runaway train. What started as a small home based business to keep Isabel busy soon had its own department in the Gregg Warehouse. Isabel eventually had to have some of her range manufactured in Sydney as Harris Clothing couldn't cope with the volume of work.

Matthew was incredibly proud of the achievements of his beautiful wife, his darling Isabel.

It sometimes bothered Matthew that the war had in fact been so good to him. The business was doing extremely well and he had sold the house in Potts Point and together with Isabel purchased a beautiful villa in the suburb of Mossman with stunning views down to Sydney harbour bridge. Life was good.

After qualifying as a doctor Alexander spent the remainder of the war working at a repatriation hospital near Sydney. Although kept extremely busy, he was occasionally able to spend some leave with Matthew and Isabel.

However, towards the end of the war he was sent to Burma where he was part of a team providing medical care to soldiers liberated from the camps. The experience had a profound effect on him.

Eventually the war would end and everyone's life was set to take off in a new direction.

CHAPTER 31
Peace Declared

May 8th 1945 saw the longed for V.E. Day. Victory in Europe was celebrated but it wasn't until 15th August of that year when V.J. Day was declared that Australia felt the war was indeed over for them. But at what a price - on August 6th and 9th atomic bombs were dropped on Hiroshima and Nagasaki, there was not an adjective sufficient to describe the resultant carnage. People all over the world had been horrified when the concentration camps in Germany were liberated and the world discovered true cruelty. Now here was yet another example of man's inhumanity to man.

Thankfully, for the Johnstone family young Samuel was starting university in 1945 so he never realised his dream of being a fighter pilot.

The war didn't just end on an arbitrary date, it was a slow and gradual return to some kind of normality.

At H.Q. there were changes, as the government contracts started to dry up. Laurelei Couturier was once again extremely busy as people wanted to get out and enjoy life again. Alongside her exclusive couturier pieces, Laurel started to design ranges of affordable stylish outfits, the manufacture of which kept Harris Clothing busy.

One blessing was that over the following months letters from Europe slowly started to arrive with more regularity.

Coatbridge

My dear family

At long last the war is over. Here in Coatbridge V.E. Day was heartily celebrated on 8th May. There were big dances in the Gartsherrie Institute and the Airdrie Town Hall and the bairns had two days off school. We held a wee celebration at the refuge which everyone enjoyed.

Apparently it was fair jumping in Glasgow, the pubs all ran out of drink and George Square was mobbed with people celebrating, I bet there was plenty of sore heads the next day. Apparently folks who didn't even know each other were hugging and kissing. It was just the same here in Coatbridge after all the years fighting we could now stop worrying about youngsters being called up.

The worst thing I find is actually seeing the evil committed by Hitler and his nazi party in all the papers and apparently it's on the Pathe News in the picture houses, horrors like you can't possibly believe, I expect it's all over your newspapers as well. What with cities on both sides ravaged, children playing on bomb sites, refugees trying to return home - Europe is in a mess, it will take years, no decades, to fully recover.

Thankfully Andrew and I married before the war started so we were able to support each other all through the conflict.

Maria, remember the two big boxes of dried fruits and other luxuries you sent to us, you have no idea how much they were appreciated. The two that went to the refuge provided many a wee treat for the ladies. Our two almost lasted for the duration and it was so nice of you to remember the Law family, Agnes was thrilled and her supply was partly used for family celebration cakes.

Jennie and I are still on the women's refuge committee but Mary and Jessie Law are now the guiding hands, together with our Mary. Liz doesn't have the energy now to get involved on a daily basis but she still attends meetings and is a wise sounding board. I think Ella Millar would be proud how we have used her legacy to help women in need.

The shortages all over Great Britain are terrible, but we have just got to manage as best we can. It's very hard for people with young bairns.

Well the big election is on 5th July, will it be Clem Attlee or Churchill? There is definitely a groundswell for change among those who served in the war, do you know it wouldn't surprise me if Labour win. I said as much to Agnes Law, she was horrified. Bless, she just pointed to her wee statue of Winnie and said, 'That man got us through the war how can you imagine he won't be our peacetime prime minister, Jessie I'm pure ashamed you could even think he might no win'. I didn't argue with her, I just let it go.

Can you believe I've been in demand making hats. Andrew

says he is a 'kept man' and I am the money earner now. Not really,
I just make them for family and friends, it's been a challenge using
bits and bobs which I've actually quite enjoyed.

Tom, Agnes and Emily are all well, Emily has now been
demobbed from the Wrens and is hoping to start university soon.
According to our Agnes she is keen to study architecture, not the
first subject you would associate with a woman but I'm glad to say
times are changing and perhaps Emily will be an equal in a man's
world.

Well my dears I'll post this letter with joy in my heart knowing
there is a good chance it will actually arrive in Australia.

With all my love to my beloved family

Ma

* * *

Glenboig

Dear Maria and Sam

At last it's over. Pray to god this will be the last war we will
know. The years of fighting were bad but even worse was the ending.
The newsreels of what happened in the concentration camps have
been horrific. VE Day was well celebrated all over Britain then a
few months later victory in Japan day.

V.J. Day was very much an anti climax here, partly I think
because of how we won. I know the wee Japs were evil devils and
what happened to our boys in the east was inhumane. But what a
wicked weapon the Americans have unleashed, an atomic bomb, now
the genie is out the bottle there will be no putting it back in again. I
fear for future generations, I really do.

Our ma is still doing well, she goes to Mass most mornings and
always says a prayer to St Joseph. I think it's to give thanks to him
and the good lord for taking my pa up to join them.

Ma loves all her children and grandchildren, her only real
sadness in life was losing our Michael in the first war and then our
Maureen.

Maria, ma is so proud of you and all her Australian family.
It's just so sad she will never meet you again. We are all getting
grey and lined now, I wonder if we would still recognise each other.

Still a lot of shortages here in Scotland. Goodness knows when *rationing will end. Mind you when you see the devastation to the German cities on The Pathe News you realise how lucky we are. Honestly, after all the fighting and loss of life, there are certainly no winners in war.*

I've been going out fishing during the war to help supplement the ration, I can sometimes swap some for a rabbit. Last week I got a half pound of sausages and a good portion of lambs kidney from the butcher for two fine trout. What a treat, Clare cooked the sausages and the kidney with vegetables and Bisto gravy, she served it with mashed tatties. I tell you it was absolutely delicious, I could have licked the plate.

I'd better finish now. Well, who knows what will happen in the country now that the election is not far off.

Hope to hear from you soon
Love from Dan and all the Riley family

* * *

Dan's letter had arrived in the morning and Maria read it on her way to work, in fact she read it several times. That evening after dinner she handed it to Sam, saying, "Sam, read Dan's letter carefully and tell me what part you think I simply can't get out my head."

Sam read the letter several times then said, "I know he talks of the horrors people are having to face up to, same as in the letter from my mother that arrived a few weeks ago. However, I would take a bet on the words that you've taken to heart are, 'We are all getting grey and lined now, I wonder if we would still recognise each other'. Am I right?"

Maria smiled, "As always you can read me like a book. Sam, Australia has been good to us, we have plenty of money in the bank. Alexander is a qualified doctor, Isabel is happy in Sydney with Matthew and building her own career with Lingerie by Isabella. Joshua has now been demobbed and Laurel is over the moon to have him safely home with her and the girls. Our last wean, Samuel, well we have packed him off to university in Sydney, heaven help Sydney! We have an empty nest my dear, I think it's about time we did something just for us two.

"Sam how do you feel about taking a trip to Scotland? We could see both our families and Walter and Fiona in Edinburgh. What do you think?"

"As always Mrs Johnstone, you are right," agreed Sam. "We've plenty of money in the bank account and you no longer need to produce uniforms for the war effort. My darling you have done your bit. Laurel, Alice and Faye can look after the business and let us have a long trip back home. I bet you know what I'm going to say next."

"Yes I do," Maria laughed. "You're going to say 'Cape Town'. Oh Sam, wouldn't it be wonderful to see Ishbel and Robert and meet Charles and Elize and Anna and the wee lad Fraser.

"Sam there is something else I want to suggest. You are into your fifties now and you have worked so hard during the war years. Considering the damage to your lungs in the first war don't you think it's time you retired from the brickworks? I don't mean retire altogether, we have the property portfolio to manage. Now that Mr Green has retired I think it would be a good idea for you to take a greater interest in our investments. You'd be your own master and if we want time off together well we can have it. Samuel Johnstone, I love you and I want to spend time with you. The war years seems to have flown past full of work. Sam this is going to be our time.

"Just talking about it is making me quite excited. I'll take a couple of hours off work tomorrow and visit the travel agent."

True to her word Maria disappeared from H.Q. for a few hours and returned with an itinerary in her handbag ready to discuss with Sam over a glass of sherry that evening.

Maria had priced the trip first class, with a two week stopover in Cape Town staying at the Mount Nelson. Built into the itinerary was two nights in Madeira, staying at Reid's Hotel. On arriving in Southampton they would take the train to London where they would have a few nights stay before travelling on to Glasgow and then Coatbridge.

After including meals, spending money and gifts the total cost was eye watering. However, Maria couldn't wait to get home to discuss her ideas with Sam.

Maria prepared the dinner thinking, 'This is just like the old days before we had Alexander, with me cooking dinner before Sam came home from work and looking forward to spending the evening together plotting and planning'.

After supper they got out Maureen's farewell notebook, Maria always used it when she was working out something important, it was her way of keeping her sister close.

Carefully she finished the calculations and showed the final figure to Sam, "I know it's a jaw dropping amount and we could bring it down quite a bit by travelling second class but you know the auld Scottish saying 'there are nae pockets in a shroud'. What do you think? Will we go and visit Scotland?"

Sam put his arms around his wife, kissed her passionately then declared, "My darling girl, of course we will go to Scotland, and we'll go in style. There is no way we are going to go home in separate dormitories. Do you remember the night of our blessing in Cape Town when Captain Thorn kindly gave us a first class cabin for the night? Maria, that is what I want for you, for us, first class. Our reward after nearly thirty years of hard work and bringing up five bairns."

The following weeks were positively manic and Maria couldn't imagine that she would ever complete her 'tick list', but busy as she was, she felt lighthearted. Every evening she looked forward to returning to 'The Brig' and spending the evening with Sam updating their plans.

Sam too felt the years roll back. Retiring was something of a relief. During the war years, regardless of his health, it would have been impossible as he felt deeply that he had to do his bit for the war effort. However, it was over now and it was time for him and Maria to enjoy the fruits of all their labour.

Before leaving on their adventure home to Scotland, Sam and Maria decided to take a trip to Sydney to visit Matthew and Isabel. It would also be an opportunity to catch up with Samuel and Alexander.

The military hospital on the outskirts of Sydney where Alexander had been working was scheduled to close later in the year. After much thought as to what he would do next he had decided to go back to university and qualify as a psychiatrist. Matthew and Isabel had been very supportive of his decision and insisted he stay with them while he was studying. They had also offered accommodation to Samuel but he rejected their offer in favour of halls of residence.

In the blink of an eye it was time for Sam and Maria to catch the train bound for Sydney.

Back in Coatbridge two mothers opened letters they never expected to receive.

Northcote

Dear Ma and Andrew

I know Maria writes to you more than I do giving you all the family news but I thought this is a letter that should come from your son.

As you can imagine life has changed a lot here during the war years, the children are now finding their own way in life and the business is once again changing. No more contracts from the military but that is more than compensated by work from Laurel and Isabel.

I have decided to retire from the brickworks. Maria and I work well together and it will be wonderful to work with her in the family business. Also, I will be my own boss and I'll be able to take a bit more time off work. To celebrate we are off to Sydney next week to visit Isabel and Matthew. Alexander will arrange a few days leave from the hospital while we are in Mossman and hopefully Samuel will get some time off from university.

Can you believe all these years in Australia and we have never been to Sydney. Actually, I have never been out of Victoria although Maria has been to Canberra on business for military contracts. Visiting Sydney is a big adventure for us both.

However, Maria and I have decided that the time is now right for us to have another <u>huge</u> adventure. Ma, we are coming home, we are coming on a trip to Scotland. We are sailing via Cape Town where we will once again meet Ishbel and Robert and be introduced to their families. Maria has also arranged that we stay two nights at Reid's Hotel in Madeira where Ishbel treated us to afternoon tea on our journey out to Australia.

The ship lands in Southampton and we thought it would be good to spend a few nights in London before travelling by train to Glasgow and then home to Coatbridge. We anticipate arriving early July 1947, we will give you the exact date soon, any changes and we will send telegrams.

It's all a bit hectic here at the moment, please tell Agnes and Mary about our plans. No doubt you will also tell Jennie, the Law family and all your other friends.

We are very much looking forward to meeting Andrew, and are so grateful that he has looked after you with such kindness and love.

Ma, is there room at the bungalow for us to stay with you or would it be easier if we booked into a hotel, you can let us know which would be best.

I never thought I would write this letter, you can't imagine how excited we are to be coming home. In a strange way we seem to be turning into the Sam and Maria who sailed to the other side of the world nearly thirty years ago. We have had an incredible life here in Australia, brought up a wonderful family, own a lovely home, Maria is a successful businesswoman and I have done well at the Northcote Brickworks. Ma, now it's time for us to come full circle.

Looking forward to seeing you both in July.

With love from Sam, Maria and all the family

Northcote

Dear Ma

It has been wonderful to be able to contact you directly since my father passed on. So sad, so many years out of touch, thank goodness we had our Dan to bring us together. You know my pa missed so much I wonder what made him such an auld curmudgeon.

Anyway, the exciting news. We are coming home on holiday, yes you read right. It's been mayhem here getting everything organised but we are due to arrive in Coatbridge early July this year.

Ma, I promise you I will accompany you to Mass and we will both give thanks to St Joseph.

Sam has retired from the brickworks and I'm taking a long break from the business, Laurel, Alice and Faye can manage quite well without me (did I tell you Mrs Wilson has retired). Before we leave for Scotland we are going to visit Matthew, Isabel, Alexander and Samuel in Sydney which is all very exciting.

Sam and I have had a good life here and we thought while we are still fit to travel it was the right time to return to visit our roots. On the way we will stop at Cape Town where we received the blessing from Robert. I always felt that was the moment when we were properly married.

Please tell the others our news and tell them how much we are looking forward to seeing them all again. I will write to Dan as well but I'm not sure who will receive the mail first, you know what it's like!

All the family are well and that's our youngest, Samuel, away in Sydney at university now. The Johnstone's in Northcote have an empty nest.

We will write on our travels and let you know when we will be in Glenboig. Now there is a sentence I never thought I would write.

With all our love
Maria and Sam

* * *

Two women who lived only a few miles away from each other, women who had never met, felt the same emotions on receiving their letter. First a wee tear, then overwhelming joy.

After sharing the good news with Andrew, Jessie spent the next hour telephoning the family, Jennie, and the Law girls at the women's refuge. Then she put on her hat and coat and took a Baxter's bus over to Gartsherrie to share her news with her old pal Agnes Law.

Annie Riley did not own a telephone so she instantly put on her hat and coat. First stop our Lady and St Joseph's chapel to give thanks. Before leaving the church she put five shillings in the charity box and lit a candle in gratitude. Then she visited all the family, except Martha who lived in Glasgow with her husband Joe, she sent her a postcard. On the way home she couldn't resist calling in to see her friend Teresa, who was so delighted at the news she got out the remains of the Hogmanay whisky and and they enjoyed a wee dram in their tea.

As Sam and Maria settled into their first class seats on the train to Sydney. Maria asked Sam, "Does this not take you back to our train journey from Glasgow to Liverpool? I think the worst thing was each of us only had a roll on cheese to eat the whole day, we were famished."

"No need to be famished today, once we are on our way we will have a nice breakfast then a read at the papers, I see you brought a couple of magazines. Maria, it's so nice to see you getting time to relax and read something that's not related to work."

On arriving in Sydney, Matthew, Isabel and Samuel were there to greet them. Matthew had booked them all into the Sir Stamford hotel at Circular Quay for the night. As they drove to the hotel everyone seemed to be talking at once, so happy were they to be together again.

Before going to bed the family sat in the lounge and had hot chocolate with biscuits. Samuel piped up, "This is just like the old days, hot chocolate then bed. I used to be so jealous of Alexander, he was allowed to stay up late while I was packed off to bed. Even Isabel was allowed an hour more than me, I was very hard done by as a child."

His father replied, "Well you're enjoying life now. I hear you refused Matthew and Isabel's kind offer of a room in Mossman in order to stay at the university residence."

"Course I did pa! Can you imagine having your big sister making you hot chocolate and ensuring you eat plenty of veggies. No thanks! I'm a student and I'll eat pies."

Everyone laughed and it was the start of a wonderful week for Sam and Maria. Alexander managed to get a weekend leave and on the Saturday evening Isabel prepared a special family dinner. Sitting on the stoop before eating, the ladies enjoyed a glass of wine while the men drank a beer and ate potato chips.

Matthew caught Isabel's eye then said, "Attention everyone, I have an announcement to make. I'm only sorry that Laurel isn't with us but four out of five together is quite good these days. Sam, Maria, I am delighted to announce you are going to be grandparents, my darling Isabel is going to have a baby."

Alexander cried, "What, I'm a doctor and I had no idea, obviously not a very good doctor. Congratulations! We are all so happy for you both, when is my new niece or nephew due?"

"Isabel is twelve weeks pregnant, we've another six months of a full nights sleep."

Maria suddenly realised the tears were coursing down her cheeks. She remembered so vividly Isabel's birth and how happy she had been to have a little girl, and now her little girl was going to become a mother.

That night in bed Sam and Maria held hands. Sam whispered, "Isn't it wonderful, we're going to have our trip to Scotland and we'll be home before baby Gregg is born. That's some news to tell the families back home in Coatbridge. Also our Walter, he will be delighted, he was always besotted with Isabel, she had him under her thumb. I can't quite believe we're going to be grandparents again.

"Do you know it's nearly thirty years since we sailed up the Yarra and set up home in Northcote, before the end of the 14-18 war. We could never have imaged bringing up five children, six if you include Walter. Maria you are my beautiful girl with the strawberry blond hair."

"Not so blond now Sam! My hair has plenty of silver."

"You're still my beautiful girl, inside and out and I'm so thrilled we are going off on our trip together. The Adventures of Sam and Maria Johnstone."

Before they left to catch the train south, Isabel presented her parents with a Leica camera as a going away gift from all the family. "Remember use this well, we want you to record everything and when you come home we can make up albums, and perhaps when you're on your travels you could also send us a few photographs through the post so that we can follow your adventures and feel we're joining in with your trip"

—

CHAPTER 32
The Circle Completed

After returning home to Northcote from Sydney, the following days seemed to fly past for Sam and Maria they were so busy preparing for their trip. Then suddenly it was time to leave. Their trunks having already been sent on board the ship Joshua and Laurel collected them at 'The Brig' and drove them to the docks in Melbourne.

Friends and family of first class passengers were welcomed on board for cocktails and canopies before the ship sailed. The atmosphere was fun and exciting, the ballroom adorned in bunting and the staff, wearing white uniforms, dispensed delicious canapés and cocktails from silver trays.

In all the noise and excitement Laurel took Maria aside, saying, "Don't worry about the business. We'll look after Harris Clothing while you and Sam are on your well earned trip. You're leaving behind a good team, me, Alice and Faye. Maria, we're doing now what you did for Walter, but please don't stay in Scotland. Come home we need you both back in Australia.

"Incidentally, I thought it was very nice of you to give the girls such a good bonus. I know you told them it was 'just a wee something' but Alice and Faye were absolutely blown away with your generosity."

Just then the siren sounded and there was an announcement that all the visitors must leave the ship.

Laurel and Joshua walked down the gangplank and stood on the dock waving to Sam and Maria as the Auchincloich set sail.

The ship was taking them back home on the reverse of the route they had travelled out to Australia on a third class passage as penniless immigrants. This time they were booked into a first class cabin and Maria had a trunk full of beautiful clothes.

As they were preparing to go to dinner on their first night at sea Maria pondered, "Sam, I wonder what the other people at out table will be like? I hope we don't repeat Walter's escapade and meet a Mr and Mrs Perriman."

"Too true," agreed Sam. "I just want us to enjoy our time aboard the ship. Incidentally, talking of Perriman, when we were in Sydney Matthew told me that the prison authorities had informed him that his father is terminally ill. He's made the decision not to tell Laurel or visit him and I can't say I blame him. I think what he can't forgive is watching his mother grow old in the nursing home. He still visits every month but apparently she's no better. She takes great interest in things like talc or a new scarf or biscuits but she has no foot in reality. Matthew thinks she has no idea she ever had children, he let her see photographs of his wedding to Isabel but her only reaction was, 'pretty dresses, very pretty dresses. I do like pretty dresses'.

"And talking of pretty dresses, Maria you look absolutely beautiful in that gown!"

"Thank you kind sir! It's one of Laurel's creations. I must say I'm thrilled with the wardrobe the girls have put together for me. Poor Sam, you just have your evening wear and some smart day outfits and I'm dressed up like a dish of fish. But onward and upwards my dear, the first class dining room awaits."

They were not disappointed, the evening was everything and more than they expected. Their table companions were three pleasant couples in the same age range as themselves, all travelling straight to Great Britain to reconnect with family and friends after the war years. Everyone was agreeable, and during the voyage their delightful dinners together were often followed by a game of cards.

All in all the journey to Cape Town was thoroughly enjoyable without any diversions into the world of criminality.

At last the ship sailed into Cape Town harbour. Standing on deck Sam and Maria watched as Table Mountain silhouetted against a blue sky drew closer, their excitement growing at the thought of seeing their friends once again.

Ishbel, Charles and Elize were at the dock waiting to meet them. The years had invariably brought about changes but they immediately recognised each other, hugs and tears all round.

Sam and Maria, together with their luggage, took a taxi to the Mount Nelson hotel while the Hofmyer family followed in their car.

As soon as they were registered and the luggage taken to their bedroom, the friends met for coffee in the lounge.

"Robert is so terribly sorry he couldn't come this morning but he is lecturing," explained Charles. "However, he and Anna together with young Fraser Charles will join us for dinner this evening."

Ishbel and Maria could scarcely talk for crying. They so wanted to catch up on the nearly thirty years they had spent apart.

Elize ordered coffee and scones leaving the men to get to know each other and the women to tearfully talk ten to the dozen.

That evening as they were preparing to go to Rondebosch for dinner. Maria tied ribbons around the presents she had brought in her trunk. "You know Sam, I still can't believe we are actually staying in a bedroom at the Mount Nelson, we could never have believed such a thing possible way back in 1918."

"Well my dear, the lord has been good to us and now we must get a move on. I've booked the car for six o'clock. Put your hat on and we can get away."

Maria and Sam couldn't remember an evening like the one they enjoyed at Rondebosch. The wine flowed, delicious food was served and best of all was the conversation.

High on the agenda was the royal visit when the king and queen together with the two princesses had arrived in Cape Town to begin the royal tour of the Union of South Africa, sailing into the city on 17th February 1946 on the HMS Vanguard to an ecstatic welcome. After which they toured Southern Africa in a special train.

At one point in the evening Elize beckoned Maria, "Come upstairs Auntie Maria I've something I want to show you."

Elize led her upstairs to her bedroom, she opened the door and there was Sylvia sitting in a little wicker chair. "Isn't she lovely? Sylvia always used to sit on my bed then one Christmas Uncle Robert and Auntie Anna gave me the chair, it was just meant for her.

"Auntie Maria I used to love your letters about Alexander and Isabel growing up in Australia. Then Matthew and Laurel joined the Johnstone clan and of course Samuel, they all seemed to have such fun together. Now we are all grown up and involved with our careers, even young Samuel is at University.

"I always wanted to meet Alexander and Isabel when I was a youngster growing up. Being an only child I always thought it must be wonderful to have a brother or a sister. I know Robert is technically my brother but I've always called him Uncle, besides there is a big age difference."

Maria replied, "Well why don't you visit Australia? At the moment Alexander, Isabel, Matthew and Samuel are all in Sydney. You could go and stay with Isabel and Matthew, they have plenty of room in their house in Mossman. Besides, and I haven't even told your mother yet,

Isabel is going to have a baby. It would be really nice for her to have another girl around to balance things up.

"What are you doing work wise at the moment Elize?"

"Well, I'm at a bit of a crossroads at the moment, as you know I qualified as a pharmacist then during the war I started studying again and I'm now a doctor of medicine. I've been thinking about training as a G.P. I'm working in obstetrics at the moment and that also has an appeal. I might drop Alexander a note and ask him about studying at Dunedin. It gets a very good name and now I can I'd like to travel a little bit. Anyway, what is Alexander doing at the moment?"

"Quite a story really," explained Maria. "He's decided to go back to medical school and qualify as a psychiatrist. As you know he's been working in a hospital near Sydney treating returning soldiers. Well, he has found that in many cases the mental health issues are just, if not more complex, than the physical injuries, particularly with men who have been in the prison camps. With the hospital closing, he feels that it's the right time for him to take on a new challenge.

"His father and I have always encouraged the children to follow their heart, after all it's what we did, so we are supporting him one hundred percent.

"We had better go back downstairs now they will all be thinking we have got lost."

The fortnight Sam and Maria spent in Cape Town created a scrapbook of wonderful memories. Ishbel, Robert and their family and friends showered them with true South African hospitality. The Leica camera was well used to record their stay.

Highlights included, visiting Anna's family on their farm near Paarl, which gave them the opportunity to see the Klein Karoo. A day spent with Charles and Ishbel driving down the coast road through Simon's Town and down the peninsular to Cape Point, the views from which were indeed spectacular.

They hosted a dinner at Mount Nelson, travelled along the west coast, seeing zebras, springboks and other animals in the wild. They visited Groote Constantia winery and drove up the Helschoogte Road near Stellenbosch en route to Franschhoek where they saw more delightful wine and olive farms.

One of the highlights for Sam was travelling up on the cable car to the top of Table Mountain. Charles and Sam enjoyed a long walk atop the mountain while Ishbel and Maria had coffee in the cafe.

"I'm sorry to be such a cowardly custard," said Maria. "It's a truly fabulous view but heights just aren't my thing at all, besides it's lovely to get a chance to have a blether just the two of us. Dinner at your house tonight then it's off on another ship tomorrow morning to Southampton. Can you imagine our feet will actually touch British soil again. Ishbel, truly I never thought we would ever return home, it's exciting and frightening all at the same time. Did you and Charles never think about a trip back home?"

Ishbel replied, "That's just it, it's not home for Charles, he is South African, he has no family or close friends in Britain, only a few medical acquaintances he corresponds with. I still write to my two boys but if I'm being brutally honest, we're not close. They've made their lives in Scotland and Robert and I in Africa. Worlds apart! Over the years I've travelled all over the Union of South Africa and into Rhodesia but I have no real draw to go back to Perthshire.

"Not only did I find love in Africa, I give birth to my beloved Elize, I've seen my son married to a kind and beautiful woman, who has given me a fine grandson in Fraser.

"I love this country, it's in my bones. My only real sadness has been losing Sophie. Even after all this time I still miss her. She saved my life when I had the Spanish flu, she was a true friend and over the years we laughed a lot together.

"Maria, when you see Walter please give him our best wishes, such a fine young man and he was very kind to Sophie, she often spoke about him. Please tell him his thoughtful words and letter meant a lot to her. He will know what you mean."

The men joined them, they had another coffee and it was time to take the return journey down to the city in the cable car. Maria just kept her eyes closed while everyone else marvelled at the view.

Once again the Johnstones' were onboard a ship heading for home. As they were sailing out of Cape Town harbour Maria was pleased she had organised another stopover in Cape Town on their way home.

Sailing into Funchal harbour during the northern hemisphere summer was magical. They arrived in the town on the tender and were met by a representative from Reid's who transported them to the hotel.

The hotel had recently reopened after being closed during the war and there was the newness of fresh paint and polish in the air.

Madeira was a two day idyll, Sam and Maria were on their own in the beautiful surroundings of Reids, they felt like young honeymooners. They were able to reminisce about days gone bye. However, on this visit to Reid's they were wrapped in security, the security of a successful business, ownership of property and land, money in the bank, but best of all their beloved family.

Maria had not been looking forward to the final leg of the voyage through the Bay of Biscay but this time they were sailing through the northern hemisphere summer thankfully they reached Southampton without major incident.

At long last the ship docked in Southampton and Sam and Maria once again set foot on British soil.

They travelled by train to Waterloo Station in London and then, as instructed by Sam's sister Mary, took a taxi to the Savoy Hotel. After registering, the receptionist informed them, "Mr and Mrs Johnstone your luggage will be taken to your room by the bellboy. I wonder if you would care to accompany me to the lounge for a welcome drink?"

Sam and Maria followed him through the elegant Art Deco lobby to the lounge where he indicated a comfortable sofa, "Would you like a glass of champagne or would you prefer a tea or coffee?"

A voice behind them said, "Oh I think today calls for champagne my big brother is back home."

Sam and Maria turned round and not only was Mary behind them but his mother Jessie was standing beside her.

The four encircled each other and the tears flowed. By the time the waiter appeared with the champagne they were all seated and holding hands. Mary said, "Ma and I thought we would come down to London and surprise you before you come home to Scotland. Everyone is so excited at the thought of seeing you both after all these years. When you left could you have imagined in your wildest dreams that you would one day return and stay at the Savoy?"

Sam replied, "Australia has been good to us but it's the work ethic we learned from our families that has carried us through the years. There is only one regret, I won't see my pa. Even now I can scarcely believe that he is not with us and I will never again hear his Ulster brogue ending a sentence with, 'so I did' or 'so I will.'"

Jessie took his hand, "Son, I never thought I'd be able to live again after I lost Alex. He was everything to me! However, I had to carry on my work at the women's refuge, that's what got me through the black days. Over the years Andrew was my friend, we became close and marrying him was a good decision. We look after each other and we enjoy each other's company. Sam, I hope you will accept him as a special person in my life."

Mary added, "Sam, Andrew is a really good man. He doesn't try to take pa's place, he is our friend and he cares for us all. Agnes, Tom, Emily and Liz all get on well with him."

They drank their champagne and tried to do the impossible, catch up on almost thirty years.

During the following three days in London, Mary insisted that they see a bit of the city including Buckingham Palace, St Paul's Cathedral, Tower Bridge and the Tower of London. However, they also saw the many bomb sites that scared the city and Londoners still queuing for groceries and other basics. Having known pre war London so well, Mary found it very sad to see the damage that had been inflicted on the capital city.

Jessie was quite happy to forgo the sightseeing in order to sit in comfort in the Savoy reading or writing her daily letter to Andrew, fortified by cups of tea served in delicate china cups.

On their final morning in London everyone enjoyed a delicious breakfast at the Savoy before traveling by taxi to Euston to catch the train north.

At last the long journey was over and the train steamed into Central Station. Waiting to meet them was Andrew with Agnes's husband Tom and their daughter Emily. More cuddles, more tears.

They made their way back to Coatbridge where Agnes had organised a welcome home tea in her bungalow in Drumpellier. Agnes put her arm around Maria and led her into the sitting room, where waiting to meet her, was her mother, brother Dan and his wife Clare.

More tears and cuddles. Maria felt as though she would never sleep again she was so pumped full of happiness.

Eventually Andrew managed to get Sam on his own, "Sam, I know you must have very mixed feelings meeting me. However, I just wanted you to know that I cherish your mother and I will always look after her."

Sam replied, "We have been receiving letters from ma telling us about you through all these years. I feel I know you from hearing about your life with my mother. Also, you are always included in letters from Mary and Agnes, so I know that you are a huge part of their lives too. While we have a quiet minute, I'd like to thank you for all you've done for the Johnstone clan. You have saved my mother and brought her happiness. What greater gift."

The following weeks in Coatbridge were happy, fun, sad and reflective for Sam and Maria.

As promised Maria went with her mother to Mass, her first time since leaving Glenboig. While worshipping in the church stirred up memories of her childhood, she knew in her heart she was no longer a Catholic, nor could she ever be a Protestant or an Anglican, her belief system was much simpler and didn't need the dogma. However, she would never hurt her mother my telling her how she felt.

Annie Riley would never have understood Maria's feelings. Annie's beliefs had sustained her well, particularly through the years married to Patrick when there was so little joy in her life. Watching her children take their first communion, accepting the wafer and wine that joined her to Jesus, listening to the hymns soaring to heaven, these and many other moments in the church were her spiritual blessing.

Sam and Maria were very comfortable staying with his mother and Andrew. This home was very different from where Sam had been brought up at 130 Long Row, it had lovely furniture and soft furnishings also a beautiful garden, Andrew's pride and joy. The kitchen boasted the latest work saving aids and there was a lady from the refuge who came in three times a week to help Jessie with the housework. However, in the important things it was exactly the same, Jessie brought warmth, laughter and the smell of delicious home cooking, just as Sam remembered from his childhood with his sisters and the Law family.

The company of the Australian visitors was much in demand from friends and family. In order for them to meet with all the family and friends from Glenboig, Dan and Clare decided to arrange a get together at the church hall. What started as a gathering of about forty people, mainly family, like Topsy, grew and grew to more than double that number.

Mrs Riley extended an invitation to Sam's family and what could never have been envisaged in 1917 happened in 1947, the two families joined in a celebration. And, a wonderful evening it was, everyone had contributed a plate of food, and like the parable of the loafs and fishes, despite rationing, there was plenty of food for everyone.

The parish priest made a welcome speech and said the grace. There was much 'blethering' and the evening finished with Rose Kelly playing the piano and the younger guests dancing and playing games. Perhaps the most poignant meeting of the evening for Maria was with Neil, who had been married to her sister Maureen. They found a quiet corner and shared memories.

The evening ended with an enthusiastic rendering of Auld Lang Syne before everyone returned to their homes.

When Sam and Maria arrived back with Jessie and Andrew to the bungalow Andrew insisted on them all having a wee dram to toast a wonderful evening.

The days flew past, Sam and Maria visited all Maria's siblings, Martha and her husband and son in Glasgow, Rose and her husband

Gerry and Frank and his wife Marianne in Glenboig. Time spent with
Dan and Clare was especially precious after all the years of
correspondence. They spent time with Liz and Mary in Airdrie, the
Law family in Gartsherrie, Jennie her husband John and daughter
Louise, Agnes, Tom and Emily. They also spent an afternoon at the
refuge where they were able to appreciate first hand the amazing
project initiated by Jessie and made possible by the generosity of Ella
Millar. Afterwards Sam was full of pride at what his mother and her
team, Ella's Friends, had accomplished, providing a safe haven for
abused women and children.

Maria spent time alone with her mother in the wee house that she
thought she would never see with earthly eyes again, and enjoyed being
introduced to her ma's friends.

All too quickly it was time for Sam and Maria to travel to
Edinburgh to spend a week with Walter and Fiona, leaving their travel
trunk with Jessie. Andrew ran them to Sunnyside station where they
caught a train to Glasgow then changed trains for Edinburgh Waverley.

Alighting from the train at Waverley, Sam and Maria immediately
caught sight of Walter and Fiona. Maria hugged her boy and erstwhile
business partner. Once again tears of happiness, Maria couldn't
remember a time in her life when she had cried so much.

Walter whisked them in a taxi to Cadogan Crescent. After settling
into their room Sam and Maria enjoyed a wonderful catch up lunch
with their hosts. Maria could immediately see why Walter had fallen in
love and married Fiona so quickly, she was an intelligent, beautiful
woman but there was an air of kindliness about her that reminded
Maria of Ishbel.

"We too have an empty nest now," said Walter. "Alice and Samuel
have both left home, Alice is at Glasgow university studying history
and Samuel, well, he must have inherited the Macpherson mathematics
gene. He is also in Glasgow training as a chartered accountant.

"Our tuition business is still up and running, although we have a
management team taking care of most of the day to day work. Fiona
and I have been involved in a bit of property development. I inherited
properties from my father and we have since added to them, good long
term investments, our old age pension."

Once again the days seemed to fly past, as well as catching up on
family news they visited North Berwick, the East Neuk of Fife and
had an enjoyable day in Edinburgh's old town where they explored the
castle. Walter also insisted on taking them to Musselburgh to show
them the bakers shop where he had proposed to Fiona. The tables and

chairs were long gone but the shop still sold paradise slices.

The night before Sam and Maria returned to Coatbridge they all decided to visit the North British hotel for dinner. Always a memory jerker for Walter and Fiona.

After their meal they retired to the lounge for coffee and a whisky. Walter announced, "Friends, can I have the floor for a few minutes? Fiona and I have been talking. As you know if circumstances had been different we would most likely have settled back in Melbourne and well, I'd love for Fiona to see my home country. How would you like company on your return journey? There is absolutely no reason we can't have four or five months away from Edinburgh. It would also be wonderful for me to see Ishbel and Charles again and give me the opportunity to show Fiona the most beautiful city in Africa. What do you think?"

Sam replied excitedly, "What do I think lad? What do I think? I think it's the best idea I've heard in many a long day! The children, well they are not children now, but you know what I mean, will be absolutely thrilled."

Maria, well Maria was in tears yet again. They spent the remainder of the evening plotting and planning the trip.

It was much easier to leave Walter and Fiona when they returned to Coatbridge knowing that they would all be travelling back to Australia together.

Sam and Maria spent another four weeks staying with Jessie and Andrew. During this time Maria booked a twin room in the Savoy Park hotel in Ayr and spirited her mother down to the Clyde coast for a few days. Annie Riley had never stayed anywhere remotely like the Savoy Park and those days with Maria in Ayr, where they were blessed with beautiful weather, were a precious memory for them both.

Andrew organised a trip to the Trossachs. From their base in Drymen at the Buchanan Arms they had a little adventure each day. They drove along the shores of Loch Lomond and meandered in the village of Luss with its historic church, explored McGregor country and spent a day in Stirling where they visited the castle and the Wallace Monument.

The men also enjoyed some country walks while Jessie and Maria were able to have time together really getting to know each other.

All good things come to an end, and eventually it was time for Sam and Maria to return to Australia. On their last evening they arranged for the Riley, Johnstone and Law families to have a steak pie dinner at the Georgian Hotel. Walter and Fiona, who were spending the night with Agnes and Tom, joined the company. Walter was delighted to see Dan, Clare and dear Jessie. Also, Mrs Riley who was proudly wearing the gold locket Walter had given her all those years ago.

The goodbyes were not easy but said they had to be and then one last sleep in Coatbridge and it was time for the foursome to catch the train to Glasgow and onward to London. Jessie did not go to Sunnyside Station, she said her goodbye at the bungalow and then cried her heart out before getting a tea tray ready for Andrew's return, when they would sit and discuss how blest they had been over the past weeks and look at the photographs.

The foursome had a short stopover at the Savoy in London, a luxurious treat.

Two days later, another train journey to Southampton, and it was time to board the liner bound for Cape Town.

Their first dinner onboard was bitter sweet for the Johnstones. Although excited about visiting Cape Town and then returning home to see the family, and the anticipation of becoming grandparents again, Sam and Maria were conscious of the fact that this trip had been the time when they really had said farewell to their families in Scotland.

Walter and Fiona were simply excited to be taking the journey after all these years that should have been their honeymoon.

The journey to Cape Town mirrored the outward journey for Sam and Maria but this time they had the joy of seeing how thrilled Fiona was with all the sights. Sailing into Madeira and enjoying two nights in Reid's hotel was particularly thrilling for her and Walter. Sam and Maria felt like old experienced travellers, this being their third visit.

As they got closer to Cape Town everyone was feeling excited and happy about seeing glorious Kaapstaad once again and introducing Fiona to their friends. They planned staying on the Cape for almost three weeks and Walter was hoping to take Fiona up into the Klein Karoo to see the spectacular scenery.

Seeing table mountain and sailing into Cape Town was thrilling as always, but seeing Ishbel and Charles waiting on the quay, Sam and Maria felt they were returning home.

As well as giving Sam and Maria a warm welcome, Ishbel and Charles were delighted to see Walter again and meet his wife Fiona. His quest to find his father, which had began in Cape Town all those years ago, now fulfilled.

—

CHAPTER 33
Letters and Romance

Cape Town

Dear Alexander

We have just had a bon voyage dinner with your mum and dad, they are now heading home to Scotland.

No doubt they will be writing to you with all the details of their stopover, they had a lovely visit to Cape Town and beyond, the mums couldn't stop talking. The dads got on very well, so all in all a good time was had by everyone.

One evening I was talking with your mum and she said that you were going to study to become a psychiatrist. I too am at the stage where I feel the need to reassess my career. As a woman I am presently working in obstetrics and gynaecology, now there is a surprise - being encouraged to think about a consultancy down that route, always a shortage of female birth doctors don't you know!

I understand you studied medicine at Dunedin. I would like to take the opportunity to travel while I continue with my studies. Would you be so kind as to write to me with your opinion on the medical faculty at Dunedin, also any particular areas of speciality at which you think they excel.

You probably know I have a degree in pharmacy as well as medicine. I've always thought taken together it gives me a good background to become a G.P.

Since the war finished I've felt the need to stretch myself, have new adventures. My mother would probably say, 'you don't know what you want young lady'.

Alexander, I would be most grateful for any advice you can give me regarding Dunedin or in general for that matter.

Hope you are well and looking forward to your course starting in September.

Kindest regards

Elize

* * *

Sydney

Dear Elize

Lovely to hear from you. When we were children and received letters from Cape Town we always thought you had it made, you were an only child, you had servants and your mum didn't have to work. ...sounded good to us.

You seem to have followed your father into medicine, now that's hard work. I graduated in Dunedin and then I was sent to work at a hospital for returning soldiers near Sydney. War, no career choices for me. Saying that I have gained a lot of experience. Then I was seconded to the Far East to work with the liberated troops. To be honest while overseas I didn't think much about my career, that was when I truly realised the price of war. It was as much as I could do to get up each morning and keep working day after day seeing sights I couldn't wipe from my mind.

When I returned to Sydney I really started to think about mental health issues, the hidden cost of war, hence my decision to study psychiatry. There is an excellent course here in Sydney which will allow me to carry out paid work so I won't have to rely on my parents or clean out all my savings.

Another plus about studying in Sydney is I will be staying with Matthew and Isabel. Very comfortable billet! Samuel also had the opportunity to stay here but he prefers halls, he is enjoying himself! I can't criticise, I enjoyed Dunedin.

I have written to a friend in Dunedin and asked him to forward to you brochures on the up to date offerings at the medical school. I thoroughly enjoyed my time in Dunedin. It's not exactly the centre of the universe, unless you are addicted to chocolate, in which case it is. You can smell the stuff all over the town and everybody knows somebody who works in the factory, so no shortage of chocolate.

Seriously, the university gets a very good name, particularly the medical school.

Otago is quite beautiful, I used to enjoy hill walking, no poisonous snakes in New Zealand, actually no snakes. And, you have to follow the rugby, it's obligatory.

Let me know what you decide to do, decisions, decisions.

Best wishes

Alexander

* * *

Cape Town

Dear Alexander

Thank you so much for your letter, yes in some ways I was spoiled, not only did I have my mum and dad but I had Sophie and Uncle Robert. Robert married Anna then it was a good many years before their son Fraser was born so they were always very good taking me out on treats and buying presents. You were probably right, I had it made.

I studied pharmacy mainly because I've always been interested in plants. Living on the Cape, well you can't not be, the fynbos is amazing. Before I completed my course I had already decided daddy was right all along, I graduated and immediately started studying medicine.

Gynaecology wasn't my first choice but because of the war it was desperately understaffed. I work in Groote Schuur, its a fairly new hospital and very well equipped, it's also about ten minutes from home, Elize is spoiled yet again.

Thank you, I received a lot of information from your friend Alan Ashton at Dunedin. I've also spent time in the library absorbing information about New Zealand. It looks a fascinating country with incredible scenery. It might not have poisonous beasties but it certainly has its share of scary earthquakes and volcanoes. Rotorua sounds terrifying, have you ever visited?

I've also been reading up about Australia. It seems so new compared to the Cape, we go back to Jan van Riebeeck in 1652. As well as English I had to learn Afrikaans at school. I even lived with Anna's family in Paarl on a number of occasions to improve my accent as Afrikaans is their first language. My father is bi-lingual and Uncle Robert speaks very well but you should hear my mother, she was taught kombuis (it means kitchen) Afrikaans by Sophie, factor in her Scottish

accent, she is totally hilarious. Anna's family are always very polite
when she tries but they must squirm as she truly murders their language.

Back to career, I have discussed a number of possibilities with my
dad. His view is I must do what will make me happy and not worry too
much about income. He was very pragmatic, he said. "Elize my dear you
have been our joy but your mother and I are no longer young, before too
many years you will inherit the family home and a sum of money. There
is a trust fund in place for young Fraser and Robert will not be
overlooked. Why don't you take a sabbatical and clear your head.'
Phew!

Alexander your mum said if I wanted to visit Australia perhaps
I could stay with Isabel and Matthew. What do you think, is Sydney
a good place for a sabbatical?

After what Dad said I think I should swiftly get myself onto the
career path I intend to follow, less worry for them.

Will you ask Isabel if I can come and visit, alternatively is there a
small hotel in Mossman where I could stay?

I'm fairly busy at work, still managing a bit of a social life. On
Sunday I'm going to Silverburn on a hill walk with a group of friends,
afterwards fish and chips. The following Saturday one of the midwife's
is getting married, after the service the family are having a marquee in the
garden, something to look forward to.

Bye for now, I'm taking Mum to have tea with Anna and her
mother, going out with the oldies, to be fair they are quite good company.

With best wishes
Elize

* * *

Mossman, Sydney

Dear Elize

Alexander told me all about your letter. Of course you are welcome
to stay with us for your sabbatical. No more talk of hotels. Just let us
know your arrival details and we will gladly meet you.

We are all very excited about seeing you, perhaps we could do a girls
side trip down to Melbourne so that you can meet Laurel and her
family. Laurel would be so upset if we all met you and she was left out,
her husband Joshua is very nice and her girls are a pure joy. They are
very like Laurel and have inherited her artistic ability. Laurel

converted to Judaism when she married Joshua, she does great Friday night dinners!

You could also investigate the medical school and hospitals in Melbourne if working or studying in Australia is of interest.

I am going to have a baby in late October, we are over the moon. I'm taking a bit of time off work, partly because I want the staff to be able to manage without me before I'm off completely for quite a few months. The bonus has been organising the nursery. I've just realised I'm like my mum, I enjoy creating a nice home. Nesting? Or is there a medial term? In any event I'm driving the gardener mad with ideas for outdoors and driving myself (and Matthew) mad with paint charts and material samples.

Looking forward to hearing from you with your arrival details.

Kindest regards
Isabel

* * *

Sydney

Dear Elize

No doubt you have received a letter from Isabel, there is to be no further talk of hotels, you will be very welcome in Mossman.

While you are here we would love to take you along the coast road and perhaps up to the Blue Mountains. You must also sample the ferries, we take them for granted. Visitors are always intrigued how we travel on a ferry in order to reach various suburbs. The harbour bridge is also quite an engineering triumph.

Between Isabel's and my ideas it looks more like we are planning a sightseeing route march rather than allowing you to have a thoughtful sabbatical to plan your future career. Please just say stop if we are going overboard.

I did once visit Rotorua with some fellow students, it's unique, I'll tell you all about it when we meet in Sydney.

Give our best wishes to your parents and thanks for spoiling Mum and Dad, we have received letters from them telling us about all the kindness they received in South Africa.

Awaiting your arrival details.

Best wishes
Alexander

Cape Town

Dear Isabel

Things have been moving fast here, I have booked a flight, quite scary but I thought I'd start my adventure on a 'high' note. I will arrive on Sunday 15th June at 10.15am.

My parents are delighted that I will have the opportunity to visit Australia. If it hadn't been for the war I think they would love to have visited your mum and dad in Melbourne.

Congratulations, you must be so excited getting ready to welcome baby Gregg. Enjoy your pregnancy and eight hours sleep every night, after baby makes an appearance life will never be the same.

The idea of having a holiday in Melbourne sounds rather good! The folks are all in favour of my visit to the Johnstone family.

I'll stop now as I want to catch the post, besides we will have lots of time to blether (Scottish mother) after I arrive.

Best wishes
Elize

* * *

On the appointed day, Alexander, Samuel, Isabel and Matthew were at the airport to welcome Elize to Sydney. Over the years they had seen photographs of her as a child but somehow they were not ready for this beautiful woman who combined a formidable intellect with film star looks. Elize was wearing a simple light wool suit against the chill of the Australian winter. Isabel's first thought was 'she would look stunning in a Laurelei creation'.

The party took two taxis to Circular Quay, where they caught a ferry to Mossman. Standing at the rail looking out towards the Sydney Harbour Bridge, Elize was mesmerised by the view. Living in Cape Town she couldn't imagine any other city being nearly as beautiful as her home town but her first impression of Sydney was one of awe.

Dinner that evening was a jolly affair with the five young people getting to know each other and talking about their hopes and dreams for the future.

The following day Samuel returned to university and Alexander returned to the hospital where he was due to finish working at the end of the week.

After seeing the boys off, Elize confided in Isabel, "For the first time in as long as I can remember I feel free, I can read a book just for pleasure, walk in the garden, go shopping, without having work responsibilities or studying. It's altogether a strange feeling but I can understand now why my dad put his work on hold a number of times when I was growing up, he used to say, 'I need to smell the flowers.' "

"That is exactly what we will do Elize," agreed Isabel. Now let's get ready and go into town and I'll give you the orientation tour, perhaps a little light lunch then a birl around the shops. Birl just means…" Elize laughed, "Of course I know what birl means! I had a Scottish mother too, remember."

The two women had a whirlwind day in Sydney ending up in David Jones Department Store in Market Street where they enjoyed tea and a scones. Isabel was known for her sunny nature but also for asking straight questions. "Tell me Elize, have you got a young gentleman in your life at present? I guess not or you wouldn't be in Sydney."

"Isabel you are incorrigible," laughed Elize, "and you're quite right, nobody special at the moment. I've gone out with a fair few doctors but nothing serious, we always ended up talking shop. I had a fairly serious relationship with a cousin of Anna, Uncle Robert's wife. However, I finished with him a while before I left for Australia. He's a very nice man but I'm just not cut out to be a farmer's wife, certainly not a good Afrikaner wife. I thought it was better to end the relationship before one of us got hurt. So here I am young, free and single and on a different continent.

"Actually, I'm not looking for love at the moment, I want to think about my career."

"I know what you mean," agreed Isabel. "During the war I got caught up in mum's business, it wasn't what I wanted to do but I didn't really have an option. Then I met Matthew, well I didn't exactly meet Matthew, I've know him forever. It was a change in circumstances, just like you I came to Sydney for a hiatus to sort out the direction I was going to travel in my life. Being with Matthew in a different place we saw each other in a completely new light. We didn't waste any time, we had a lovely family wedding in Melbourne and I've never regretted taking that trip to Sydney, not for a single minute.

"We had better get down to the dock now and get a ferry home." Before dinner Elize wrote to her parents.

Mossman, Sydney

Dear Mum and Dad

Firstly, thank you so so much for suggesting my taking a trip to Sydney. What a warm welcome I have been given and I feel so relaxed and lazy!

The Gregg homestead is beautiful and the setting....wow we travel by ferry from Sydney to Mossman. Matthew keeps a car at the office and Isabel keeps her car here in Mossman. From the back garden I can see down to the harbour and I can also see the new harbour bridge.

Alexander finishes at the hospital this Friday. Isabel is giving a dinner party on Saturday to celebrate his 'unemployment'. It's a few months until he starts his studies in Sydney so like me he intends to have a break from work. Actually, I think he needs a bit of time to himself, he had a harrowing time towards the end of the war at the liberation of the camps in the Far East. He saw and heard things nobody should have to deal with.

Alexander is definitely very like his father and Isabel her mother. I think the fairies sent Samuel, he is a complete dare devil and I think he could be a right mischief but he is great company. According to Matthew he is very clever but he is jolly good at hiding his abilities.

Thank you for being such wonderful parents and funding my trip to Australia, I know how lucky I am, honestly.

Please give my love to Uncle Robert and Aunt Anna, I hope she has forgiven me for finishing with her cousin Johan, I really did like him but I was never going to be an Afrikaner Frau.

With all my love
Elize

* * *

On meeting Elize at the airport Alexander had immediately been very taken with her. However on the Friday evening when Alexander arrived with all his belongings he had taken one look at the alluring Elize and thought, wow I think I could fall in love with that girl.

Saturday morning dawned and Isabel co-opted Elize into her dinner party arrangements. Over breakfast she announced, "There will be ten of us altogether, Matthew and me, Samuel and his latest, I believe she's called Margot. Our neighbours, Lilian and Tony, Matthew's colleague Jim Brown and his wife, I haven't actually met her but I'm sure she'll be nice and of course you and Alexander."

Elize didn't miss Isabel's comment 'you and Alexander'. Well she thought, 'if you think I am going to be paired with another doctor you are very much mistaken Mrs Isabel Gregg.'

The evening of the party Elize wore a dress based on Christian

Dior's new look style that she had bought in Sydney. Isabel had persuaded her not only to have the dress but to buy a pair of elegant high heeled black patent shoes to complete the outfit. It cost considerably more than Elize would normally have considered paying for an outfit but hey ho she was on an adventure.

After getting dressed and applying her make up Elize looked at herself in the mirror and thought, that's not me, not me at all. Elize Hofmyer wears white coats, and she certainly does not have her nails painted red. There was a knock on the door, "It's only me Isabel, I just wanted to see, wow, wow, wow. Gosh Elize, in all due modesty I was right, that was the dress for you, you look fabulous! Give me a minute to go downstairs and then, make your entrance."

"But Isabel, I'm not the sort of glamour girl who makes an entrance."

Isabel smiled, "Tonight you are. Now do as I say, one minute then come downstairs."

Everyone was sitting out on the stoop enjoying a gin and tonic while looking out onto the harbour and the twinkling lights of Sydney.

When Elize came through the patio doors leading out to the garden, you could hear the intake of breath. Samuel muttered, "Cor, she scrubs up well!"

"Be quiet," muttered Alexander, "she is a vision!"

Mathew poured Elize a G & T and introduced her to their friends.

Everyone had a lovely evening; excellent food, superb wine, and best of all interesting conversation. After the guests had left Samuel said to Matthew, "How about breaking out the whisky? A wee dram for a nightcap would go down rather well."

Wearily Matthew replied, "You are welcome to raid the drinks cabinet but I'm off upstairs, some of us have been working all week."

Samuel tried his brother, "What about you Alexander, a drink to celebrate your new career plan?"

By way of an answer Alexander took Elize's hand, "We are just going to have a wee walk in the garden. Sorry you'll have to drink your nightcap alone, I think Margot has already gone upstairs."

Before she could argue Alexander whisked Elize into the garden which was still lit with fairy lights.

They walked to the bottom of the garden holding hands illuminated by the twinkling lights. It was like fairyland. Alexander broke the silence, "Elize Hofmyer, I think I am falling in love with you."

Elize replied, "Alexander we hardly know each other! The only thing we know we have in common is that we are both doctors and your parents travelled on the SS Trojan with my mum and uncle in 1917. You can't possibly have fallen in love with me."

"Elize, do you remember Walter who visited your mum and dad when you were a child?"

"Of course I remember Walter, he brought me Sylvia. Besides he was very handsome and he had all sorts of adventures. And, he was extremely kind to a little girl, he even gave me a gold bracelet."

"As you probably know Walter was supposed to sail back to Melbourne with his bride Fiona but his father took a stroke and they settled in Edinburgh to look after him. What you probably don't know, is Walter proposed to Fiona days after they first met and she accepted, they just knew. I've never felt for a girl the way I feel for you. Tomorrow can we spend the day together, just go off on an adventure, I'm sure Isabel will let me have her car for the day."

"All right, tomorrow an adventure," agreed Elize, "but Alexander Johnstone much as I like you, and I do like you very much. I didn't come to Australia to fall in love, and I can't let the freedom from work and the romantic setting here in Mossman turn my head. In this dress I'm Cinderella at the ball, eventually I'll have to dress in a white coat and comfy shoes and become Dr Elize Hofmyer again."

"Elize you will be just as wonderful in a white coat. Now I'll take you back into the house. Promise me we will meet at nine o'clock in the kitchen, quick breakfast and then we spend the day together."

Secretly Elize definitely wanted to spend the day with Alexander so she agreed. "Nine o'clock it is, see you then." She ran upstairs before he could steal a kiss.

Isabel had been watching them in the garden from her bedroom with the lights out. Matthew told her to get into bed and stop being so nosey. "Honestly Isabel you really are the limit trying to matchmake your brother with Elize. Granted she is very nice but it's none of your business. Now stop this nonsense and come here and give your husband a cuddle."

The following morning Alexander and Elize rendezvoused in the kitchen as arranged. Isabel was already making toast and coffee, she said, "I thought we could just have a coffee now and I'll make a proper cooked breakfast later."

Alexander, wanting to put his plan in place said, "Isabel I was wondering if I could borrow your car for the day so that I can show Elize a bit of Sydney, coffee and toast will do us just fine."

"Of course you can have my car big brother. Matthew and I were just planning to have a lazy day at home and get some work done in the garden."

By now Samuel had also shown face, "What's this, you two off on a jolly in Isabel's car, can Margot and I join you?"

Having no intention of including Samuel, Alexander informed him. "Not on your life, we are off who knows where. You will just have to sort yourself out. Perhaps you and Margot could help Matthew with his gardening."

Elize crammed the last piece of toast in her mouth and they were off with Isabel's cry of "if you want dinner tonight phone me," ringing in their ears.

They took a drive through the suburbs happily chatting with no awkwardness between them. Eventually they ended up in Manley where they parked the car and walked hand in hand along the beach.

"You are not in a Dior style dress today Elize, I just want you to know it wasn't the dress I fell for last night, it was you. Ever since I saw you at the airport I knew you were special. Please don't think I'm some sort of Lothario who goes around falling in love with every beautiful woman he meets, nothing could be further from reality. The truth is, it's Samuel who is the man about town in our family.

"When I was in the Far East I saw so many men die without the chance to marry and have a family life and well, I don't want you to disappear back to Africa without me having the courage to say how I feel."

Elize stopped walking and looked at Alexander, "Of course I rather suspect I'm falling in love with you but I've got to be honest, I'm terrified! It's just being here in Australia, no work, my spirit feeling light. I have to be sure you'll want an African girl for the rest of your life. Now race you to the ice cream stand and you can by me a wafer."

"I'll race you Elize but there is a cultural difference, it's a pokey hat."

She laughed, "Of course it is, my mum is Scottish too. We can't possibly marry the children would be trinational, I'm sure it's not a word. But can you imagine poor wee souls speaking Afrikaans, Australian and Scottish?"

They raced to the kiosk where Alexander bought them ice creams and they found a bench to sit and enjoy them. Elize asked, "Is it really true Walter got engaged within a few days of meeting Fiona?"

"Perfectly true, apparently they met on the Saturday with friends, had a dinner date during the week, following Saturday they went off to the seaside for the day and he proposed. They bought the engagement ring on the way home. Mind you, Walter inherited loads of money so

he probably bought her a whopper of a diamond. I'm just an
impecunious doctor."

"So Alexander Johnstone, on the basis of the Walter and Fiona
romance are you suggesting we buy an engagement ring on the way
home?"

"I wish we could but it's Sunday and the shops are all closed. What
about Monday?

Alexander didn't beat Walter's record but three weeks later he
bought Elize a Kimberley pink diamond, surrounded by white
diamonds, from Fairfax & Roberts Australia's oldest established jeweller.

In celebration of the engagement Isabel organised a little family
soirée for which Matthew supplied some excellent champagne. Elize
apprehensively telephoned Ishbel and Charles to tell them of her
engagement to Alexander. She needn't have worried they were both
delighted. Alexander then spoke to his prospective parents in law and
reassured them that he would do all in his power to make their
daughter happy.

They then tried Andrew and Jessie's telephone number in
Coatbridge, no reply.

"Never mind," said Samuel, "we'll catch up with them soon and I
would put a lot of money on them being well pleased. Now brother in
law are we going to toast our engagement in champagne or just admire
the label."

—

CHAPTER 34
The Planning Meeting

Later that night after the engagement celebration when Isabel and Matthew were lying in bed, Isabel whispered to her husband, "I've had a spectacularly brilliant idea! It will take a bit, well a lot of organising. Before I say anything to the others can you give me your opinion, I'd like to know if you think my plan is do-able?"

Matthew listened carefully to all Isabel had to say before replying, "My darling, you never cease to amaze me but if you can pull off this feat of organisation you should be running the country never mind Lingerie by Isabella. I'll leave you to speak to Alexander and Elize tomorrow after I leave for work. Isabel darling, don't be too disappointed if they have other ideas, please don't push them, after all it is their wedding."

Matthew was breakfasted and was off to work before Alexander, Elize and Isabel met in the kitchen for breakfast. Samuel too had eaten an early breakfast and headed back into town.

Isabel started to make French toast while her brother made a pot of coffee and Elize set the table. As they were enjoying their breakfast Alexander said, "French toast always reminds me of Sunday mornings before we went off to Sunday school. Remember Dad would make us breakfast while Mum was preparing the vegetables or the pudding for dinner, for some reason there was always an extra slice and Dad would cut it between how many of us were sitting at the table."

Isabel thought 'no time like the present'. "While we are talking of Mum and Dad, you two have announced you are engaged and going to get married. Elize I know you will want your family to attend and Alexander you will want Mum and Dad and the rest of us to cheer you both on. Well, I was thinking. Mum, Dad, Walter and Fiona will all be arriving in Cape Town in about six weeks or so. Why don't we all fly out and have a big family wedding in Cape Town? Matthew is up for it and we could phone Laurel in Melbourne. Samuel, well he will just do as his big sister tells him. We could keep it a secret from the parents until they arrive in Cape Town.

"Matthew says I should mind my own business that you might have other ideas but I just wanted to throw my idea into the ring."

Whatever reaction Isabel imagined it was not Elize bursting out laughing and saying through her laughter, "Honestly Isabel, you really are totally incorrigible. How on earth can we organise a wedding and get everyone to Cape Town in five weeks? It's a brilliant idea but we could never pull it off."

Isabel replied, "Never say never to a Johnstone! If you two really want to get wed with the all the relatives in attendance I'll wave my magic wand and you shall go to the wedding."

Alexander piped up, "Don't underestimate my wee sister Elize. If you want to take her up on her idea say 'yes.' She will go into whirlwind mode and it WILL happen, of that you can be assured. Or, if you would prefer we celebrate in some other way that's absolutely fine but speak now or forever hold your peace."

"Isabel, do you really think we could pull it off? The two families plus Walter and Fiona all attending our wedding in Cape Town, it would be a tremendous feat," said Elize.

Alexander and Isabel just looked at each other and smiled, "We were brought up on carrying out the impossible, were we not wee sister? But if we are going to get this show on the road I think the planning meeting starts now."

They quickly cleared the kitchen table, got out lined notepads and Isabel started issuing instructions. "First we must decide on the wedding date, Elize, using the timeframe when my parents are in Cape Town can you go and telephone your minister and see if he will agree a date? That's the starting off point, and make sure your mum doesn't write to our mum with the engagement news."

Isabel knew the phone bill at Chez Gregg would be off the Richter scale by the time that the wedding was organised but she didn't care a jot. By lunchtime, a wedding date had been agreed. Charles and Ishbel were in on the plan and they had agreed to organise a venue for after the service and send invitations to Charles's family in Durban and some of Elize's friends and colleagues.

Elize's measurements had been given to Laurel and they had discussed dress ideas and it was agreed Miriam and Sonja would be bridesmaids. Elize also wrote a letter tendering her resignation to Groote Schuur hospital.

Isabel had contacted her travel agent and was awaiting to hear from him with proposals regarding flights.

Lunch consisted of a pot of tea, sandwiches and fruit. Alexander laughed, "Isabel, how many of these working lunches did we eat prepared by Mrs Wilson at H.Q.? I can hear Mum saying, 'Right troops we need to make a plan.' "

Isabel replied, "The plan this afternoon is you need to let Samuel know what's happening, I assume he will be your best man and Elize needs to contact her Uncle Robert and Aunt Anna personally. Also write to her two half brothers in Scotland. I know you've never met them Elize but as a courtesy you really have to inform them, besides your mum will appreciate your staying in touch with the Scottish family.

"Elize, I thought this evening I could sit quietly with you and sketch your ideas for your wedding dress. We can send it off to Laurel tomorrow so that we're all singing from the same hymn sheet."

"Isabel, I was thinking," said Elize. "When I was bridesmaid to Anna and Robert I had a little cream dress with a Stewart tartan sash. I absolutely loved that dress and wore it to parties until it was too small, in fact I still have it in the back of my wardrobe. Do you think we could do something to include the Stewart tartan for Miriam and Sonya's dresses, there is no Hofmyer tartan?"

Isabel thought for a couple of minutes, "Elize, am I right in thinking Stewart tartan is mainly red? If so why don't we take one of the darker colours like the blue or the green, make the dresses of the darker colour and trim in the tartan. The girls are blonde and they would look lovely in a darker colour, what do you think?"

"Sold! I think I'd like to go for the blue. Perhaps we could make their posies white or cream with little blue touches, and add a little flower clip to their hair.

"As for me, I know what I don't want, I don't want anything too elaborate, definitely not a meringue, and not anything awkward to wear or glittery just something elegant and simple."

"Sounds lovely!" agreed Isabel. "This is what we must do, make decisions not spend ages analysing everything in depth."

Just then Alexander came back into the kitchen. Isabel said, "I have another good idea, I think I'll phone Matthew and have him bring home fish suppers for tea, anyone object?"

"You won't get any objections from us about having fish suppers. Now I think it's time for a coffee break, I'll get the pot on," said Alexander.

The next few days were more of the same with Isabel issuing

instructions and making notes.

Ishbel telephoned and confirmed that she had taken an executive decision for the reception and booked a private room for a champagne afternoon tea at the Mount Nelson, and that she had arranged to have some invitation cards printed. She also instructed Elize that she must contact the minister to confirm hymns and let him know if she required the choir to sing.

"I've also organised a florist my darling. I've booked two arrangements for the church, also your bouquet, two posies, sprays and buttonholes. However, I said you would let me know your chosen flowers and I'll pass on details. The hotel will supply table flowers but again they want to know your chosen colour scheme.

"It's all so exciting. Just let me know what I can do at this end. Your father is so incredibly proud that he will walk his beautiful daughter down the aisle.

"I'd better go Elize, I dread to think what the telephone bills are going to be. Bye my darling."

The girls had a five day trip down to Melbourne where they stayed with Laurel and Joshua. True to her word after talking with Elize Isabel had sent Laurel some sketches of ideas for both the wedding and bridesmaids dresses. By the time they arrived in Melbourne to their delight Miriam and Sonya's dresses were complete, and work on the wedding gown was well underway.

As well as completing the dresses they were able to get a lot of other ends tied up, including finalising flights and booking the accommodation. It was truly a marathon of organisation but through it all the three girls, together with their trusty helpers, Alice and Faye had lots of laughs.

Isabel and Laurel took Elize to visit Mrs Wilson and update her on all the goings on. Isabel had asked her to come to the wedding but she reluctantly refused.

"It's very kind of you to offer to fly me to Africa and I would love to have attended young Alexander's wedding but at my age I'm not going on one of those airplanes, you couldn't pay me to go on one. If the good lord had intended us fly he would have given us wings. However, I have a wee something I'd like you to take to Cape Town."

Mrs Wilson produced a large silver coloured tin, decorated with white ribbons, inside was one of her rich fruit cakes, beautifully iced and secured with soft tissue paper. "I would be honoured if my wee blond Alexander and his lovely bride has one of my cakes as part of their wedding celebration."

Elize took the elderly lady's hand saying, "Mrs Wilson we would be honoured! I promise you your cake will take pride of place at our reception." And, it did.

Meantime Sam, Maria, Walter and Fiona, we're all blissfully unaware of the arrangements being prepared for Alexander and Elize's wedding in Cape Town. In fact they were totally unaware that they were even engaged let alone that there was a wedding in the planning.

—

CHAPTER 35
The Glorious Reunion

After their happy reunion on the dockside, the travellers from Scotland together with Ishbel and Charles headed for the Mount Nelson where they had made reservations.

As they walked into the lounge for coffee the entire Johnstone clan was waiting to welcome them together with Charles's family from Durban, Alice and Faye, Robert, Anna and Fraser

Sam could hardly mutter, "What on earth is going on?"

Alexander brought forward Elize, saying "It's a long story Dad but Elize's is now my fiancé and we are going to be married on Saturday with all our family present."

Not only was the family crying tears of joy but some of the waiting staff were moved, especially knowing the reception was going to take place in the hotel.

Laurel handed Maria a large box saying, "Mother of the groom outfit, keep it to open in your room, you want to surprise everyone on Saturday."

Sam was also presented with a box from Laurel, "For you daddy, your father of the groom kilt outfit, naturally Johnstone tartan."

The following three days passed magically, one of the highlights was a pre wedding dinner. Charles and Ishbel had taken over a room in the Kelvin Grove Club for the evening and hosted a glorious celebration with a quartet playing dance music after the meal. Samuel danced with Miriam and Sonya, the girls thought this was turning into the best holiday they had ever had, and there was still bridesmaid duties the following day. Their mum and dad had also promised they would go on a train journey and they would see elephants, giraffes and zebras in the wild, absolutely 'joe terrific'.

Saturday dawned a beautiful morning. There was a jolly breakfast in the Hofmyer house. Laurel, Joshua and the girls had stayed over to help dress the bride. They had hardly finished eating when the hairdresser arrived. On her heels was Isabel and Matthew.

Charles said to Matthew and Joshua, "I think this is the cue for us to depart for an hour or so. Why don't I take you both down to my club in Newlands, we can have a read at the papers and enjoy a coffee in a girl free environment, what do you say?"

"I say that's an excellent plan, we're probably just a nuisance here anyway," agreed Joshua.

The waiter had just brought the escapees a tray of coffee when Robert arrived, "I've just dropped Anna off at the mad house. Can I join you three for coffee and a wee bit of sanity? They are dressing wee Fraser up in a Stewart tartan kilt. Poor wee man! He's the only boy surrounded by women, I felt terrible deserting him."

"Not that terrible," laughed Charles, "or you wouldn't have hot footed it down here to join us."

"Don't imagine I'm getting off that easily, my mother has organised a Stewart tartan kilt for me too."

Joshua chuckled, "Lucky for us Charles, no Hofmyer or Stern tartans methinks. We'll just have to make do with formal attire."

During the wedding planning, Isabel managed to track down Johnstone tartan kilts for her dad and her brothers, also a McDonald for Walter. This was indeed going to be a Scottish wedding, down to the piper playing them into the kirk and then welcoming the guests at the Mount Nelson.

The preparations were eventually completed and everyone arrived at the kirk, taking their seats to lovely organ music being played in the beautiful sanctuary. Somehow the calm seemed to affect all the family and guests. The plotting, planning and hurly burly was over it was time to think on higher things.

As he proudly walked down the aisle with Elize on his arm Charles thought on how different his life would have been without Ishbel and he suddenly thought of Sophie and sent up a prayer of thanks to the woman who saved his wife's life and helped bring Elize into the world. Sophie too was present at the wedding of her darling Elize.

The marriage service which was in English and Afrikaans was touching. Alexander thought his bride the most beautiful woman to have walked God's earth.

The reception was joyous and much to Samuel's chagrin Margot caught Elize's bouquet when the newlyweds set off on their honeymoon.

Alexander and Elize were taking the train north to Pretoria, after a few days in the capital they planned to travel to Rhodesia where they would spend several weeks, including a visit to Victoria Falls.

In the days following the wedding there was a busy round of activities. The only people to return to Australia a few days after the wedding were Alice and Faye, Samuel and his girlfriend Margot.

Joshua, Laurel and the girls together with Matthew and Isabel had decided to holiday for a month in Africa as this would give them an opportunity to spend time together before Isabel's baby arrived.

Their trip finished in Cape Town and all too soon it was time to return to the airport and board the flight for Johannesburg, from where they would board separate flights to Melbourne and Sydney.

Sam and Maria found it difficult to say farewell to Ishbel, Charles, Robert and Anna at the docks when it was time for them to board yet another ship, this time heading for Melbourne and home.

Charles took Sam's hand saying, "Our two families are now joined as one, we are forever part of each other." Maria and Ishbel held each other tightly tears mingling with tears.

Fiona put her arm around Maria, "It's time my dear, we have to board." A final kiss and Maria walked up the gangplank supported by Fiona.

As the liner sailed out of Cape Town memories flooded back to Sam and Maria of the day almost thirty years ago when they had reluctantly left the Cape to start a new life with very little except their wits and a capacity for hard work.

During the final leg of the voyage Maria just wanted to get home, however she tried to keep her thoughts well hidden from Walter and Fiona as she was well aware they were now thoroughly enjoying the honeymoon trip that had been so cruelly cancelled because of John's illness.

Eventually they sailed up the Yarra, home at last, home from a trip that had exceeded their wildest expectations, culminating in the wedding of Alexander and Elize.

From their base in Northcote at 'The Brig' with Sam and Maria, Walter organised sightseeing trips for him and Fiona. Not only did they travel the tourist route but Walter took Fiona to visit Mrs Wilson and on a nostalgic trip to H.Q. He also visited his mentor Mr Green who was now long retired but his mind was as nimble as ever.

Their final adventure was to board the train to Sydney where they would once again meet up with Matthew and Isabel and enjoy some sightseeing in and around Sydney for a month before returning to Melbourne to say their goodbye's to Sam and Maria.

Sitting in the kitchen of 'The Brig' a few weeks after Walter and Fiona had left for Sydney. Maria poured Sam another cup of tea, "You know Sam it was wonderful seeing everyone and my goodness didn't the Leica capture some amount of memories but do you know I'm quite content sitting here having our breakfast, just the two of us. I might not be your lass with the strawberry blond curls anymore but I love you just as much as when we worked together at the brickworks back in Glenboig."

"Maria, I feel exactly the same, just the two of us, perfect. Tonight I'll percolate some coffee and we can enjoy it with a wee bit of shortbread while we once again pour through all our photographs.

"Now, can I leave you with the dishes? I'd like to go and fill the bird feeders then give the shed a tidy and sort out my seed packets." They kissed and set out to do their respective chores.

When Sam hadn't shown up for his morning tea and scone by ten past eleven Maria went into the garden calling his name.

"Sam, I've just made a batch of treacle scones. If that doesn't get you out of that shed I don't know what will."

She opened the shed door, Sam was slumped forward in the rickety old rocker chair with the seed packets still in his hand. Maria knew immediately he was dead, at last he had lost the fight with the mustard gas.

The family quickly arrived from all airts and pairts. Everyone gathered to say a tearful farewell to the head of the family, Samuel Johnstone.

On the day of the funeral Sam's coffin was sitting in the heart of the well loved sitting room in 'The Brig' as the minister conducted the service. Maria looked around the room at her beloved family. Matthew and Isabel, Laurel, Joshua, Miriam and Sonya, Alexander and Elize, Walter and Fiona, and young Samuel. Maria's heart, while breaking, was full of pride that she and Sam had created this wonderful extended family.

Sam left 'The Brig' for the last time to the strains of a piper playing 'Over the Sea to Skye'.

THE END

EPILOGUE

MARIA never got over losing her beloved Sam. 'With great love comes great sorrow'.

Although still contributing her expertise Maria took a backseat in the business with Laurel eventually taking over from her completely. Alice and Faye both continued to work with Laurel until they retired.

Maria's remaining joy in life was her five children, their partners and her grandchildren.

SAMUEL JOHNSTONE JNR fulfilled his ambition to fly, not in the military but with Qantas, where he became a senior pilot. He travelled all over the world but his home was always Melbourne.

He eventually married 'late in life' but never had any children.

MATTHEW AND ISABEL. Matthew's business went from strength to strength and eventually he left it to his two sons, Duncan and Samuel. Their daughter Jessica took over her mother's business, Lingerie by Isabella. This allowed Matthew and Isabel the freedom to enjoy their retirement, travelling all over the world.

ALEXANDER AND ELIZE eventually settled in Melbourne. As well as conducting his private practice Alexander became an imminent lecturer in psychiatry while Elize worked as a G.P. This career path allowed her to work part time when their two daughters, Charlotte and Alexandra were young.

They took many long trips back to Africa, eventually buying a small cottage as a base in Cape Town.

LAUREL AND JOSHUA'S two daughters were brought up in the Jewish faith and to the delight of their family both Miriam and Sonya married Jewish men.

When Laurel eventually retired the girls took over the business, yet another generation running Harris Clothing.

Like Matthew and Isabel, Laurel and Joshua also enjoyed travelling, they often made up a foursome on their adventures.

DOCTOR CHALMERS lived a long interesting life and passed away quietly during the war years (when his malts ran out). He left his entire estate to be divided equally between his two nephews and Walter.

ISHBEL AND CHARLES were devastated when the nationalist government brought in apartheid after winning the election in May 1948. Ishbel often thought of her dear friend Sophie as she contemplated the iniquitous regime.

They lived well into their nineties and passed away within weeks of each other. Thankfully Elize and Alexander were with them at the end, lives well lived.

ROBERT AND ANNA also found apartheid difficult to reconcile. In order to try and put something back into society they paid for the education of their maid's children and ensured that she received a good wage.

After retiring they bought a house in Franschoek where they enjoyed the country life. Their son Fraser became a minister in the Dutch Reformed Church.

WALTER AND FIONA. Like Maria, Walter lost the love of his life far too young, Fiona died from leukaemia in her early 50's. After losing his wife Walter travelled back to Melbourne where he bought an apartment.

Once again the Johnstone family were always there to support him.

His children Alice, a lecturer and Samuel a chartered accountant gave him a reason to regularly return to Edinburgh.

ANNIE RILEY. The visit to Scotland from her beloved daughter Maria with her husband Sam was the crown of her life.

Her four remaining children, together with their families cherished her as the heart of the family during her remaining years.

Retired and looking for a new interest, like many of my generation I started to research my family tree.

I was saddened to find that Gartsherrie, a place that my mother had greatly loved, appeared to have been almost wiped from the pages of history.

With the demolition of Wm Baird Iron & Steel Works and the flattening of the Rows and Gartsherrie Institute to make way for new council housing the history of Gartsherrie and its people, during the years when it was so closely affiliated to Wm Baird & Sons, 'The Works', appears to have simply vanished.

The books are my small contribution towards keeping the memories of Gartsherrie and it's people alive.

I have now completed the trilogy:

The Laws of Gartsherrie
Beyond Gartsherrie
Escape from Gartsherrie

Since writing the first book I have been delighted with the response I've received from all 'airts and pairts'. There are many folks not only in Coatbridge but all over the world who have roots in Gartsherrie and it has been a real privilege to share their memories.

Alexandra J Morris

www.AJMorris.me.uk

Printed in Great Britain
by Amazon

82263904R00190